dixi
books

Tadej Golob

Tadej Golob (1967, Slovenia) is a unique best-selling author with a thematically broad range of works, who put Slovene crime fiction on the map of world literature. He won the Slovene Novel of the Year Award for his debut, has written several biographies, two YA novels, and a book about the first person to ski from the summit of Mount Everest, also conquered by the author himself.

Gregor Timothy Čeh

Gregor Timothy Čeh was brought up in a bilingual family in Slovenia. He studied Archaeology and History of Art at UCL, taught English in Greece, returned to England to complete a Masters at Kent, and now lives in Cyprus. He translates contemporary Slovene literature for publishing houses and authors in Slovenia, with translations published in both the UK and US.

Tadej Golob

Lenin Park

translated from the Slovene by
Gregor Timothy Čeh

dixi
books

Dixi Books
Copyright © 2018 by Tadej Golob
This book was published in agreement with Založba Goga

Lenin Park
Tadej Golob
Original title: Leninov Park
Published by Založba Goga in 2018
Translator: Gregor Timothy Čeh
Editor: Katherine Boyle
Proofreading: Andrea Bailey
Designer: Pablo Ulyanov
Cover Design: Jurij Kocuvan

 Co-funded by the
Creative Europe Programme
of the European Union

"The European Commission's support for the production of this
publication does not constitute an endorsement of the contents, which
reflect the views only of the authors, and the Commission cannot be
held responsible for any use which may be made of the information
contained therein."

I. Edition in English: February 2022
Library of Congress Cataloging-in Publication Data
Tadej Golob
ISBN: **978-1-913680-44-2**
1. Thriller 2. Crime 3. Detective 4. Slovenia

© Dixi Books Publishing
293 Green Lanes, Palmers Green, London, England, N13 4XS
info@dixibooks.com
www.dixibooks.com

Tadej Golob

Lenin Park

translated from the Slovene by
Gregor Timothy Čeh

dixi
books

The Voice of the New Age

Monday

CHAPTER 1.

Hanging on the wall was one of those antique clocks with pine cone weights. Surprisingly, it showed the right time. Nine thirty-six. His phone was two minutes fast but he had set it this way deliberately so as not to be late.

Taras was sitting on a chair at the dining table next to the open window, hoping to catch the breeze that should have been created by the draught, had the air outside not have been just as hot, stale and still as inside the flat. He had just had a shower but droplets of sweat were already appearing on his forehead and were about to trickle down his cheeks and neck...

He stood up and stepped to the sink that, with a narrow dishwasher and a ceramic hob with two burners created a kitchen corner, tore off a couple of paper towels from the roll and sat back down in the chair. Then he stood up again and pulled the chair closer to the window. It made no difference, though he could now hear all the noise from the street, conversations that reminded him of the hum at a badly attended football match where you can make out the individual voices of spectators but not make much sense in terms of what is being said. Not that sense is what one might expect at a football match or indeed a place like the joint just below the window of this flat.

He could have guessed the time, at least approximately, by the fact that the sun, at its strongest in mid-June, had already moved behind the Opera and waiters at the café on Cankar Street were putting away the last sunshades. As in the flat where

Taras was sitting, it made little difference. Even in the shade the thick, scorching humidity pressed down towards the ground with the same intensity as before.

Ljubljana was, as anyone in the know was quick to point out, experiencing its hottest summer on record. The hottest *beginning* of summer, Taras thought whenever this was mentioned. It was only the middle of June and they had already had fifteen consecutive days with temperatures no lower than thirty degrees, often rising close to forty at midday. What was worse – this was no dry, desert thirty plus. The heat that lingered over the town had arrived as a cloud of humidity and comparisons with places like Singapore were not far out. It was – as one weatherman on state TV had said in desperation over not being able to offer a better forecast – so hot you could just drop dead.

The gushing sound from the bathroom stopped and a little while later Tina's dark head appeared at the door connecting the kitchen with the hallway. Behind it her naked body of which little more than her neck and shoulders were visible.

"Won't be a minute. Do you have time for a coffee?"

He checked his watch, even though he had only just done so before, and nodded.

"Fifteen minutes."

Tina also nodded and her head disappeared behind the door.

The clock on the wall was still at nine thirty-six. Just as it had been three minutes ago, half an hour ago, and would be in an hour's time. As someone who didn't believe in coincidences, should Taras have taken this as some kind of an omen?

He used another paper towel to wipe his brow. He hated the heat and all it brought with it. He didn't mind sweating when he ran or cycled but he couldn't stand it when he was standing in a queue in a shop or at the bank, or when he leaned over a bowl of hot soup, or in front of people like Drvarič and Kristan. Were it not for Brajc who was even worse off, Taras would have believed he was the one person in the entire world least able to handle the heat.

"What was it that you wanted to show me?" she called out from the bedroom.

"In the hallway, in a plastic bag."

She put on a pair of shorts and an oversized T-shirt that made her look like a student, one not even close to graduation. She held the supermarket bag he had hung on the door handle in the hallway. In it she found his standard issue Beretta.

"What's this? Why did you bring this with you?"

With the index finger and thumb of his right hand Taras formed a gun like a young child might do, playing at kindergarten... though kids at kindergarten these days probably don't play games like that any more.

"Bang, bang..."

"Bang, bang?"

"My annual firearms training and assessment. I couldn't just leave it in the car."

"What, this late in the year? I thought we were all supposed to have completed it in the spring?"

"I couldn't get to the previous one."

He was not a bad shot, especially not when he used to enjoy it and practised a lot. Even now he would achieve a solid result, though after the age of forty his eyes were no longer as reliable in focusing between the sight and the target. Previously focusing, the alignment of the focus, happened so quickly, so automatically, that he used to think he could see both the sight and target in focus at the same time, but now... it was either one or the other, with a kind of slow-zoom adjustment in between. And while he used to see exactly where he was sending the nine-millimetre bullet, it now left the barrel on more of a zen Buddhist may-the-force-be-with-you kind of decision. Somewhere into or out of the mist. Of course this also showed in the results.

Tina put the weapon on the table and went across to the dishwasher to take the coffee pot. In which she wanted to make the coffee. Filling it with water, she placed it on the smaller of the two elements before sitting down on the only empty chair by the small round table.

"And, how did it go?"

"Well enough for me to pass."

He told her his score.

"Thirty?! That's borderline, and ten points lower than me!"

She laughed and when she laughed she was unbelievably

cute, not just beautiful or sexy. Why was it that, at their first meeting, he had kept asking himself whether he liked her or not? He looked at her as if this was the first time he was seeing her and she appeared to be blushing.

"What is it? Anything wrong?"

She knew there wasn't.

"Can I give you some advice? Colleague to colleague, police officer to police officer?"

"Police officer and colleague?"

"Police officer and colleague."

"Go ahead, colleague."

"When it comes to weapons, don't rely on your shooting abilities. They're relatively unimportant. It is *never* like on the shooting range."

When it comes to weapons, people are capable of all kinds of stupidity. He had even seen someone turn towards their colleague when their gun had jammed.

"It doesn't work..."

The bullet was probably low quality and perhaps damp. The firing pin had done its work but the primer kindled and kindled, only to ignite properly at the exact moment the barrel was pointing at the left lung of the innocent observer. He survived but only just.

"Oh? And what *should* I rely on?" she asked him.

"On actually *using* the gun once you have drawn it."

She saluted.

"I get it, Mr Eastwood."

She stood up and finished making their coffee. They both knew that he would drink his, look at his watch and say he had to leave, but for now, at this moment, he could still afford to pretend that he was not in a hurry.

"Although I thought it was more like: drawing my gun means I *am* ready to use it."

"It isn't."

Tina thought he would explain but he didn't. He picked up the gun on the table, lifted it up and tried to straighten his arm. Then he gave up and put it back on the table.

"I can't extend my arm because of my elbow."

"Oh? Is it still the same?"

"No change. Sometimes I think it's better... but it isn't. No change."

When, about an hour ago he had shot a round of bullets, his eyes clouded over with pain. Just as well he scored what he had done. In fact he would not have passed the assessment were it not for Petrič. They were about the same age and knew each other from the police academy. Petrič saw that Taras was having difficulties, tapped him on the shoulder, stepped into his position and shot three bullets into the black centre. This gave him the score he needed to successfully pass the test.

"It'll get better," she said, putting the two cups of coffee on the table.

"But that was not what I wanted to show you. Look at this!"

Out of the bag he pulled a round, flat, silver gadget.

"Is that...?" she asked. "What were these called again?"

"It's a *Discman*. They weren't popular for very long. I found it by chance when I was moving some junk the other day."

"And what's so unusual about it?"

He didn't even know himself. Perhaps it was that, at the time he had bought it, the *Discman* represented the height of technological achievement, something that would define his and everyone else's future, but it turned out to be merely a blind alley in technological advance. A tiny silver non-flying saucer.

"Nothing," he laughed. "Forget about it. It just looks like such a silly device."

"I'm trying to remember if I ever actually used one."

She pressed a button and the tiny silver saucer opened.

"It still has a CD inside!"

She took it out of its slot.

"Motörhead, *Ace of Spades*. Into one-note screeching were we?"

It was a clue as to exactly when he had last used it.

"Does it work?"

He looked inside the bag and shook his head.

"No batteries. I seem to have left them in the car."

"Shame," she said, put the CD back into the slot and closed the cover.

"Did you park at the station?"

"No, not far from here, on Župančič Street."

On his way here he had been trying to find a parking space when, miraculously, he found one he could squeeze his Citroen C8 into one just a three-minute walk from her flat.

"Oh, then you must have walked through Lenin Park?"

"Lenin Park?"

"That green triangle between Župančič Street and that tiny street along the side that points in this direction, next to the Fig-ovec Inn. The park has had various names, they changed it to Park Ajdovščina some years ago, now I think it is called Park Argentina or something like that."

"I know the name. There used to be a petrol station close by where kids would buy booze. Not a night went by without someone reporting disorderly conduct and breach of the peace. I'm surprised *you* know it."

"When I was a little girl, my grandmother would take me there. To her it was always just Lenin Park. This I now find rather interesting. She came from one of those old Ljubljana families that had lost so much after the war, and was the last person to endorse anything to do with 'communism', as she called the era. But to her the park was always just Lenin Park, even later."

"*In Lenin Park there are trees.*

In Lenin Park there's even a warehouse of seeds."

"What?"

"Some song from the time when the park still belonged to Lenin. I only remember these lines. And it is now not even called Park Argentina any more, its official name is Slovene Reformation Park. Why do you want to know if I came through the park?"

She frowned for a moment, took a sip of coffee, wanting to gain a second before saying what she was going to say.

"Why?"

"Then you must have seen that homeless bag lady?"

"Yes, I did."

When he had walked along the pavement bordering the park and not the diagonal path across it that Tina was thinking about, the old woman was lying on one of the benches a few feet within the grassy area. There were plastic bags everywhere around her, some of them on the bench, others under it. Taras could recall the woman tirelessly dragging her plastic bags around town ever since he had first come to Ljubljana, meaning at least the last thirty years. She was not someone you wouldn't notice, and she didn't seem to change at all over the years. This was why he was so surprised when he noticed her this time. She looked very old and tired, terrible even for an old homeless woman.

"Every time I see her, and lately this has been often, because it seems she barely moves from the bench in the park any more, I get a guilty conscience. I should do something but I don't know what. The other day I tried to give her some small change. She didn't even want it. It was as if she had not even noticed me. And the stench. Could you smell it?"

He had done.

"It's as if she is rotting away alive. Isn't there some service in this country to look after people like her?"

Taras shrugged his shoulders. There probably was.

"If she can still be helped at all."

"What do you mean?" she gave him a surprised and accusing look. "There's always something that can be done."

"Really? A while back, about a year ago, I ran over a cat. It was one of those stray cats..."

The animal had jumped out of a bin and run straight out in front of his car. He hit it and the cat, despite its injuries, picked itself up and shot into some bushes beyond the ditch at the side of the road. He had thought about just driving on, but stopped and went across to the bushes where the dying animal stared at him with huge eyes he would never forget.

"I'm not talking about a cat," she said. "A person is not a cat."

She waited for him to agree, or at least add something, but he checked the clock on the wall, picked up his gun, thrust it in its holster and placed it back into the plastic bag. Only when he was putting on his trainers did he add, "Once, when I was still with the uniformed police, some writer was brought in one night and put into prison."

Taras had been on night duty and the writer was drunk so he had spent the night in the cell. In the morning, when he woke up, and before he was released, he had had a coffee with the police officers and he told them a story...

A story about how he and his mother had been deported to Germany during the Second World War and how he survived the Dresden bombing. He had been placed with a German family on the outskirts of town and when the bombs began falling he was standing at the top of the stairs leading into the cellar. The force from a nearby blast threw him down the stairs and he broke his arm but that was not what stayed with him, what hurt him most...

After the bombing he had gone into town and down by the river – Taras had forgotten which river runs through Dresden – he saw SS officers shooting people who were in flames due to the phosphorus from the dropped bombs. There was no help for them, phosphorus cannot be extinguished. Not even by jumping into the river.

"They did the only thing they could."

Taras stroked her hair and gave her a quick kiss. This always made her feel uncomfortable, dirty. It felt as if a guilty conscience was creeping its way into Taras, as if he could hardly wait to leave and sort out in his head what he had to sort out before going back home.

They did the only thing they could. Tina shuddered.

*

He unlocked the car on the passenger side and placed the bag with his gun onto the seat. Then he walked round the car and climbed in, put the key into the ignition and turned it. Even such a simple movement caused him pain in his bad elbow. When the engine started, so did the radio, and he caught the end of some bland and pointless song in English. He opened the glove compartment, found the pack of batteries and fitted them into the *Discman*. He tucked the earphones into his ears and turned up the volume.

> *If you like to gamble, I tell you I'm your man,*
> *You win some, lose some, all the same to me...*

*

Aleksander called her. He would be home in half an hour. Routine, this hiding of ours is becoming more and more of a routine, she thought to herself as she went around the flat, checking there were no tell-tale traces of Taras anywhere. The bedroom, the bathroom, the kitchen where she washed up one of the two coffee cups. Then she went to the refrigerator, took out a yoghurt and sat down in front of the TV.

She flicked through the channels. All the films that were just beginning seemed silly or at least uninteresting, the watchable ones were half way through, Eurosport was showing cycling on some plain stage and, flicking though all the channels for the third time, Tina realised that she wasn't at all in the mood for TV. Repeatedly her brain returned to the image of the tiny old lady surrounded with all those plastic bags that looked like drooping, deflating balloons.

Could Taras have walked past her without being touched in the slightest way? She stood up from the sofa, opened the fridge and found some cheese and salami with which she made a sandwich. Then she looked in the fridge again and found a chocolate milk. She put both in a bag, put on her sandals and left the flat.

There was still a crowd outside the cafés on Čop Street, noise that died down as soon as she disappeared into the passage under Nebotičnik. Silence then followed her all the way to the park where she found the bench with the old lady surrounded by bags. She hung the one she had brought onto the green slats above the woman's feet, hoping only that the old lady would notice it among all the others when she woke up in the morning.

Tuesday

CHAPTER 2.

"How can you be bothered..." Alenka muttered.

Almost as soon as Taras silenced the alarm clock on his mobile phone, his wife fell back to sleep. It was five in the morning and he hoped that the air outside would not be as stale as it was in their bedroom, even though they had been sleeping with the window half open.

Fifteen minutes later he was leaving the outskirts of Ljubljana and cycling along the regional road towards Polhov Gradec. He was on the mountain bike that he had fitted with thin, smooth tyres because he mostly cycled on asphalt. The road was almost empty and at the speed of just over twenty kilometres with which he was pushing his way through the heavy, still air, it seemed almost bearable, though he could not, even at this early hour, say it was fresh. The hot night had not cooled him down, and when the sun that was just rising behind his back would reach him, he would probably boil.

To begin with he did not exert himself excessively, just tried to get into a rhythm at what you might call the 'upper boundary of comfort'. He was saving his strength for the last six kilometres when the road climbed upwards, and would then push harder were he to still feel like it. An hour and a half after leaving home he was at the church on Črni Vrh. Even though he had been cycling for a number of seasons, he had only discovered the route this year, and after he had been to the church three or four times he even googled it to find out more about it. It was dedicated to Saint Leonard, protector of prisoners and women in labour.

This too he had had to find on the internet. Of all the years of catechesis, the only one he could remember was fire-fighting Saint Florian.

On the bench in front of the church he changed his sweaty T-shirt for a clean one from his small backpack. He then spent some time looking at the surrounding hills and the valley below from where a hazy mist was rising and, as he always did, he could not help thinking how beautiful Slovenia is. Not only here, in these low-lying hills in the surroundings of Ljubljana, but everywhere. He checked his phone, switched to silent mode before his ascent. There is nothing more annoying to someone exerting the last of their strength to ride up a hill than persistent, merciless ringing. He did not expect to have any unanswered calls, but there were two. One from Drvarič and one from Brajc, and a message from Drvarič.

Nine o'clock, my office.

Taras stood up, sat on the bicycle and pushed off towards the short but steep hill that led from the church to the settlement stretched out along the road, and from there into the valley. On the way he greeted an old lady who was clearly on her way to the graveyard next to the church. She did not return his greeting; maybe there was something about him she didn't like.

The slope must have had a gradient of at least fifteen degrees (probably more). There was a coffee bar with a terrace next to the road at the bottom of the hill and Taras would have loved to stop for a coffee, but it was only open at weekends. He would have to wait until he got to work. If he pushed hard enough, he could be there in time for one even before half past eight, well before Drvarič.

*

"I know," he interrupted her as she was about to tell him about the nine o'clock meeting. "Did he say what it was about?"

"No."

He thought about taking her for a coffee before the meeting and letting Drvarič wait, but he knew that they would not be able to enjoy it this way. Idiot or not, the man was still the boss.

"Never mind, let's get this over with and we can go for a coffee afterwards. Although by then Brajc and Osterc will also be here..."

"I think they were here before me today. Brajc called me at around half past seven, but he didn't say why."

"Yes, he called me too."

Taras walked down the corridor behind her and could not take his eyes of her tight-fitting jeans. He could not care less about what Drvarič wanted to tell him. Not now, not ever.

*

"Sabina, you go to the park with the children who are here already," the older teacher told her younger colleague at the France Prešeren Nursery School located close to the American Embassy with the National Museum across the road on one side and the Foreign Ministry opposite it on the other. Distinguished company that gave the nursery school distinguished status and clientele. Parents of children at this school did not have to get up as early as those in the suburbs Šiška or Fužine who then had to travel into town, so there were only a few children around at seven o'clock in the morning. It was these whom the older teacher, in charge that morning, was trying to get out into the park, possibly also making her own job a little easier on this stuffy morning. The one thing this nursery school didn't have was a decent playground. On dry summer days the ground, which seemed unsuitable for growing a lawn of any sort, produced clouds of fine dust that would eat into all and everything, causing widespread coughing.

"Of course it's possible," said the man from the maintenance company that had been called in, after the school had requested help from the town hall with solving the problem. "But it means you should stop operating for a year or so."

"Stop operating?"

"Yes, because of the kids. No grass in the world can grow if you walk all over it every day... How many do you have here?"

One hundred and forty-two in seven classes. Two meetings later the idea of grass was abandoned and it was decided they would get Tartan playground tiles instead.

"Should I take them to Tivoli?" the younger teacher asked.

The teacher in charge shook her head. The playground equipment there was neatly fenced off but it was a little too far away and she would never take the children there alone. The slides were too big, too dangerous for a single escort, especially because the playground area was split down the middle with a line of bushes, rendering it impossible for one person to keep a constant eye on the entire area and all the corners where lively children might wander off or hide.

"Take them to the other park, Park Argentina or whatever it's called now. You have to be back by breakfast anyway."

There were five children and the teacher lined them up in pairs, holding the hand of one of them herself. She was not actually certain whether she was really allowed to take the children beyond the high fencing of the nursery school compound alone; she had never studied the rulebook in detail and Greta, the older teacher who was in charge, had never thought much about sticking to the letter of the law and preferred a more liberal interpretation of the Pre-School Institutions Act that, among its list of rules on the standards for providing pre-school education, also regulated what criteria needed to be met when children were taken beyond the school enclosure. Sabina did wonder whether her colleague was a little too lax about the rules, but she kept quiet about it. Greta was from an era when the first thing parents did when their child came home with a scratch or graze was not rush off to the family lawyer, only later seeking medical attention. This was also the reason the school's headmistress was counting down the months until the end of the year when Greta was due to retire.

As long as they reached the park without any problems. Sabina glanced at the group following her. She was holding Jan, the liveliest child by the hand. Traipsing behind her were Maja and Tilen, and behind them Jaka and Lina. She had organised them into pairs herself, otherwise they would never have been back before breakfast. If Jan does not cause problems, and there was no indication he would have a bout of his usual stubbornness at this time of day, then this should be a perfectly acceptable outing. And it really would be too hot to go out later on in the day.

She released them among the chestnut trees by a low wall built of large, dressed stone blocks, their tops smoothed with a layer of concrete, and sat on one of the benches. The park, split diagonally down the middle by an asphalt path, was almost empty. On the other side of the path, on a triangular patch of grass, someone had allowed a dog to run around off its lead; apart from them there was nobody else. Well, there was someone; on a bench at the far end of the section which included the playground and the trees lay a woman whom Sabina had seen there on a number of occasions. A homeless woman with lots of plastic bags around her. Clearly she was still asleep.

"Miss, can we play *Who's Afraid of the Big Bad Wolf?*"

Standing in front of her was Lina, a sweet, slightly chubby four-year old with long plaits and thick glasses. She was holding a soft toy, a large fluffy grey rat with three baby rats sewn to its belly. The child would not go anywhere without it and often found herself in a tug of war with Jan or any of the other children who tried to separate the baby rats from their mother. Sabina had a soft spot for her and tried to be encouraging whenever she could, hoping that Lina would grow into a beauty, more beautiful than some of the other perfect but spoilt little princesses her group was full of. She stood up.

"Anyone else for playing?"

Jaka and Maja joined them, Jan and Tilen chose the slides, and before letting them go there – to a distance of about ten metres – Sabina instructed the boys, "Only on the smaller slides, and you're not to go beyond the path."

In the middle of the other equipment was dinosaur-shaped horizontal tree trunk with its branches partly sawn off and stripped of its bark. Intended for climbing, it had become so smooth and slippery through use and re-varnishing, that she would not even try climbing onto it herself, let alone allow a four-year old to do so.

"And you're not to climb the trunk. Is that clear?"

Tilen nodded.

"Jan?!"

The future ruler of the world gave her a cheeky look, but eventually also nodded. Sabina wanted to add that they would go straight back to the nursery if he disobeyed, but there was not much point. She would have to keep a constant eye on him anyway.

Who's Afraid of the Big Bad Wolf was a simple game, especially the way they played it. She would stand on the path that crossed the park and shuffle her feet on the spot for a while and the children would sneak up behind her and touch her. When she turned round and shouted "Boooo!" at them, they would then run to a wooden house about fifteen metres away and hide inside it. She would then roar for a while and hop around the house while the children would scream with excitement. This would be repeated... up to twenty times.

She was not counting, but it must have been after five or six times, when she suggested a short break.

"No, no, no..." the children shouted.

"Just a brief break. The Big Bad Wolf is tired."

She sat on the bench and checked her phone. Another fifteen minutes and they would have to go back, otherwise the cocoa or tea, or whatever was for breakfast today, would be cold. In this heat, that might not be bad, but still. She glanced at the three children hiding in the wooden house; they had clearly found some other game to play. Sabina was twenty-five and could not imagine what it would be like to have someone waiting for her at home after a day spent with children at the nursery school. She would need to consider it at some point, she was thinking, as her gaze moved towards the dinosaur trunk. The boys were not there. They were crouched behind it, picking something up from the ground. Then they stood up and threw that something into the direction beyond the playground... She could not see where, because the boys were obscuring her view. She stood up and called out.

"Jan, Tilen..."

They did not react. Once again they threw what they had found on the ground. She walked up to them, followed by the other children from the house whose attention had been drawn by her shouting.

"Hey, you two!"

They were throwing whatever they were throwing at the woman on the park bench. Sabina ran up to them and grabbed their hands.

"What do you think you're doing?"

"But she isn't moving," said Jan, trying to wriggle his way out of her grip. She gave him a furious look and pointed with her finger to show him he should move away. He took a step back and stopped, "But she isn't moving."

She turned towards the woman, lying on the bench about three metres away, surrounded by plastic bags that must somehow have been attached to her, otherwise they would long have been blown away. What could she possibly keep in them, Sabina wondered and stepped closer.

"Wait there," she instructed the children she could sense behind her back.

She was almost right next to the woman, wondering what would happen if she woke up, when a slight breeze moved away one of the plastic bags that had been lying across her face. It revealed something that Sabina could not make out initially. It was as if someone had poured some kind of putrid yoghurt with something else... over the woman's head, over her hair, which looked partly singed. She stepped closer, close enough to pick up the smell of a human body that rarely washed or changed its clothes and notice in the yogurt, which was not yoghurt at all, tiny white worms feasting on human blood and brain tissue.

She screamed and ran towards the children who screamed along with her and ran, laughing and shouting into the small wooden house.

*

"How are we all?" Drvarič asked, pretending to be in a good mood.

Drvarič was one of those people who have a curious, constant, ever-felt absence of genuineness. Such people do not smile when something is funny but only if they have planned to do so in advance. They are utterly skilled in suppressing their primary reactions and Taras could not imagine Drvarič swearing, for example, or at least crying out, were he to hit his finger with a hammer, unless such a reaction was pre-scripted. Drvarič and his kind are not even put off by the fact that this makes them appear to react with a slight delay, almost as if they were actors in an amateur theatre production who have set themselves a goal beyond their capabilities. Do they not notice that everyone else knows they are pretending to be something they're not, Taras asked himself every time, including this one.

"All right," said Tina.

"And we're about to be better," Drvarič continued, giving Taras a fleeting look of barely noticeable accusation, as an actor on stage might glance at a fellow actor who had forgotten their lines. "I have something for you two."

"I didn't hear the phone in the morning. I was out on my bike," Taras said.

Tina glanced at Taras out of the corner of her eye. Why does he insist on working Drvarič up even when it is totally unnecessary? Like now, for example. Of course anyone can be anywhere they want at half past six in the morning, without explaining to the boss that they could not be bothered to pick up the phone because they were exercising.

"You went cycling in the morning?"

"Yes, so I don't get put off my day before it even starts."

There, again.

"Right, right," Drvarič muttered, either unwilling to argue with Taras or to understand what Taras was really saying.

"Well, I have a nice little thing for our young lady, if you'll agree?"

Taras stayed silent.

"I've already sent Brajc there, but I thought Tina might take over, with your assistance, of course. You're going to be busy over the next few days anyway, aren't you?"

"No," said Taras. "Not that I know of."

"I thought you had a meeting with Petan at court the day after tomorrow?"

Taras hissed contemptuously through his teeth.

"That'll take just a couple of hours plus the journey there and back."

Drvarič shook his head. "Hopefully. But I'm sure you won't object to Tina taking on her first, so to say, murder case?"

"I'm excited," said Taras.

Perhaps it only sounded that way and it was probably just another pick at Drvarič, but Tina felt a little hurt as Taras' response might also be interpreted differently.

"Is the team complete? I mean, leave and holidays. It *is* summer. Nothing longer than two days for the next fortnight please."

"Brajc and Osterc are going on a union trip tomorrow, but it's only one day."

Plus the two days it will take Brajc to recover.

"Where are they going this year?" Drvarič asked.

"Budapest."

"Budapest? For a day?"

He then mulled over the Budapest-in-a-day thing for a while, before concluding,

"Well, right, I suppose, one day, then."

"Excuse me," said Tina. "What case did you have in mind?"

"Oh, haven't I mentioned it yet? Well. In that park, the one behind the GPD, I can never remember what it's called…"

"Lenin Park," Taras helped him.

"Lenin? And it's still called that?"

Taras nodded.

"Really? Well, a dead woman has been found in that park. Brajc is there already, and I assume the NFL and the IFM as well. Now they're waiting for the head of investigation."

"This dead woman," Tina asked, "doesn't happen to be the bag lady who slept on the bench in that park?"

"Yes," said Drvarič. "Do you know her?"

He smiled and looked at Taras.

"No worries, your colleague here will help you."

CHAPTER 3.

Brajc's alarm went off at seven. It was a small red radio clock with angular orange numbers that they had been given as a wedding present. It had somehow escaped the Excel divorce spreadsheet and for this reason Brajc was especially fond of it. He only used it as an alarm clock, even though he could of course use his mobile phone for the purpose and thus avoid waking up to the most inhumanely penetrating, metallic-digital and unpleasant sound there was.

He sighed and turned to the right to reach it and switch it off, dragging his nose across the pillow soaked with the sour stench of the damn summer he hated as much because of the heat as he hated the winter because of the cold and the spring and autumn because of the damp or the leaves he should, though never did, rake up in the garden, or whatever else he hated it for. If he had it his way, people would not settle in places where the temperature falls below eighteen degrees or rises above twenty-five, and also not in places where it rains all the time or where it doesn't rain at all. He had once spent some time looking on the internet to see whether such a place even existed, and just as he discovered almost with relief that it didn't and that there is something wrong with everywhere else in the world and that billions of people are hardly, if at all, better off, the Google search window came up with Las Palmas with the lowest January temperatures at around eighteen degrees, and the highest temperatures in August rarely exceeding twenty-five.

"Just look at them..." he bleated in disappointment and for a while stared at photos of the largest town on Gran Canaria. "Palms and all that," he added after a while and looked out of the window of his living room, his gaze getting settling on the solitary spruce surrounded by three silver birch trees.

Pillow under his arm, he walked out onto the balcony on the first floor of the family house that had been designed for two families and in which he was now living alone until he and his former wife could decide what would happen to it. He pegged the sweaty pillow to the washing line. "Nothing better against bacteria than UV radiation," he was once forced to listen to Golob. "If you were to hang a plastic bag of dirty water on your backpack... let's say you're somewhere in the wilderness. If you were to walk around with it all day in the sun, you could easily drink its contents by evening..." Blah, blah, blah. What idiot would walk around the wilderness all day in the sun with a plastic bag full of water? Probably not even Taras would do that.

He threw a knob of butter into the frying pan and waited for it to almost melt before adding a little more, and, fuck it, you only live once, a third helping as well. Then he carefully, without breaking the yolks, added three eggs. Once they began to coagulate he also threw in a couple of slices of bacon. While this combination was pleasantly sizzling away in the pan, he put the coffee pot on the stove. Waiting for everything to cook and boil, he stepped to the window as if to check what the weather might be like today even though he had been outside on the balcony just a moment ago. Creeping up a clear blue sky from round the corner was the glowing sphere, and in his thoughts, because he could not be bothered to say it out loud, Brajc cursed the sphere and the blueness, and then also the missing clouds, despite the fact that both these scourges, the blueness and the lack of clouds, were in effect the same thing.

When his phone rang he was already back in the bedroom where he picked out from the wardrobe what he would wear that day, annoyed by the realisation that he would need to put a few things in the washing machine or he would run out of clean clothes very soon. As it rang, he glanced at the flashing angular numbers on the red radio clock. It was seven thirty-five. Irritated, as he had been since he had woken up, he reluctantly pressed the button.

"Yes?" he asked and then added another 'yes' or two, and an

'ahaa' and finished with an "I'll take care of it." He then searched through his contacts and called Taras. As far as he knew Taras was still his boss and Brajc wasn't sure why they hadn't called him.

Taras was not answering.

"Surely he's not still asleep?" Brajc muttered as he called Osterc's number.

He let it ring for a long time and just as he thought that Osterc had finally picked up, the line went dead. His way of telling me to sod off, Brajc wondered, or had the phone just run out of beeps, letting him know that there was no point in persisting? He called again and this time Osterc's number was no longer available. Miffed, he found Tina's number. Is there anyone who actually still works in this country?

"Yep," she said and sounded happy, as if right now she was somewhere else... somewhere like Las Palmas on Gran Canaria and not in the Ljubljana bracing itself for a hellishly hot summer's day. He moved the pan from the stove at the last second before burning everything that was inside it. Such a possibility merely aggravated him further.

"Are you still at home?" he asked.

"Yep," she said again. "Just finishing breakfast. Anything urgent?"

"Basically... well, no, I'll sort it out myself."

He rubbed his stomach. Nothing more urgent than breakfast. And just as he would not allow anyone to cut short his own, he would not cut short anyone else's either. He shook some salt over the eggs and bacon (more than he had lied to the doctor about, and there were also more eggs than he would admit to) and some pepper (that he had not asked about at all), and cut a thick slice of bread, sighing with content. For a moment, a terrifying moment, he had even thought that the dead bag lady might spoil his breakfast. Well, she wouldn't. Whatever the case, he liked to eat in peace and quiet. There is a Slovene saying that even a dog likes to be left alone when eating.

*

While Brajc was emptying his frying pan, Osterc was getting his two kids into the car in order to drop them off at school and before that drive his wife to her work, if that would even be possible, considering the late hour at which they were setting off from home and for which his wife, this time, as always, was blaming him. Not entirely justified, although it was true that Osterc sometimes simply did not know how to do things quickly, especially because he was not selective. For example, if his phone rang just as he was putting shoes on his younger son, who should of course be putting his shoes on himself as one would expect from a child in third grade, but who as a clever child discovered that in a time constraint he could successfully pretend to be a helpless toddler, Osterc, without any qualms, dropped the child's heel and shoe, found his phone in his pocket and looked at the screen...

"Are you nuts?" his wife shouted at him, pulled his phone from his hand and switched it off. Not only cut the line, she switched it off entirely.

With an upset face Osterc completed the task with his second son's shoes and clenched his teeth all the way to Ljubljana. When they reached the petrol station at Barje he finally spoke,

"It was Brajc. There might be something wrong at work."

"It'll wait," said his wife, figuring out in her mind whether it was easier for her as a part-time librarian, to be late for work, or whether the kids could, once again, be late for school.

"Where are we going?" Osterc asked as they reached Tržaška and they had to make their minds up. To get to their kids' school at Bičevje he would need to turn right in a hundred metres, to take his wife to work in Šiška, he would make a left turn and take the road under Rožnik... He did not get an answer and, as the turning was inevitably approaching, he tried again,

"Where..."

"School," she responded sternly.

She'd rather have to listen to her boss reprimand her than deal with the class teacher of her younger son – she could be hellishly vicious.

*

"Why don't we walk?" Tina suggested.

"I can't be bothered."

Can a person who gets up at five in the morning to cycle for two hours before coming to work really not be bothered to walk the less than five hundred metres distance from the police station to the park?

"No, I don't feel like it, I've done my stuff for today."

Driving twenty or thirty metres from the parking lots at the station, they stopped at the first set of traffic lights.

"I took her some food yesterday," she said quietly. "A sandwich and some milk."

"Who?"

"This woman."

Taras looked at her with surprise.

"When yesterday?"

"After you left. Now I'm wondering whether she might already have been dead even then."

"You didn't speak to her?"

"No, she was asleep. At least I thought she was asleep."

The traffic lights switched to orange and Taras drove on.

"Were you being serious when you said that shooting her in the head might be the best way of helping her?"

"I said that I was afraid that there was no way of helping her, and that the SS shot people in the head when they were burning because of the phosphorus."

"As an example of what to do with people who cannot be helped."

He looked at her.

"It doesn't matter what I or anyone else said. The fact that you were concerned about her and I wasn't neither helped nor hurt her."

Taras swore when someone pushed in in front of him from a one-way side street and for a moment Tina worried that he might, agitated as he was, overtake them and stop in front of them. Clenching his teeth Taras drove behind the car until it disappeared round a corner. When they reached the park of a thousand names he drove up onto the pavement and stopped the engine. Behind the trunks of the trees that surrounded the park and beyond the playground area he could see a group of people, standing out from which was a figure in white.

*

Brajc didn't stop at the police station. He drove directly to the General Police Directorate and parked in a space reserved for staff. He began swearing as he tried to find his permit in the glove compartment. Where had he put it? He tapped his fingers on the dashboard, trying to remember why the hell he would have moved to somewhere else something that is only ever useful in the car. He couldn't think of a reason and dismissively waved his hand.

"Whatever..." he said to himself and stepped out of the car, locked it and made his way towards the entrance of the GPD. It was only twenty metres away, enough for the first droplets of sweat to appear on his forehead.

"Hi Brajc," said the man sitting inside the glass booth at the entrance.

Brajc did not bother with morning courtesies. He had never understood this good morning-good morning stuff. Why would anyone want to wish anyone else a good morning? Does it make it any better? He found a packet of paper handkerchiefs in his pocket and mopped his forehead.

"Hot, isn't it?" the man behind the glass tried.

"That's a fucking understatement," said Brajc. "Babnik, apparently you've got a carcass down in the park? Is anyone with her?"

Babnik nodded.

"Two cadets are keeping watch over it for you."

Brajc half turned to Babnik as he was leaving.

"The grey Omega out in your parking lot is mine. I hope it's not towed away by the time I come back and I have to rush around to retrieve it."

He stepped outside and found himself in the sun. Tiredly he glanced at the sky between the building of the General Police Directorate and the Nebotičnik, looked in the direction of the park that, despite living in Ljubljana and its outskirts all his life, he could not remember the name of, and set off in the opposite direction, towards the coffee bar in the deep shade of the passage between Štefan and Cankar Streets. The body could wait.

This was where Osterc found him, at the table next to the outside wall of the bar. He was leaning against the large glass wall that was cracked with long pieces of tape stuck over the damage.

"What happened to this?" Osterc asked.

"I don't know and I really don't care," said Brajc and pointed to the empty chair.

"Wouldn't it be better if..." Osterc tried but still sat down.

He then ordered a juice because his usual green tea would take ages to cool in this heat. He drank it instantly, throwing a contemptuous look at Brajc who only slowly finished off his cappuccino, wiped his brow with a handkerchief and beckoned to the waitress.

"Your turn," Brajc said to Osterc who was still fiddling around with his wallet trying to find the right change as the student waitress waited patiently with a bored expression on her face and her hand extended. He then hurried after Brajc who was already swaying down the passage towards the blinding sunlight.

Standing by the body lying on the park bench, behind the police cordon that separated the bench and its immediate surroundings from the outside world, stood two young police officers in uniform. At the other end a figure clad in white plastic was bending over, scratching the ground under the bench. Brajc lifted the tape and made his way straight to the man in a white Tyvek protective suit, while Osterc, showing his police ID, calmed down the two policemen who had leapt towards him.

"So what do we have, Golob?"

Golob nodded and continued collecting whatever it was he was collecting from under the bench. Brajc leaned over the body and grabbed his nose.

"Urgh, Jesus Christ, how long has she been here?"

"Not very long," said the voice under the bench. "Judging by the *muscidae* larvae, specifically those of *musca domestica*, ten or twelve hours at the most. The stench is... partly due to the heat, partly antecedent."

"Yuck," said Brajc, "Yucky yuck."

With disgust on his face he leaned over the old woman's dead body from which Golob had already removed all the plastic bags, carefully placing them into his own bag. In the middle of the head, among the matted and filthy hair that was almost the same ash grey colour as the woman's skin, gaped a small, almost perfectly round hole. Wriggling inside it were tiny white larvae. Golob had transferred some of them into his test tube in order to later, in the peace and quiet of his own lab, weigh and measure them and, taking into consideration the day and night temperatures of the specific micro-location, estimate the time when the bullet shot through the barrel of the pistol – for he was almost convinced that it was a pistol – penetrated the skull, flew through the gap in between the planks of wood on the bench under the victim's head and hit the metal bracket with which the bench was fixed to the ground, flattening and shattering as it did so. He picked up the fragments of lead, tin, and, as he assumed rather than established at first sight, also copper, which would lead to a definite conclusion that this was a case of a full metal jacket bullet or FMJ as forensics might say in some American movie, in which Golob would be played by...

"Don't you have the case?"

"Let me do my job, please," Golob barked at Brajc.

No, he didn't have it. If he had had the cartridge case he could, with some luck, not only determine the type of weapon, but even find its owner if the firearm was in the databases of any country with membership of Interpol. These fragments he was picking up from the ground with tweezers wouldn't be of much use to him.

"Just wanted to help," said Brajc, moving backwards out of the way and then turning round towards someone he noticed on the horizon.

"There! Here comes Taras," he said over his shoulder. "Golob, you'd better make up what you don't yet know."

CHAPTER 4.

"Hello everyone," said Taras and stood next to Osterc who gave him a surprised look as did Brajc and Golob. Normally he would first go and look at the body and after the mandatory "What do we have here?" allow them to give him a rundown of the basics. This time, before anyone had a chance to ask anything, he pointed at Tina.

"Her case."

"Really?" Golob cried out, rustling in his one-piece white Tyvek suit as he looked up from above the body. "Well done, congratulations."

He took off his glove and shook Tina's hand. Brajc and Osterc followed suit, Osterc automatically, as usual, and Brajc with a genuine excitement. He continued to smile even a few seconds after he let go of her hand, until he realised that this probably didn't signal that anything would change for him and, if anything did, it would certainly not be for the better. As a novice she was certain to be a little confused and over-keen at the same time... Well, we're in for some spectacle, he thought to himself, glancing at Taras who was standing indifferently to one side, rubbing his elbow.

"Well, what do we have?" Tina asked, trying not to sound uncertain but realised with irritation that she sounded like a poor version of Taras.

Despite this, Golob gave her an encouraging nod and began explaining. As if all this had little to do with him, Taras sat on the low stone wall that ran along two sides of the park. Relieved, Brajc joined him, only Osterc stood somewhere half way between them and the bench.

"I'll now tell what the forensic doctor ought to be telling you *if* he was here and I don't know why one hasn't arrived yet but it doesn't make much difference. So, we have a shot at close range, clear from the typically star-shaped wound due to the effect of gasses, a straight shot, proof of which is the regularity of the circular contusion ring. The bullet entered the cranium just above the forehead, right here on the hairline," said Golob, lifting the lock of grey hair that was hanging across the wound though not hiding the burned patch of skin around it. "It went straight through the skull, passed through the gap in the bench and hit this metal base where it shattered. We unfortunately don't have the cartridge case. Clearly this is the work of someone who knew what they were doing."

Tina stepped closer to the body on the bench. Of course the first thing she looked at was the wound on the woman's head. It was impossible to avoid and with the brutality and raw force of what had caused it, it was in strange contrast with the expression on the old woman's face. In her work and in general Tina had so far not seen many bodies and those she had were... She was looking for the right term and, yes, 'contorted' or 'grimacing' would be the closest to what she was trying to describe. All of them faces of people who had not wanted to die. This was so even for the few that she had seen who had not died some violent death. Yet here it was almost as if the woman had fallen asleep and been dreaming happy dreams when this happened to her. She appeared calm, peaceful.

It was hard to say how old she was. Had this been a woman who lay in her bed every evening, warmed some milk every morning and poured some oats into it, a woman who would go and have coffee with her friends once a day and in the evening join some activity group, like her aunt Dora who went to a reading club... Apparently they had recently gotten into reading crime novels, and Dora, who was not in fact her real aunt but they all called her that, had completed some kind of reading list on the theme and would now, whenever she saw Tina, cross-examine her on a variety of police matters. "Is it true that..."

When she had last seen her, Dora was interested in how police officers wear their weapons during the summer season so they are not in full view of everyone. In fact, more often than not they don't, and if they do they keep them in a holster against their hip and there's also a discreet police belt mount that some use. Then there is Taras who brought his in a plastic shopping bag.

If the old woman on the bench had been one of these ladies with an orderly life, Tina would guess she was around eighty. She knew, however, that with a life like hers, she might well be barely sixty. Life on the streets is tough.

"There should have been a bag with a sandwich and a chocolate milk hanging from the bottom end of the bench," she said.

Golob gave her a surprised look. Taras was standing behind her, so he could not see his face.

"But how...?"

"I live close by and yesterday I felt sorry for her and I brought it here."

"Yesterday?" Golob asked almost shyly.

"At around half past ten, quarter to eleven. I don't know if she was still alive. I didn't see. At the time I thought she was just asleep."

She turned towards Taras. With the palm of his left hand he was smoothing his stubble. His right hand was resting on his leg, his palm holding his knee. He was watching her and when their eyes met she picked up on his barely noticeable smile.

"What a coincidence?" said Golob. "Perhaps you were the last person to see this woman alive."

"Or the first to see her dead," Tina said quietly.

"Does anyone know when this happened?"

"Cvilak will be able to give us more details and, before that, also the gentleman approaching..." he pointed towards the ambulance that had just stopped behind Brajc, out of which stepped a man, a very young man, almost a boy, in white. "But based on the temperature of the body that I was able to measure, not of course in the way they can measure it on the dissection table, so please take this only as an indication, I would say that no less than ten and no more than fourteen hours ago. Then we also have the *musca domestica* larvae..."

"The common fly," Brajc muttered from the wall he was sitting on, annoying Golob -he didn't have many opportunities to talk and even now he was being interrupted by some bore with a couple of A-levels and a *Schnellkurs* in criminology.

"Would you like to take it from here, Brajc?" he rebuked him.

"No, no..."

Brajc waved his open palms turned towards Golob and, as he happened to be holding a soggy paper hanky he had been wiping his sweat with, it looked as if he was waving a white flag of surrender. Or it would have, had he not quietly but loud enough for Golob to hear, added, "...just get to the end of it today if possible, please!"

Golob decided to ignore him but it was too late anyway. The unknown face in the white gown, younger than any of the others present, even Tina, was already standing next to Taras.

"Wow," he cried out. "My first solo inspection and I get this. Crazy! Have you finished? Can I take a look?"

Taras pointed at Golob. With a kind of conceited caution Golob waited for his young colleague, patronisingly showed him the body, explained what he had already told Tina, Taras and everyone else, and then moved on to the flies, or rather the *muscae domesticate*...

"...which are not some kind of non-existent *common* fly, as we heard here today, but what is officially known as the *housefly*..."

"Fly as in fly," the young doctor said in good humour, earning himself an accusatory glare from Golob.

"...and if we know that, depending on the temperature, which..."

"...is so hot you could just drop down and die!" Brajc muttered.

"...which during the night was still around twenty-five degrees, I would say that it is most likely that the death occurred between ten and fourteen hours ago. A rough estimate."

The forensic doctor nodded and during Golob's explanation produced a smart phone from his pocket and tapped the screen a few times. When Golob finished, he commented, "You're probably right. This thing here also says more or less the same thing."

Only when the coroner and his two assistants approached

the corpse with a body bag did Taras step closer and take a brief look at the woman.

"I don't know if you noticed," Golob said keenly. "This so-called ring of dirt," he circled round the wound with his finger. "It always appears in shots at such close range, or in our case point blank. As you can see, there's nothing inside the contusion ring, no traces of soot or fat, although there usually are at least some..."

"Which means?" Tina asked.

"This means that before it was fired, our gun was very well cleaned. At least as well as any decent gun should be. And there is another detail I want to point out to you."

He turned towards Taras who interrupted him.

"You will write it in your report, won't you?"

Taras turned round, went back to Brajc and Osterc and sat on the wall.

Golob looked at Tina with surprise.

*

Half an hour later Taras, Tina, Brajc and Osterc were sitting in the passage between Štefan and Cankar Street, ordering coffees though this time Osterc had his usual green tea. Taras was about to lean back on the glass partition but realised it was taped up so he kept to carefully swinging in his chair. There was a slight draught through the passage and Brajc's melting, after he returned with a few paper towels from the toilets on the first floor, did in fact ease slightly. The damn steps were so steep he had needed to sit on the lid of the toilet seat to catch his breath, inhaling the stench of chlorine cleaning products. What idiot had thought of putting the loo on the floor *above* the bar?

"You're sweating too?" he asked Taras whose T-shirt had a dark arc along its edge. "See why I'm not into sports. Not worth it."

Taras didn't pay him any attention. He looked at Tina and beckoned to her. She didn't respond. With an absent gaze she was holding the handle of her cup, as if unable to decide whether to lift it or leave it on the table.

"She was found by a teacher from a nearby kindergarten," said Osterc when he noticed Taras' move. "I will send you the write-up of her statement by mail."

"Send it to Tina," Taras corrected him.

"Do we know who she is?" Tina asked, finally bringing the coffee to her lips.

Osterc shook his head.

"We found no ID, but then what do you expect from people like this? What use was an ID to her? Perhaps Marn will find something when he looks through her pockets."

"It's not certain we will find out. Not all of these people are in the register," said Brajc.

Tina looked at Taras who nodded.

"Don't let it get to you," said Brajc, trying to put her at ease. "I mean, the…"

He fanned the hand he was not holding a paper towel in through the air, as if wanting to push enough oxygen to his brain to find a more appropriate word than *old bat* which was about to come off the tip of his tongue.

"…well, she's probably better off this way. She was just suffering. And God did she stink!"

Tina looked at him and finally put her cup on the table.

"Isn't she?" Brajc continued. "Osterc, you tell her."

Osterc took the first sip of his green water and showed no sign that he might have wanted to say anything.

"Well, I mean, was that a life?" Brajc kept looking at each of them.

"You're not the only one to think that," said Tina and glanced at Taras.

"Only yesterday did I express something along those lines," he admitted.

"For this old woman or in general?" Brajc was surprised.

Taras nodded.

"For this very one."

"But, how? She was still alive yesterday?"

Taras nodded once again.

Tina placed her cup on the saucer and moved a lock of hair that had fallen across her forehead. If she were to stand in the park for an hour, Taras would have been only one of a hundred passers-by, and all of them would think the same thing Brajc was now trying to express. And what had she done for this woman who was now being transferred from the red and white van into refrigeration? She had brought her a sandwich and half a litre of chocolate milk in a bag.

"Taras, where were you yesterday?" Brajc asked.

Taras smiled.

"Yesterday evening?"

"Yes," said Brajc, calculating a little. "Somewhere between nine, ten, eleven p.m.?"

They all laughed, even Osterc this time, and Tina made an effort to also turn her mouth upwards. He was in the park with his police gun, and then there was that story with the cat... She closed her eyes for a moment and shook her head ever so slightly. She did not think anyone would notice buy Brajc did.

"Come on, don't let it get to you! She was just a homeless woman. You will have all the time in the world to find out who it is that won't allow us a moment's peace."

*

Taras and Tina stood in front of the bench that reached from the wall almost to the path that crosses the park diagonally, still cordoned off with police tape, though the body of the woman was long removed.

"Did I miss it, did they say anything about when they would do the autopsy?" Taras asked more in order to say something than out of any real interest. This time it would not be necessary to hack the body apart to find the cause of death.

"Tomorrow morning. Why do you want to know? They expect me to go, don't they?"

"If you don't want to, I can go."

"Thanks, Taras, but this is my case."

If this had been his case, he would probably have been tempted to merely call Cvilak and ask him to simply sign the autopsy report. Why on earth should he hang around a body with a perfect round hole in its head? Even Drvarič noted that she had been shot.

"Shall we start work?" he asked and waited.

She nodded and looked around the park. To the north and west of the bench there was quite a lot of empty space, a little further along were some trees and only a hundred metres or so away the first buildings that were hidden from view by a huge plane and a few smaller trees growing at that end of the park. Behind their backs was a four storey building with flats, built in the 1930s, and its northern face looked right across the area of the park with the bench next to which Taras and Tina were standing.

"Canvass?" he asked.

She seemed lost. He never imagined that the responsibility would paralyse her in this way.

"Canvass?" she repeated.

"Yes, a canvass. We question every window that overlooks the crime scene."

"Oh, yes, of course," she said, as if she had only just awoken from a heavy sleep. "Taras?"

"Yes?"

"Are you OK with me leading this case?"

"Of course. Why?"

"I got this silly feeling that you didn't approve."

He laughed.

"It's not that. This is not about my ego. I couldn't care less about rank and experience. What makes me just a little miffed is knowing that these things don't ever go the way Drvarič thinks they do. He has long been far from reality. Did you ever have the impression that there is any kind of enforced hierarchy in our little group?"

No, she hadn't. Taras was in charge and nobody else tried anything much anyway.

"And one other thing; this case might not be as simple as it seems from behind an office desk and if anything will get complicated Drvarič will be the first to forget about you."

He did not need to tell her all this, she knew it anyway.

"But if you feel this way, perhaps you should pair up with Brajc."

It sounded wicked. She shook her head.

"I don't want to be there when he has a heart attack. I don't want to be the one who will have to resuscitate him."

He laughed even though it did not sound like a joke and he

had thought of it himself. Over the last few days, with the heat killing the town and himself trying to limit any physical activity to the minimum, whenever he was with poor old Brajc who was out of breath and groaned even just going to the toilet, Taras had often wondered how much the man must be suffering, how much more he could take, how hard his heart must be working to prevent the system from collapsing. There were days he could not be bothered to go cycling in the morning but just the thought of Brajc's veins made him change his mind.

They went round to the entrance of the building, the front of which overlooked Župančič and Puhar Streets. Tina stepped into the foyer and looked at the nameplates of the residents next to the bells on the entrance panel. No foreign, immigrant surnames, all of them old Slovene family names, Koren, Levstik, Kalin... It was similar in the block of flats she lived in and in most of the old, middle-class, residential buildings in the centre of town. When one of the original residents of these flats died they were passed on to their heirs who most often got married to owners of similar town flats, and it was a closed social circle, almost without any newcomers.

Tina pressed the first button. There was no response for a long time and she was already aiming at the second surname when someone answered the intercom. Tina could not decide whether all the crackling was due to the antiquated system or the venerable age of the male voice that answered it.

"Yes, what do you want?"

She introduced herself, told him that she was a police officer and asked him to open the front door because she and her colleague were gathering information about... She paused for a moment.

"... about what happened in the park last night."

"About what?" the voice asked after a delay of a few seconds.

"We can explain when you open the door," Taras almost shouted from behind her. "We're from the Police, didn't you hear that?"

The door eventually opened.

"I'm sorry," he said as Tina held it open for him. "If I had to spend a second more in the sun, it would be me who'd need resuscitating."

CHAPTER 5.

"Hello again, Babnik," Brajc chirped, leaning with his elbow, one of the more healthy parts of his otherwise exhausted body, onto the counter in front of the window in the foyer of the General Police Directorate, merely a good hundred metres from the bench on which the dead woman had been lying just a little earlier. "Taras said that you were responsible for everything that dies in the park. I have one outside, wrapped in a blanket. Around seventy kilos, I'd guess. Where should we deliver this?"

"Take her home, Brajc!" came from behind the glass. Then the door opened and the tall guy in a police uniform walked out in the corridor. Slightly overweight with a blond moustache under a partly bald head with a few remnants of hair. Overweight but far from Brajc's dimensions. "What is it that you want now?"

He sounded rude but there was a trace of fondness in his voice.

"We've come for the tapes from your security cameras, Babnik," Osterc explained.

Brajc gave him a miffed look, as if he had wanted to tease Babnik just a little longer.

"What do I want?" he then turned to Babnik. "I'd like you to show me the shots you have from that lovely camera you have above your door over there. So we can check whether anyone walked past here with a gun in their hand at, let's say..." he paused and waved the thumb of his right hand through the air as if trying to estimate the approximate time. "... about twelve hours ago, plus, minus two hours. Would that be possible or are you still too busy with Kennedy's assassination?"

*

"Do we need to pay anything?" Brajc asked mockingly when he signed the receipt and was given the USB key with a copy of the tapes.

"Happy viewing." Babnik appeared satisfied. He probably imagined Brajc sitting hours on end in front of the screen, making notes on all the people walking past the camera, without any real hope that anything would come from this.

"No worries," said Brajc and, almost as if he was guessing what his blond colleague was thinking, added, "We'll stick it on fast forwards, and that'll do it. Before you can say knife. Definitely before you get off work today."

They stepped out of the building. In the meantime, the sun had already reached its zenith right above Štefan Street and Brajc reluctantly blinked, searching in his bag for his sunglasses. Donning his Ray-Ban Aviators, exactly like those worn by Tom Cruise in *Top Gun*, he immediately felt a little more... let's say sharp, even though as he was now, he would probably not even fit into the cockpit of a fighter plane.

"Well," he turned to Osterc. "What now? Shall we go to the station and check this out?"

He waved the envelope through the air.

Osterc stepped a few steps towards the middle of the road and looked up at the security camera on the building of the General Police Directorate. There were two cameras, each pointing in one direction down Štefan street.

"This we've got," said Brajc, once again waving the envelope.

Osterc returned to the pavement.

"Go ahead, spit it out," said Brajc. "What's bothering you?"

"Why don't we just walk around once more and check whether there might be any other cameras anywhere? On one of the houses or shops?"

Brajc looked at him with disdain and shook his head. He already had sweat trickling down either side of his face. He found the paper tissues in his bag and mopped it up. All he wanted was to fall into the chair at his desk back at the office and switch on the desk fan, the only thing they used as Taras could not stand the air-conditioning. Even now he was having difficulty breathing with all this ozone, and here's Osterc suggesting they walk around…

"I think we should help the kid," Osterc suggested. "Do you think she'll manage herself? With Taras the way he is?"

Brajc wanted to dismissively wave his hand but stopped mid-gesture to mop up a couple of further droplets of sweat before they trickled across his face. He sighed and took another breath, as if awaiting a new deluge. He had to admit that in his concern for his own well-being he had not even thought about this.

"What way is that?"

*

They went through the swing door into the hallway. The air was stale and, even after Tina pressed the switch, the light was poor, faint with a strange yellow glow. They walked a few steps along the corridor and almost missed a turning to the left towards the flats that must look out across the park. This corridor was narrower than the main one and began with a couple of steep steps at the top of which, quite without purpose, was another swing door that the residents must swear about every time they return home holding shopping bags, let alone were they moving in or out, needing to get any furniture through it. The door was now wide open, held in place by a couple of wooden wedges and when Tina and Taras walked up the steps a faint smell of fresh paint wafted their way on a barely noticeable draught. Someone must have recently repainted this part of the building.

Walking up these steps and through the swinging door they reached a lift in the middle of a staircase that spiralled up alongside it. Tina followed the stairs and on the first landing saw a door that was slightly ajar. The surname engraved on the nameplate was Baloh. She paused hesitantly and was about to knock when a voice from inside called out, "Come in!"

Tina pushed the door open to step into the hallway, a fairly typical entrance space for flats in Slovenia with a shoe cupboard, a wooden panel on the wall with hangers, a stool to sit on when putting on your shoes and a mirror mounted on the wall in such a position in the long narrow space that it could barely be used for its purpose.

"Do come in!"

She pushed the door open and came to a halt. It was as if she had fallen into some other world.

The room was white. All the walls were white, everything had been freshly painted and the furniture, which she initially did not even notice because it was all covered in white sheets, was moved away from the walls. Because everything else was white, the set of sofas in the middle of the room was all the more striking. Four massive seats covered in red fabric with gilded wooden legs and a small cupboard, a kind of chiffonier of a darker wood, cherry or olive, and a small coffee table. Tina had studied computers and psychology and neither helped her in determining the style of the furnishings in this part of the flat, if indeed it was any kind of style at all. The word *Biedermeier* came to mind but all she knew was that it had some connection with bourgeois taste in some previous century. Are curved, gilded legs part of that period?

Reigning in the middle of this red and gold island was an old man, his hair combed back, just as white as the sheets covering the furniture. He was wearing some kind of dressing gown the same colour as the sofa on which he was sitting. His trousers were black corduroy and on his feet wore a pair of slip-ons. With a hint of satisfaction, he watched her looking around the place.

"A pity you came at such an inappropriate moment with everything covered up. There are plenty of things here I could show you. It took me quite a long time to collect all this stuff. Well, time is something I have plenty of."

And money, Tina thought. When she approached the old man she noticed two paintings leaning against the sofa. The frames of these, oils, in as far as she could gather looking at them, a portrait of a black woman and a landscape, were also carved and gilded in a similar style to the furniture. In all this gold and curved antiquity, the only thing that stood out was a photograph on the chiffonier. Not very big but the only one without a frame, stuck onto a piece of glass, it had been placed on some kind of stand. From where she was standing she could not properly see what it showed. A group of men posing... Nor was the photograph recent.

"My name is Tina Lanc," she began. "And this is my colleague..."

"Taras Birsa."

"We're from the Ljubljana Police Directorate and are gathering information about the death of an elderly lady here in this park of yours."

"Sit down, do sit down..." the old man said, his eyes not moving off Tina. "Can I offer you anything?"

It was as if he had not even noticed Taras. He sat back on his sofa and waited.

"Thank you," said Tina and carefully sat on the sofa, as if afraid it was some museum piece not really intended for sitting on. "I'm fine."

She smiled and the old man returned a smile.

"How can I help you?"

She took her notepad and biro from her bag and placed them on the coffee table.

"This morning an elderly woman was found on a bench in the park that I believe your flat overlooks. She was dead."

She looked at him.

"The bag lady?"

Tina nodded.

"Yes, she regularly slept there on that bench. No, I didn't know."

Her gaze must have been inquisitive because he continued.

"The window from my bedroom looks out onto the park. I cannot recall the park seeming any different today to what it is usually. There were children in the park in the morning. Loud, but children should be loud. If they aren't, something is wrong. We, old people, need to be quiet instead of them. But I do get up early," he added as if in apology. "You younger people probably get up a little later. Can I ask you what kind of a death the woman died of?"

Tina thought for a moment about not giving further information about the death to the man but there was little point. It would be in all the newspapers by the morning, on TV tonight...

"A violent one."

She observed his face. He did not stir.

"She was shot."

"I see," he said and she found the way he said it strange. As someone used to news like that, the way Cvilak would react, or perhaps Taras.

"Don't you find that..." she was looking for the right word.

"Odd?" he helped her and without waiting for her response added, "We're all different."

He brought the tips of his fingers together and used his thumbs to scratch his smoothly shaved chin.

"And now you are probably interested whether I can give you any further information?"

Tina nodded.

"We would like to know if you saw anything."

He shook his head and Tina unwittingly thought about how very different this interview would be if it was being conducted by Taras. He had a way of making the person opposite him feel accused, guilty and subdued. This old man was not at all intimidated, he didn't feel he was under any pressure from the policewoman sitting in front of him. Tina glanced at Taras. He was indifferently observing the old man, his gaze occasionally travelling round the flat. Nervously she moved the lock of hair that had fallen across her eyes when she leaned over her notebook.

"Just to make it clear. We're not here to find the perpetrator but anyone who might have any kind of information that would help us."

The wretched hair fell across her face again.

"Of course, if we do find the culprit as we are doing so, so much the better," Taras added.

He did not like the old man and inferred as much. Perhaps that was what held their attention? Perhaps it helps not to like people?

"Yes, of course," said the old man, almost as if Taras had not spoken. "Of course. No, I didn't see anything, though I did hear... Well, and also saw."

Her hand stopped mid-gesture towards her hair and returned the biro to the notepad.

"I was watching the news..."

"The evening news?" she asked.

"News at Ten. Is that not what they call it?"

She nodded.

"Well, I was watching the news read by that moustachioed guy. It had only just started. They were showing how that developer guy being taken to prison... What's his name again..."

Tina reminded him of the name.

"...yes, that's the one. Well, there was a big bang outside. I thought it was a firecracker. When the item about his developer was over, I went into the bedroom because I needed my glasses to check the TV programme guide, and I looked out of the window. That firecracker, which clearly hadn't been a firecracker, was still glowing. I noticed a little yellow circle down below the window. I should have known what it was about. She was shot at close range, wasn't she?"

Tina scribbled in her notepad.

"This means it must have happened a little after ten?"

"A minute or two past ten. I usually watch the first couple of minutes of the news. I'm not interested in what happens in Nether Nowhere."

"And you didn't see anyone down in the park?"

"No."

She wrote a big zero under her previous notes and crossed it out. It would probably be too simple for her first case if she were to find the first witness after only five minutes.

"And why did you say that you should have known what it was about?" Taras spoke. "And that the woman was shot at close range?"

The old man flinched, as if he had only just noticed his presence, and then smiled, pointing towards the chiffonier about a metre behind him.

"Would you be so kind as to bring that photo there, from the shelf...?"

Tina stood up and went up to the cupboard he had pointed towards. She picked up the photo and looked at it carefully before sitting back onto the sofa. Three men, three young men...

"Recognise me?" he asked.

She thought he could be the one in the middle. The only blond in the photograph. The old man's thick, combed-back, silver hair might have been blond in his youth.

"This one?"

"Exactly. And do you know what this is?"

"Some kind of army?"

"No, it's the Foreign Legion. The French Foreign Legion, not just some kind of army. But that's all I can tell you."

She gave him a questioning look.

"It is not something that is talked about," said the old man, zipping his finger across his mouth.

"We're not really that interested in what army you served in," said Taras. "What we would like to know is if you own any weapons. We'd need to take a look."

The old man smiled. He didn't seem at all intimidated by Taras.

"I have born many weapons in my life, you wouldn't believe how many. From an FG 42 onwards. Alas..." he added with regret, "I have no use for any weapons now. What I own is in that cupboard in the top drawer, together with my licence."

Taras stepped to the chiffonier and opened the top drawer. What he saw was not what he expected. An Austrian Glock 19 handgun, a neat, small, compact, ultramodern weapon. Somehow it did not fit in with the old man or the gilded legs of the chairs and table. Beside it was a booklet on the leather cover of which was an emblem with crossed guns and the Slovenian coat of arms. He picked it up and looked inside. Franz Baloh, born 24 January 1928 in Celje.

"You know, I wouldn't change that with your Beretta. It *is* Berettas you're issued with, isn't it?"

"For some time now."

Taras put the gun licence back into the drawer, crouched next to it and leaned across the handgun as if wanting to read the miniscule writing on it.

"And have you used this at all lately?"

The old man laughed, his grin revealing yellowing teeth.

"Do you want to know if I shot this woman?"

He grinned again and it seemed as if he got some satisfaction from being asked this question. Then, all of a sudden he stopped and, for the first time since they had entered the room, stared straight at Taras. He crossed his hands in his lap, leaned back and asked.

"Why would I do that?"

Taras stood up, closed the door and returned to the table. He beckoned to Tina who handed him the photograph. He took a closer look. Three soldiers in light trousers, white shirts with dark, tasselled epaulettes on the shoulders and white *kepis* with black peaks on their heads...

"That was our parade uniform," the old man said.

Taras put the photograph on the table.

"You didn't answer my question. When did you last use this handgun?"

The old man looked at him calmly, speaking with a tired tone in his voice.

"Long ago, so long ago I don't even remember it any more. Anyway, do take it with you and check, if you want. You guys can do that, can't you?"

From his small backpack Taras produced a transparent plastic bag, stood up and went across to the cupboard. He opened the drawer, stuck his pen behind the trigger guard and gently lifted the gun into the bag. With an expression of satisfaction on his face he turned to the old man.

"I just need you to sign the form that we are taking this to be tested. You wouldn't believe all the things *we guys* can do."

CHAPTER 6.

"Let's take a walk round the park," Osterc suggested. "It'll take five minutes and if there ain't no camera anywhere, then there ain't no camera."

Brajc didn't think it was worth responding and Osterc turned north towards the Figovec Inn where, as far as he could remember, there was a jeweller's shop and jewellers usually have cameras, but clearly it had either moved or closed down. Instead there was a workshop that cut keys and keys are not something people steal, so it had no camera. Figovec also didn't have a security camera. They then crossed the park and went past a café with a garden concealed behind a huge plane tree and, even if they had had a camera there, it would not show anything. When they reached Župančič Street they came across a fence erected around the gap created after the demolition of a huge old building. This was known as the *Kolizej* and was the last of four multi-functional buildings built in the mid-1800s when Slovenia was still part of Austria-Hungary. These buildings were created to serve as army accommodation with various sections including horse stables and a brothel. After the old building had been demolished a few years ago, the site was left derelict and the hole had become an overgrown jungle that didn't need security cameras to protect it from intruders. Brajc was barely able to walk. Then, all of a sudden...

"There!" Osterc shouted out.

They stopped in front of a small, unassuming hotel, which had a security camera mounted on the wall under the canopy above the entrance.

"I hope it's not just decorative," said Osterc, looking at Brajc who was trying to catch his breath. "And that it takes in a little of the street as well."

"You go," Brajc rasped and collapsed onto the stone wall that ran round the park. "I'll wait here."

*

Tina rang the doorbell on the floor above. The nameplate said *Vasle*. Nothing. She put her ear against the door to determine whether there was any movement inside. Nothing. She rang the bell again and looked towards Taras but he was already on his way up the stairs.

The next door they reached said *Jaklin*. *Dr Jaklin*, in fact. Tina rang the bell and this time there was a response. Barely audible steps coming from inside the flat that fell silent when the person inside stopped in front of the door. A second or two later the door opened slightly and behind it stood a woman in her mid-sixties.

"Hello. Can I help you?"

Tina introduced herself and Taras whom the woman could not see, and she showed her police ID. The woman looked at it distrustfully and looked up at Tina.

"And what is this about?"

Tina explained briefly.

"...and that's why we're here now. Did you not see anything? We've been down under your window all morning."

"Oh, no, no..." the woman said and seemed confused for a moment. "That's not my window. It's my son's..."

They waited for her to finish the sentence but she didn't. In a kind of hope that Tina would solve the situation by thanking her and leaving, she stood at the door with her hand ready on the handle.

"Despite this, we need to talk to you," said Tina, pointing with her hand towards the flat. The woman still did not comprehend.

"Could you give us a little of your time?"

It didn't sound like a question and the door briefly closed so the woman could unlatch the security chain and then opened, though only just enough for Tina to squeeze past. Taras had to make himself cough so the woman understood that he too wanted to enter the flat.

The place was, in terms of size and space, the same as the one two floors below, but it took Tina a while to realise this as it was furnished very differently. If the one below was filled with furniture from some past century, time in this one had come to a halt at some point in the 1970s. It was as if she was visiting her own Grandma, Tina thought. Straight lines, fading colours, where there were any. Upholstered chairs in earth colours with an addition of green, dark brown cupboards with shallow brass notches instead of handles, all already a little warped. A few paintings on the walls, landscapes, probably by unknown, unimportant artists. A TV jutted out of one of the cupboards, a classic thick screen with a cathode ray tube.

"That D R on your door is your...?" Tina tried.

The woman shook her head.

"That was my husband. He's been dead for a long time."

She pointed to an area behind a round table with three chairs. Old fashioned, they seemed like something that might now once again be fashionable in some circles. Wood with a padded seat, all cracked along the edges. Tina sat on one carefully and placed her notebook on the table.

"Your downstairs neighbour, the one on the ground floor, says he heard a bang last night at around ten that could have been a shot from some kind of gun. Were you at home at that time?"

The woman nodded.

"Did you hear anything like that?" Tina continued when it became clear the woman was not going to say anything else.

She shook her head.

"Nothing? A shot from a gun so close by is hard to miss. How come?"

The woman became confused, her gaze moving from Tina's face to her hand holding the biro, ready to start writing...

"I don't know, I can't remember..."

Tina sighed, put down her pen by the notepad, and looked straight at the woman.

"You said that the window looking over the park is your son's. Your son's room? Is he at home?"

The woman appeared confused again, her eyes wandering

towards the table and Tina's notepad, and then almost plead-
ingly back to her face.

"Is he at home?" Tina repeated.

"He is, but he is resting."

"I'd like to talk to him," Tina insisted. "We are investigating
a murder."

The woman stood up and hesitantly made her way to the
door leading to a corridor. Tina could hear her knock and then
open the door.

"Leave me alone!" came from the room after a brief pause
during which the woman must have been trying to explain what
this was about – Tina could only assume this as they could not
hear the woman at all – then another, "I told you, just leave me
alone!"

Tina stood up and resolutely stepped along the corridor towards the woman who was standing at the half opened door
looking confused. Gently she pushed her out of the way and
opened the door fully, finding herself in a darkened room. The
only window was closed with blinds that allowed so little light
to penetrate the room that for a few moments Tina stared into
darkness. Then she noticed a bed in the corner and someone on
it. Reaching with her hand towards the wall, she found the light
switch.

Sitting on the bed was the son, a man of around thirty. She
was puzzled by his black tracksuit and shaved head. Above him
on the wall was a flag or a banner with *Blood and Honour* written on it. Next to it a picture of Adolf Hitler. On the other wall
was a new, flat screen TV and on the desk by the window a computer. It seemed the light was switched on just in time, before he
shouted another one of his leave-me-alones.

"Sorry to disturb you," said Tina and waved her police ID at
him. "But last night someone shot a woman under your window.
We would like to know if you saw or heard anything."

He continued to blink at her and it didn't look as if he was
going to respond but he eventually spoke.

"What, the old bag lady?"

"Homeless woman, you mean," said Tina in an icy voice.

"Oh, was she homeless? I thought she was just camping in

our park."

He forced a loud laugh.

"No damage done there, if you ask me. Anything else?"

Taras appeared at the door. The skinhead looked at him but clearly Taras did not have any particular effect on him.

"We want to know..." Tina said, realising that her voice was trembling slightly, so she stepped to the window and raised the blinds. "...if you saw or heard anything. Your downstairs neighbour heard a loud bang at around ten in the evening."

"I didn't hear anything. Shame." He gave her a look of hatred and contempt. "Anything else?"

Tina peered out of the window. Below them, set only three metres back from the asphalted path, was the bench, now empty. There was no better place to aim at a person on the bench than from the windows in this building. Had Golob not said that they were dealing with a close-range shot, she would put this idiot at the top of her list of suspects. Of course she would first need to have a list.

"Right, I need your name," she said as she turned towards the man sitting on the bed. "Your name and a statement on where you were last night between ten and twelve."

"Yeah, you bet."

He plugged in his earphones and pressed a button on his mobile phone. Defiantly he looked her straight in the eye and began wildly shaking his head in some kind of grotesque dance.

His dance took Tina by surprise and she just stood there, half way between the window and the door where Taras was standing, looking as if none of this had anything to do with him. She was overcome by a terrible sense of powerlessness. What could she do? Without a warrant he was not obliged to talk to her. What would Taras do? Would he, like her now, slowly, trying to maintain her dignity, leave the room?

Clearly he would. Even before she reached the door he had turned round and disappeared. She followed him with a mixture of relief and regret. A part of her, a large part of her, wanted Taras to slap the idiot across the face, treat him the way he had handled that spoilt brat at Lake Bohinj when she first came to work with him, the hearing about which was due at court the day after tomorrow. She closed the door after her and saw Taras disappearing through the front door.

"Can I have your names, please," she said to the woman. "Yours and your son's."

"Marija, and he is," she glanced around the room as if she was afraid he might hear her. "He's Ignac."

"Just another thing, please," Tina said quickly, anxious to catch up with Taras. "Who lives on the floor below you? There was no answer when we rang."

"There wouldn't be," said the woman. "The lady who lived there died half a year ago and the flat has been empty ever since. I think her son has put it up for sale."

She caught up with him on the corridor where he was trying to remove some paint from the back left side of his shorts with which he must have leaned onto a not quite dry wall.

"I was afraid you might hit him."

He grabbed his right elbow with his left hand and grimaced.

"It did cross my mind, believe me it did. I think," he muttered, "that I've seen this moron somewhere before."

On the stairs leading to the upper, fourth floor, they came across a man of around twenty-five. Tina was about to stop him and talk to him when he saw Taras and smiled.

"Oh, hello, Inspector," he cried out. "Don't you know me?"

Taras looked at him for a moment or two, having to think before he remembered.

"Celje?"

"Yes, but I'm in your department now, on training. What are you doing here?"

Taras explained and the young man smiled awkwardly.

"Well, unfortunately I won't be able to help you there. Whenever I am in Ljubljana, I stay with my aunt," he pointed up the stairs. "Well, great aunt, she's my grandmother's sister. I'm on the afternoon shift today and last night took up the chance to go out. I only got back from town around two in the morning."

"What about your aunt? She was probably at home?"

"Oh, yes, she wouldn't go anywhere anyway because of her dogs. If anyone will know anything, she will. She is, well, you'll see, she's quite a character. She helped half the family until they were able to get jobs and careers."

*

At reception, small as the hotel itself was small, Osterc showed his ID to the girl, a polite student with long hair gathered into a bun, and asked about the tapes from the security camera. She did not even know that they had a camera that recorded anything at all, so she called the owner. After a long conversation during which she handed the receiver to Osterc and after searching the computer, they eventually found the folder where the data from the camera was saved and self-deleted after twenty-four hours.

The camera was placed so it took in the hotel entrance, the path leading up to it and part of Župančič Street with the pavement and also the pavement on the opposite side of the road. It also caught the bottom part of the wall that separated the street from the park and Osterc could see Brajc's feet and hands resting on it. The western entrance to the park was not in the shot. Better than nothing, he thought and once again checked the screen showing the current view of the road outside the entrance, stuck his USB in the slot, marked the shot and copied it. Brajc's feet had in the meantime disappeared.

*

Tina pressed the bell with the surname *Opeka* next to it, almost instantly triggering a bout of barking by what seemed to be more than one dog inside. There must have been at least two tiny hysterical canines within and they now ran up to the door, growling angrily. After a while they could also hear a voice calming them down.

"Shushhh, shushhh, my princesses, shushhh!"

The door opened and at it stood a woman with completely white hair pinned up in a bun. She was wearing a black skirt and a black cardigan. Next to her, jumping over each other, were two dogs of the same breed, white, with patches of brown and black across their ears. They were yapping like crazy, but the old woman ignored them.

"Follow me," she said when Tina explained why they were here.

They followed her into the living room amid the growling and barking of the dogs that hopped around her feet and she had to push them out of the way a number of times.

"Sorry, they are very territorial," said the woman, trying to make the dogs go away. "Give them five minutes."

"Jack Russells?" Taras asked.

The old woman shook her head.

"Parson Russells. Similar, apparently the breeder was the same man. Do you like dogs, Inspector?"

Taras nodded.

"Surely not terriers? They say these are big dogs in small packaging. I only found out later, or I would not have taken them. They need someone who can chase around with them and not me, a cushion-comfy old woman. The next lot will be poodles, if there will be a next lot at all."

"So, ma'am…" Tina began when the woman and Taras had finished their dog discussion. "We'd like to know whether you saw or heard anything."

"No," said the old woman.

Your neighbour, the man living downstairs, said he heard a bang. You didn't?"

"No."

Tina put down the pen she was holding and tried again.

"Where were you last night? Were you at home?"

"I'm always at home," said the woman. "I don't go out."

"What about the dogs? Surely you have to take them out for a walk?"

"Yes, that of course. They have to go out morning and evening."

Tina sighed and did not try to hide it. She picked up her pen and notepad again, so the woman might see that she was expecting more from her, something that she could make a note of.

"So, when were you out yesterday?"

"As usual," said the woman. "Six in the morning and eight in the evening. Now that it is hot, perhaps a little later. Before and after that I was at home."

Tina scribbled something on her notepad and looked at Taras.

He was gazing at the old woman with a sort of ironic smile.

"You didn't know the woman who died?" he asked.

"No."

"How come?" he continued as if he had something in mind, as if this was a question that might lead somewhere.

"I did not consort with people like that..." said the woman and for the first time her answer faded away, losing its resolute sharpness.

"Oh, I see," said Taras. "Like what?"

The old woman's eyes suddenly lit up. She looked at Taras, then Tina, and with no help forthcoming, at the terriers now lying at her feet and then back above the table.

"And how do you know what the woman did if you didn't know her?"

The old lady suddenly stood up, as if she had thought of something urgent. She clapped and cried out, "I didn't offer you anything! Can I get you some tea?"

Without waiting for a response, she hurried with surprising agility to the door that obviously led into the kitchen. Tina gave Taras a questioning look.

"I'll explain," he said, pointing his finger to the door.

They sat in silence for a minute or so and Tina felt like some extra in a film, watching the main character act out a scene she had not read or prepared for. Then the old woman returned with a tray with two cups, shuffling her feet along and placing it on the table.

"Now, what was it that you asked me, officer?" she asked obligingly.

"I wanted to find out how you know what the victim did, as you said you didn't know her."

"Oh, that," said the old woman. She reminded Tina of a theatre actress trying to ensure that her voice and gestures would also be noticed by those sitting in the back rows. She dismissively waved her hand, as if to say, of, course, I should have thought of that myself earlier, or something like that.

"I did not know her *personally*, but of course I often saw her in our park. It's hard to miss a character like that."

She looked at Taras, as if wanting to check the effect of her words. Taras smiled.

"And how did you know that the victim was the homeless woman? My colleague here only mentioned that the victim was a woman."

"I saw you lot from the window," said the old woman. "In fact, I noticed her before you arrived and thought that it was odd that she was still asleep."

Taras nodded and looked at Tina.

"Can I take a look at the window from which you can see down into the park?" Tina asked.

A little hesitantly the old woman nodded and led Tina, dogs following, into the bedroom. There was a cover over the bed and the room was neat and tidy like the rest of the flat but the air was stale and smelt of medication. Tina stepped to the window and glanced out of it. From here the bench was partly hidden behind a branch from a nearby horse chestnut, but despite this, if one happened to be looking, it was possible to see what was going on around it.

"Thank you," she said and turned towards the door.

When they returned to the living room, Taras was already standing by the table and when he saw them he made his way to the front door. He was already holding the handle when he turned to the woman, as if he had just remembered something, and asked, "And how's your health, ma'am?"

The woman gave him a surprised look, only briefly, and then – it once again reminded Tina of a theatrical performance – replied in the previous obliging tone.

"Thank you, officer. I'm managing. Doing well for my age."

"Well, I'm glad of that," said Taras, opened the door and stepped out into the corridor.

CHAPTER 7.

"What was that about her health?" Tina asked as soon as the old lady on the fourth floor closed the door behind them.

Taras smiled and turned down the staircase. Tina followed him.

"Before you came to work with us, last year, in the summer or towards the end of spring, I can't remember precisely but it isn't important, they re-surfaced the parking lots at the office with fresh tarmac. For the period it took them to do this, the ministry sent us seasonal parking permits. Not for the nearby underground parking below Republic Square but for the open-air spaces down in Tivoli Park. Well, OK, at least they gave us something. And it happened to pour down with rain for the two weeks, so I didn't cycle to work. Well, there, in front of the parking machine in Tivoli, I regularly noticed an elderly lady. She stood there, shaking, huddling under the canopy above the parking machine in order not to get wet. She held out her hand and shook. The consequences of childhood meningococcal meningitis, she told us. I felt sorry for her, and I always gave her any small change I happened to have. I believed her, even though I've been a criminal investigator for over twenty years."

"And?"

"It was her."

"Oh, come on!"

"Yes, believe me. Without the dogs, but it was her. I am glad she is cured of it."

They stepped out into the sun and Taras was about to turn south towards the police station when he saw something, or rather someone, on the wall by the park. The man was lying on the wall and a bewildered older couple was standing next to him, asking him something. Taras went a few steps closer. Brajc. Not only was he totally sweaty, he was having difficulty breathing, was trying to catch his breath and looked as if he was having trouble simply keeping himself alive. Taras thanked the man and woman who turned around and left with great relief, though they did keep looking back.

"What's up with you, Brajc?"

Brajc looked at him, grimaced, and uttered, "I don't feel that good. This heat... It's killing me."

His lips were ash grey, his face also.

"Do you feel dizzy? Headache? Dry mouth?"

Brajc nodded faintly.

"Did you have anything to drink today apart from that coffee earlier?"

"If I drink, it just makes me sweat more."

Taras rolled his eyes.

"Look after him for a second," he told Tina and crossed the road towards the hotel. He returned with a glass of water and Osterc. Brajc took a few short sips but Taras insisted on him drinking it all.

"Tina, go and get my car..."

"Ours is here at the GPD," said Brajc in a weak voice and pointed behind his back.

Taras looked in the direction he was pointing and then at Osterc who nodded, looked in Brajc's bag, found the keys to their car and disappeared.

"Tina, are you going to the station anyway?"

She nodded.

"Go with them, put Brajc in the shade, right in front of the fan, make him drink a lot of water or, even better, buy him some isotonic drink. If he's not better, take him to the hospital."

"No, no..." said Brajc weakly but as firmly as he could. "Tomorrow we have the union trip. No way I'm missing that. I'll be fine, Taras, it's just this damn heat..."

Taras felt guilty when he left them and, after about twenty metres or so, he turned round and looked towards Brajc and Tina who, next to the collapsing hulk she was sitting with, looked even younger and more petite than she did otherwise.

*

Alenka was already sitting at the table in the covered garden of the restaurant in the Knafelj Passage. She had a bottle of mineral water on the table and was, despite the shade, still wearing her sun glasses. Clearly she had been waiting for a while and not passed her time by messing with her mobile phone, which Taras was pleased about. She didn't even have it on the table.

"Hi," he said and leaned down to kiss his wife.

He had stopped at the station and changed his T-shirt, but already had sweat marks on the front of the new one after just a few minutes' walk. He pretended to ignore this. Alenka had no less of a walk to the restaurant but she looked as fresh as a flower. She put her glasses down on the table.

"Busy?"

He nodded. The restaurant was too. When he'd arrived, he had glanced at the other customers. Men in pinstriped shirts and watches on their wrists, women in suits and uncomfortable shoes. He had caught a snippet of conversation between two of the men in striped shirts.

"This thing does not drink water..." he caught one of them saying. Of course Taras didn't have a clue what thing this might be.

There was definitely nobody else there wearing a blue T-shirt with a faded *Sound of Silence* written across it. Taras had never really wondered what the phrase was supposed to mean. It was Alenka who had bought it for him, albeit in some other times, and instead of protesting about his sartorial choices of the day, she decided to ignore it.

"They found a dead woman in Lenin Park."

"What park?"

"Slovene Reformation Park, that used to be..."

"Lenin? That name hasn't been in use for quite some time. Now it's...? What is it called? Isn't it Park Argentina?"

"That also."

He thought she would nod and they would order because over the years they had become used to not talking about his cases more than was essential. This was not to do with any kind of professional vow of silence. He knew inspectors who liked to offer their company even the tiniest and often strictly confidential details of an investigation, he knew lawyers who would disclose far more about their clients than they might want them to, and doctors who showed around various pictures of their butchered patients. Perhaps he was not like that because he was more of a quiet type anyway, or perhaps because he never drank.

This time, though, Alenka went on.

"A woman?"

"The homeless bag lady."

She shook her head. She didn't know who he was talking about.

"And since when are dead homeless people of your concern? Would not this be a case more suited to your young assistant?"

"Since the homeless people have a bullet hole in their head," he said with a hint of irritation. "And besides, it *is* her case."

He checked the table.

"Don't we have a menu here?"

She smiled.

"As opposed to policemen, doctors like people. The person approaching us will explain in person what is available in this place in terms of food today."

A short man in white, looking more like a cook than a waiter, was approaching them on the paved path through the tables. From afar he gave them a happy and welcoming smile.

"Good day, Mrs Birsa..." he said with an inquisitive nod towards Taras, who offered him no help, so Alenka intervened. "...and Mr Birsa."

"Oh, you're the lucky man! We were wondering who the beautiful lady belonged to."

"How come? We've been here together before, Stane, haven't we?"

There was a touch of embarrassment in her voice though it was unnecessary. She had told him that she came here for lunch with her colleagues and had often suggested they met here. How come he agreed today? The heat perhaps? It took less effort to agree than to say no and then try to explain this no and try to find a more acceptable alternative. Perhaps it was the prices.

"No we haven't," said Taras. "This is the first time I am here."

"Indeed, I have not had the honour of meeting the gentleman," Stane the host confirmed and sat down on an empty chair.

"For today I would recommend..." he listed around ten different dishes in various combinations, using numerous diminutives.

"Stane, this time you've not come across the right audience," Alenka stopped him. "Mr Birsa couldn't care less what he puts in his mouth as long as it has enough calories and vitamins."

Stane exaggerated surprise, half pretending and half for real.

"And minerals," added Taras.

"That's not possible. I will bring you something that will awaken your taste buds..."

"Don't bother," Taras interrupted him. "I have Glock Syndrome. I can only taste salty, bitter, sour, and that's it. You can bring me sawdust and I wouldn't know the difference."

"Glock Syndrome?" Alenka asked when the man had left.

"I couldn't be bothered to listen to him."

Taras chose the gnocchi, not for the taste but because they were soft and he didn't need to cut them. Pressing the knife against the surface and moving it caused him pain in the elbow that he could handle on its own were it not a constant reminder that his hand was useless. Useless for training, useless for push-ups, useless for any kind of exercise that would maintain his body in shape.

"Can I continue with push-ups or planks?" he had asked when he went for a check-up.

"God forbid!"

He used his left hand for the gnocchi.

"Is it still painful?"

He nodded.

"With every move and it feels as if it's causing throbbing in the head."

"You need to be patient. What does Doctor Wolf say?"

"He's not a doctor. He's a physiotherapist."

This respect for anything medical annoyed him, not just with Alenka. People never forget to add a title whenever they see someone in a white gown.

"What does Wolf the physiotherapist say?" she repeated.

"That I need to be patient."

Wolf was the first physiotherapist he trusted since he had begun to feel pain at recreational boxing training sessions he attended three times a week. The pain appeared on the outer side of his right elbow, where the tendons attach to the bone. Wolf was the third specialist he visited after ignoring the pain for a long time and then asking Alenka to find him someone. He went first to see a doctor who was an expert in pain management therapies and she had injected his elbow with some cocktail of anti-inflammatory drugs. He had held his hand up in the air for two days, initially causing the pain to spread but then miraculously disappear and lay low for three months. His hand was like new and he had had full use of it. When, however, the pain returned, it was worse and Taras blamed himself. Wolf was the only person he saw who gave the impression that his problem was curable and, above all, he was the first who did not, like all the others, try to tell him that...

"...certain things at your age..."

"I do know how old I am," he would cut short such a conversation and then called off any further treatment.

Wolf, on the other hand, looked at the elbow on the ultrasound and showed Taras various light and dark patches, commented on them and spent ten minutes explaining the causes of his troubles and tried to clarify certain points by sketching on a piece of paper. Taras tried hard to believe him, especially after he said that he too had had a tennis elbow...

"...and I also have never played tennis."

"Well, if there's anything I do have, it's time and money," Taras now said to Alenka.

"Sorry?"

She did not get the joke that he had heard... From someone.

"As Bob Dylan would say, *Time is on my side.*"

"Rolling Stones," she corrected him. "*The times, they are a-changin'*, that's Dylan."

Well, great, dementia on top of everything else.

They finished their food and drank their mineral water,

Alenka paid the overpriced bill and they ordered coffee.

"So, you're with your intern...?"

"You mean Tina? She's not an intern. And in this case she's with me. She's in charge of the woman in the park."

He bit his tongue but it was too late. She had thrown the bait and he had grabbed it.

"Hey, keep your socks on! I didn't mean anything like that."

Sometimes he wondered how he would fare if he was on the receiving end of an interrogation. If they sat him down at a table and tried to extract an admission from him or catch him out on some inconsistency? Would the knowledge he has gained from his work help him? He knew the methods and approaches of various criminologists and knew most of them personally anyway. They certainly couldn't shine a light into his face and say, "I can see inside your head, I can see everything, just admit to it!" Above all, he would know that he could demand a lawyer and that this would interrupt any interrogation. Once for a joke, he had asked Mozetič to conduct a test on him on the polygraph. He tried hard to stay calm at the questions he lied about and believed he could easily trick anyone with his persuasive answers. Cool as a cucumber is how he saw himself. Not the machine. At every lie it consistently drew out a jumpy, jagged, hysterical curve.

Guilty!

"They can say what they want, with normal people the polygraph is one hundred percent accurate," Mozetič explained to him at the time. "There are a few problems with psychopaths but there are ways of getting round those too."

But how does it work in a situation like this when you're being interrogated but both the interrogator, Alenka, and the interrogatee, him, are pretending that this is just an ordinary conversation? A conversation in the middle of which you simply cannot stand up and say, I'm not doing this any more, where is my lawyer, and for which the standards are proven to be very low, lower than those of the mafia, because the accuser and the judge is one and the same person. A single wrong gaze, a nervous blink or hesitation in giving an answer are enough for a guilty verdict.

"Alenka, I'm a policeman," he said, looked at her and smiled. "If you want to know anything, you only have to ask. You dismissively call her an intern because you think that I like her. If she's an intern, then what am I? Some kind of foreman? And if we forget that I don't, that I find her quite plain and ordinary, does a man after all these years not deserve a little trust?"

He should bite his tongue again. Were someone he was interrogating to come up with, 'Don't I deserve a little trust after all these years...?' Well, in fact, no. The fact that you did not kill anyone in the last twenty years does not mean that you're innocent. There's always a first.

Lucky for him, Alenka did not have this kind of experience. Embarrassed, she looked away at the white tablecloth in front of her, grabbed her cup of coffee and held it hesitantly – just like Tina earlier, he thought – took a sip, as if she needed a moment to think, and then put the coffee back onto the table and started talking without looking at Taras.

"I wouldn't be jealous at all if it hadn't been for that stuff about Prelc... I never was before."

It hurt, almost physically. He could not stand hearing his name, even though it has been six months since the revelation.

"I don't want to talk about that."

She looked up.

"That's exactly it. If it is so hard for you that I... that you by chance found out that years and years ago, long before we ever met, I once slept with my professor, then you sleeping with a colleague twenty years your junior might, in your eyes, seem like some kind of just retaliation."

He pulled a face, almost grimaced.

"I'd like to know where I stand."

He tried to keep calm. He wanted to grab his coffee cup but instead rested his elbows on the table in front of him, nervously twitched with his right hand when the painful point touched the surface, so instead he grabbed the edge of the table with his palms, as if he needed a point of support not to topple over. If he could talk about it, were it not to appear ridiculous, self-humiliating, he would have said something along the lines of, 'I thought that I had been someone special and that was why you went with me...' And this 'went' would be a euphemism for slept, had sex with, fucked... '...but clearly not. The criteria had obviously been much lower and if you got laid by a married guy who was in the circles you moved in considered one of the worst womanisers on the planet, then you should hardly be bothered, and why would you care, if I did the same with a colleague? Why would he be able to have it and not me? And after that, how could you work with him all those years, laugh with him, social-ise with him and even invite me along? Just as well Prelc didn't have a dog. I could have offered to take it to the park for him if he didn't have the time.'

Is there a conversation that could solve all these questions?

"I really don't want to talk about that," he said. "Not because I would have anything going on with my colleague. I'm not ac-cusing you of anything. I will process all of it in my head, just don't mention him to me. At least not for a while, right?"

Did what happened with Tina really happen because of Alenka and... that man?

Now it was Alenka who lowered her hands to the table and looked straight into his eyes.

"I am not proud of *all* the things I've done in my life, least of all the one thing that bothers you so much. Do not, however, de-mand some kind of regret from me. What happened, happened; I cannot change it. It is a part of me. It is also because of this that I am who I am and also because of this that I'm with you, howev-er silly that sounds. And just in case you've forgotten, with what-ever it is that is swarming inside your head, I do love you, Taras."

CHAPTER 8.

"Right, let's go," said Cvilak and stood up from his office on the third floor of the Institute for Forensic Medicine in Ljubljana. He smiled at Tina, opened the door for her and a little later gallantly gestured with his hand for her to enter the lift, pressing the button to the basement, and waited for her to step out into the corridor leading towards refrigeration where bodies waited for autopsies on one side, dissection on the other. The corridors of the faculty, so full of people during the day, were menacingly empty. When Cvilak had said that the autopsy would be at nine, she had understood nine in the morning, and he had to stress that he meant in the evening.

"We can't do it during the day," he said as some kind of explanation.

He was probably busy during the day with the profit-making activities of the faculty, determining and proving paternity, for example, which was not covered by the national health system. The dead, especially anonymous ones, could wait.

"We will have company," he said and pointed at a group of young people waiting outside refrigeration. "Medical students. Because the case is both straightforward and also very rare, we will allow them to watch. There are about twenty murders in Slovenia every year, give or take one or two. Of course they are not all caused by a shotgun. And beside..." he hesitated uneasily for a moment. "We will conduct a complete autopsy. It would be a pity to waste a perfectly useful body."

Tina smiled, even though she did not feel like smiling at all. She tried to see autopsies as an essential part of the process of criminal investigation and the dead as evidence, but she could not get rid of the thought that what was lying on the table every time had a day or two earlier been breathing, speaking and doing whatever it is that people do, her included. She could not overlook the similarity between the flesh – the muscles, veins and bones – into which Cvilak was cutting, sawing or hammering with his tools and everything offered in the meat sections of supermarkets in shopping centres, in fact they looked the same. After every autopsy she attended she had a period of being vegetarian. She thought that she would get used to it after a while but with every autopsy the time span it took her to get over it was longer and she thought that if things continued this way these periods would eventually merge into one. What she found particularly horrible was the weighing of the liver and other internal organs. Fresh, served…

"Stay with us for the first part and when the students are doing their training you can leave as far as I'm concerned. It will be like a lesson," Cvilak continued as if he had guessed her thoughts.

"I'll take you up on that offer. I've not even been home yet today."

There was one difference she noted. Butchers were full of pieces of healthy, young animals. On Cvilak's table the yellowish fat that had accumulated around the internal organs was the least obtrusive.

Besides, with her knowledge she could not determine anything that Cvilak might miss. The fact that the criminal investigator in charge needs to be present at the autopsy is probably a remnant of some law from the era of the Empress Maria Theresa when the one brandishing the knives and the one responsible for getting the perpetrators of the crime locked up was one and the same person. As in American crime stories today.

"Get ready for a little stench. The bacteria have taken their toll."

"How come? Didn't she die only last night?"

"Yes, very probably not before then," Cvilak nodded. "But with this hot and humid weather the bacteria don't wait for the usual twenty-four hours. I remember some woman who hanged herself in her bathroom; she had sealed all the gaps in the door

and put on a heater – when we broke into the place we measured fifty-eight degrees. She had been hanging for less than
twenty-four hours and was totally blackened, bloated, a rotting
bulk. That's how quickly a person can go to the dogs when they
stop fighting."

He shrugged his shoulders and scratched the back of his
neck.

"So it isn't quite true that we are dust and return to dust.
Over time yes, but a whole load of other things before that. If
you take humidity out of the equation, for example, you would
get cured ham. The same body in the Karst area would become
mummified."

The group of young people outside the door almost stood to
attention when they saw Cvilak and Tina. Two female and three
male students in white gowns.

"What's up, kids?" Cvilak almost shouted. "Your first client?"

They nodded. One of them even smiled. Tina glanced at their
faces. A mix of curious expectation and fear. She was probably
just like that half a year ago. An eternity ago.

*

"The gateway of death?"

The students looked at each other in confusion until one of
the girls tried to respond.

"*Atria mortis*?"

"I know what the Latin term for it is. Does anyone know
which gateways we are looking at?"

"Oh, right," three of them said almost simultaneously and
began listing them all at once. "The lungs, heart or brain."

"And why? In the right order."

He pointed at one of the young men who had been silent so
far.

"Because death can occur mostly because of the failure of
respiratory, vascular or nervous systems."

Cvilak nodded.

"In our case this is – I hope we all agree – the brain, the
crown of the nervous system in all vertebrates to which we all
belong, including the poor woman we have before us and whose
violent death we shall try to explain. Well, let's take a look then."

*

Tina sat on the chair next to the woman taking notes and listened to the long description of the gunshot wound, including a determination of the direction of the shot, its distance, once more no different to what she had from Golob the previous day. There was a confirmation of the time of death, which Cvilak narrowed to twelve hours prior to the discovery of the body, plus-minus one hour. She listened attentively to Cvilak talking, asking questions and commenting on the shot and the wound, which, on their victim, was irregular with large radial destruction...

"Which means what?"

The students stayed silent and Cvilak was about to irritatedly give them the answer when the silent student spoke up.

"That we are looking at a projectile of supersonic velocity."

"Precisely. And what else proves this?"

"The exit wound."

"What about it?"

"It is larger, a few times larger than the entry wound, star-shaped, the skin defect with everted edges..."

With the students Cvilak took longer than usual. From an educational point of view this was probably praiseworthy but for Tina who had not only not been home at all today but had also not had anything to eat since breakfast, it dragged on painfully. Thus, while waiting for Cvilak to get the autopsy saw going, she...

"That you have undoubtedly seen elsewhere in this facility. Where would that be?"

"The casting room at orthopaedics," said the more silent of the two young women.

"Well done! It is exactly like the saw they use to remove plaster casts from legs. What will we find when we use it to get to the inside of the skull?"

He looked at the young man who had given all the answers previously but it was the girl who spoke.

"The secondary shot channel... A wound cavity formed by projectiles at a velocity twice the speed of sound."

"Bravo, Miss. And, as you said, due to the radial forces that are immense at such speeds, we will in here..."

With his latex gloved finger he silently tapped the head of the dead woman.

"...come across a cavity."

Well, at least any hunger Tina had felt before had gone away.

She listened to Cvilak's lecturing as he veered off into various subjects, using the opportunity to convey as much course material to his students as possible. Thus she found out about the often-unsuccessful suicide attempts with captive bolt pistols used for slaughtering animals, when the person trying to commit suicide aims at the frontal lobe and survives because in doing so they do not damage the vital centres, and how...

"...with a bolt pistol we are essentially not dealing with a shot wound but a stab or puncture wound."

Then he talked about stab wounds for a while, rat, mouse or swallow-tail shaped wounds, and the basics about axe, stab, saw, cut and bite wounds. And with the human brain being designed so it most easily remembers the most bizarre information, she will forever remember the fact that stab wounds can also occur during illusionist tricks.

"Now there *is* one thing here that is interesting," said Cvilak with a change of voice and repeated it so she understood that it was directed at her. Tina stepped closer to the body. The autopsy saw was ready next to the woman's head.

"This."

Cvilak moved his finger around the area of the wound where there was a pale, barely noticeable pink ring.

"This is what we call an abrasion collar. It is interesting in this case here because it is very pale, almost without hyperaemia."

"Hyperaemia?"

"An excess of blood."

"Which means?" asked Tina.

"Which means?" Cvilak repeated after her and looked at the students.

They all stayed silent.

"It doesn't mean anything," said Cvilak. "It would if it had not been there at all."

He looked at Tina.

"If, however, these faint signs of assault on the organism were entirely absent, then we would be justified in concluding that this gun shot was created *post mortem*. But in this case... Due to age-related degeneration, she probably had relatively poor circulation, and this is all the poor woman could manage."

*

Tina moved back to the seat she had been sitting in and by the time she eventually heard the clatter of Cvilak's scalpel as he laid it on the metal tray, she had already been sinking into a torpor in which the thoughts in her head alternated without any hierarchical order between gunshot wounds and all other kinds of wounds, a cold shower and an even colder beer by the river. This way she missed him cutting into the skin on the crown of the woman's head and removing the scalp, pulling it across the deceased woman's face. She only stirred at the piercing sound of the saw, its sharp blade and high speed cutting through the bone to get to the dead woman's brain, all the way round the skull so that Cvilak was able to lift off the lid and place it on the metal tray. By then the faces of most of the students were as white as their gowns and most of them were probably wondering whether they had chosen the right profession.

"In short..." Cvilak turned towards her when she stood up to go towards the door.

In short, she had been shot at close range with a short-barrelled weapon that Golob had also recognised as a nine millimetre calibre and from its remains concluded it must have been an FMJ. She had known all of this before she made her way to the Institute of Forensic Medicine.

Finally leaving, she was grateful to be able to breathe in some air, which, despite the late hour, could hardly be called fresh, but, compared to the stench of formaldehyde, it seemed nothing less than invigorating. By now she already knew that she would get rid of the sickly smell of rotting flesh after a few minutes but that the taste of it would linger in her throat for a day or so, regardless of how hard she tried to rinse it away.

*

Her phone came into action now that she had left the basement and it was once again receiving messages. She didn't look at them. At the top of the stairs that lead down through a small park and the Štorklja Inn through to the road leading into the town centre she wavered as she thought about the inn, the tables, the people around them, living people with glasses of beer in front of them, people out for a stroll, an ice cream in one hand, the other around their girlfriend or boyfriend, or holding a Border Collie or something similarly fashionable on a leash. None of them were thinking about *atria mortis*, dissecting a head, evisceration of internal organs and such. She didn't feel like going home and needed something that would clear her brain of the taste of death, even if she couldn't get rid of it from her throat. Brain... It would take her a while to not associate the image of the old woman with the crown of her skull removed whenever the word brain would come to mind.

She thought of Taras. How nice it would be if they could sit at some table near the Butchers' Bridge and have a beer together. If she could touch him, even if they can occasionally, as if in passing and apparently unintentionally do so during their coffee meetings in the presence of Brajc and Osterc...

She shook her head and went down the stairs. You're an independent and unattached woman and you can go and have a beer alone she thought to herself and then remembered bitterly how she was not in the right frame of mind to call Aleksander. Was he even at home?

In the faint light of a streetlamp a few metres outside the Štorklja Inn stood a group of people. Three of them. Two women and a man stood guard with banners and leaflets against abortion. Surely they can't still be collecting signatures for a petition at this hour? They now turned towards her.

"Good evening," the man greeted her but she stuck her police ID under his nose. She really couldn't be bothered to deal with these people. Not now and not ever.

"This issue also concerns you, officer," the man continued. "You too will one day be a mother, you too will one day have children..."

She gave him a tired look. Had this been the morning she would have told him where to go, but right now she simply did not have the energy. And how does this dimwit know that she doesn't already have children?

"This is about them. Just a signature and you will soothe your soul."

Despite the heat, he was wearing a buttoned-up jacket with a white shirt and tie underneath. Smooth black hair combed to one side and a face without any wrinkles whatsoever, even though he was not in the prime of youth. No other signs by which one might judge his character. Like some kind of android, she thought. Why do they all look so alike? Do they clone them? He stuck a lined notebook in front of her face. It had a numbered list of names and signatures.

"You too will one day be a woman..."

She took his pen, smiled at him, and wrote FUCK OFF! in capital letters into his book.

The smile that appeared on his face when she had taken the pen froze and turned into a grimace. She returned his pen.

"This was not the cleverest of moves, Miss Lanc," he said and she could not but admire his observation skills - he had not seen her ID for more than a couple of seconds. "Slowly this country is moving in the right direction and things like this will simply not be allowed to pass."

Tina showed him the middle finger across her shoulder. When she reached Zalog Street and turned towards the centre of town and the river, she wondered whether she was perhaps not spending too much time with Taras. What on earth was she doing?

Wednesday

CHAPTER 9.

"There's air conditioning on the bus," Brajc mumbled when he looked out of the window at a quarter to four in the morning. The sky had begun to turn a lighter hue of blue.

He pegged his pillow on the washing line and went into the bathroom where he took a quick shower, slapped on some deodorant that he then packed into a small bag emblazoned with YASSA[1] next to the characteristic line of stars, and made his way to the kitchen. He wondered whether to go for his usual eggs for breakfast but settled for two slices of bread with ham. It would be a long trip but last night he had already prepared sandwiches with dried salami and, he smacked his lips at the mere thought, Budapest was the culinary capital in a world as he thought the world should be. Just in case Taras was right about that dehydration stuff, he also had a cup of tea with his sandwich. He had to look through the whole cupboard above the kitchen table to find a box of mountain tea with two teabags of not exactly fresh ground herbs. Even the slightly faded design on the box betrayed the fact that the tea he had found was probably well past its expiration date.

In a world according to Brajc, every important meal would

---

1 YASSA was the logotype for a Yugoslav sports brand. It is an acronym for Jugoslavenski Asortiman Sportskih Artikala (Yugoslav Assortment of Sports Items) and was promoted especially during the 1984 Winter Olympics in Sarajevo. Here it is an indication that Brajc still uses an old-fashioned sports bag, probably from his school days, to pack the things he needs for the day trip to Budapest.

start with some kind of soup. Beef soup, if no other was available, and Brajc could list at least three or four Hungarian soups. Soup with small liver dumplings, for example, then there is goulash soup, bean soup with meat... On a similar trip in the past they had once stopped at Lake Balaton and there Brajc tried a fish soup with carp and apparently the catfish stew was just as good. In fact he had tried a kind of improved recipe called drunken fish soup which is a good way of using up bits of fish that are not normally used in other recipes. There is no need to point out that by the time they reached Balaton on the second day of their Hungarian tour Brajc was already rather tired and that he would probably put any soup he was served above beef soup on his list.

After this warm-up expanding the muscles of his stomach, he would choose meat for his next course. Pork, beef, veal and poultry, in this order of preference, only adding the poultry in case none of the first three were available. Although *paprikash* with flour dumplings... Basically, meat! Roasted, fried or cooked, with the addition of *lecsó*, a kind of mixture of peppers, tomatoes and onions, if he remembered correctly and he had little doubt that he did. To this ecstasy of meat he would also add a thick beef soup with onions, diced potatoes and paprika which is, although they call it a soup, a dish on its own and works wonders for curing a hangover. After that a leg of goose, liver, turkey breast, stews of various kinds, veal... Somewhere he had read that waiters in Hungary send people who ask for meatless dishes to Romania. It's a good job he knows. If they ever organise a trip to Bucharest, he won't be on it.

On a planet where Brajc would be the one forming tectonic plates of dietary habits, every meal would end with a dessert. It could be strudel, gibanica, baklava with a coffee and a shot of local brandy, but he would also be happy with a dobos torte layered with chocolate buttercream and a caramel topping. Of his last visit to Budapest three years ago, apart from the crowds at the Café Gerbeaud on Vörösmarty Square, it was Advent season at the time, he best remembers a special dessert called *Túró Rudi*, a kind of sweet curd coated in dark chocolate. *Cukrászda*[2]

2 Patisserie

was one of the rare Hungarian words he could remember. As well as *Jó étvágyat³*.

"There is air conditioning on the bus, and in taxis as well," he repeated, making a list of inns and *cukrászdas* he intended to visit without walking more than a hundred metres. All day.

Osterc was ideal company for such trips. He didn't drink and ate little, so Brajc could indulge in celebrating with guardian angel Osterc by his side. And talking of celebration, an ideal way to usher it in is with a beer and a *pogácsa*, a savoury pastry, or *lángos*, a deep fried potato dough with various fillings. Brajc preferred the classical cheese and sour cream. When he'll roll off the bus, full and drunk, good old Osterc will load him into his car and take him home and also pick him up the following morning to take him to where he had left his own car. He just hoped that Osterc would first deliver his wife and children to their destinations. Brajc feared Osterc's wife even more than he feared Taras.

Five minutes before half past five Brajc had thus arrived at Dolgi Most on the western outskirts of Ljubljana and eyed with satisfaction the large Scania bus that promised a bearable five-hour journey to the Hungarian capital. In the half-light he tried to find Osterc but could not see him. Instead, waiting on the pavement in front of the bus, was Osterc's wife.

*

Osterc did not feel any particular need for Budapest, let alone a wish, but Brajc's persistent enthusiasm and eventually pestering made him agree. In a way Brajc was right, he never went anywhere and just staying at home makes you stir crazy. The problem was that he had only told his wife two days before the trip and an even greater one that he had not been anywhere with her for some time, at least not without the children.

"It is almost a kind of obligation," he presented her with his plan.

"Is Taras going?" she asked him.

He had to admit that he was not.

"And your new colleague, Tina?"

She neither. In fact, he and Brajc were the only ones from the Ljubljana Police Directorate. They would pick up most of the

---

3 Bon appetite!

passengers on the way, in Domžale, Celje and Maribor, something which Brajc was looking forward to since all these people
joining them would also bring along some local brandy so none
of them would be bored on the flat Hungarian plains.

"Aha," she said and Osterc knew what was coming. Silence
until departure and also for a day or so after his return.

Then, the day before they were due to go, Patrik, his eldest
son fell ill. When they went to collect their sons at school, Patrik
was waiting with his Art teacher, a teacher who was fond of
him. He was snivelling, had a headache and a sore throat. When
they measured his temperature after they got home, the ther-
mometer showed thirty-eight point four. Maja Osterc was becoming desperate when her husband found a solution to two of
his problems. Budapest with Brajc that he was not at all looking
forward to *and* the stubborn silence of his wife who was to stay
at home.

"Do you know what," he said just as she was about to burst
into tears. "I can't leave you alone here with all this and I think
that I was too quick to agree to this Budapest thing."

She gave him a suspicious look. It was a promising start but
what was this leading to?

"The problem is that I cannot cancel the trip now. So I was
thinking… what if you went instead of me?"

"Can you do that?" she asked, more surprised by her own response than by the suggestion. She had not believed herself that
she was prepared to do anything in order to avoid the insoluble
puzzle that was awaiting her the following morning. How to get
one child to school, look after the other and keep a cool head
about it all.

"Would I not be the only woman if I did go?"

"Only as far as Budapest," Osterc confirmed. "After that they
will all go their own ways and you will be the only one on the
guided tour. If you want to go, of course."

Maja thought about it. She called the head of the library
where she worked who agreed on the condition that she would
in turn fill in for her whenever her boss decided that she needed
her. Then she went off and packed her things into a small black
bag. She thought about looking on the internet to check the pro-

gramme of the trip but changed her mind before even switching on the computer. In fact she did not care, as long as she went somewhere, as long as she would not be at home.

*

"Ping."

A 00:00 flashed on the screen and Anna moved the device on the trolley and used a paper towel to wipe away the gel from his elbow that was supposed to increase the effect of the laser and ultrasound therapy.

"Now flossing and we're done."

"I can't wait."

"Is it that bad?"

"Not as bad as it is odd," he said and it was her turn to smile as she took two rolled up wide elastic bands from the shelf in the cupboard, one red and the other blue. In the end she chose the red one and placed it on the bed on which he was leaning with his elbow, returning the blue one to the shelf.

"If you ask me, this is the only thing that's effective."

He stretched out his arm and watched her use the red band to wrap his elbow tightly, applying all her strength, even by leaning her knee against the bed. His fingers initially lost all their colour and became white then soon turned into bluish-purple spuds.

She placed a yellow rubber ring with some kind of nodes on it, a little like some creature creeping along the undiscovered depths of the ocean.

"Hold onto this and squeeze it," she had told him at their first therapy session. Now he already knew what to do.

He pressed on the bright yellow squid until he lost all the strength in his hand that was left twitching helplessly, barely able to hold on to the ring.

"Good," she said and took hold of the rubber wrapped arm, bending it so that the back of his hand was pinned against the bed and twisting his arm back at a right angle, a way of stretching the tendons attaching the muscles to the elbow.

"Imagine," Anna had said at one of their earlier sessions. "a tendon that is losing its flexibility. With every microtrauma injury it swells, calcifies... It can even snap but more often it just tears or rips at its point of origin on the bone. As in your case.

And because that is the point where it is has the poorest circulation, it takes a long time to heal."

Two months had passed since then. Two months, fifteen sessions and a thousand euros later and – no change. The incomparable pain at an indeterminate spot on the top right outer edge of the elbow, as first described by his GP when, after the effects of pain blockers had worn down, he referred him to a sports and work medicine specialist and then to a physiotherapist who went on about how the screen that projects the ultrasound is on the blink and it would take the National Health Agency at least a month to approve the purchase of a new one, which would need to come from Japan, so if he was in a hurry and was prepared to pay, the best thing was to go privately. He noted four addresses on a piece of paper that Taras could have found on the internet from the beginning rather than having waited for three weeks for the GP appointment.

In fact, it was not the same. After two months without dumbbells, he felt as if he was turning into a kind of spider, a plump creature with thin limbs.

Anna unwrapped the elastic band and waited for a couple of minutes for the blood in the fingers to start circulating again as he stretched his arm to help it do so.

"Well, let's do it once more," she said, stretching the elastic. This time she placed a soft ball next to the yellow rubber ring on the bed.

As he was driving back into town, the sun was already high above the Stožice Arena. He looked towards the giant oyster[4] nesting between the motorway ring road and the high-rise blocks of flats, the pointed outlines of which rendered them similar to ballistic missiles and indeed earned them the nickname *pershings* when they were first built. God knows what they are called today, if anything at all. He massaged the sore point with two fingers, trying to find out if there had been any progress at all or of it was still as bad as it had been before.

---

4 The Storžiče Arena is a multy-purpose arena, the largest in the country, located on the outskirts of Ljubljana. It opened in 2010 and became an instant landmark with its iconic oyster shape.

CHAPTER 10.

At the traffic lights he checked his phone which was switched off during his therapy session. Drvarič had called him and, when he didn't get him, sent him a message.

"Check *Slovenske novice*[5]!"

He checked the time – twenty to eight – and called Tina.

"Yes?" she said. He had woken her up.

"I'll check."

As he turned from Tivoli Street towards the office, a message came through from Tina.

"Will bring. Five minutes."

*

Stopping at the coffee machine for his usual morning dose he almost bumped his head on a sign saying *OUT OF ORDER*.

He switched on his computer, went straight to his inbox. The newest email was from Tina. No subject, no text, just a shot of the front page and the article in today's tabloid. *Did Nazis Murder a Homeless Woman?* was the headline.

He had just began reading when Tina stepped through the door.

"Are you subscribed to this thing?"

"I went to the newsagent and for the first time in my life bought this shit," she said, placing the hard copy of the paper on his desk. "I took a snapshot of the article and sent it to you. Some of us do live in the modern world. By the way, you owe me ninety cents."

The article was surprisingly level-headed for a such newspa-

---

5 A popular tabloid

per. It summarised what the police had already told the public, gave some statistics about homelessness in Ljubljana and correctly, without any sensationalist what-the-hell-are-the-police-doing tones, concluded that there are few specific indications – none in fact, Taras thought – as to who might have committed the murder, wondering in the final sentence whether the answer as to who had carried out such an incomprehensible deed might not hide in the graffiti that appeared at the scene of the crime.

The accompanying photo showed the green park bench on which someone had written *Sieg heil!* with white spray.

One might have expected much worse from the tabloid. Taras looked at the bottom of the article. Only the author's initials P. V. were given. He tried to think of any journalists he knew with these initials. There was a Peter Valič from the broadsheet *Delo*, but why would he be writing for a tabloid?

He called Drvarič.

"Have you seen *Slovenske novice*?"

"Seen and read," said Taras.

"And?"

"I'll check it out. When we were at the park yesterday, the graffiti wasn't there."

"Call in at my office before you go, so we can coordinate things, right?"

Taras was unsure what there was to coordinate, but fine, he would do so.

"Tina as well? She *is* in charge of this case."

Drvarič fell silent, as if he had forgotten all about that. After a long pause, he eventually responded.

"Yes, her too. Let's say half past eight."

Taras re-read the article.

"And?" said Tina. "Of course I immediately thought of that Nazi from the third floor."

"Who wouldn't?" said Taras, glanced at the article one more time and checked his phone book.

"How can I help you, Inspector?" the voice at the end of the line greeted him. "How come you are only calling me now? I expected to see your name on my mobile before the ink had dried."

"I'm getting older, that's it. You tell me. How come you found the graffiti? Don't tell me it was by chance?"

"Wouldn't think of doing that. We got it the same way we get more or less everything we print. Someone sent it to us."

"Someone, whom we both know, also probably wrote it."

"Yes," said the journalist. "That much I would agree. Sign of the times."

"Wrote it but not signed it?"

"Of course not. I can forward it to you, if you want. The photo we published is ours. The one sent to us was not the best quality."

"A name?"

"Can't remember. I do have it on the computer at work but I am not in the office right now. Give me ten minutes. Is your address still the same?"

"It is."

Taras thanked him and said goodbye. On his way to get coffee from the machine he remembered the damn thing wasn't working. Checking the time, he asked Tina if she wanted a coffee from Pisker. Silva the owner had recently begun using paper cups, mostly for the students from the nearby economics college.

"I didn't think that you'd ever use them."

It was quite possible that with age his taste buds were letting him down because Silva's coffee and coffee from any other shop didn't seem any different to the stuff their vending machine spurted out.

"Sign of the times," he said to himself and remembered that he had forgotten to ask

Valič something.

He put down the coffee on the counter and redialled his number.

"Yes, Taras?"

"Tell me, since when do you write for tabloids?"

A brief silence.

"Well, firstly I don't. And secondly, since it would not really be a good idea to publish this article in *Delo*."

"Because?"

"Anything published in *Novice* is trash. Everyone will have forgotten it by this afternoon." He fell silent again. Taras was clearly not going to make things easier. "Did you sleep through the elections?"

"We only have them every four years."

"Indeed, until now, and our sector goes in high gear every time. Only that this time round nobody is smiling. I can't say more on the phone."

"That bad?"

"Unfortunately."

He was about to cross the road at a red light when he noticed two kids with schoolbags next to him. Catching his balance by grabbing hold of the post at the crossing, fortunately with his left arm, he smiled at the surprised children and waited for the lights to turn green.

*

"So, you've seen this?"

Drvarič lifted the paper to show them the front page.

They both nodded.

"And, what do you think?"

He put the paper down on his desk and gave them a quizzing and almost worried look. Where now his confident stance that no one would be interested in the case because nobody would miss the murdered woman... etc.?

"I don't know," said Taras. "Haven't got a clue."

"Is there anything in it?"

"It would be almost too good if there was. People used not to sign a murder."

Drvarič smiled bitterly.

"Or create a political drama out of one."

"What drama?"

Drvarič waved his hand dismissively.

"You'll see."

"A member of these neo-Nazis lives in one of the flats above the park. It is possible that he is the author of the graffiti," said Tina.

"Do we have anything on him? Anything that would warrant an official visit?"

He looked at Taras.

"He is police unfriendly."

Drvarič pulled a face.

"Then we should conduct house searches for around two million Slovenes."

It looked like waiting for this morning report was worth it. What a privilege, being treated to Drvarič's humour.

*

"What now?" Tina asked.

"My mate who wrote the article has forwarded me the mail with the picture of the bench," said Taras. "Let's see who the author of the message is."

Valič's message was at the top of the list of unread mails. He opened it to find the sender's address: düa41@gmail.com.

"Our young Nazi?" Tina spoke.

The message was brief: *Park Argentina, crime scene – a few hours later.*

He clicked on the attached photo.

"He didn't even need to sign it," she said.

He enlarged the photograph. It showed the bench taken from above, the graffiti upside down and partially obscured. As if it said only *ieg hei.*

He printed out the photo and the message and pinned them to the board.

"Is it not possible in this day and age to find out where the message was sent from?"

Tina nodded.

"Yes, in a roundabout way. Every computer has an IP number on the internet with which it identifies itself to other computers.

"When sending an email, the IP of the sender isn't visible but what is, is the address of the mail server at the sender's provider. We can put in a request with ARNES[6] that provides all IP numbers in the country…"

"They probably wouldn't give it to us. Sending photos of benches is not yet a criminal offence in this country."

"…but, if you allow me to finish what I was saying, I could look at my list of friends from my computer degree and call a couple of them who are employed there. I'm sure they would be

6 The Academic and Research Network of Slovenia, the government institution managing the Slovenian Internet Exchange.

prepared to help for just a cup of coffee."

Taras nodded and underlined the düa41@gmail.com on the printed out message he had pinned to the board.

"And now?" he turned to Tina.

"I have arranged for a meeting at *Kings of the Streets*[7] at eleven. Apparently they are the people who deal with the homeless. Do you want to come along?"

He nodded. What else was there for him to do?

"Should we call in on the young Nazi before then?"

He stared at the snapshot of the bench.

"You don't believe he's the one who shot the woman?"

"I believe," he said with a cynical smile, "that the world will one day come to an end, but haven't a clue when."

He moved away from the board and looked at her. At last. They were alone and yet he was being more distant than when Brajc and Cvilak were in the office.

"How did it go with Cvilak?" he asked.

She held her head.

"What? Did she jump off the table?"

She shook her head.

"No, but almost."

*

She walked down Zalog and then Trubar Street and near the Butchers' Bridge walked down to the river and found an empty table outside one of the three, almost totally full bars. It was noisy and lively, as she expected it to be. She needed a little of the kind of peace a lonely person can only find in the middle of a crowd.

There were more people than usual in this end of town, partly also due to the performance of a woman acrobat jumping about on some netting attached to a float in front of the bridge, accompanied by some guy on the shore playing an electric guitar. Her drink arrived and she felt an almost burning sensation when the pleasant taste mingled with the one glued to the mucous membrane of her throat by the dissection room. Perhaps she should have a few more to wash it away. She would have

---

7 Slovene: *Kralji ulice*, society for help and self-help for the homeless, an NGO established in 2005 that works with the homeless in Slovenia.

ordered another but even as she was having her first drink it was necessary to deal with three idiots who, after asking whether they could sit at her table and she, without thinking, agreed because there was no space anywhere else, almost immediately attempted to chat with her.

"So, out alone, are we?" one of them asked as he fiddled with his phone.

"Yep," she said and congratulated herself for sounding totally indifferent.

"Well, then you must be glad of our company," another concluded and the three of them laughed as if he had just said something highly amusing.

She took a couple of sips of her beer and pushed the glass away, even though it was nowhere near empty. Standing up she said, "No, not really."

She could feel their gazes on her back or thereabout as she left. At least they hadn't said anything else.

*

Just before midnight she arrived at Cankar Street above which the light in her flat was still on. When did Aleksander intend to call me, she wondered. At two in the morning? Not even then? Right at that moment her phone rang. Finally. But it was Cvilak.

"Am I too late?"

"No, I've only just arrived home."

"I only realised the time after I had dialled your number. I know it's late..."

She waited patiently for him to mumble an apology.

"...but in our routine checking we did find something interesting. Something I've never seen in all these years."

Now it was Cvilak who waited for her, "What's that?"

"When we reached the lungs we discovered that they were badly eaten away by cancer."

"Eaten away?"

"Spread stellar shaped into neighbouring tissues, already into the pleural membrane and, what is particularly interesting – along the way it penetrated the pulmonary artery."

She had only had one beer, albeit on an empty stomach, but

now she was feeling a little tipsy.

"After death?"

"No, of course not," she heard Cvilak's annoyed voice. "After death all the processes end, the cancer also dies."

"Could it mean that she did not die because of the bullet, because of the gunshot wound?" she asked and realised with surprise how relieved she sounded.

"I don't know," said Cvilak. "I did note certain, albeit weak signs of vital reactions around the shot wound. To be honest – I don't know. This continues to be an academic question that needs to be answered."

*

"Hi," Brajc greeted Maja Osterc as she stood by the bus. "Where's your husband?"

"Patrik has fallen ill and Zoran stayed at home."

"At home?" Brajc repeated after her, the shock on his face so obvious that Mrs Osterc quickly tried to explain.

"It was he who suggested I come instead of him. I hope that's fine with you. I'll only be travelling with you. When we get to Budapest I'll go off on my own."

Brajc nodded and continued to nod for quite a while; he looked like one of those toys, dogs or penguins with nodding necks that people used to put on the dashboard of their cars, bobbing their heads on a journey. She will travel with them? And go off on her own in Budapest?

Of course they sat together. The seats were allocated in advance. Brajc offered her the window seat. She leaned on the edge of her seat and stared out across the town, waking up as they were driving past it on the northern bypass. The thin blue line in the sky was widening, turning orange. Brajc did not see it. He was staring at the seat in front of him. Number twenty-two, it said on it. And he had been looking forward to this trip so much.

In Domžale the bus picked up the first passengers who had applied for the trip and were not from Ljubljana or places to the west of the capital. Like Brajc, those who were, had to arrive at Dolgi Most by their own means. A tall, rather rounded gentleman boarded the bus and noticed Brajc from afar. He grinned at him. He had a bag similar to Brajc's hanging across one shoulder, his other hand was holding a bottle of brandy. He waved at Brajc across the still half-empty bus and made his way towards him. Brajc watched the bottle moving towards him but not with quite as much joy as he would have hoped.

"Hi there, Brajc," the man almost shouted when he came closer.

When he spotted the tiny woman sitting next to Brajc, his hand dropped.

"Hi, Artnak," said Brajc. "This is Maja Osterc, Zoran Osterc's wife, you know Osterc, don't you?"

Surprised, Artnak shook hands with the only woman on the bus and when she turned back towards the window he silently raised the bottle and waved at Brajc with it.

"Thanks, but I don't really seem to be in the mood today," Brajc looked at it longingly.

Artnak shrugged his shoulders and made his way to his seat.

Brajc leaned his forehead on the number twenty-two in front of him and felt like crying.

*

Osterc had dropped off his wife at the bus stop ten minutes earlier than the time they had arranged. He really could not face Brajc and his accusing eyes, so he didn't even get out of the car. By the time he returned home it was daylight. The children were still asleep, even Patrik who was coughing and snivelling but was at least sleeping.

At seven he woke up their younger son, made him breakfast and took him to school at half past seven. Forty minutes later he was back at home. Patrik was still asleep. Osterc made himself a cup of tea, gazed out of the window and wondered how he could spend his day usefully, providing his son's illness would allow it. He stared at the grass growing in the yard around a small garden that he had created on the rocky patch overlooking the Ljubljana Marshes. The grass was thin but already quite tall and he decided he would tackle it.

In the meantime, Patrik had woken up and wandered into the kitchen. Osterc offered him tea and biscuits and took his temperature. Thirty-seven point six, which was quite high for the morning, but when asked how he was feeling, the boy replied he was fine, just had a slight headache. He gave him half a paracetamol and sent his wife a message letting her know that his temperature is a little lower and that Patrik is feeling well.

Thanks. Look after him, said the instant return message.

Sitting Patrik in front of the TV, he went out to the shed where he kept his tools and winter tyres, and dragged out the push mower.

He stood at the western end of his plot, eyeing the ten by eight metres of lawn that awaited him and thought that he would probably finish before it got too hot.

Twenty minutes later he was totally sweaty, squatting by the mower, wondering why the blade was stuck. Most other people, Brajc or even Taras, would be put off by something like that. Not Osterc. Almost enthusiastically he took the mower into the shade behind the shed, found his tools and began taking it apart. He always liked this kind of work.

*

It is about a kilometre from the Ljubljana Police Directorate on Prešeren Street to the offices of Kings of the Streets, the society for help and self-help for the homeless on Pražak Street. At half past nine the sun was already high above town and Taras wore a baseball cap and sunglasses that were not exactly cycling glasses but he used them for cycling. In his short, knee-length linen trousers he looked like some Norwegian tourist on a walk round Ljubljana. He was probably also the only criminal investigator in the country wearing bright white trainers – Alenka's choice – and a cycling backpack.

More than once Drvarič had tried to persuade him to at least abandon the shorts. "Right," Taras had said at the time, "when the temperature falls below thirty. Not before that because I will melt." Brajc was having a much worse time handling the heat and had been wearing some light grey trousers for the last few days, the sweat trickling down his back creating a dark patch below the belt where it was absorbed by the fabric.

Tina who would usually just wait for an opportunity to tease Taras at least over his white trainers if not the backpack, said nothing this time. It was Taras who broke the silence after a few minutes.

"Have you already checked the footage from the cameras?"

"When? I'll do it today, hopefully."

They reached the bookshop on Slovenska Street. He stepped into the shade and beckoned to her.

"I don't know how far the cameras from Štefan Street reach or the ones from the hotel on Župančič Street, but if they are at all useful for us, then they also recorded me."

She listened to him and waited to see if he would say anything else, but he stayed silent.

"I cannot delete you, if that is what you are thinking."

"Yes, of course not. At least leave me out of the report. Nobody will look over the footage once you've seen it."

He turned away to continue along the road.

"Taras..."

He looked at her across his shoulder.

"If, for some altruistic reason you did something you should not have, tell me. I can handle it and will understand..."

He looked at her in shock and shook his head in disbelief, turned around and walked away. She followed him.

Was it sincere?

They walked on in silence until they reached a rundown block of flats on Miklošič Street where Taras stopped.

"And besides," he said slowly. "You could not handle it, believe me, you couldn't."

CHAPTER 11.

Tina and Taras went up the stairs and in the corridor on the upper ground floor greeted a homeless person hanging around there. The corridor stank of stale sweat and urine. In a small space to the right were some tables and chairs and two other homeless people were playing chess.

"Hello," Tina greeted them.

They turned towards her curiously.

"Excuse me, where are the offices?" she asked.

A tiny, lively man with a bristly beard and brown teeth jumped up and hurried down the corridor.

"I'll show you," he said and turned to the other man at the chess board. "Don't think about moving any of the figures, I've got all the positions worked out."

"I also have him worked out," he added as he led them down the dark corridor through a set of double doors into a space beyond which, at least by comparison with the corridor, seemed rather bright. In it was a row of tables with various young people working at them.

"Who was it that you were looking for?" the tiny man asked.

"The one in charge," said Taras.

"Štefan!" he shouted. "Štefan, you have visitors!"

Tina was expecting that Štefan would appear from some space she had not noticed at the end of the office, but he just stood up from one of the tables a couple of metres away.

"Bobi, we're not deaf."

"I brought them, 'cause, you know... I was playing chess with Feder..."

"Thanks, Bobi. You can go back now, you know what Feder

is like!"

Bobi slapped his forehead, turned around and disappeared down the tunnel he had brought Tina and Taras along.

"He's great, our Stanko," the man smiled. "But I don't recommend him as a chess partner. In his better times he was the municipal champion. We call him Bobi..."

"After Bobby Fischer," said Taras.

"Are you into chess?"

"Not really," Taras shook his head. "But I know him. Before I joined criminal investigation I worked as a police officer out on the street."

"We have police officers here often, fortunately not criminal investigators," said the man.

The eyes of everyone else in the room were glued on Tina and Taras.

"Štefan Vraz, president of the society, public relations, sport section and volunteers. It was you who called me on the phone, was it not?"

He first shook Tina's hand, then Taras's and pulled two chairs from the other tables, somehow managing to fit them between his table and the next, sitting at which was a girl in her mid-twenties with electric blue hair, piercing on her lower lip and a sleeveless vest. Taras nodded and sat next to her. After a brief hesitation during which the girl was unsure how to respond, she chose to smile.

"How can I help you?" asked Štefan.

Tina produced a photograph of the victim from her bag and showed it to him.

"Do you know this woman?"

He looked at it and nodded.

"Of course, she's the lady with all the bags, isn't she?"

"We were hoping that you might be able to tell us her name."

He shook his head.

"I don't know it. We don't have a list, we're not the police," he laughed. "Jana, could you take a look at this?"

He showed the photo to the girl with the blue hair next to Taras. She got up and leaned forward, leaning on Taras's shoulder as she did so. She was not wearing a bra under her vest and

Taras could not help but notice the contents of her cleavage.

"Any clue who she could be? Did we ever have any contact with her?"

"No," she said. "I know who she is but we have never worked with her."

She returned the photograph and took her time in moving her hand from Taras's shoulder.

"I thought," said Tina, "that at least you would have some kind of overview of everyone on the streets."

Štefan put the photograph down on the table and shook his head again.

"No, not even close. There are many for whom nobody knows who they are or where they come from, people wandering the world without an identity, without an ID, people whom no one would miss. Just now we were thinking about going to the police... meaning to you guys, of course, because there is someone we haven't seen for two weeks. Usually these things don't end well."

The girl with the blue hair returned to her previous position. She propped up her head, resting her elbows on the table, almost touching Taras. Of course everyone else was eavesdropping but, with her, Tina could not stop but wonder whether she was one of those creatures with a more Mediterranean attitude to personal space.

"We don't even know how many homeless people there are," he continued. "All we know is how many people come here. Some research was done, the first data is from 2004. It was largely on the basis of when our society was established. So the statistics are there but, oh, I hate numbers because what we should first establish is a proper definition, something we don't have in Slovenia, so we really don't even know the true extent of the problem."

"Can we offer you coffee?" the girl next to Taras suddenly asked.

"No thank you," said Tina.

"I'd like one, if possible," Taras nodded and smiled, even though he had already had one earlier.

"Everything is possible. How do you take it?" the girl said

and swayed off to the coffee machine by the wall.

"People are simply not interested in these things and I am glad if I get the chance to explain it to anyone. We are a non-profit organisation," Štefan continued. "We work differently to the State and keeping records wouldn't help us in the work we do with these people. The homeless should really be looked after by the State through social work centres but why do they just hand it over to the non-governmental sector? Because working with the homeless is a complex issue, you need to be fairly flexible, something we, the NGOs can be. Social services only carry out official functions, those given to them by the state, and they are very rigid in doing so. A homeless person who wants to sort out everything at social services would need to knock on quite a few doors whereas with us a single person helps them sort out various matters. Social services would need someone to go out 'in the field,' but few are prepared to do that. We have programmes with which we apply for funding and if the State authorises us, we, in a way, do the job for them."

She was wearing very short trousers, cut-offs. As a woman it was hard to judge. Exuberant, might be one word that came to mind. Who knows what she will be like in five years' time but what was now swaying through the room would definitely stop the traffic on the main road, that much Tina would admit.

"If we consider only people on the streets, the visible homelessness, the numbers are much lower than when talking about all persons who live in uncertain or unsuitable conditions."

"People with roofs over their head?" Tina asked.

"Yes, but even that is uncertain. When you rent you are at the mercy of the landlord who can throw you out at any time. And there is another key moment, or problem... I too lived in a flat until recently without a proper rental agreement, but I have a social network. These people have none. If the owner one fine day decided to throw me out, I know a few people who would take me in. If we then take the numbers from the people in the streets to this, a much broader definition of homelessness, according to some research done in 2010, the most indicative we have, the numbers in Slovenia increase from a couple of thousand to seventy thousand individuals."

The girl returned with two cups, put one on her table and gave the other to Taras.

"And of this, how many in Ljubljana?"

"A few hundred in those who are visible, the ones in the streets."

"A few hundred?"

The girl with the blue hair spread out in her chair and folded her arms on her belly, stretching her vest even further, her nipples protruding through the thin cotton. Taras half turned to her and nodded to thank her for the coffee.

"You wouldn't think it, would you? I said before that we don't keep records. Well, we do keep some because the people financing us demand them, and these records, though only estimates, clearly show that numbers are slowly increasing. When we began recording the numbers a few years ago, our day centre, which is just one of our programmes, handled around three hundred and fifty different people in a year, now it deals with four hundred and thirty. Every week, every day, almost, we notice new faces, and it is also true that in the meantime some also find their way out of the situation, go somewhere else, or die. There are some who have been with us from the start and will stay with us until the end, and some who use us on a temporary basis. However, we can only help them if they agree to it. We don't force anyone. We cannot do that anyway. Some are also in a situation so bad that they cannot be helped."

Tina glanced at Taras and expected at least a trace of a meaningful victorious smile, as if to say, told you so, but Taras was too busy trying to divert his eyes from the cleavage of his new friend. Suddenly Tina thought how a coffee might have come in handy after all. She would pour it over his head! Almost as if Taras had heard her thoughts, he finally moved his gaze from his neighbour.

"And do these homeless people today socialise at all?"

Štefan turned towards him and shook his head.

"Depends. Looking at them like this, one might say they are friends, but I know that, at least on the junky scene, anyone who dies is first robbed and only then the police are called. They are not friends. They are together because they have found themselves in the same situation but I don't know whether they would be if it weren't for this. There are also loners, if I can call them that."

"Like our woman," said Tina.

"Most possibly. She never called in here. Can I ask what happened to her?"

"She was shot," said Taras.

The girl next to him nodded. Tina thought she could almost hear her say, 'Wow!'

"Are there," she said impatiently and louder, as if wanting to drown out the inaudible 'wow', "any other places on Ljubljana where they might know anything about her?"

"Yes, of course. Ljubljana is relatively well organised as far as the homeless go, at least the basics like food, showers and such. The only thing is that you need to be is mobile, I mean capable of walking, at least a mile or so, because it starts in the underpass from Congress Square under the main road. There is a day centre there where breakfast is available. A proportion of our people move around. They first hang around there, then we open at ten and sometimes have a few cakes, bread rolls, pies and stuff that has been donated, though we essentially don't handle food. At eleven they start serving lunch on Poljane Road where there is a homeless shelter, the oldest in Slovenia, something that is unfortunately also rather apparent. Not exactly a place to be proud of. An evening meal can be available at the Society of Saint Vincent, the SVP, back in the underpass where they were in the morning, and it is quite decent. They cook it themselves and it's much better than the food in various canteens. Sandwiches are also handed out by nuns twice a week next to the church on Prešeren Square. Showers are offered by two programmes, so you can, if you are relatively mobile, look after yourself, food and clothing, even if you sleep in a railway carriage. This is why there are in fact not many real street homeless, people living on park benches. Closest to here is a man in the park in front of the courts. He has been on the street for thirty years. It will probably really be best if you go and visit one of these centres and enquire about your woman. There you may be able to find someone who might at least know something about her."

"Do homeless people have something like a 'territory' of their own?"

"The visible, legendary ones, are more or less on the same spot all the time. Everyone knows them and they in fact don't need to beg. The man in the park at the court does, you've probably seen him, but he begs just to pass time, out of boredom. They also don't come here for lunch because people bring them food."

"Thank you," said Tina and looked at Taras who nodded.

They stood up.

"This year we had one freeze to death," he said as they turned towards the corridor. "This is not something that happens often. Those who are on the street for a long time know that they shouldn't fall asleep at minus five, minus ten, and find shelter in some underpass or the public areas of blocks of flats. In shelters they put them in rooms with five, ten people... you must be quite drunk in order to sleep over in those."

"Thank you very much for your kindness," said Tina.

"I'm sorry I wasn't of any help. This will be a hard one, you know. There are more and more people coming here, as you can see," he indicated the space behind them with his hand. "We do what we can."

"Tell me one more thing," said Taras. "Why would someone shoot an elderly homeless woman?"

Štefan shrugged his shoulders.

"Some people don't like the homeless."

"Specifically?"

He smiled.

"Have you not seen the anti-migrant posters, Inspector? And what else is a homeless person but a migrant?"

Taras nodded.

"Thanks."

"If you need anything else, just call in."

The girl next to Taras also stood up and smiled at him.

"We open at ten and have free coffee, no questions asked."

*

They walked back in silence until they reached the lively pedestrian zone from where they could see the park in which only a day ago someone shot the homeless woman. There Taras turned to Tina,

"She's barely any older than my eldest daughter. And even if she hadn't been. OK?"

There was a little embarrassment in his smile and without waiting for her to respond he turned up the main road in his silly cyclist backpack and white trainers. Tina stood there, staring after him. In the hundred metres she needed to walk to the Šestica Inn she would find three better looking guys, another three in the next hundred metres to the Nama department store, but... Would you call what he has a presence? Besides, she thought as she set off after him, she was herself not much older than his eldest daughter.

CHAPTER 12.

It was one of those days again when by five o'clock in the afternoon she will be able to congratulate herself if she doesn't slap the brat across the mouth or at least twist his ear. She had had to stop him three times from grabbing Lina's toy rat, each time just in time before he ripped off the rat babies sewn onto the fluffy mother.

"Jan, this is the last time I am telling you this," she said as she held his hand, trying to stop herself from squeezing it so hard it would bruise. "And if you continue to be naughty, I will call your grandma. Did you understand me?"

It was her only weapon. Threatening him with his mother or father didn't help. The spoilt brat just laughed. How could he be any better than his parents who were the only ones not to take off their shoes at the bottom of the wooden stairs leading up to the first floor where their classroom was located. The only person capable of making him leave the nursery without screaming his head off or anything worse was his grandmother.

He scowled and removed himself to the far side of the playroom. There he found a plastic gun in the pile of toys the children had brought from home – there was always a gun, a sword or a plastic knife among them even though the kindergarten tried to avoid toy weapons of any kind. With it he aimed at Lina. She paid him no attention. Then he lifted something metal in the air, held it against his cheek and pretended, bang, bang, to be shooting with a gun.

She went across the room towards him. He moved his hand behind his back.

"Show me!"

He shook his head.

"Jan, show me what you are holding!"

"No!"

She pulled her phone from her pocket and pretended to dial a number.

"Hello, is that Jan's grandma?"

He shouted in a huff and threw what he was holding across the room. It hit the wall, bounced off and fell onto the wooden floor. She picked it up. It was a small brass cartridge case, the remnants of a bullet.

*

Tina stuck the USB into the computer and clicked on the folder with the data from the camera at the General Police Directorate. For a moment she feared that the programs used there might be so old that her laptop, far newer than anything they have ever seen at the GPD, would not recognise it. A few long seconds later the program managed to run the footage. The camera was placed above the entrance to the police station and covered a section of Štefan Street and the entrance to the passage under the Nebotičnik that lead through to Cankar Street, the street she lived on. It did not include the Park but from the direction people were walking in it was possible to determine who was about to turn towards its south entrance or who was coming out onto the road from that entrance. Brajc and Osterc had downloaded the data for a long time frame and Tina decided to check three hours of it, from eight to eleven in the evening, the time during which Cvilak was convinced that the woman had died, in one way or another on the bench in the park of a thousand names, as Taras called it whenever he did not call it Lenin Park in order to confuse the likes of Drvarič. Even if she fast forwarded the footage and only stopped it whenever something was happening, she was in for a couple of hours' work.

Taras sat at his computer listening to old TV news and she almost had to admire the see-if-I-care calmness with which he was passing time in the office. Whenever Osterc was looking up his own stuff during work time, it was pretty obvious by the way he sat, even more rigidly than usual, and the cautious alertness with which he was ready at any moment to click on work if anyone happened to get close enough to see what was on his screen. Brajc, well, whenever Brajc wastes time on the computer he just plays solitaire and, if caught, merely asks whether anyone has any work they need help with because he has finished his. Perhaps in his laid back appearance he was a little like Taras but, at least with Drvarič, Brajc would twitch and try to put together at least some plausible explanation about why he was watching some old TV news. Taras wouldn't bother. Perhaps this was also why Drvarič almost never appeared in their office and always demanded that Taras came to his. He felt safer on his own turf.

Štefan Street is not one of the busiest roads in Ljubljana, even though located almost in the centre, very close to the old town. It is used by the occupants of the flats in the houses that line it on either side, lead to the entrance to the Nebotičnik skyscraper with its restaurant at the top, but this was out of the range of the camera, and to the entrance to the offices in the same building a little further down the street that the camera did record but which was not used by anyone in the evening.

Tina thus stopped the tape every time someone appeared in the shot, grey, out of focus, unrecognisable, so she sometimes did not even know whether it was a man or a woman. The image was also mute. She had hoped that the camera might have at least recorded the sound of the shot but clearly this would not be the case. There were fewer and fewer people appearing in the footage as she wearily watched various dots move on the screen. There was little point. Up to the point she had checked, the only people who might have turned into the park were two couples, both of them holding hands, and she could not imagine that the handbags they had across their shoulders contained anything more than their phones and wallets.

Then her attention was drawn to the unmissable figure of a person in grey shorts and white trainers, holding a plastic bag in his hand. She thought about the couple with the handbags containing their phones. Perhaps she should have taken a closer look at them because, if she had not known what he was carrying with him, it would never have crossed her mind the person in the shot was carrying a gun around in an ordinary plastic bag that could come from any supermarket. At 21:59:01 Taras walked from the passage towards the park and at 21:59:11 disappeared from the shot.

She let the tape run, trying to swallow the lump in her throat, though she knew that it would not reveal anything else. She glanced at Taras who was still looking at the news and writing something in his notepad. Then the phone on his desk rang and he lifted the receiver.

"Coming," he said.

"Anything happened while I was dealing with the dead?" she tried to say jokingly.

"Not really," he mumbled more than said before standing up and putting his notepad and phone in his backpack. He finally looked at her.

"If anybody asks for me, I'll be back in about an hour."

So much about her leading this investigation. She stood up from her computer, stretched, and went to the corridor to get a glass of water from the dispenser. What a case. Someone shot a nameless woman who perhaps didn't even die from that. A motive? Because she got on their nerves? If this is now enough for murder, they could all start getting ready to work overtime.

When she returned to the computer she noticed that she had forgotten to stop the footage that was now running at four minutes past ten. A woman appeared on the screen, a young woman who stepped out of the darkness of the passageway, looked towards something, then picked up her phone, typed something, clearly a number, and after a brief conversation went back into the passage. Had anything else happened in the two minutes she had wasted on Taras and the water?

She wound back the footage. At 22:02:45 a man in dirty white trousers and a T-shirt leaped out of the passage and drunkenly staggered across the street, past the camera into the direction Taras had left. Ten seconds later the girl she had already seen appeared from the passage. She let the tape roll and since there was nothing for the next few minutes she forwarded it until about eight minutes later a police car stopped outside the passage. She sighed. What is this called? The left hand not knowing what the right hand is doing?

At that very moment Taras was once again stepping out from

the passage under the Nebotičnik. He walked in the same direction he had done two evenings ago, though this time without his gun and without a plastic bag. He turned round the building and stopped at the bench, kneeling in front of which was a technician who was taking samples of the paint of the graffiti and taking another photograph the sprayed on message *Sieg heil*!

"So the Boss is busy, is he?" Taras asked.

The technician nodded.

"His latest ballistics software is on the blink…"

"Ouch!"

"You can imagine, can't you? It was his brainchild and now because of him the entire ballistics department is on hold. You have something with us, don't you?"

"This thing," said Taras and handed him a brass cartridge case in a clear plastic bag. "Tell Golob that it's a gift from the amateur forensics at the nearby kindergarten."

*

While Tina was checking the footage from the cameras, Taras sat looking through his notepad where he had jotted his observations during the conversations with residents from the flats above the park. Notes that only he understood and, anyway, Tina will have to write up the official observations. He began from the end, with the old lady, owner of the pair of close relatives of Jack Russell terriers, and flicked the pages to the young Nazi and his mother, the empty flat with nobody living in it, to the former member of the French Foreign Legion. Baloh. What had he said, that he heard something that could have been a shot?

Taras checked his notes. The man had been watching the news about a developer being sent to prison when he heard a bang outside.

At least they will be able to establish the precise time of the murder. He clicked on the web and found the rtv.slo site with the archive of programmes. He found Monday's news bulletin and the unmissable 'moustachioed guy' as the old man had called him. Indeed, in the headlines he announced an item about the jailing of the director of the last big Slovene construction company on corruption charges relating to the construction of the second of two recent tunnel projects. Some other director of some other firm was already in jail because of the first.

Taras, like the news anchor, waited for the item announced but it never came. He noticed the presenter getting nervous, checking his notes twice, as if to see whether they really contained the announcement of the item, and eventually cleared his throat.

"I apologise. As the announced item does not seem to be ready, we shall now move on to parliamentary news and return to the report at the end of the programme."

Taras watched the bulletin to the end and all there was was another apology from the newscaster. The report had gotten lost somewhere in the computer quagmire and, as a fan of analogue, Taras could not but help smile smugly. It seems the former member of the elite unit of the French Army was the only one who actually saw it. Then his phone rang.

"They've brought the pistol you requested from the NFL. And one more thing, the kindergarten on Prešeren Street called and said that one of the kids who were in the park yesterday found a bullet. They said bullet, but judging by the description, it is just the cartridge case."

"Coming," he said.

*

"Baloh, Baloh…," he mumbled to himself, found the surname and pressed the bell.

"Yes?" came a voice from the door phone, much quicker than he expected. It was a woman's voice.

Waiting for him at the door was a woman of around fifty with a worried and questioning expression on her face.

"Don't be alarmed," he said. "Mr Baloh…"

"My father," she said.

"Yes, Mr Baloh and I have already spoken and I would like to go over something I am not entirely clear about."

"About that woman?" she said and pointed with her finger over her shoulder, vaguely towards the park.

Taras nodded.

"Terrible, but what does my father have to do with that?"

"He apparently heard the shot," said Taras and politely but determinedly turned past her, through the hallway into the dining room where the old man was sitting on the same sofa. The coverings, sheets with which the furniture had been covered on their previous visit, had all been removed and the furniture was all back in place against the walls. If the flat had previously reminded Taras of some theatre storage room, it now looked like a museum. Would he want to live in a place like this? Could he? On a sofa and a gramophone on which he would play Beethoven's Moonlight Sonata, drinking a glass of... water?

"Oh, it's you," the man said in place of a greeting, looking across his shoulder until he discovered with disappointment that there was nobody else apart from his daughter there. "Are you alone today?"

"Yes, today I am. My colleague is going through the footage of the cameras around the park."

He watched the old man's face. He did not seem in any way unnerved.

"I didn't know we had cameras in the park."

"Around the park. In the streets around the park. What is interesting is that they did not record anyone at all at the time you mentioned."

Of course he was bluffing. Without seeing the footage, he knew that, if nothing else, the cameras must have caught at least him.

"Yes, and?"

Still, or even more obviously, he had the face of someone who need not fear anything, the sovereign calmness of a person handling the situation.

"It means that the person shooting must have come from this house."

Or from any of the three directions not caught by the cameras.

"When was it that you said you had heard the shot?"

"Did I say I heard it?"

This time the old man's voice shook and, as if looking for help, he briefly leaned towards his daughter and then turned back to Taras, trying to achieve his previous, cool look.

"I can read out what you said to us."

"Well, go ahead," said the old man but it was more than obvious that his self-confidence had vanished.

From his backpack Taras produced his notepad, opened it

and held it quite a distance from his eyes to be able to read it.

"Yes, and?" said the old man when Taras finished.

"Well, there was no news item about the developer who was taken to jail on the news."

The old man gave him an even more confused look. It was obvious that he did not know at all what Taras was talking about.

"You said that you had heard a shot during the item about the developer but this item was actually not in the news. It was only announced in the headlines."

The old man shook his head. He did not understand what Taras was aiming at.

"Someone who watched the beginning of the news would hear that announcement, and if they stopped watching the TV after the headlines, maybe even left the room or the flat, they wouldn't know that the item was in fact not included in the news at all."

It took another second or so for the old man to comprehend. He then put on a broad smile before pulling a face.

"And that is why you now think that I killed her?"

"I am just asking how it was possible that you watched a news item that was not on the news."

"Oh, come on. You policemen are the same everywhere. Here, in Paris, anywhere. You are never just asking."

"You said you were in the Foreign Legion, yet you don't want to talk about it. Why? Surely nobody can accuse you of anything now?"

The old man looked at him with contempt.

"It is not about anyone accusing me of anything. It is a case of a promise. I don't know whether you can understand that."

"The FG 42 was not a French machine gun but a German one."

The old man gave him the same blank look he had done when Taras was talking about the news item.

"When I was first here," said Taras impatiently, "you mentioned that you carried all kinds of weapons as a soldier of the French Foreign Legion. The only one you mentioned by name was an FG 42. The FG 42 was the machine gun used by the German parachute units during the Second World War."

The old man nodded and smiled cynically.

"Well done! Who would have thought. Well, I will make a tiny exception and tell you just as much as I am allowed to say. Then you don't ask any further questions. Right?"

Taras didn't nod but the old man continued anyway.

"I was sixteen when I was mobilised in Hamburg where my mother, a German national, found refuge after my father from Celje was sent to the East. I was trained as a parachutist and sent to defend the Atlantic Wall. Have you heard of it? That was where I was caught by the British who handed me over to the French and at the time that bode no good. I survived because of my young age and because I accepted their offer. That was how I came to be in the Foreign Legion. For a long time my unit was made up entirely of Germans. That much as far as my time in the Foreign Legion goes. As far as the woman is concerned though..."

He pointed with his finger to the drawer on the chiffonier by the wall.

"...I gave you the gun. You could by now have checked it to find out it has nothing to do with her."

"Not yet," Taras had to admit. "I am returning the gun but as far as the ballistics go... We are having some technical problems."

*

The woman escorted him to the door and, once she had closed the door to the living room, put her hand on his shoulder as if wanting to stop him, and spoke in a quiet voice.

"Inspector, the person who killed this woman is certainly not my father."

She sneaked a look back towards the door, as if afraid her father might be able to hear her.

"He has dementia, though he does not want to admit it. He would prefer to be accused of being guilty than admit that he cannot remember anything. Did you not notice that he often does not know what you are talking about? And the things he does remember, I have to listen to day in day out, three, four... ten times a day he tells me the same thing."

"I am not claiming it *was* him," said Taras. "Just checking the facts."

"And besides," she spoke even quieter. "He cannot even walk. Have you seen him off his sofa? You haven't, no? He hides his wheelchair in the pantry. There is no chance he could get himself to the park. Were it not for me, he would die of hunger."

*

Outside he found some shade and called Golob.

"Thanks for the cartridge case," said Golob.

He must have been excited though he sounded reserved.

"When will we have the ballistic results from the shooting in the park?"

He sensed an unease transmitted through the receiver by Golob's silence.

"Is it very urgent?"

"I wouldn't be calling you if it wasn't."

The silence now lasted even longer than the first time.

"Well, we of course conducted all the ballistic experiments we needed to with the pistol you were in such a hurry with. We saved everything. Now we also have the cartridge case to compare the data with. We have a problem though," Golob eventually uttered. "The programme that compares databases, this Evofinder that we have only just purchased, has crashed and we are now waiting for an authorised programmer. We are not allowed to touch it ourselves."

"You're waiting for the repairman?"

Golob had to admit that Taras was right. Authorised programmer sounds better, but in fact they were waiting for the repairman.

"You don't need to compare what you have with all the guns in the system from Reykjavík to Lisbon. Just check it against the one I gave you. Surely you can scan the cartridge case separately."

The silence this time was so long that Taras wanted to check the line wasn't dead.

"The scanner is part of the package and works only with this ultramodern system. We no longer have the old one. Nobody expected we would need it again."

"When then?"

"I don't know. Certainly not before Monday."

Taras sighed loud enough for Golob to hear him.

"I am sorry, but as far as I understand, the owner is not about to run away, is he?"

Taras said goodbye. He will almost certainly not run away, more likely he would die of old age before Monday.

CHAPTER 13.

The bus stopped at the last motorway resting place before Budapest.

"When we reach Budapest," the tourist guide had told them previously, "we shall take a drive around the town on our bus to see the main sights, giving us more time for individual visits and any guided tours you might want afterwards. Your choice."

As he was pretty certain that nobody would want a guided tour he smiled – he would get paid anyway and not have to do anything at all.

Maja Osterc went to use the loos while Brajc hesitantly joined the group he knew and with which he was hoping to spend his time on the trip. As there was not much time at the stop they were just ordering double shots of *pálinka*.

"What's good for jam is just as good for pálinka," one member of the group repeated an old Hungarian truth and waved at the waiter when Brajc joined their table.

"No, no," Brajc shook his head and tried to explain to the waiter that he wanted a "Coffee, long... *Kaffe verlängerter.*"

He used his stomach as an excuse, remembered Taras and added that he was having problems with acid reflux, it was bad and there's no playing around with these things. The group nodded sympathetically and downed their first round. Brajc sipped on his coffee and with a mix of horror and to him unexpected relief, realised that he had not consumed a single drop of alcohol on this trip.

Maja Osterc was the only person in the world in front of whom he did not wish to appear drunk, though he didn't even know himself why not. He used to have a wife in front of whom he was often drunk and even now that they were divorced he had no problem appearing before her in a state of inebriation. He drank in front of his son and on a trip like this he would even drink in the presence of Taras, say what he may. Before the petite librarian with smoothed black hair tied back in a ponytail, the wife of his colleague, however, he could not. He might on one of the picnics he organised and also invited the Ostercs to but there he was on his own territory and had huge amounts of food so any units of alcohol consumed were offset and lost the battle with all the glycerides circulating in his veins. Here, however, on this long-awaited trip he had been so looking forward to, he just couldn't. Even if most of the companions on the trip would not understand.

This is how, for the first time since the world was created, Brajc arrived in the Hungarian capital more sober than he had been on any union trip, and for the first time also actually listened to the tourist guide talking about Heroes' Square, the People's Stadium, the Parliament, St Stephen's Church, bridges, Elisabeth Bridge, Széchenyi Chain Bridge, Margaret Bridge...

And when the bus stopped and the guide asked whether anyone was interested in a tour of the Castle Hill in Buda, and only the tiny hand of Mrs Osterc was raised, Brajc's fat hand followed with a couple of seconds delay to the shocked silence of the entire bus.

"What?" Brajc rebuked them. "This is the seventh time I am in Budapest and I have never visited Buda. Am I not allowed to?"

The guide stared at the two hands sticking out of the crowd, sighing to himself. There is no such thing as an easy victory.

*

At half past twelve Tina went for lunch and had a salad from the self-service canteen in the underpass near Cankarjev Dom. She could not get anything else down her throat in this heat. She sat down, surrounded mostly by students and thought about how, until recently, she was one of them. Not now. She was a thirty-year-old woman living with a guy she had nothing in common with, whom she was not in love with, and now that she was messing about with Taras, she wondered whether she had ever been. Was she in love with Taras?

"Better not," she said to herself in a low voice. "Better not. That would be catastrophic."

She discreetly looked around to check whether anyone at the other tables in the busy dining room noticed the woman talking to herself but it was an unnecessary concern. Most of them were on their phones, in some way or another looking as if talking to themselves anyway.

When she returned to the office there was still nobody there. Brajc and Osterc were in Budapest anyway and who knew where Taras was. In terms of what she was doing this suited her just fine.

She quickly forwarded the tape from the second camera to 22:00 hours. It showed the pavement on the opposite side of the road, not the side at the park, and both lanes of traffic for about thirty metres left and right of the hotel. The camera was placed so that it caught a side view of the passing cars and she could not read any number plates, but she recognised Taras's Citroën C8 by the dent on its right side acquired in the parking lot at work when he missed a newly installed metal bar that was supposed to protect the aluminium gutter on the corner of the building. Taras would previously always do a tight turn around it. The footage showed the front part of his car, almost to the door, and it drove away from the parking space on Župančič Street at 21:59:15, something that initially didn't make sense. He could not have driven away before, according to the footage from the first camera, he had even arrived at the car, but then she realised that the cameras were probably simply not synchronised.

She let the film run, as if hoping that Taras's car would be one of many, but for a long five minutes there was nothing at all. The next car to drive past was a white van. She stopped the tape and moved it back and forth by fractions of a second until she was able to discern the sign on the side of the car. *Franc Zupet, painting and decorating*, it said and below that in smaller letters that she was unable to read at this resolution, probably the place and phone number of the said business. In the first camera the painter came two minutes after Taras, in the second he appeared five minutes after him. What was he doing in the interim three minutes?

She rewound the footage and checked it again from the second Taras disappeared from the first camera to the moment the white van drove past. There was nothing. For the few cars that drove past just before Taras they could probably not determine the owners but she noted them carefully, for example a grey Volkswagen Golf at 21:59:00 which made her think of the huge number of Slovenes she would need to question if ownership of a car of this make and colour was a sufficient criterion, then a white Renault (of similar popularity), a black Mercedes and then Taras's C8. After that nothing until the white van.

And nothing. She found nothing at all. If she ignored the footage of Taras there was nothing apart from the painter and decorator Franc Zupet.

*

"In the thirteenth century Béla IV ordered the building of a fortress on the banks of the Danube, wishing to protect the town from raids by Tartar-Mongol hordes that had previously attacked Pest and then crossed the frozen Danube to Buda..."

They were standing in the shade next to Matthias Church in which, as he found out, various Hungarian kings were crowned, including Franz Joseph I of Austria who was also ruler of the territory that is now Slovenia when that belonged to the Austro Hungarian Empire. They were the only group in which the guide was not using a taped tour. The heat was just as relentless as in Ljubljana, four hundred and fifty kilometres away and to Brajc, the no more than hundred metres that he thought he would have to walk today had extended to quite a few hundred, the distance between the church, the renaissance palace and the library...

"...the *Bibliotheca Corviniana* established by Matthias Corvinus, known to us as King Matjaž..."

...Trinity Square, the Fisherman's Bastion and the Royal Palace. At first he listened to the guide's explanations, then he simply tried to survive.

"Well," said the guide after an hour or so, satisfied in the end that he had found someone who was prepared to listen to his knowledge. "I think that that will probably be enough for a first impression of Buda and the Castle Hill. More information would just confuse you."

They were standing in front of a fountain with figures showing King Matthias hunting and Ilonka, who had fallen in love with him, standing to one side. It all ended tragically, at least for Ilonka when she discovered the true identity of the man she had loved and died of a broken heart.

"Any other questions?"

Brajc shook his head. Close to the Matthias Church he had noticed a *cukrászda* that was apparently where Franz Joseph himself ordered his cakes and if it was good enough for the Emperor it would be good enough for him.

"If madam and sir might want a boat ride on the Danube, I know of a very good offer."

Brajc have him a tired look, looked at madam and nodded. He had not heard this madam and sir thing in a long time.

*

It did not take long for Osterc to find out that it would not be possible to mend the mower. What was broken was the axle onto which the blade was attached and he could not understand how this happened. Had the boys had anything to do with it? He would have become angry if that had been in his nature but instead he put the mower away in the shed, then spent a while moving some tools from one end to the other and, as he had nothing else to do, then back again. And what now? The car was, in as far as that was possible, of course, flawless, oil, filters, water in the cooler, screen wash storage tank full, everything hoovered and clean. For a moment he felt unuseful but then he remembered he was at home because of his sick son. He went back into the three-bedroom house and found Patrik sitting in front of the TV in the kitchen.

"Are you hungry?" he asked him.

"No."

The TV was showing three men each forging their own knife or sword, some kind of weapon. This looks like it could be interesting, Osterc thought and sat down next to his son.

*

"Thanks for the company," Maja Osterc said to Brajc somewhere under the Széchenyi Chain Bridge while the loudspeakers of the riverboat blasted out Strauss' *Blue Danube*, even though the river in Budapest was dark brown. "I hope I didn't spoil any plans you had?"

"Oh," said Brajc dismissively waving his hand towards the shores on the Pest side where he assumed that most of their group was. "I'm glad you came. These people go on trips like this just to eat all day and get drunk. Not much fun."

She nodded at him encouragingly.

"And how are you in general?" she asked him when the boat turned round at the Rákóczi Bridge. "Still alone in that big house?"

"Yes," he said and, even though he did not intend it to, this 'yes' sounded sad. "But it has sort of suited me until now. You see, I had to come clean with a few things but it's time now I start handling things differently."

They disembarked at the Chain Bridge and with the Saint Stephen Basilica close by they went to have a look in there as well. Brajc had the feeling that he had already once stood in front of it, though things had been very different, all he could recall was the dome but that could not have merely hovered mid-air, so he must have seen the rest of it as well. When they reached the steps in front of it and he looked down on the square across which they had come, he remembered why it all looked so different. What was missing were the stalls of the Christmas market that were of course not there in June.

The bus returned to Ljubljana in a similar manner as it had left, in silence. Those still left on it were asleep. Including Mrs Osterc. Only Brajc sat, awake like an owl, thinking. He had been waiting for and looking forward to the union trip for over a month, fantasising about the food and alcohol he would indulge in, now he was returning home sober and so hungry he could bite into the right hand of Saint Stephen that is paraded around his church every August. He should have been disappointed but he was unusually calmed. Tomorrow he would wake up and not need sunglasses to go to work. He could hardly wait to see Taras. And just maybe it was time he got his act together. Before Saint Never's Day, or, as the Hungarians would say, before the Basilica is finished.

*

At just at about the time the fifty-two seater Scania was turning towards the Malence junction, the British drag performer Cheddar Gorgeous stepped onto the stage at the gay club Tiffany on Metelkova, advertised by some as the only true squat between Christiania and Beijing[8]. With lips painted blue, blue eye liner and glitter on his cheek and forehead he stepped out in front of the enthusiastic audience, not only the gay men from Tiffany's but also lesbians from the Monokel Lesbian Club next door, located in the same building at the north side of Metelkova. Among them was a couple who had argued loudly before the show and did not stop even when the British artist began his performance with which, as he had announced before his arrival in Ljubljana, he was inadvertently indulging in something political.

"I think that everyone playing with gender in an extravagant way is in their own way an activist," he explained but right now the arguing lesbian couple was threatening to overshadow this message.

And because the girls, one in jeans and a leather jacket, despite the heat, the other in yellow shorts and a blue sleeveless T-shirt, did not stop making a fuss despite the ever louder protests of other customers, the security guard had to separate them and show the more aggressive of the two the way out of the club.

"You'll regret this," she shouted but the security guard still removed her from the venue and Cheddar Gorgeous was able to continue with the performance he had prepared for the evening.

An hour later they were arguing again, this time in Monokel, once again full after the performance next door was over. With the sound of techno music and the darkness of the club under a brand new disco ball, their argument seemed like some kind of fresh performance, especially when a circle that formed around

---

8 Metelkova (full name the Metelkova City Autonomous Cultural Centre), named after nearby Metelko Street, is a squat and cultural centre located in the former headquarters of the Yugoslav Army in Slovenia that were taken over by a number of alternative and youth organisations.

was soon taking over the whole dance floor and their argument seemed to be leading into a brawl. The girl DJ was playing *schranz*, a hardcore type of techno, and glanced towards them nervously. In a minute or two the scene from Tiffany would probably repeat itself but there was a massive bang outside. At the same time the glass frontage and the disco ball above the dancefloor shattered. Everyone, not just the argumentative couple, froze, the women looked towards the window behind which a shadow, an outline of a figure was disappearing. They then looked down at the shattered glass and the gaze of the girl who had been made to leave during the performance at Tiffany's became fixed on the bare legs of her friend. For a moment there was no other sound in the place but the hundred and fifty beats per minute, then the music was interrupted by a scream.

There was blood trickling down the inside leg of the girl in shorts.

Thursday

CHAPTER 14.

Alenka was lying in bed in that transitional stage when one is no longer asleep but also not yet awake, waiting semi-consciously for the alarm clock to ring. When instead of the clock the phone rang, she was confused and tried to switch off the alarm which was not an alarm. It was Taras.

"Good morning," he said and she could hear the unease in his voice.

"Can you come to collect me?"

"Why? What happened?"

"My chain snapped," he said and with the way he said it she knew she was not getting the whole story.

"Where are you?"

*

Taras liked fast bicycle descents. One of the things he enjoyed every so often was overtaking cars on his return from Vršič or other roads with lots of bends. If he was unable to overtake them – he wasn't crazy enough to cut a blind corner – he would get on their nerves with his cheap mountain bike that they could not lose from their back bumpers. Alenka, who occasionally went cycling with him, had often said that one day this would not end well.

This morning he had cycled to the church of Saint James above Katarina, along the asphalt road to the last inn and then another kilometre or so up the dirt track to the hill on which was the small church, basically just a larger chapel, visible from afar.

He was doing well, pedalling as hard as he could, close to the top where the road was steepest. Reaching the last five metres where he always had difficulties, he came across an unpleasant surprise. The last stretch of the hill had been cemented over and no longer presented a challenge. At the top he sat on the bench under the lime tree for a minute or two, he did not need to change because it was already so warm that his wet T-shirt will probably feel pleasantly cool. Then he sat on his bike and set off back down towards the valley. He could not recall whether his thoughts were elsewhere or whether he came across some sand or leaves on the corner. What he does remember is the front wheel slipping and that for a second he thought he would still be able to straighten it, but the following moment he had already crashed onto the asphalt and was sliding across to the other side of the road. The impact was so hard that, although he was almost certain that he had not hit his head, he had blacked out when, after freeing himself from the bicycle, he tried to crawl on all fours to the side of the road to avoid being run over by anyone who happened to be driving to work from Katarina to Ljubljana at half past six in the morning. He had stopped on the verge and for a moment thought he would need to throw up but in time the pain settled. Only then was he able to check his wounds.

*

Alenka picked him up in the valley to which he had descended on his bike without the chain that he wrapped around the handlebar. He was a sorry sight. His right side that he had fallen onto was covered in blood. The palm of his hand, his elbow, the right, painful elbow, his cycling shorts ripped on the hip exposing grazed skin underneath and his knee, all scratched and grazed with blood oozing out of all the wounds. His cycling glove on the right hand was completely torn and the hand was not only bloody but all greasy from the chain that he had to pull from the sprocket. Despite this, he seemed to be in a surprisingly good mood.

"You should have seen that," he said when she stopped at the side of the road with the Citroën in which they could easily fit two bikes when they collapsed the back seats.

"Spectacular like Primož Roglič[9]."

*

By the time he arrived at the office the other three were already there. With a bandaged hand, elbow, a plaster on the hip and the knee so the bloody patch would not ooze onto his trousers.

"I fell with the bike," he said before anyone had a chance to ask him anything and for Tina's quizzing eyes added, "I'm fine, just a little skin damage."

He sat at the computer and switched it on, glancing across towards Brajc. But Brajc was ready for that.

"Shame you weren't with us," he said to Osterc for the second time today, loud enough for Taras not to miss it. "Old Buda really is something special."

Taras looked up across the top edge of his computer screen.

"Osterc's elder son fell ill and Maja went instead of him," Brajc explained. "Did you know, Taras, that the German army, as they were retreating from the Russians, blew up the Széchenyi Chain Bridge, the oldest bridge in Budapest, and the Hungarians re-built it but it is a metre wider than the original and that the new bridge was opened exactly one hundred years after the original?"

Taras did not know that.

"Someone called Pestner called you from the police station," Tina quickly said before Brajc had the chance to list the particularities of the eight remaining Budapest bridges.

"Did he say what he wanted?"

"He said it was something to do with Metelkova."

"Metelkova?"

She clicked on her computer, picked it up from her desk and turned it towards Taras. He stood up and moved closer. On screen was an article about a *New Attack on the LGTB Scene* with a subtitle claiming this was the *First Time Fire Arms were Used*.

He read the report on how during a party at the clubs Monokel and Tiffany, organised to raise funds for the Pride Parade,

---

9 Slovene racing cyclist, in 2017 the first Slovene to win a Tour de France stage, came second overall at the 2020 Tour de France after his countryman Tadej Pogačar, and was in 2020 ranked World No.1 road cyclist at UCI World Ranking

someone had shot through the window at Monokel and hit a girl on the dancefloor in the leg. The bullet, which had bounced off various hard surfaces, fortunately only caused a superficial wound and she was discharged after being treated at the nearby medical centre. Members of the LGTB scene were outraged...

"This was last night?"

"Yes."

Taras checked his phone book and called the police station, asking for Pestner.

"What good news do we have today, Mr Pestner?" he addressed him.

"Lots of good news, as always. Have you heard about Metelkova?"

"Just read an article, but what is it supposed to have to do with me and my group?"

"Maybe nothing," said Pestner. "In general it is me and my guys who are responsible for Metelkova. However, when we went to take a look at the scene last night, we found a piece of graffiti on the building next door that might be familiar to you, something that brought attention to the case you are working on. You've probably guessed?"

"*Sieg heil*?" Taras asked.

"Precisely. Fresh graffiti. It is of course possible that it has nothing to do with the shooting, mine or yours, but in case there is some connection it would be good if we all knew about it. There is no point in each of us trying to invent the wheel separately."

"OK. I'll send you what we have and you get your information to me. Would there be any problem if we go and check the scene as well?"

"As you wish," said Pestner.

Taras put down the phone and looked at Tina.

"In fact the call was for you. Pestner should have spoken to you."

"Should have," she said, "but didn't."

"I'm sorry, old habits die hard."

Taras did not give the impression he was particularly remorseful.

He went across to their board and wrote *Metelkova* next to *Sieg heil!*

Then he turned towards his trio and informed them about his conversation with Pestner. When he finished he stared at Tina.

What she wanted to say was that they should just stop pretending and that he should take over the case as he does every time one comes their way. Instead she said, "Someone should go to Metelkova but I have another hour's work with these." She pointed to the pile of papers accumulating on her desk. "There's too much of it to leave for later."

"I can't go either," said Taras without an explanation and turned to Brajc and Osterc.

"Why do I have to deal with this now?" Brajc protested. "Someone is sure to come along again and accuse me of being a homophag or something!"

"A homophag?"

Taras gazed at Brajc, confusing him a little. "Well, someone who hates gays. You know they will have a go at me. I don't hate them at all as far as they leave me alone but as soon as they see me they will start. Police this, police that, and if I don't drag in from somewhere the drunken brat who thought of blowing up their disco ball and if they don't consider him to fit their notion of the perpetrator, then... then..."

"A homophag?" asked Taras.

"We just don't fit together, that's it."

Angry, Brajc fell silent. He was annoyed and whenever he was annoyed no cooling fan on his desk could help. With his already soaked paper towel he wiped his brow again, leaving tiny flakes of paper behind. Taras had made his mind up and if Taras makes his mind up nothing can change it, he knew that much, but he tried again anyway.

"Taras, just be sensible. For fuck's sake, am I now supposed to go round these clubs of theirs, or what? At my age? Would this not be something Tina could do much more easily?"

"Well, don't then," said Taras.

Brajc was about to thank him but something told him it was better to wait.

"Don't?"

"Of course not. We live in a free country and anyone who doesn't want to work can just go along to human resources and hand in their notice."

*

"What is it with this guy?" Brajc growled as he and Osterc drove to the chain at the barrier preventing vehicles access to Metelkova. "Hand in my notice just because I expressed mild displeasure over having to deal with these weirdos? It's not my fault he can't ride a bike properly!"

After driving for twenty minutes around various diversions due to roadworks they reached the Belgian Barracks, as it used to be called even though there were probably never any Belgians in it. Leading up to it from the east is Friškovec, a street named after an execution site where serious criminals were beheaded in the middle ages. The last execution was in 1707 when some woman was decapitated. What her crime was is not known.

Brajc stopped the car and beeped his horn. Nothing happened.

"Osterc, go and find someone to open the chain," said Brajc nervously tapping the steering wheel until Osterc reappeared from the Celica Hostel[10].

"Wouldn't this be better with some kind of ramp?" he then barked at the poor student accompanying Osterc and who was trying to unlock the old padlock in order for Brajc to drive into the courtyard or rather main square of the Metelkova City Autonomous Cultural Centre.

"And where is this thing?" he asked the student as he finally succeeded in lowering the chain.

"Where is what?"

"These two clubs for these people," said Brajc, leaving the unfortunate student to wonder what clubs and what people the red-faced, sweating criminal investigator in the grey car was talking about until Osterc explained.

"Oh, you mean the clubs Tiffany and Monokel?"

"Yes," said Brajc, annoyed with Osterc's intervention.

---

10 The Hostel Celica located within the Metelkova area is a former prison - celica means (prison) cell in Slovene – that has been converted into a unique and now very famous Youth Hostel.

"Over there, that's where the shooting was, over there."

Brajc waited for a while, looked at Osterc as if to say, told you so, and turned back to the student, "And... where is there? We're not all homosexuals, you know!"

Thirty seconds later, when they had driven along the entire length of the only street in Metelkova, they stopped outside a blueish building covered in graffiti, dominated by the word *justice*. Its outer wall was the northern boundary of Metelkova.

Brajc grabbed the handle to open the door but it was locked. On it was a large piece of white cardboard with *Protest – tonight at 21:00* written on it. He checked the doorbells, first pressing the one that said *Club Monokel*. When there was no answer he also pressed all the others, without success. Wearily he looked at Osterc who took the copy of the police record that, as was noted at the top, was taken by the on-duty patrol at half past two in the morning after Golob allowed them to finish the job. Osterc then tried one of the phone numbers on the report, then a second and a third, but without success. It was already past eleven. Surely they're up by now, he thought, and tried all three numbers again. No answers. Then he stepped to the police cordon which protected the area around the shattered window, one of many windows, all with metal frames mounted together to form one big window. Through the hole he could see in the dark interior the remnants of the glass ball on the floor. He felt round the metal frame with the missing glass. There was a long groove on the vertical side on his right.

"Where is the graffiti?" asked Brajc.

He compared the photo of the graffiti on the wall that Pestner had sent them with the outside walls of the clubs Tiffany and Monokel. Yes, the photograph was taken in the middle of the night but this was not the same wall. This one was covered in graffiti whereas in the artificial light the one in the photo appeared monotone, a light, off-white colour. He turned to look at the neighbouring buildings and on a large elongated building about fifty metres away saw a large dark, black, rectangular patch that someone had clearly painted in order to cover something.

"It's gone," said Brajc. "Bye."

Osterc continued to try ringing the various phone numbers he had. Brajc dragged himself to a nearby park and sat on a bench in the shade of a bushy lime tree. Bored, he gazed at the surrounding buildings and the groups of tourists who had come to this Southern Christiania, taking snapshots of the place, waving angrily at some cheeky young girl who tried to immortalise him on her phone, mopping the droplets of sweat on his face with some new paper handkerchiefs he had found in the glove compartment of the car, before they merged into the Zambezi on his already soaked T-shirt.

The tourists moved along slowly, almost cautiously, as if they had lost their way and ended up in a zoo where, as an experiment in order to see what would happen, the animal enclosures had been left open. Their caution was unnecessary. At this time in the morning there was more probability of coming across a tiger on Metelkova rather than any of its residents or users.

"Nobody is answering their phones," said Osterc.

Angrily Brajc twitched the hand in which he was holding a soggy ball of tissues and then, as if he had run out of energy for anything else, just sighed and took a few deep breaths of the heavy, scorching air, sitting with his eyes fixed on a green façade of a building covered in purple sea creatures. A huge octopus at ground floor level and jellyfish under the roof but what drew Brajc's attention were all the giant squid in between.

So they sat for a minute, Brajc with his gaze fixed on the squid, Osterc waiting, passing his time reading Pestner's report.

"Do you know what I find odd," he eventually said.

Brajc mumbled something incomprehensible, although it could also have simply been a slightly louder sigh. He did not try to move his eyes away from the street art on the wall. In recent years he had developed an unusual affinity to ugly animals. If Discovery Channel showed some documentary about pandas in Sichuan he switched to *Bones* or some similar crime investigation series, but when they showed hyenas or other animals, which everyone else he knew found repulsive, he watched with interest. His favourite was a tiny ugly crab from southern seas that uses a kind of piston, a hammer it launches at bullet speed, smashing into the unsuspecting fish's head, allowing the crab to then drag its victim into its hole in peace. And these squid... He once saw a programme about huge Pacific squids, giant cannibalistic monsters from the depths of the ocean that they process into cat and dog food in Peru. He felt sorry for them.

"If someone shot from the outside, close enough for those inside to see him, clearly with the intention of hitting the ball..."

"Mhmm," said Brajc.

"How come they hit the frame?"

"The frame?" Brajc repeated.

"The window frame. If they hit it and the bullet bounced off to the disco ball, then the disco ball was not what they were aiming for."

Brajc looked at Osterc and then past him to the broken glass at the Monokel club.

"And what does that have to do with us?"

"And if he wanted to sign his own work, why choose this house and not the one he shot at?"

"Pfha..." Brajc huffed but before he could explain this 'pfha' Osterc's phone rang.

The conversation lasted for about a minute during which Brajc once again became immersed in the painting on the wall on the opposite side of the road. When Osterc finished, Brajc cleared his throat.

"Well?"

"That was the woman in charge of this club, Monokel. She said she is not in Ljubljana right now but that we can come this evening at around nine when they will hold the protest march against this attack and she would make time for us then. Apparently everyone who was here last night will also attend."

He expected Brajc to start complaining and was prepared to take charge of all the necessary conversations and enquiries because he did not think it was worth both of them ruining their evening over this but, to his surprise, Brajc just said, "Right, meet you at the station at half past eight."

Osterc stared at him, almost expecting an explanation, but Brajc was already once again contemplating the squid.

CHAPTER 15.

Taras turned up in the park outside the courthouse with a bottle of the cheapest wine he could find in the shop across the road. He knew that there was not much point in buying anything better. In their years on the streets the homeless have developed a taste of their own and anything above one euro fifty was too sweet.

There were three in the park. Taras got them to gather around, gave them the wine and showed them the photo,

"Oh, that's Mici," said the oldest among them.

Despite the heat he was dressed in long corduroy trousers and a black jumper. He stank like the porters in Nepal.

"Mici? Mici as in Marija?"

"No, that was just what we called her," said one of the other men with a Carinthian accent. "She didn't talk to anyone. She wasn't from round here."

"She used to talk to herself. Non-stop," added the third man, as if afraid he needed to say something or he would not be allowed a swig from the bottle.

"And in which language did she talk to herself?"

"Bosnian."

"Actual Bosnian? Not Croatian or Serbian?"

The guy in the corduroy trousers had in the meantime opened the bottle with his lighter, took a swig and passed it on to his Carinthian colleague.

"Isn't that the same? What's the difference?"

*

Taras visited other places in Ljubljana where homeless people gathered. The shelter on Poljane Street where he waited for the food distribution and then showed them the photo of the woman as they were all stuffing themselves with minced meat macaroni. He went to the passage connecting Plečnik and Congress Squares where the SVP was based and then returned to the station without calling in at the office, picked up his work car and drove to the Caritas centre in Moste and talked to the nuns in the Sisters of Mary Shelter. He then drove along the bypass to Ježica and the Shelter of God's Mercy and forced a conversation from the Missionary of Charity who in principle did not receive male company on that particular day. He could have spared himself the trouble of doing all of this because he found out nothing that the three guys outside the courthouse had not already told him. They all knew her, many even had contact with her because she used to come for food to their shelters, though not recently. Some of them had other names than Mici for her but Taras was pretty sure that none of the names they gave him was her real name, and besides, nobody had given him a surname. None of them had the faintest idea why anyone would want her dead.

"Someone must have just done it for the hell of it," said the Carinthian guy at the courthouse.

*

When he got back to the office it was empty. Osterc and Brajc had clearly already left but Tina's bag was still hanging across the chair at her desk and her computer was still switched on. He sat at his desk and stared at the folder he found on it. Just as he opened it Tina walked in, drying her hands with a paper towel.

"Did you take a look?"

He shook his head.

"I've only just arrived. What is it?"

She went across to his desk and leaned across the folder.

"I don't know whether you have ever seen such a well-organised..."

His hand stroked her back and slid down to her buttocks. It was summer and of all the bare skin processed by his pituitary gland in town today could not compare to the half inch of exposed skin above the belt of the otherwise dressed woman before him...

"Taras!"

He moved his fingers higher up and she thought he would move his hand away when he slipped it behind her belt and past the elastic on her knickers.

"Taras, not here!"

"Why not?" he buried his face in her neck. "We can lock the door and anyway, the next person to come in here will be the cleaning lady at eight in the evening."

He used his other hand to undo the button on her trousers...

"Taras," she cried out, composed herself and pushed him away. "Stop this, damn it!"

He took two tiny steps back in disappointment.

"Right, right."

She did up the button on her trousers.

"If you're not in a rush to go home... at least... what about a coffee?"

Even before she had a chance to nod, the door opened and Brajc and Osterc barged into the office. Taras's hand dropped to the desk and Tina reflexively turned round and pretended to be busy with the folder, opening it pointlessly and then closing it again.

"Anyone mentioned coffee?" Brajc asked. "Are we invited as well?"

She wanted to hit Taras across the head with the folder.

*

"How's the kid?" Brajc asked and found out that Patrik was better, that he still had a slight temperature but that Maja went to work despite this.

"He's sitting in front of the TV having a good time. Apparently yesterday you were..."

Osterc was looking for the words with which to convey the assessment of Brajc that his wife had given him when she said that he had been surprisingly normal.

"Yes," Brajc helped him. "I was bored of..." and he stopped because he could not find a way of describing drinking and gorging without admitting to this openly. "Well, I wanted for once to see Budapest like all..." He did not want to say 'normal people' because that too would be an admission that he himself did not fit into that category.

Tina was not following the conversation of unfinished sentences. Taras sat on the far side of the table with bandages on his wrist and elbow and, as she had noticed earlier, plasters all over his hip, but with his surprising good mood he reminded her of a satisfied teenager. She shuddered at the thought of what might have been had Brajc and Osterc stepped into the office ten seconds earlier. Or, God forbid, if... they were to have entered ten seconds later.

"I went to see the old man," said Taras.

"The old man?"

"The Foreign Legion guy. Yesterday."

"And?"

"I returned his gun and am now waiting for the ballistic report which will unfortunately not be ready before Monday. Monday at the earliest."

"Ballistic report of what? The shattered bullet?"

"Oh, yes, sorry," Taras smiled. "The cartridge case was found." He told them about the phone call from the kindergarten.

"And why would you think that the old man might have shot the bag lady?" Brajc asked. "Didn't you say he was almost an invalid?"

Both Osterc and Brajc had finished talking and were listening to Taras.

"I don't know whether he is or isn't an invalid. His daughter says so. What I do know is that someone has recently used this gun. Golob was also able to confirm this. The barrel stank and it wasn't oil."

"And the motive?" Tina asked with relief as if this conversation would finally end the episode in the office. Never again, she had said to herself, like some alcoholic who sobers up after a night on the binge and finds out that they miraculously didn't smash the car or knock over some innocent pedestrian. Thanks for another chance. No more messing around.

"I certainly can't see one?"

She looked at Taras who did not pay attention to the fact that she was primarily addressing the question to him.

"There's always a motive," said Osterc.

She waited for him to explain this further but he just continued to squeeze the teabag with his spoon.

"Because?"

"Because, why would anyone kill anyone otherwise?"

Yes, indeed, why? Well done Osterc!

Tiredly Brajc looked first at her and then Osterc and when Osterc was clearly not intending to add anything else, he turned back to Tina. Hanging around Metelkova had clearly exhausted him.

"If you ask me, the bag lady was killed by someone who wanted to brag about something like that in front of his sick mates. This new-age Nazi who danced about when you visited him – did you check his Facebook profile?"

She would have slapped her forehead if this wouldn't make it so obvious that she hadn't. And this from Brajc, a drunken and neglected forty-something who barely got through secondary school and finished a course on criminal investigation, asking her, a new generation graduate in computer engineering, information technology and psychology.

"Facebook..." Taras repeated quietly.

She thought he was nearly as embarrassed as she was.

"Facebook," he repeated again as if learning the pronunciation of some complicated foreign word. "Well, what about it?"

"Nothing," said Brajc. "It's just that people these days post all kinds of things. Facebook, Instagram, all kinds of social media stuff. They can't fart without reporting it."

Taras looked at Tina. She briefly shrugged her shoulders with embarrassment.

"I'll check."

"Don't forget, that we are going to Novo Mesto tomorrow," said Taras.

She nodded. No, she had not forgotten.

"To do with that stuff in Bohinj?" Brajc asked.

"Yep."

"If you want us to, Osterc and I can go as witnesses saying you would not hurt a fly."

Taras smiled gratefully. He felt bad for saying the stuff about Brajc handing in his notice. Tina also smiled, bitterly. She too should not have any problems swearing that Taras would not hurt a fly.

*

He expected to find Alenka at home but she wasn't there. He called her but her number was unavailable. Five minutes later Anja called him and asked him whether he knew where mother was because she could not reach her on the phone. He talked to his daughter for a while. She was in the middle of her exams and appropriately nervous; this was probably why she wanted to talk to her mother.

He switched on the TV and caught the end of the afternoon world cup match between France and Peru. He had forgotten entirely about the world cup. There was plenty of time until the evening match between Argentina and Croatia and if they went for a walk or a jog now, as he had promised when she came to collect him when he had fallen off his bike this morning, they would be back before the match. Well, now she wasn't here. He sat on the sofa and for a while watched the after-match discussion where they kept repeating the same phrases about defence and attach formations, and fell asleep.

He was awoken by the commentator shouting when Modrić achieved the second goal for Croatia and the match was almost over.

No lights were on, so he assumed that Alenka had not yet returned. He called her again, without success. Her phone was switched off. Then he called Anja and asked her whether she had spoken to her mother. She hadn't. He called her work where there was, of course, no answer at this hour.

She had never done anything like this before and surely wouldn't. He became worried. He rang the Medical Centre and asked whether, God forbid, she had been taken there... She hadn't. He had no phone numbers of her friends and colleagues so he sat in the car and drove off to the clinic. It was closed, all the lights inside were switched off. He tried calling her again and once again her number was not available.

What if...? All kinds of scenarios went through his mind. Calm down, he kept telling himself. Perhaps she went to the cinema... if she went to the cinema, surely she would go to the one close by, Kinodvor, she wouldn't go elsewhere, would she? And if she went to the cinema alone, without telling him anything, was something wrong? Whatever it was, it could all be sorted out, just as long as she was fine. He drove to the cinema and waited for a quarter of an hour for the last showing to finish. She was not there. He jumped back into the car that he had left on the pavement outside the entrance to the cinema, rushed home, and decided to search every room, starting with the cellar. When he reached the bedroom, he found her. She was fast asleep.

He leaned over her and could smell alcohol. For a while he stood there, confused, a thousand questions rushing through his head, then he composed himself, tiptoed round the bed to her night stand and picked up her handbag. He carried it into the living room and quietly emptied it onto the table. Among the usual clutter, phone, lipstick, perfume, handkerchiefs... was a photo. He picked it up and stared at it motionlessly for a while.

So, this is why, went through his head.

He had thrown twenty-five years out of the window. Not that he did not deserve it.

He put it down and then picked it up again, as if it would be any different this time.

And when he was about to put it down on the table for the second time, a tiny detail drew his attention. He was, after all, a policeman. He stared at it, then closed his eyes, hoping that when he looked again this tiny detail would still be there.

CHAPTER 16.

Being unorganised was not the worst thing Maja Osterc persistently and without any change in his behaviour accused her husband of. They had met when she travelled by train from Ivančna Gorica to attend lectures for her librarianship course in Ljubljana and Osterc was at the time working as a policeman on the railway, checking the documents of people travelling on the train who, to put it bluntly, did not look white enough or Christian enough for the places they were travelling through.

Osterc became a policeman because his uncle who was a policeman had mentioned this possibility when he had to decide what to do after finishing primary school.

"All right," Osterc had said even though he had not until then shown any inclination to this profession.

So he became a policeman and, after he got married, Maja came across some kind of handbook for future criminal investigators in the library where she worked. She attached the appropriate codes to the book and, instead of placing it in the shelf in the reference section, she took it home. Osterc looked at it, nodded, and put in a request at work to re-qualify as a criminal investigator. His application was approved, he finished the course and was allocated to Taras who was, after an initial cross-examination, very happy to get this otherwise silent man on his team. No one else knew how to find the right tyres at the price Osterc could. He was very talented in practical technology, without really knowing what to do with this talent.

"How can you be so without ambitions?" Maja often asked him, the last time after she returned from the trip to Hungary when Osterc had spent the afternoon helping the neighbours solve various problems with anything that spins and can be broken in doing so.

"Why don't you open an afternoon workshop and charge people for all this?"

Unsure what to say, he mumbled that he needed to go back to work and, instead of leaving at eight to get there for half past when he had arranged to meet Brajc, left half an hour early. Brajc found him at the computer, browsing a site that sold lawn mowers. Out of something over five hundred and forty thousand possibilities he reduced his search to a Makita DUR365UZ cordless grass strimmer, 'an excellent choice for use on public surfaces in residential areas and other urban spaces'.

"You're looking for a mower? Don't you already have one?"

Two. Osterc had two mowers, a motor one he now never used, and the push mower that would more than suffice for his tiny patch of lawn on the Karstic terrain outside his house – he had bought it over the internet second-hand because his wife wanted one, saying she could not stand the roar of motor mowers.

"It's bad enough all the neighbours use them, I really could not handle another one in our garden," she had said.

It was true that Saturdays and Sundays were often dominated by the piercing sound of lawnmowers coming from left and right, from close by and from further away.

"What about getting an electric one…" Osterc tried.

"The boys can use the push mower," said Maja. "It will do them good."

This was how Osterc ended up with the push mower, though it was he who pushed it back and forth on the rugged tufts of grass that would never become a decent lawn even with generations of such treatment. The boys had a go when he first bought it, found it fun to play with for about five minutes, got bored and went off to do their own thing. Very soon, but not for the same reasons as the boys, he too became bored with the push mower. A mechanic at heart, he missed the hum and even the exhaust fumes of a 'proper' mower. He bought the motor mower in secret and used it whenever his wife wasn't at home but it was a hassle to bring it out of the shed and get it running.

He did not know why, but the promised performance under

the image of the Makita DUR365UZ got him into a good mood, even though he knew he would never buy it. It was the most expensive in its category.

Brajc eyed him suspiciously. He felt uncomfortable in the presence of happy people.

"Shall we go?" he said grumpily as if his continual bad mood was Osterc's fault. Only when he turned did Osterc notice that he had his gun attached to his belt.

"What's that for?"

"Don't you know where we're going Osterc? Just in case one of these poofters grabs my arse, I'll show them the hell!"

He made his way to the door and as he waddled past, Osterc inadvertently thought that there was probably no real danger of such a thing happening.

*

It was getting dark when they arrived at Metelkova and Brajc demanded that Osterc drove right up to the graffiti-covered building that houses the clubs Monokel and Tiffany. It was impossible to drive right up to the entrance because of the gathered crowd. Osterc estimated there were a few dozen people present. When they parked the car and opened the doors, they were hit by loud music, stuff neither of them listened to – in fact neither of them actively listened to any kind of music anyway. If the radio was on, they would listen, if it wasn't, then it wasn't and whatever happened to be on at the time was fine with Osterc and got on Brajc's nerves. Oliver Dragojević[11] least of all.

"What's this now?" Brajc growled, stepping out of the car. "This place should have been cordoned off. Did they just go inside, or what?"

The police cordon that had been placed round the building from the broken window all the way to the entrance had been removed, the door to the club was open and there was a bouncer standing outside. Walking past him, coming out of the club, were two men holding hands. Brajc pulled a face and turned towards Osterc.

"Call the creature you arranged this with and tell her to

11 Croatian singer and song writer, he was a household name throughout the former Yugoslavia, famous for his easy-listening blend of traditional and pop music.

come out here. I'm not going in there even if they chuck me out of my job for it."

*

"Are you two from the police?" asked, or rather shouted, a girl, the long haired half of a couple approaching the car against which Brajc and Osterc were leaning. In vain Brajc tried to find any sign of weirdness on her. Fortunately, her short-haired friend had a ring in her nose. Osterc nodded and shook hands with both girls. Brajc just stood behind him, stunned, but it didn't seem like the girls noticed this.

"What's this?" Brajc eventually shouted. "Who let you in?"

He was shouting but the music was so loud that the girls had to lean closer to him were they to understand what he was trying to tell them.

"You can't just break into the place! There was a cordon there that said Police all over it and you're not supposed to cross it. Nobody is, not even you."

The girl with the short hair and the ring leaned towards Brajc and shouted, "This is Metelkova. How do you think it was created?"

"What?"

"Shall we go somewhere a little quieter?" She pointed at a building some fifty metres away.

They ascended a few wooden steps, went past a sign offering drinks such as *gin chronic* and *mojito brujito*, and reached the interior of the place that was even stuffier and hotter than outside, but at least entirely empty and it was just about possible to have a conversation. A young man with dreadlocks came along and asked them what they wanted to drink.

The girls looked at the criminologists.

"I'd like a Coke," said Osterc.

Brajc stayed silent. Sitting down peacefully at a bar with two lesbians and trying to decide what he would have to drink was too much for him.

"What would you like to drink, Inspector?" the short haired girl asked him again. "We'll have beer, won't we?" she added.

The long-haired girl nodded and though what appeared on Brajc's face was not exactly a smile, it was definitely something that smoothed out the wrinkles of his scowl.

"OK, I'll have one too then," he said.

*

The girl with the long hair was Milena and she ran the club, the other, Jana, was the club's main DJ.

"First the glass shattered, then..." Milena stopped and shook her head. "No, that's just me rationalising it. It all happened at once. A flash, the window and the disco ball above the dance floor, it all shattered at once. Our first disco ball. At Tiffany's they had one from the very beginning, now we girls acquired one too. For fun, though some of the girls were against it."

"Did you hear the shot? See anyone?" Osterc asked.

Milena shook her head.

"The music is always pretty loud and the glass is frosted so we don't get people gawking. And then, after it shattered, there was nobody outside. In fact, it's not really strange that there wasn't anyone."

She gave Jana a loving glance. "Jana knows how to make a party."

Jana smiled and raised her glass.

Brajc automatically raised his as well and joined in the toast.

"Hang on, there must have been someone," Osterc interrupted them.

"The report we got from our colleagues says that some people in the club saw someone outside who ran away after the shooting. That they saw the flash and the shooter."

"That's what we thought yesterday, yes, and we also told the police," said Milena shaking her head. "But today this guy has appeared here and says he was not involved in the shooting. Would you like me to send him over so you can talk to him?"

Brajc and Osterc looked at each other.

*

A man of around forty appeared and came up to their table. Dark haired with signs of developing baldness, jeans and a white T-shirt that failed to hide his round belly. He introduced himself and, embarrassed, sat on the chair offered.

"Apparently you were outside when the window was shattered?"

He nodded.

"But," said Brajc, tapping on the sheet of paper in front of him. "You aren't mentioned in the report our colleagues wrote last night. Here it states that witnesses saw someone outside the window when the flash occurred and the window and the disco ball shattered and that this person then ran away."

He sighed and looked at Osterc, as if hoping he might give him the strength to explain.

"When it all happened, I got scared..."

There were no signs he was going to continue, so Brajc helped him.

"What of?"

He groaned once more, ran his fingers through his hair and looked at Brajc.

"I was not supposed to be here. That's it. I have a partner at home, we've been going out for a long time. But yesterday he went on a business trip and I went out. I just came to have a look, I swear that that's all it was. But my partner is jealous and if he found out I came here... You can imagine."

He rolled his eyes to the ceiling.

"And you preferred to break the law?" said Brajc.

The man looked at Brajc and the glass of beer in front of him.

"Well, basically, yes."

"That's not good."

He raised his glass, finished the beer in it and beckoned at the waiter.

"What, he would break up with you if he found out?"

"I don't know. But there would certainly be high drama."

The guy with the dreadlocks came up to the table.

"I'd like another beer," said Brajc. "And my colleague... Another Coke?"

Osterc shook his head.

"Nothing then. What about you?"

"Well, I'll have a beer too then."

Brajc waited for the waiter to bring the beers, raised his glass to the man in front of them, drank the first half inch from the glass, settled comfortably in his chair, folded his arms in his lap, or rather across his pot belly.

"I'm listening. Everything, from A to Z, please."

*

In fact, the guy had first gone to the cinema. He had come back from school, the secondary school where he taught Physics. He was posted there after five years of sending requests for a transfer, hoping that his secret would not come out at the primary school in a small settlement in provincial Lower Carniola where he was teaching IT.

"These people," he explained to Brajc and Osterc, "still think that gays will grab their arses and harass their children. It's unbelievable!"

Brajc nodded in agreement.

He explained that he felt bored after coming home and decided to go to the cinema. When some Pakistani film he chose finished, he thought he might call in at Metelkova for half an hour to see what had changed since he was last there.

"Nothing has changed."

Everything was as if not a day had gone by since his last visit. The same scene, the same people, compartmentalised into groups according to some internal rules, incomprehensible to others.

"Do you know what once happened to me in Tiffany's, some time ago?"

He had had a boyfriend, they had got on well together. One day they happened to meet by chance at Metelkova and the guy who was there with a group of other friends did not even acknowledge him, ignored him completely.

"Anyway, last night I paid the entrance fee, went to Tiffany and on the way peeked into Monokel where everything was still very alter, but a kind of lax alter, if you know what I mean, and indeed, two of the girls were staging a psychodrama in which we were all supposed to participate."

"A psychodrama?"

They had been arguing so loudly that, for a moment, he had thought it was a performance.

"I mean, I find all that so pointless."

So he went outside for a cigarette. At the precise moment he lit up there was a whizzing sound.

"Whizzing?" Osterc asked.

"Yes, like some insect on steroids. The glass shattered, people started screaming, I got scared..."

And he ran away.

In the morning he read the news on the net, in various articles and forums, and became ashamed of his actions.

"Would it be possible not to mention my name?"

The gathering outside the club, at least the official part, was clearly over and people spread around, some into the buildings, others across the unkempt park outside. Brajc and Osterc stood outside the window with a gaping hole in its metal and glass structure. Blasting through it was music that Brajc and many others would describe simply as dubba-dub.

*

"If this man is telling the truth," said Osterc, "then the bullet was not shot from close range outside the window but from somewhere..."

They turned and looked towards the building that is known as Pešaki[12].

"That *Sieg heil!* was in fact written on that building and not this gay disco," Brajc added. "Tell you what, Osterc, why don't you call your two girlfriends again."

*

"Where could we get the keys to that house over there?"

"Tito has them," said Milena and looked at Jana. "Have you seen him at all today?"

"I think I did. I don't think he would miss today's protest..."

She disappeared through the door.

"Tito?" Brajc asked.

"Our Tito[13]."

Milena smiled and at that moment Brajc felt something that seemed like regret. Jana was indeed a more robust type of woman and that nose piercing was a little disconcerting, but Milena was... You'd never have guessed.

"Former Mayor of Metelkova, one of the 'natives'. He was

---

12 Plural of *pešak* - infantryman, Metelkova is a former army barracks.
13 'Our Tito' (orig. *Naš Tito*) was a slogan used in support of Marshal Tito during the Communist period in Yugoslavia, here Milena is of course referring to their friend Tito but smiling because of the double meaning.

among those who climbed across the fence in 1993. He has his studio," she pointed towards the building, "in Pešaki."

*

It took about ten minutes for Jana to return accompanied by a long-haired, bearded man of around sixty who, judging by his looks, the way he walked and the greeting he directed at Osterc and Brajc, one would be justified in calling a hippie.

"Look, look, a pair of coppers, wha's up?"

"Apparently you can unlock this for us," said Osterc and pointed to the solid wooden door closing the entrance to the former assembly centre of the Austrian army.

"Yep, but do I want to?"

He raised his chin staring provocatively at Osterc.

"Open it if you don't want any fuss," said Brajc, more fed up than threateningly. Ageing hippies would rank highly on the list of people he could not stand.

"Right, right, no panic. I was going to anyway."

Hairy and bearded Tito produced the keys from his pocket and leaned over the lock.

"By the way, do you know some guy called Taras? What was his surname...?"

"Birsa," Brajc helped him, pretty sure there were not two people called Taras in the Slovenian police force.

"Yes, him, how's he doing?"

"He's our boss," said Brajc and not exactly gently pushed the former Mayor of Metelkova out of the way and entered Pešaki. Inside everything was dark and he was not happy to have to wait for the hairy guy to make his way past him and press the light switch on the wall, illuminating a short corridor that led to a more modern wooden and glass door, or more like a partition wall where the corridor had a left and right turning though it also seemed to continue beyond it.

"There's a terrace upstairs," said Tito.

"We'd like to go to the terrace also," said Osterc and Tito walked along to the next door, opened it and walked up the stairs beyond it. Osterc thanked the girls who hesitated briefly as if wanting to go with them, but then turned round and went back towards the clubs.

*

The terrace was dark and remained so even after Tito had hit the switch. Osterc found his mobile and switched on the light. He shone it on the floor and noticed a thin dark line on the concrete. He followed it to the left and after a couple of metres it became thicker and ended in a puddle of dried up... It looked like paint that had spilt and all its moisture evaporated out in the sun, leaving only a hard layer of a crackled substance.

He flowed the line towards the right and came across the wooden door to a kind of improvised shed.

"And what's this?"

"A storage shed. For paints, brushes... all kinds of things," said Tito. "I have the keys."

He made his way to the door to the shed, Osterc and Brajc behind him, and when they had almost reached the door Brajc held his nose. Tito unlocked the door and was about to open it when Osterc grabbed his shoulder, indicating that he should move out of the way. Touching the handle with a paper handkerchief he gently pushed the door open. Previously only faint, they were now hit by a strong stench of decay.

"Phew," Brajc's face turned sour before he had a chance to even look into the space. "Another one, is it?"

Osterc used the light of his phone and amongst the junk in the shed, in the middle of pots of half dried up paint, leaning on the back wall, half sitting and half lying down, was a man who looked a little like their guide, bearded and hairy. The only difference was that in the middle of his face, where the nose reached the forehead, was a dark stain.

*

"Do you remember the lecture the idiot Golob gave us after all that stuff with Verbič?"

They moved to the concrete wall that ran all the way round the terrace. It was easier to breathe there. Osterc nodded. He had actually found what Golob had told them interesting but it was probably better he did not let this on to Brajc.

First they were treated to a detailed explanation of the penetrative power of 4.6x30 millimetre calibre bullets used by the special forces in the attack on Verbič, and comparisons with usual nine-millimetre bullets used in hand pistols, but when Osterc asked a couple of extra questions, there had been no stopping Golob. From his drawer he produced the latest research that the ballistics department had conducted under his supervision.

"This will interest you. We've started on guns. According to our own and also other research," he said as he smoothed out the paper, almost as if stroking a pet, "the life-death boundary is already at three to four joules of the bullet's energy, assuming that the bullet is shot at the most vulnerable parts of the body."

He pointed to his eyes.

"Included in these are all the areas where the major veins are exposed. Note!" he almost shouted. "Depending on the circumstances this boundary can also be much lower, though it is usually much higher."

He flicked through the pages.

"Aha, here. Look! With the EBV4, that's our ballistics software, we've reached the following conclusions."

From this point on he had read out the report. Even he could not remember all of this off by heart.

"With a shot at a thirty-degree angle that ensures a longer range without intermittent obstacles, the bullet has a range of two hundred and fifty metres. During its entire path, the energy it is charged with is more than three joules, so it is deadly. The energy of the bullet, however is considerably reduced in the first third of its path, as much as around eighty-five percent.

"At a straight shot, with an angle of nought, without intermittent obstacles, the bullet has a range of around one hundred and seventy metres and it hits the ground with an energy of around two-hundred and twenty joules."

"You remember, don't you?" said Brajc as he tried to find Golob in his list of contacts. "With a little luck, I will now be able to return this kindness."

"Hello, Golob!"

Brajc waited briefly but not long enough for Golob to compose his thoughts and respond. With what right was he disturbing him at half past ten in the evening after he had spent the whole day trying to get fingerprints from around twenty plastic bags that were found around the body of the unknown woman in what's-it-called park? Still unknown, even after Marn, the criminal investigation technician went through all her stuff. All he was able to find out was that "she had no identification document with her, nothing in fact that would in any way help with her identity. I will compare her photo with those we have on our records and we'll see."

"Hello, Golob!" Brajc repeated, leaning on the concrete wall of the terrace overlooking the building with the gay and lesbian clubs.

"Do you know where I am right now?"

Brajc had disturbed Golob in the middle of reading the latest issue of the German magazine *Kriminalistik*, a journal for criminal investigation science and practice first established in 1926. More precisely, Golob was just in the middle of thinking about the results of research described in an article in the *Kriminaltechnik* section titled *Sicherung und Untersuchung von Blutspuren* and a subtitle *Software zur fotografischen Sicherung und Winkelberechnung* written by the husband and wife team, doctors Mark and Ines Benecke. Golob knew and respected the authors of the article even though, during an evening social gathering at a seminar in Hamburg, he had almost mistaken Mark Benecke with all his tattoos and playing in a punk band for what he often publically called criminalist hipsters who had seen too many American crime series and attempted to model their image upon those.

"No, Brajc, I don't know," he responded not without agitation in his voice.

"Well, I'll tell you then," said Brajc. "I am on Metelkova."

Once again he paused. Keep the arrogant toad in suspense.

"And?" Golob asked in a voice in which the agitation was mixed with caution.

"We came to speak to people who were here last night for the assassination of the disco ball. You won't believe what we have just found."

"What have you found, Brajc?"

If there was anything in the tone of his voice now, it was resignation.

Brajc was onto something that he would use to get back at

him. That much he now already knew.

"We have found the answer to the question on the kinds of motives that drive a person to carry out such a horrendous crime. It was a brand new disco ball, still a child."

"Get on with it Brajc, tell me."

Brajc paused for a little longer, as if thinking about whether he should torture Golob further or whether this was enough revenge for all the torture he in turn had inflicted upon them.

"The people in the club made it into a huge issue. It will be hard for me to explain that the bastard with the gun was not after them at all. The real victim is in the building next door, on the first floor, or rather in some makeshift shed on the terrace. As you can imagine the victim is not going anywhere and has a hole in the forehead. Interested?"

There was silence at the end of the line and Brajc had to make an effort not to laugh.

"Earth calling!"

"Coming," Golob sighed and hung up.

"He's finished. I'll tease him till the end of time over this."

Friday

CHAPTER 17.

"Ay, ay," said Anna when she looked at his elbow. "The whole thing is one giant wound. Where am I supposed to attach the electrodes?"

She shook her head.

"It won't work. What were you doing?"

"Brushing corners," said Taras and stood up.

There would be no therapy. In fact this suited him.

"How is the arm otherwise?"

"Now it is not only painful at the tip of the elbow but the entire elbow, the entire arm."

She laughed and Taras did too. In a way he preferred it this way. He was used to things hurting because of scratches and bruises. He said goodbye and was almost out on the corridor when the curtain separating one area of therapy and another moved and he saw a face he had not seen for at least twenty years.

"I thought it was your voice," said the man behind the curtain. "I don't know whether to be happy or not, but... I finish in fifteen minutes and if you have time, I invite you for coffee."

Taras smiled.

"Happy? That would be something new with you. Do you know the hotel across the road? I'll wait for you at the bar."

*

"How long has it been, Taras?"

"It will be twenty years at the end of June. I can tell you the exact date."

"Where did you disappear to after Dhaulagiri? I thought that was going to be only our beginning and admit that I thought you were one of those who would never give up as long as they could walk."

Taras smiled. He too had thought so, both the first point and the second.

"I became a father, had a daughter, then another... and work, mortgage... What about you?"

"Two, both at secondary school but I continued for at least another ten years. I still go climbing now occasionally."

Aljoša Malus. One of his fellow climbers from twenty years ago. At the time he had got on Taras's nerves, he was as competitive as everyone else but wouldn't admit it and could be as irritating as hell. Now, however, he was happy to see him.

"Why were you at Wolf's?"

"Hernia. Two operations, and if I had listened to the doctors I should have gone out to buy a wheelchair. But I refuse to listen to them."

They chatted for half an hour, particularly about fellow climbers from Dhaulagiri. About those who were no longer alive and those who had vanished, each into their own black hole.

"You know what?" said Malus as they parted at the top of the steps outside the entrance to the hotel. "It will be twenty years since our last expedition. I think that calls for a trip to the mountains, go climbing somewhere to celebrate?"

Taras smiled and pointed at his injured elbow.

"Yes," said Malus. "And I have a hernia and am not supposed to wear a rucksack. But if you take some of my gear and get it to the wall, I can climb any grade three from there."

"Which grade three?"

"Any one. We'll find something."

"Close to a road, with a good rock face and no crowds," Taras suggested.

"None like that round here. But are you in?"

Taras used his left hand to rub his shoulder. It hurt but after a long time it was a different pain. It was as if the cycling injury had devoured the previous one.

*

He was at the office at half past eight. Tina was already there. There was a folder on his desk.

"I've checked the online social life of our boor and this is what I found. Printed out for a colleague from the analogue era."

There were some printed photos in the folder. Four of them.

"A selection from his Instagram account."

The first one was of the old woman in the park, a portrait with her eyes closed but without a trace of the shot and an entirely different expression on her face than she had had when they found her. It was the grimacing face of a person in agony. The green bench was visible in the margins of the shot and the caption under it said:

Clean up the country? About time too!

The other photo was of the same face but it already had the hole in the upper part near the hairline. The caption:

We've cleaned up the country! Sieg!

The third photo took in a wider angle. In it were Golob in white, and Taras and Tina with half of Brajc and Osterc cropped out of the frame. The sentence under it read:

Once upon a time there was an old Sow with three little Pigs.

"From the story of three little pigs building their houses. Out of straw, wood…"

"I know it," said Taras.

He also knew the fourth photograph. The bench with *Sieg heil!* written across it and the caption: *The end for some, for all the others only the beginning!* It was not the same photograph as the one sent to Slovenske Novice, but similar, from the same series.

"This really is only the beginning," said Tina. "I then checked his Facebook page. He has two accounts. The first has more of this shit, the second though, a private one that uses a pseudonym that is not hard to link to the owner and this much I can prove, reveals a few interesting things."

"Does a private profile not mean that…"

"Yes, that it is not public and he had created it so that everything he published did not appear elsewhere and that only friends of friends could request friendship, so I first had to

become friends with someone called flak88 and when he confirmed me... You wouldn't believe all the things you can sort out
relatively quickly with a fake profile and a photo of Emma Stone.
These idiots clearly don't watch musicals."

There was a three-page printout of the correspondence between the author of the photo of the dead woman and various
friends.

The skinhead from the third floor in the block of flats on Župančič Street that overlooked the park was looking for someone
who might sell him a gun.

"If you have five hundred euros you get it today," someone
with the user name Gustav wrote.

"I have," came the answer.

"Do you see the date?" Tina asked.

It was the day Mici was killed.

"I don't know, but I find it extremely stupid. Is this not like
bragging in the booth outside a packed pub that you have killed
someone?"

Tina nodded.

"I know someone who once claimed that criminal investigators are incredibly stupid people."

Taras once again browsed over the printout.

"Perhaps," she continued, "he didn't intend to kill her to start
with and then things got out of hand. He had bragged in front of
so many that he could not back off because it would make him
look soft."

"Were there any responses from his friends after this date?"

Tina shook her head.

"None. He blocked all comments."

"Package this in a way that even Drvarič will understand. After the court thing today, we will go for a visit."

"That's not all," she said.

"Yes?"

"My friends from ARNES called."

"About the mail with the photo of the bench?"

"Yes. It was sent from a computer with an IP that belongs to
the Oton Župančič Public Library."

He smiled.

"Across the road, isn't it?"

"Yes, across the road."

*

The State Attorney's Office is housed on Šubič Street, in a building almost adjacent to the one where Taras and Tina worked. At five minutes to nine a man with a black briefcase stepped out of the grey building and glanced at the sign above the door. He had still not got used to the fact that his place of work was no longer called the Public Legal Aid Department, and if it happened to come up in a conversation he did not miss the opportunity to quote Shakespeare's 'that which we call a rose by any other name would smell as sweet'.

Taras and Tina waited for Alič, for that was his lawyer's name, in their office. At nine o'clock precisely he knocked on the door.

"Good morning, Taras! Glad to see you again. Ay, ay, ay!"

Alič was a grey-haired gentleman, six foot three, and surprisingly straight and lively for his age – he was a year or so older than Cvilak and could have asked for retirement a decade ago, though, like Cvilak, he did not want to. If he was to be believed, he had trained himself to stand straight when he discovered that at court an imposing height is just as important as broad knowledge, careful preparation, ferocity, experience, reflexes and all the other qualities of lawyers, so if you are lucky enough to be blessed with it, it is worth working on maintaining it.

"Clint Eastwood made a career out of it," he often repeated. "Robert de Niro, Dustin Hoffman, and their likes had to learn how to act instead."

He had always been a lawyer, meaning since some time in the fifties when he graduated and specialised in Public Law. He still introduced himself as a public attorney even though he and lawyers like him are now officially known as State Attorneys. In fact, saying 'he and lawyers like him' is doing him an injustice. He was a white crow among the otherwise unmotivated and incapable administrative clerks, as he himself called them. "In France I would have been respected and on a par with the chief judge, here I am the last hole on a transverse flute," he liked to say.

"Same here," Taras returned his greeting. "Did we forget any applications today that will cost the State a million or two?"

"It was nine, Taras," Alič reminded him, referring like Taras to the notorious case from a few years earlier when a public attorney missed the date for sending in the application for a case to the European courts, costing the State the mentioned amount.

"What is saddest of all is that he actually forgot. It was not that they could say he had amnesia. Roguery I can understand and to a certain degree respect, incompetence not at all."

He offered Tina his hand.

"That is, after all, why with all my jaunty public attorney heart I represent unscrupulous cops like our colleague here. Tina, if I am not mistaken, who will attest to Mr Birsa's version of the truth in court?"

"The very one."

"I am glad, Taras, that there is always something new, that we aren't getting repetitive. I mean that we are going to the district court for the first time and that we have reached the record value of dispute – twenty-three thousand euros."

"If anything, I have time and money," said Taras.

"If not, the wife will provide it, won't she?"

When he had left home she was still asleep.

*

The road to Novo Mesto was empty at this hour and in this direction, so they arrived almost forty minutes before the hearing. Taras and Tina went to a nearby café and Alič went, as he said himself, on a stakeout.

"I met Petan," he said when he returned. "He seems to have grown an extra centimetre since I last saw him and he was not exactly a shorty before. And, what's more important, I found out about the judge assigned to our case. He is called Vovk. I happen to know him..."

Taras did not doubt this. Alič happened to know just about all the judges in all the courts in Slovenia.

"...and remember just one thing: whatever you say, be as brief as possible."

When they arrived outside the courtroom, Petan's team was already there. The accuser, Tilen Rezman, and his three friends from the weekend house in Bohinj, and three others who, like

Petan, looked very serious but at the same time also somehow embarrassed. Among them was someone who Taras knew from somewhere and after a few seconds also recognised. He was a doctor whose name he had forgotten but was certain that Alenka had once introduced him to. He also knew what the man was now thinking. That next time he would see Alenka she would rip his head off.

"Well," the judge began the proceedings. He was a tiny, thin man who kept clearing his throat. "Let us not drag this thing out..." he said although they had not even begun. "We can probably establish straight away that if so far you have been unable to reach an agreement are also unlikely to reach one now, so we can get down to business. Am I correct? Of course I am," he said without waiting for confirmation by the lawyers.

"So, let us begin with you, Mr Petan. What do you have to say?"

Petan stood up and, this much Taras had to admit, conveyed a fairly accurate description of events. He admitted that his client's behaviour was inappropriate, even repeated the abusive language he had used on Taras and especially Tina, leaving out only that he had been kicking the seat in Taras's car and embellishing the account by adding that when Taras was pushing his client's face into the snow, he had shouted: *Die!* Taras had done nothing of the sort, in fact he had not said anything at all.

"We will prove," Petan concluded, "with the help of three medical experts," he listed his names, "that the events caused my client permanent physical and psychological harm. It is no secret that my client's father is a wealthy and well-respected man..."

Well-respected, indeed, thought Taras, the man was under house arrest.

"...so this is not one of those cases where a beaten up loser wants to make some money out of their misfortune."

"Yes, yes, yes, point taken," the judge interrupted him.

"Defence."

Alič stood up and in the briefest defence statement Taras had ever heard in a court said that almost all the things Petan had said up to the moment about which we are all here instead of outside enjoying the sun, were true, but not from that point onwards, and that there is also a witness able to confirm this.

Then he sat down. The judge nodded, checked the time and ordered a break. After just fifteen minutes of the hearing.

Alič nodded at Taras and Tina, and whispered, "He's a chain smoker. Fifteen minutes – maximum."

*

"Rozman…"

"Rezman," Tilen Rezman corrected him and stood up.

"Well, Rezman then. Will you tell us anything new?" Judge Vovk asked after the break.

"Excuse me?"

"Will you tell us anything we have not yet heard or merely confirm what your lawyer has already told us?"

Confused, Rezman looked at Petan.

"Excuse me, but we consider this a key testimony."

"Why? You told us everything. There is no jury here that you need to impress. Same goes for you," he then turned to Alič who just nodded politely.

"You three? Will you all say the same?"

Tilen's friends looked at each other, turned to Petan and then nodded to the judge.

"Well, then choose a representative and may it be noted that the other two agree with what has been said."

He looked around the courtroom with satisfaction and flicked through the pages in front of him.

"Well," he said. "That part is over then. Now as far as your expert witnesses go. One is an ENT specialist you brought here because of the damage caused by the choking, and the other a psychiatrist, if I am not mistaken."

"Yes."

"Who will undoubtedly testify to the psychological traumas of the accuser, et cetera, et cetera."

"Yes."

"The third is a urologist. Why is he here?"

"As I explained, my client has…"

"Urination problems that are the result of this and this. I know. And, so it says in your report, these problems are of a psychological nature, yes? And the psychiatrist is here as an expert in that field, is that not so?"

"Yes, but the urologist would explain about the way the urinary system is physically affected..."

"Look, Mr Petan," said the judge, nervously tapping his fingers on his desk. "This is not Doctor House. We are in a courtroom. Choose one or the other. We don't want two of them prattling on about the same thing. Who will it be?"

"The psychiatrist," Petan uttered through clenched teeth and Taras could see the man he knew in the opposite team breathing a sigh of relief.

"Now that we all agree, I suggest we take a break."

*

After the break Tilen's friend was called to the witness box and explained what happened after Tilen had returned to the house once Taras let him out of the car.

"He was like a zombie," he said. "I've never seen him like that."

Alič did not ask him any questions.

Then it was both doctors' turn. First the ENT specialist. He described the damage that they observed on the accuser when he visited the medical centre and which are permanent and could have occurred as a result of asphyxiation caused by the actions described...

Alič let him say what he had to say, then looked at the judge. When he gave him a sign that the witness was now his, he asked him, "You say that the damage could have occurred in the way described?"

"I am fairly convinced that these ruptures that did not just occur on their own and that have become a chronic problem, happened in the way described."

"And you did not check whether the mucous membrane in the nose is also damaged in the same way? What about the nasal septum?"

"Why?"

"Because that would prove that the damage occurred due to other reasons. My client – as stated in the report, so we don't need to waste the court's time – found the group in the middle of a cocaine orgy..."

"Excuse me!" Petan intervened. "What cocaine orgies! This cocaine you keep mentioning is entirely made up."

"If it is made up," said Alič and looked at the judge, "why does Mr Rezman not go with a court representative to the medical centre ten minutes' walk from here and submit a blood sample for toxicology tests?"

The judge sighed and checked the time.

"What do you prefer, Petan, your client going for a blood test or that we dismiss his testimony?"

Taras had to hold on to the table and clench his teeth to stop himself from laughing and in as far as he could see in his peripheral vision, Alič was doing the same. Tina kicked him lightly in the leg.

"Dismiss the testimony," said Petan through his teeth.

"Well," the judge suddenly became animated, "if that's the case then there is no point in calling the second expert and we can conclude that..."

Petan shot up in anger.

"First of all, if this is how it will end, and it seems it will, I will demand an annulment from the high court."

"Good luck," said the judge. "That will take a while and I am going to retire on the first of August."

He looked at Alič.

"The way things are going I assume you will not bore us with your witness?"

"No, your honour, we see no need."

"Well, we will," Petan interfered. "I will. You should at least allow us that."

"What am I supposed to allow you?"

"To question Ms Tina Lanc."

The judge looked at Tina and turned to Petan.

"But she is a witness for the defence?"

"Never mind. I will also prove why this is so."

The judge looked at Tina, then Petan, then Alič, then checked the time.

"After the break."

*

"He is bluffing," Alič whispered to Tina in the corridor. "Just stay calm and repeat your alternative truth."

"And don't worry if he comes up with some unexpected dirty trick," Taras added. "If there is anything you can't remember just say that you don't know."

She looked at him with surprise.

"What are you talking about?"

"Just don't get put off. Everything is under control."

She looked at Alič who repeated, "He's bluffing."

Who is? Petan or Taras?

*

"The way you see the events and the way my client would describe them, had he been allowed to take the stand, differ, would you not agree?"

"Yes."

"You claim that your colleague has not overstepped his powers, that, basically, none of this shoving into the snow and asphyxiation actually happened?"

"Yes."

"Why is this so?"

Tina smiled.

"Because the way I described the events is what happened."

"Right. And the way you see the events have nothing to do with your relationship to the accused?"

"What relationship?"

"This kind of relationship."

Tina felt dizzy. She touched the table and inadvertently glanced at Taras.

"This kind of relationship, your honour," said Petan and turned the photo for the judge to see. "This kind of relationship," he repeated with the photograph turned towards Taras and Alič.

"This is becoming interesting," said the judge.

"Would Ms Lanc be able to explain to us what this photograph is actually showing."

"I don't know."

"You don't know. Perhaps your colleague might know?" he turned to Taras, holding up the photo.

What was the saying, the author of whom he could not recall? Moments like this outshine the lives of every one of us...

"Is this the same one you sent my wife yesterday? We spent the whole evening laughing over it."

CHAPTER 18.

"I am trying to remember," said Alič in the car on their way back to Ljubljana. "When was the last time I had this much fun in my life." Taras smiled but Alič was too enthusiastic to notice that his smile was forced and that Tina on the back seat was not participating in the exultation. She was leaning against the side window, staring outside without really seeing or wanting to see anything, and the only time she looked towards the front was to catch Taras's eyes in the mirror. He looked away.

At the parking lot outside the office they said goodbye to Alič.

Taras locked the car and hurried after her. He caught her just outside the entrance towards which she was escaping.

"Tina..."

"Yes."

"You know what this means?"

"I am not stupid, Taras."

She opened the door and almost ran towards the office. She did not want to hear any more.

They were awaited by questioning gazes. She smiled and collapsed into her chair. Taras entered the office after her.

"Well, how did it go?" Brajc asked.

"Smooth victory," said Taras. "Plus a bonus card."

He threw the photograph he had confiscated from the court onto the desk. Osterc picked it up and showed it to Brajc.

"Wow," said Brajc. "Is this what you get up to when you go out for coffee alone?"

Taras switched on the computer and let them wait a few seconds.

"Brajc, I give you five minutes to find out what's wrong with this photo," he eventually said. Two to Osterc. If you don't find it, perhaps you really should go and hand in your notices."

As if he was being serious, they both looked at the image of Taras stroking Tina's head until, probably even earlier than two minutes, Osterc smiled with relief.

"Better late than never," said Taras, glancing under his brow at Brajc who was still none the wiser. "And while your colleague here is still fighting for survival, where is the search warrant for Župančič Street?"

Osterc passed the photo to Brajc and mumbled.

"Well, that's another thing... There isn't one."

Taras looked up from the screen, looked at Osterc and then at Tina. It looked as if she had not even heard Osterc. She was staring at her screen with a background of a wheat field after an afternoon storm, as if unable to decide which file to click on.

"I don't know why, Drvarič didn't say."

"But there is no warrant?"

"No."

"Well, if that's the case..."

Taras stood up, grabbed his backpack and stepped towards the door. He was already holding the handle when he let go, took the three steps to Brajc's desk and picked up the photo of him and Tina.

"Still not clear?"

In embarrassment Brajc rubbed his hands and Taras opened the door and disappeared.

"Funny," said Osterc.

Brajc waited for a couple of seconds as if wanting to make sure that Taras was not going to come back.

"Can one of you finally tell me what the joke is?"

*

He called Alenka from the car. The phone rang this time but she did not answer it. He drove the couple of minutes further to the clinic and found out at reception that she had not come in to work. He found her at home, sitting at the kitchen table. She was staring emptily straight ahead and continued to do so when he appeared.

"Where on earth are you? I spent half of yesterday looking for you, I called you today and called in at the clinic. What's going on?"

"How did the court case go?" she asked indifferently.

"Fine," he said and just like he had done before with Brajc and Osterc, dropped the photo onto the table. "And I got this as a keepsake."

She glanced at the photo and for a moment awoke from her numbness. In confusion she looked at the photo and then him.

"I assume you too have already received one like it?"

She stood up, went to the kitchen, returned with the photograph, and placed it next to his on the table.

"So, will you tell me… Is there anything to say?"

He sat at the table, straightened the photos as if playing a game of memory, leaned onto the smooth lacquered maple surface and laughed.

"The other day, when we had lunch in that restaurant in the Knafl Passage the waiter called you Mrs Birsa. I didn't say anything at the time, but I found it touching."

She looked at him and pulled a face.

"He called you Mrs Birsa. I never asked you why you introduce yourself with my surname when we are not married. Do you remember what you said to your dear mother when she nagged you about having a wedding?"

"Is this important right now?"

"You said: at least we won't have to waste money on wedding rings. The rings…"

He pushed both photos in front of her. She looked at them, picked up one and looked at it more closely, then Taras and then the photo again.

"That's not your hand!"

"At last!"

"That's not your hand!"

"No, of course it isn't. It's Osterc's. The photo was taken from afar, my head is not next to hers, sitting in between us was Osterc, who, believe me, was not stroking her hair but reaching for goodness knows what and I am most probably laughing at something that Brajc had said."

She stared at the photo as if, like Taras the day before, she was afraid that the ring on the finger of the hand that was stroking Tina's hand might disappear, then she buried her face in her hands and began crying.

That's the end of that, went through his head with both a sense of regret and relief. He had been given another chance. He hugged her and stroked her hair.

*

For a while she stared at the screen, attempting to order her shattered thoughts. What was it that Taras had said his mentor, her predecessor Penca, used to say? When you know what you are looking for, you will find it? Something like that. After this photograph there was no chance she and Taras would continue what they were doing. Well, what was it they were doing anyway? Can a person who did not expect anything still be disappointed?

Osterc and Brajc were still sitting at their computers and if she was not going to start on something, one or the other would sooner or later look up and ask her what was wrong.

She opened the file with the footage from the camera on Štefan Street and watched the dark street, occasionally lit by the beams of a passing car. A car appeared, and drove past. The light appeared and vanished. Bright lights and once again darkness...

Then, as if something suddenly clicked, as if two wires suddenly connected, she had an idea.

She found the file with the shots from both cameras and forwarded the footage from the second camera to a minute before ten. This time she was not looking out for people, not watching out for anything passing by, but looked at the buildings and the lights and shadows on them. The shot at ten o'clock would probably appear as a faint flash that could also be picked up by any otherwise low resolution surveillance camera. She ran the footage at ten percent of real time speed, leaned back and from a distance, her eyes glued to the screen all the time, tried to pick up on a brief flash of light.

Was what she was looking for at 21:59:01? Fifteen seconds before Taras's car left the parking space?

She played it again and again and... There could be something but even if there was, she could not be certain with this screen and light.

She ran the shot from the first camera and stopped it a minute to ten and then switched it to the slowest possible mode. Whatever it was that flashed in the other shot, this camera also recorded it though much fainter and less specific, at 21:59:31. She checked three times. The image lit up in the right corner for a couple of moments. She switched on the desk lamp and made a note of both codes. If she could rely on this flash, there was a thirty second difference between the cameras. The first camera had a thirty second delay. Then she copied out the times.

Camera 1	Camera 2
21:57:11 T. goes into park	
21:59:31 flash	21:59:01 flash
	22:00:15 T. drives off

In order to calculate the times more easily, she switched off both cameras and set them to zero.

Camera 1	Camera 2
00:00:00 T. goes into park	
00:02:21 flash	00:02:21 flash
00:02:35	T. drives off

Taras would have had two minutes and thirty-five seconds. Two minutes and twenty seconds for around one hundred metres from Štefan Street to the bench in the park and another fifty metres from the bench to his car.

She went over the numbers twice and when she lay down her pen her head was buzzing. Taking a deep breath, she checked her contacts, found the number and called.

"Dr Golob," she said. "Can you tell me who is in charge of checking video material in your department?"

She had never before used his title in front of his surname but it seemed not to bother him.

"Computer and similar forensics are not part of our team. They are quite independent. In fact, they are not even part of the police."

He gave her the number of a certain Janez Glavan, she called him, explained what it was about, and asked him whether she could send him two inserts from the camera footage.

"Yes, please send it," the young-sounding voice said and promised that he would analyse it as soon as possible.

"And for the time being, I would like this to stay unofficial, if that's possible..."

"Ooof," he sighed. It took him a moment and then he said, "So, without filling out the official request form?"

"If that's possible."

"In principle not. But I can take a quick look and let you know whether it is worth filling one out."

She put down the receiver, looked up and met with Brajc's quizzing gaze.

CHAPTER 19.

"Did you two really win the case in Novo Mesto?" Brajc asked. "There doesn't seem to be much celebration."

Tina gathered what was left of her energy and tried to recall the hearing. She summarised all the points the judge had thrown at Petan and even his address, said that she 'shat herself' when Petan began waving the photo around the court room, which was not hard to explain because she really had done. So she told Brajc that she had no idea when Taras was supposed to be stroking her hair...

"Of course, we would know that, we were there all the time," said Brajc.

...and she finished with Taras triumphantly rising his left hand in the air, spreading his fingers and waving them.

"Something is missing, don't you think?"

"Mr Petan, this is enough," said the judge and passed his sentence.

When she finished, Brajc clapped enthusiastically. She waited for him to calm down.

"Is Drvarič in the office?" she then asked him.

"Is that warrant bugging you?" Brajc instantly guessed why she wanted to see the boss. He dismissively waved his hand as if to say, nonsense, "If I'd let it get to me every time those from above make it hard for us, I'd long be gone. Why should you care? If they don't want you to work on something, just don't."

She nodded for the sake of peace, stood up and left.

Drvarič was in the office and when she appeared at the door his eyes seemed to be searching to see if there was anyone behind her, looking for Taras, of course. He seemed visibly relieved when he realised she was alone.

"Do sit down, Tina."

"Why did we not get the search warrant for Župančič Street?"

He smiled but his smile quickly distorted into a kind of grimace. And then again, and also a third time which appeared almost comical. He was buying himself time to find an answer that he could give her. She was convinced that he had in mind a version that he would have given Taras but then she turned up. She was even prepared to hear that this was not her problem but his face eventually softened and with surprising sincerity he said, "I don't have a clue."

"The Prosecution did not offer an explanation?"

"No."

"Is this something you'd expect, something normal, considering the incriminating evidence we sent them?"

"No."

"I'm sorry for being a bore, but how would you explain this?"

Drvarič leaned back in his chair and put his hands behind his head, revealing two dark patches under his arms. Every so often he too had to go out of his air-conditioned den.

"I just don't, Tina, there is no point in us trying to find an explanation. I will not move heaven and earth for a woman who, if I am to understand Cvilak correctly, would have died anyway or might even already have been dead when someone thought of shooting her. And besides, Kristan comes back from holiday on Monday and he can handle this. He certainly gets paid more than me for doing so."

She must have appeared confused and indeed she had expected something else from Drvarič.

"And what are we supposed to do until then?"

"Write up reports and sort out the documentation. There is never enough time for that. Are Brajc and Osterc in the office?"

"They were when I left to come here."

"Can you please send them here. I have something for them to do before Monday. By the way, how come Taras didn't come rushing in here with you?"

*

"My workday began with that awful photo. Five minutes later a mother came to the consulting room who had never had her child vaccinated against anything and now wanted protection because they were going to Serbia where there has been an epidemic of measles. I told them not to go."

They were lying on the sofa in the living room and Taras was stroking Alenka's hair.

"I was in a state where I barely knew my name and the woman stood there, insisting on getting some home remedy against measles from me. Colloidal silver or anything like that. That she had heard about it being such a universal medicine. And when I told her, still very politely, that there was no medicine for measles and a bunch of other viruses and that the only safe thing to do was vaccination, she said that her husband was a lawyer, if I know what that means."

He will never leave her. He could never.

"She then added that she did not understand why people in favour of vaccination are making a fuss. That if they believe in it they should also believe that kids are protected. I told her that this was about those who for one reason or another cannot be vaccinated because they are allergic or the not-so-low percentage of those who do not respond to the vaccine and do not develop an immune response, or those we don't even know about. And she turned round and said, 'That's their problem.'"

It's time he got his act together.

"I went outside, and had a drink. I don't even remember where I went or how I came home. The rest you know."

She turned to him and looked straight into his eyes from a distance of five centimetres.

"Tonight we will go out. Together, husband and wife."

Taras forced a smile.

"Yes, Taras. For life."

*

Tina found Brajc and Osterc in a good mood. Well, Brajc was in a good mood and Osterc was like he always was. It seemed that the system falling apart, at least that was how she saw it, did not bother them.

"Friday!" Brajc almost shouted from behind his desk. "Two days and then picnic."

He looked at Tina.

"If you're free Sunday, you are of course invited."

She shook her head.

"Can't on Sunday."

She was not one for picnics.

"Drvarič wants to see you," she added.

"What for?" Brajc asked.

"I don't know. He mentioned that he needed something before Monday."

"Before Monday? It's Friday afternoon!" Brajc rolled his eyes and swore. His face darkened to a shade of purple.

"Oh, and Glavan called," said Osterc. "Apparently he had a look at what you sent."

*

"Congratulations Osterc, congratulations Brajc, you certainly embarrassed a few colleagues yesterday."

"Sod it, they should jolly well have looked," said Brajc and Drvarič nodded.

"Well, in the meantime we've got confirmation of the victim's identity. He is called Robert Vadnal. We also found his son, Jakob Vadnal. This is his address."

He handed over the address to Osterc who hesitantly took it and held it so that Brajc could also read it.

"But," Brajc said. "Does that mean that we are working on this case too, or what?"

"I don't know," said Drvarič. "On Monday when Kristan is back he will decide. I've given you this because perhaps someone should inform Jakob Vadnal of his father's death."

He placed another page in front of Brajc.

"And this is a list of people who socialised with Vadnal."

"I know, I wrote it. It is from his phone," said Brajc. "What about it?"

"Someone should talk to them."

"Today?"

"Today probably won't be possible because you need to call them first and arrange to see them. By Monday," said Drvarič. "It would be great if Kristan would get this information on his desk from us."

Brajc held the paper as if it were contaminated. There were eleven names on the list. He looked at Osterc and, despite still standing in front of Drvarič, swore loudly.

*

She should have been excited. She should have been worried, but she was strangely indifferent.

"Well," said Glavan when she reached him on the phone. "I have removed the noise and increased the contrasts from the footage. All I can say is that that momentary flash did not occur because of the camera itself but was created externally and that indeed both cameras picked up on it. The assumption that on the basis of this it would also be possible to synchronise both cameras is thus also correct. As far as your question about whether this was a reflection of a gunshot, a more detailed analysis would be needed in coordination with a few other departments."

"But *could* it be?"

"It could, this is a possibility. But why don't you fill out an order form and send in forensics so they can recreate the scene? Surely that would not be any great technical challenge."

"No, of course not, though it might be a financial one," she lied. "With the vague theory I'm working on, nobody will give us access to the funds. Thank you anyway."

"Look," he said before she had a chance to put the phone down. "If that's the case, maybe you should call in on us. Don't get me wrong, but I made a few calls, apparently you're a computer graduate."

"Yes?" Tina wondered where this was going.

"Well, we're pretty short of people here, especially ones with the right education and also experience in the field. In fact, apart from the right people we are not short of anything. Our equipment is tip top."

"I'll think about it."

"Please do."

Maybe she would.

She clicked on the video he had sent to her personal email, as she had asked him to. The flash was indeed a little stronger, more obvious. As if someone in the park had thrown a fire cracker. Six seconds later the shot ended. It was all she had sent to Glavan. An additional nine seconds and the shot from the other camera showed a grey car with a dent on the side setting off down Župančič Street. Fifteen seconds after it was likely that a nine millimetre bullet was put through the head of the woman on the bench. Fifteen seconds after this it was possible... Taras drove off in his car that had been parked a few metres away. Her hand shook as she held the mouse to close the clip.

*

"Good morning..."

Instead of replying Brajc stuck his police ID through the window.

"Where do...? What for ...?"

The girl at the reception with an impeccable hairstyle and impeccable though modest makeup, became even more confused after the first questioning look aimed at the not so impeccable looking Brajc. Osterc wondered whether it was really necessary to barge in with the ID when they could probably just tell her who they had come to see. Clearly Brajc took a different approach.

"Police matters," he said. "Tell us where Vadnal's firm is and we will find our way."

The girl checked her computer, shook her head and tried again.

"Is this a company dealing with investment consultation and cryptocurrency trading?"

It appeared she was slowly regaining the reserved calmness expected from someone who is supposed to look after the first impressions of visitors to the Crystal Palace, the office building in the BTC City business park in Ljubljana that was planned as the tallest building in Slovenia with more than a hundred metres in height. It never reached that height and construction stopped at eight-nine metres and the twentieth floor due to building regulations, but it still held the record, and there was no sign that the planned helipad on its roof would ever be completed. It was now Brajc's turn to be confused.

"You mean bitcoins and that?"

"Bitcoins, ethereum, ripple, bitcoin cash, EOS, litecoin, cardano..."

"There's that much of this stuff, is there?" Brajc was surprised.

*

"Las Criptomonedas," Brajc pulled a face when he pressed the button in the lift that would take them to the sixteenth floor. "Las Criptomonedas!" he looked at Osterc who was in his usual state of disinterest. "Do you know anything about this cryptoshit? Is it worth it?"

"No," said Osterc.

"No, as in – I don't know anything about it, or no, as in – it isn't worth it?"

Osterc took a deep breath but by then the lift had stopped at the floor they wanted.

"You can tell me later. Let's first go and inform the man that his father is dead."

They found the sign with a stylised LC. Brajc paused, found a paper handkerchief in his pocket, mopped his face and straightened his shirt, tucking it more carefully into his trousers.

"This'll be fun," he said and rang the bell.

"Yes?" came from behind the door after a while. Brajc sighed and opened it.

They stepped into what looked like some kind of reception with a desk and computer, cupboards, a coat hanger, and a plant in the corner. There was a glass wall at the back of it and beyond it they could see someone sitting at a computer, typing away. They hesitantly waited and when the person at the computer waved at them they slid open the glass door and ended up in a large office where, beside the desk where the man was typing on the computer was also a long oval table with about ten chairs around it. There was a projector hanging from the ceiling above the table and a projection screen at the end of the room. On the wall to the left of the screen was a painting, a female nude, rather explicit, without any particular symbolism.

"Kelman," said the man and stopped typing.

"What was that?" Brajc asked.

"I see you were admiring the nude. It is by Kelman."

He must have been around thirty, in good shape, his rolled up sleeves exposing his pumped up and tattooed arms. On his left wrist he was wearing a large watch, he had black hair and a black, shortly trimmed beard.

"Oh, right!" Brajc muttered. "Are you Jakob Vadnal?" he asked as he pulled his police ID out of the bag over his shoulder and showed it to the man.

"Yes?"

He looked at the ID and sniffed. The ID did not seem to make any particular impression on him.

"Perhaps you could find some time to speak to us?" Brajc pointed to the conference table and, though hesitating briefly, the man eventually nodded, got up from his desk and walked across the office with them.

"So," said Brajc when they all sat down. "I'm afraid we bring you some bad news."

He watched the face of the man that remained unchanged.

The face of someone who does not have children, he thought. If anyone had said to him that they are bringing some bad news, he would grab his heart. The guy in front of him merely sniffed again a couple of times.

"I am afraid we found your father dead last night."

There, he had said it. With the corner of his eye he caught Osterc who was looking at Jakob Vadnal just as calmly as he might be browsing an online catalogue for lawnmowers or observing the gunshot wounds on some body in front of him. It was about time he took on these chores.

"Father?" the man on the opposite side of the oval table asked and leaned on his elbows, scratching his nose with his right thumb. "My father?"

Then he lowered his hands, leaned back and fell silent.

Slightly confused, Brajc turned to Osterc.

"Perhaps you did not understand," Osterc took over. "What my colleague tried to tell you is that your father died..."

"I know what your colleague tried to tell me and, how should I put this..."

He smiled and put the palms of his hands on the table.

"...but I basically haven't had a father for a long time. If you are referring to a person called Robert Vadnal..."

He gave them a questioning look and Osterc and Brajc

nodded.

"...well, I have never actually met this person. Soon after I was born, he ran away somewhere to the West, if I'm not mistaken, to what was then Czechoslovakia."

"So..." Osterc tried but was not sure how to go on.

The guy briefly squeezed his nose and once again sniffed.

"Do I need to sign anything, Inspector? I hope they don't want me to pay for the funeral, because I won't."

CHAPTER 20.

Tina was sipping on her second beer. They were sitting at Kinodvor - she needed a drink and did not want to be alone, and, she had difficulties admitting, her own boyfriend would do. How deeply she had fallen.

"You want us to go out?" Aleksander asked. "Where to?"

She didn't want to go to the centre of town, it was always crowded by the river, so they had ended up in the coffee shop at the Kinodvor cinema. She was drinking on an empty stomach and even the first beer had gone straight to her head. She had even considered going to see some Finnish boxing film that was showing but they were too late. Never mind. She would sit down with her boyfriend and they could talk.

"Thirsty today are we," he said to her.

"Yes."

Her boss who was also her lover shot the old woman on the bench. Of course he did, he more or less said he would. And he's a man of his word. Just like he beat up that drunken brat in Bohinj, just as he had done goodness knows what else. He is dysfunctional, now it was obvious to her. He had no excuses. He shot a woman who was sleeping on the bench just as he shot that cat. He did what he could. The only thing he could. What is he, some damn SS supporter, is that it? She drank some more beer and thought of Taras in an SS uniform. She almost choked.

"What's so funny?"

She coughed and shook her head.

"Nothing, nothing, just something silly... What about you?"

"What about me?"

"How are things at work?"

"Oh, that..."

He started talking and talked and talked about the operation system and the problems they were having setting it up... if she understood correctly and she probably didn't because she was not listening to him anyway. Two days ago she was looking at the brains of a woman shot by her lover. The driver her boyfriend was having problems with or the details of whether it was a driver for Windows 10 or Android, she thought to herself wickedly, really cannot compare to this in any way.

"Total shit!"

"Yes," he was happy that she agreed with him. "And do you know what they replied? That they are aware of the faults of their new driver but that this has affected only a small number of users with smart phones or other mobile devices. And that after an update their operation system no longer registers these devices..."

Just as you no longer register anything, she said to herself and watched him as if she was looking at him for the first time. You have no idea. He smiled at her encouragingly and continued.

He looked young, young in an unpleasant kind of way. His skin was smooth, he had no wrinkles on his forehead or anywhere, not even those a man's face *should* have. He was always clean shaven because he could not stand stubble that 'prickled him.' Taras would rather die than say that something prickled him, even if it did. And he had tattoos on his hands, Aleksander, not Taras. On his right arm he had a tiger and a yin-yang symbol on his left. She tried to remember why she had found it so original. His forearms were nicely formed, he went to the gym and used dietary supplements, especially proteins. Carbs before workout, protein after it.

"Look at this carved body," he would sometimes joke and there were times when she thought it was amusing and even sexy. Now she no longer saw it as carved but bloated. He was muscular but his muscles were somewhat soft, not at all veiny like... No, she would no longer say his name, she will not even think about him.

"Aleksander..."

He would also only have one beer today, not because he was

worried he would get drunk but he was concerned about the calories hiding in C_2H_5OH.

"Yes?"

"Cheers!"

She raised her glass and he stared at her with bewilderment. Let him be confused, she was also. Things were clear as far as the facts go, but what help was that?

"Is there something wrong at work?"

"Everything is wrong," she said and it all came out. All apart from the fact that she was in love with her boss who has murdered the old woman whose murder she was investigating.

"Oh, I don't think these supposed Fascists of ours will last long," he said and this 'supposed' was like an unpleasant sting. "This is the most they can do. Shoot at homeless people."

"I didn't say that they killed her."

"Well, it sounded to me as if that was what you were implying."

"And do you find shooting homeless people a minor thing?"

He shrugged his shoulders. Clearly he did.

People began coming out of the cinema. You couldn't say that they were pouring out as you might say when people all try to leave at once when a film is over, because there were too few of them.

A small cinema, and the film had been showing for a while. Who was interested in Finnish boxing films anyway? She watched them coming down the stairs, mostly older couples, walking straight past them into the town that the evening sun had finally taken pity on, only reaching the odd corner of the street at a very low angle. There were a few younger ones, around her and Aleksander's age but mostly they were middle aged, mature. Like... she instinctively picked up the glass and brought it to her mouth, though all that was left in it was some froth.

Walking down the stairs was Taras with a woman who could not be anyone else but his wife Alenka. He was looking for an empty table when he spotted Tina. He waved at her and she waved back at him in confusion. No, not now, just not now.

He smiled and started making his way towards her, towards

them. She felt as if, sitting in the audience, she had been sucked into a film she did not want to participate in, as in her nightmares where she would sit paralysed in a car with a derailed train moving towards her. She just sat there and waited.

"Hi, how come you... you two are here?"

"Hello," she muttered and stood up as if she was at school.

"Alenka, this is Tina from the postcard."

Tina gave Taras a confused glance and offered Alenka her hand.

"I was interested to find out what the colleague my husband strokes the hair of looks like in the flesh."

"I'll explain later," she said to Aleksander, more because she was embarrassed in front of Alenka than in front of him. "Do you two know each other?"

"Have we met?" asked Taras.

"You don't know me, but I've seen you on TV."

"Oh, that," Taras smiled. "I'm trying to forget about that."

"No, it wasn't that bad."

Tina offered them the empty chairs at their table. Taras looked at Alenka who nodded.

"It's so crowded down town now anyway."

They sat at their table and ordered. Alenka a glass of white wine, Taras a mineral water, and Tina, disorientated by their arrival, a third beer.

"Apparently you don't drink?" said Aleksander.

Taras shook his head and pointed above his belt with his hand.

"Stomach problems."

"Oof," Aleksander sighed and shook his head. "That's a bummer, isn't it?"

Taras nodded. "There are worse things in the world. They say..."

They all laughed.

"So what *do* you drink then? How does it go?"

"Coffee... and when I can't take that any more, this." He pointed at the bottle of fizzy water. "I certainly *used* to drink more than enough."

In a way it was interesting that his stomach troubles happened just as he had lost interest in drinking and when a third or fourth beer no longer brought him any euphoria, just a hangover. Why drink then? With Taras's gastroesophageal reflux the world did not lose a chronic drinker, a moderate one at the most.

Tina glanced at Alenka. She was wearing a tight white dress that was clearly not from H&M and when she had appeared on the steps leading from the auditorium to the cinema café with tables and a bar, she drew quite some attention. Like some damn film diva walking down the red carpet. She was taller than Tina, more elegant and blonde, probably naturally so. It also didn't help that she was – what – fifteen years older than Tina? Even the fact that she had to guess said everything about it. And she wasn't drunk.

Taras looked as he always did, only that instead of shorts he was now wearing jeans. He too was wearing as slightly better quality, dark blue T-shirt with a white line around the collar, in combination with which his white trainers did not appear as ridiculous. Tina raised her glass. Was this tension she was feeling inside her head actually floating above their table? Aleksander certainly didn't pick up on it and continued unabated.

"I noticed you went to see this Finnish boxing film?"

"It took some persuading. He would have preferred to watch the Egypt Russia match on TV," said Alenka.

"Momo Salah," Taras explained.

Aleksander laughed. Of course he knew Salah. He liked watching derbies, Manchester United vs. Liverpool, for example, and as far as national teams went, matches between Brazil and Argentina, and decided who to support depending on which team had the prettier cheer leaders. Why did she use to not find this offensive?

"And?" Tina chirped from behind her glass, without really intending to.

"It was a good film," said Taras.

"Because?"

She bit her tongue. The ice princess in the designer dress must be aware of the way Taras starts questions with 'because'. She herself adopted it very quickly.

"I like listening to Finnish."

They all laughed and Aleksander pretended to speak it.

He sounded like... someone pretending to speak Finnish, but it served its purpose.

"Well, it was a good film. Different to all the Hollywood movies about boxing. I like those stories but when Sylvester Stallone was caught at Melbourne airport with a bag full of steroids I stopped cheering for Rocky."

Laughter.

"In Rocky Four or Five there is a scene where, during training he jabs the Russian opponent, played by Dolph Lundgren, in the muscles."

"That's Taras for you," her white highness spoke. "He notices details I am blind to. She looked at Tina and smiled.

"Are you a boxer?" Aleksander asked.

The ice princess was watching her. She could feel it and felt too tired or too inebriated to stand up to her. Tonight there will be no match. No Rocky will stand up after getting knocked out in the first round. Basically this *was* a knock out in the first round. Capitulation, as far as she was concerned.

"Well, cheers!" she said and raised her glass.

They all toasted. Taras by barely lifting his glass of fizzy water and putting it back on the table, Alenka with three fingers on the stem of the glass – you could put a photo of her drinking in any inflight magazine of any airline in the world trying to promote its Nordic image; Aleksander would also fit in well with his innocent joviality of a fool.

"Recreationally," he answered and smiled with embarrassment. "I box so I don't get fat. But now I've damaged my elbow so I haven't done it for quite a while."

Aleksander laughed.

"Are we toasting to any specific occasion?" Alenka asked.

"Oh, no... On such a day... Perhaps I have just had a little too much to drink."

She giggled.

"Don't you believe that it is all in the head, as they say?" Aleksander continued and for a change she was grateful that he had spoken.

"*No fear, just do it* and stuff like that?" her lover seemed interested. Lover until today. He smiled. Not once since he and his wife had joined them did he look at her.

"You're the boxer, not me, but we're very much on a par with our weight. So let's say we go into a ring and something clicks inside me and I succeed in getting a *lucky punch*..."

"He'd kill you," said Tina and all of a sudden she didn't care what effect her words would have. With the corner of her eyes she caught Alenka's face; her mouth turned up ever so slightly into what some might call a smile but Tina herself was not that naïve. Of course she knows, ring or no ring, she knows everything.

*

"Quite effervescent, this girl of yours," said Alenka from the bathroom.

"A hard day, first the court, then the office," he said and decided he would ignore 'this girl of yours'. He had told her – although he was not sure she was even listening to him as he was sitting on the sofa in the living room and she was in the bathroom, not really reacting to anything he said – all about Drvarič and her request for a search warrant that was not granted.

"Even I'm not unaffected, let alone her."

She came out of the bathroom, naked with only a necklace round her neck, one with a semi-precious stone, a dark star he had bought for her twenty years ago at Thamel in Kathmandu for six hundred rupees. She walked up to him and sat in his lap.

"But for now we will forget all that, and especially her, right?"

There is no better aphrodisiac than jealousy. It was nice, nicer than usual, and for the second time that day he felt like a complete shit.

*

Aleksander soon fell asleep. He had broken his rules and had two pints and then another half, and before sleep took some paracetamol and magnesium tablets. Tina lay in bed next to him, listening to the bustle in the street below dying down and she wanted to burst into tears. Never in her life had she felt this helpless. As if she had not been careful and fallen into a wild river where no amount of kicking and waving would help. Whatever she tried to grab hold of was slimy and slipped through her fingers, everything around her remained unsaid like some transparent mist above the rapids of that shitty river.

If he didn't kill her, why does he not prove it to her, why does he not at least try to convince her of it?

If he loves her, why does he not...? Why is she dreaming? He never said anything like that to her and, anyway, he will never leave his wonderful wife. With a wonderful clinic. And her wonderful electric car.

Everything seemed so complicated. The old woman in the park with a hole in her head and maggots of that..., what was it again..., anyway, some kind of fly. And the homeless artist on Metelkova, and Taras's wife or whatever she was, in white and all beautiful like Jennifer Aniston... perhaps they were even the same age... And the *Sieg heil* and the twenty seconds from the flash, which could have been the gunshot, to Taras's car. If, indeed, it was the gunshot... She could not be certain about anything. It could have been, and if it was... It also might not have been, that this would appear differently on the footage, and if it wasn't...

She stood up and went to get a glass of water from the kitchen. Her head was spinning, not because of the alcohol. Well, perhaps also because of the alcohol, but she couldn't do much about that now. She drank some water but felt no better but rather worse. If she were to go to bed now, she would throw up. For a moment she stood there, leaning over the sink, but then decided that she would not be sick, opened the tap and refreshed her face, wiped it with the tea towel and went back to the bedroom. She put on her jeans and a T-shirt, went to the hallway where she found a key from a low cupboard, and returned to the bedroom to unlock the wardrobe in which she kept her Beretta 92FS, put it away in her handbag, put on her trainers without socks, carefully opened the door and slipped out of the flat.

The bars under her window were already closed when she walked past them towards Župančič Street where she turned right and, along the right side of the road, which was not within the range of the camera from the hotel, approached the park. She waited under a giant oak for some passing merry company to get into a parked car and drive off, then she carefully, almost on tiptoe, as if she were afraid someone might hear her, made the last few steps to the bench. It still had the *Sieg heil!* on it. Clearly the words did not bother anyone. Her heart was pounding wildly so she sat down and looked across her shoulder towards the building overlooking the park. All the windows were dark. Canvass? Why is it called canvass?

Lenin Park, Park Ajdovščina, Argentina Park, Slovene Reformation Park... four names for a few trees, a patch of grass, a footpath and some kids' climbing frames.

In Lenin Park there are trees.

In Lenin Park there's even a warehouse of seeds.

She tried to look up the song on the net but could not find it anywhere.

Lenin Park, Park Ajdovščina, Argentina Park, Slovene Reformation Park.

That which we call a rose by any other name would smell as sweet...

She got her gun from the bag and put it on the bench next to her. She could easily understand people who liked firearms. A gun turns you from prey into the hunter.

She stood up and looked around. She aimed at the gravel behind the bench and pressed the trigger. It struck as if a bolt of lightning had hit the ground and she was certain that lights would start coming on in the windows above her, perhaps she would even hear sirens from the distance.

She ran like crazy to the passage under the Nebotičnik and took the shortest route home, holding the gun in her hand all the time.

She quietly opened the door and slipped into the flat, took off her clothes and lay in the bed next to Aleksander who was still fast asleep. She was shaking. Then she remembered that, silly cow, she had come back past the camera on the General Police Directorate. She rushed to the bathroom and threw up.

Sunday (and Saturday)

CHAPTER 21.

It turned out that Sunday at ten was the earliest available time for people from the list that Drvarič had returned to Brajc.

"You'd think they're some kind of grand businessmen," said Brajc whom Sunday suited even more than Saturday. If on Sunday he can tick off these weirdos by one o'clock, he can still start his traditional barbeque at two and wash away the taste of work with beer, and this would leave him free to do what he wants on Saturday.

Osterc and he asked their interviewees to come to Celica, the former military jail that has been turned into a hostel, and talked to them at the table in the corner of the dining room. Those who came to talk to the police were, as Brajc summarised after the meeting, 'shaggy, be-earringed hippies, hung over at this, for them impossibly early time of the day that desynched their biorhythms by twelve hours'. Brajc, to whom the prospect of an afternoon picnic helped offset his annoyance at having to work on a Sunday morning, felt sorry for them and paid for coffees for everybody who sat on the chair opposite him. He knows how hard it is to get around with a hangover. For himself he ordered a beer – after all it was Sunday and he didn't care if he sweated like a pig.

"To Taras," he said, raising his glass. "Who keeps telling me I can hand in my notice."

They met the woman who painted the squid and when Brajc mentioned that he thinks they are infinitely better than the smutty shit painted by someone called Kelman, if she had ever heard of him, her eyes lit up.

"He can do what he wants," she said. "He's no competition to me. I work on wall paintings of huge surfaces, that's what I love doing, the work I most enjoy. Unfortunately, it means I am more or less limited to Metelkova, the town won't give me other walls. And they all use my work in adverts, from tourist organisations, the state TV station, to the mayor. Even on some inflight magazine on a Hungarian carrier who flies to Slovenia you get my paintings advertising visits to Ljubljana. And I don't get a penny from any of it."

She of course had no idea who might have shot Vadnal.

"Ten years ago I would say it was the skinheads, but they would attack him with chains, not a gun. But we live in strange times. It's hard to know where you stand."

Brajc nodded.

A tall forty-something guy sat before them next. He brought a folder of his work along as if he had come on a job interview or to discuss his work. He looked tired, as if this was still the end of yesterday. He just stared at them confusedly when they began asking him questions and then slapped his forehead.

"Oh, yes, the police. And I thought..." he then shook his head a few times as if wanting to wipe clear his thoughts and reset his brain.

Vadnal and he would see each other almost every day and no, he did not mention anyone threatening him or having any problems.

"And what did Vadnal actually live off?" Brajc asked.

The guy with the folder thought and said with astonishment, "Do you know, I don't really know."

"And you make your living selling paintings?"

The guy nodded.

"I live quite decently from my creativity, though there's no surplus. I have to do the odd illustration here and there – with the same seriousness I do everything else and I don't do that just for the money either. I am very picky. If I wanted to be more commercially successful, I should be working on series, mass production, but sometimes it takes me up to a month, it's very personal. Would you like to take a look?"

He opened the folder.

"This is some of my work. I muddled up this meeting with an invitation to see an owner of some gallery that I have at... Oh, shit, I hope I haven't missed it."

Brajc took a look at the folder and found something that seemed to be like pictures for children and he didn't like them. Portraits of dogs of various breeds. But then he noticed that they were not at all cute little doggies from children's books but that their faces were pierced with fish hooks. Some were attached to their snouts, others their mouth, all of them hinted at fat, over-sized bodies.

"Are you interested in paintings, Mister Policeman?" the man, very much worse for wear, asked.

"Dunno, really," said Brajc. "It seems I am, a little."

Then there were dancing bears and some animals gathered around someone who was either sleeping or lying dead in a bed, and a Dachshund in the lap of a drunkard who had fallen asleep at the table, eyeing with fear the mounted taxidermy on the wall behind them. Then he reached a picture in which some animal with huge eyes, a kind of monkey, clung onto the stem of a wine-glass, climbing it up to reach the drink.

Brajc became engrossed in the painting and Osterc worried he was getting lost in his thoughts as he had done the previous day with the squids, so he kneed him gently under the table. He had to prod him again before he looked up from the folder and returned it to the author.

"Certainly better than Kelman," he said.

The tired artist smiled.

"Tell that to those who buy art. If I got for this spectral tarsier half the amount he gets for his nudes, that would be really great."

"Spec...what?"

"Oh, that's what this animal is called. I found it on YouTube."

They also met the welders, blacksmiths who were authors of the sculptures on the façade of Metelkova or along its promenade, street artists as well as people for who, even after longer explanations, they were unable to understand what exactly they did for a living. Brajc's head was buzzing from all this – Osterc, it seemed, had no such troubles. He kept his cool and did not allow any of this to get to him.

Despite the fact that all of them socialised with Vadnal, most of them right up until his death, nobody was able to give them anything useful. Most helpful was some information given to them by Tito, the ex-king of Metelkova.

"Yes, we once went to Prague together. It's thirty years since then. He had been living with some woman, I think she was a banker, or something like that, loaded with dosh, but he couldn't handle it. He packed his bags and we left. I remember I said to him at the time, 'Fuck, don't be stupid. You'll never find another woman who'll make your life as comfortable as this.' But he didn't listen. It wasn't the nicest thing he could do because they had just had a son together, but what can you do, call of the wild."

"What did he live off?" Osterc asked.

This question confused Tito as well.

"Well, dunno, really. He sometimes did various performances for which he would get some money at competitions, and he would help with various things here and there... He never had any money. He did say, though that the things were looking good for him. Well, he always said that, though."

"The former wife? Is she dead?"

"Yep. Last year, I think. He found out from the papers."

Tito got on Brajc's nerves and he did not participate in the conversation or pay for his coffee.

*

"This is early for you? First last night, now..."

She had been hoping to slip out without waking him but Aleksander was now blinking in the semi-darkness of their bedroom with the curtains still drawn.

"It will be too hot later on."

"Since when do you go running? This is shit early!" he turned round and pulled the sheets over his head.

Cankar Street leads straight towards Tivoli Park and, were it not for Tivoli Street which is now called Bleiweis Street, a sort of inner ring road around Ljubljana, one would not need to go through an underpass at all to reach the park. After just five minutes' running she left the core of the town centre and reached green lawns with bushes, flowers and trees with chirping birds awakening. Were she to now also see a squirrel, nothing unusual in the park, it would almost be too corny. Certainly very different to yesterday.

Yesterday she had woken up with a hangover, showered quickly and walked round the block to Štefan Street.

"Someone reported a shooting in the park last night."

"Really?" the man at the reception desk at the General Police Directorate was surprised. "I don't know anything about that."

She was baffled. It seemed impossible that the one hundred and forty decibels last night would not have woken up at least one person who would call the police.

"Just a second, I'll check."

He looked in his computer as Tina was having a cold sweat. Even this she had difficulties in thinking up. She had woken up at six and tried hard to get herself into a state where she dared to leave the flat by seven.

"Can't find anything," he said and gave Tina a questioning look.

"I don't know," she stuttered and hoped that the glass would stifle her hesitation. "I got a call from Taras, Taras Birsa, my boss at the Ljubljana PD."

"I know him, who doesn't know Taras," he said and Tina buried her nails in the counter. Harder and harder. Why had she just not said that she needed the footage for comparison... What kind? She'd think of something.

"Perhaps I misunderstood. I live nearby and he asked me to check the footage from the cameras on the GPD or bring them with me. I think he said that it was the GPD. You know, it's because of the case in the park... But I might have got it wrong, with all of this my head's no longer straight..."

She groaned and held her head. Was he about to call Taras and check?...

"It's this hot weather, isn't it? I don't function well in the summer either. We'll sort it out. What time span are we talking about?"

"Some time around two in the morning."

It's hard being a criminal investigator.

The man nodded.

"Do you have a USB with you?"

She found it in her purse and gave it to the man. He stepped closer to the opening.

"And if you don't need this so very officially, can we just sort it out between the two of us? I'm not supposed to give data out like this, but there is so much paper work involved..."

She nodded at him gratefully.

Fifteen minutes later she was already at the hotel on Župančič Street. Unlike her, the receptionist at the desk was very much awake and full of energy. When she showed him her badge he almost bounced.

"Oh, so that what it looks like. I thought they only used them in American films."

This time she said it was for comparison.

"I just hope," said the receptionist, "that they won't make us do night shifts because of this. From midnight onwards our hotel is without staff. It's a small hotel and the guests have keys if they come back late. If there's going to be more shootings, they are sure to tell me to hang around here at those unearthly hours. But weren't you here the other day when..."

He pointed towards the park.

"Yes, just that it wasn't me. It was my colleague," she said.

"And, have you come to any conclusions?"

She smiled and pulled her thumb and index finger across her lips like a zip.

"Yes, of course, I understand, I understand... Perhaps you might like a coffee while I get the footage ready?"

She nodded gratefully and sat at a round table in a fairly decently furnished foyer from where she could see into the dining room where the first guests were already gathering for breakfast. A few elderly couples, perhaps English or German, and a group of Japanese. Or were they Chinese? Korean?

"It might take a while, because we are having some problems with the camera footage," said the receptionist when he brought her the coffee.

Great. Were all her efforts in vain?

The coffee was good, and especially useful. When she was a student they used all kinds of strange brews as hangover cures, but nothing could beat coffee in her books. Interestingly they always discussed these alternative remedies over a coffee. 'What should I have, my head is about to explode...' they would say, holding a cup of coffee in their hands.

The guests lined up at the breakfast buffet. She typed 'difference in appearances Chinese and Japanese' and came across a forum where participants offered the following answers:

The Chinese have eyes that turn up in the corners, the Japanese turn down. Chinese people are big, Japanese are small.

The Japanese have a more yellow skin and usually rounded-oval faces, some woman wrote. *The Japanese are more pleasant, gentle, more delicately built and also more handsome. The Chinese are basically ugly, cruel, have scrawny teeth and look different, though recently both are changing for the better, they dye their hair, curl it, have their eyes fixed, so they don't all look like chunga lunga...* And, as if worried about what she had posted added, *Well, I like both because they are so hard-working, diligent and also cunning and cruel.*

Like, although they are cunning and cruel?

On occasions like this she had to agree with Taras who advocated banning the internet.

"Right, then, we're done."

She thanked the receptionist and left.

*

A day later the hangover was gone, not so the confusion in her head.

"Since when do you go running?"

Good question.

She ran towards the Čolnarna Café[14], located next to an artificial pond formerly used for boating, then through the forest behind it along the path to the Čad Inn on the road to Rožnik Hill and along the pavement to the zoo, then down the forest path to Mostec, a favourite meeting place for pensioners who like chess, families because of the playground and everyone else because of the good, home cooking and of course drinks. On a Sunday morning at seven there was nobody there yet, but she was surprised at the number of people out running. She had not thought so many people were obsessed with staying fit. She

---

14 Čolnarna means boathouse in Slovene

saw them when they ran the Ljubljana Marathon each October and read about the impressive number of participants, but she thought they just got together once a year, ran the ten, twenty-one, or forty-two kilometres, took a few selfies and that's it until the next race. She felt she didn't really fit in. Each one of them seemed to know the route they were going to run, the tempo with which they should do it, had some kind of sensible target they were working towards, and she was just...

She was just hoping to come across Taras, though he had said a while ago that he did not go up Rožnik because it was full of posers. She observed the runners coming in the opposite direction and those who overtook her to try and figure out what he meant by 'posers'. Almost every second runner had earphones connected to a phone attached to their forearm. These would certainly qualify, as would many others and she would include herself in the category. Perhaps even she would make it to the list as a beginner who does not really like running because it takes her so long to get rid of the flush when she stops.

How low she had fallen.

And no, he won't come. Had Taras chosen Rožnik, he would have been here at five in the morning, so he is probably already at home now. He has had his shower, eaten his muesli and was not thinking about where she was and what she was doing.

She stopped above the Tivoli Hall and then slowly made her way down to the road, to civilisation. She didn't know how long she had been running for or what distance she covered but she had to admit that she was feeling better. At least she had got some air into her lungs. She turned towards the northern pedestrian underpass on Bleiweis Street and just as she was about to go down the slope into the tunnel, she spotted at the bottom of the adjacent stairs an old woman who seemed familiar. It was... what was the name? Mrs Opeka?... from the flats above the park. Without her dogs, she walked slowly but purposefully. She seemed not to have any of the shaking that according to Taras she put on when she was outside. Tina nodded at her when they met but the old woman was looking at the ground and did not return her greeting.

Tina walked up the other side of the underpass. In a minute

or so she too would go under the shower, have breakfast, and if Aleksander was up for it, they could go for a coffee into the old town before it was taken over by tourists. At least she didn't have to go to the picnic.

Without knowing why, she once again turned around towards the park and on the path on the other side, leading towards the parking lots in front of Tivoli Hall she spotted the tiny figure of Mrs Opeka.

"Surely she isn't going there?" Tina wondered and followed her with her gaze until the old woman disappeared behind the trees. She waited for a few moments, then sighed and once again went back through the underpass towards Tivoli.

When she reached the parking metres the old woman was already there. She stood next to the machine, waiting for the first car to appear. Tina stood around twenty metres away so she could see her from the rear. The woman stood quite calmly and still until the car appeared on the corner and turned towards her. At that point, had she not seen it she would not have believed it, the woman's entire body began trembling, she wavered on her feet, shook from her hips upwards and this shaking surged towards her head and hands, especially her right hand that she held out in front of her. Taras was not the only one who would put a few coins in this hand.

Then the car drove on and about a second later, three at the most, the shaking stopped and the old woman returned to her calm state, maintained until her next victim appeared. Perhaps it was also the dark clothes she was wearing that made Tina think of a black widow. There was another strange thing. Tina watched her for about ten minutes. During this time there were six cars which came to the barrier, put in their parking ticket, stuck the necessary coins or banknotes into the machine, and a receipt appeared in a special slot. Apart from one, all the other drivers left the receipt in the machine. For all five, once the car was far enough, the old woman picked the ticket from the slot and put it in the bin next to the machine. Why was she doing that? Was she just keeping things neat and tidy?

Tina thought for a moment about walking up to her and, as Taras had done, enquire about her health. Instead she just smiled, turned round and made her way home. What was it that that policeman nephew of hers had said?

"She's quite a character. She helped half the family until they were able to get jobs and careers."

CHAPTER 22.

"There..."

Brajc blew at the charcoal and looked with satisfaction at the embers which were giving off a good even heat. He placed the first twenty ćevapčići on the grill and then stood over it, meat tongs in one hand, a beer in the other. He was wearing a red apron with *McĆevap* written across it.

He had bought it on a trip to Sarajevo where the Slovene police had arrived just at the time of the opening of the first McDonald's in town. That day Brajc began appreciating the Bosnians much more. There was a long queue outside the American fast food joint but it turned out not to be because of the new restaurant but because a local ćevapdžinica[15] was offering free ćevapčići to customers.

Brajc's picnics were, as he himself liked to say, so often and regular that he no longer had to even announce them unless it was to a newcomer like Tina. The season began once the day temperature reached above twenty degrees and ended when it fell below that. During this period, he held picnics every Sunday, beginning at two and ending whenever they all felt like it, as the host would explain for the sake of those who were on their first visit. Though there were very few such guests. This time it was Taras.

*

"When will it finish?" Alenka asked.

"We'll have a couple of ćevapčići, hang around a while and

---

15 Ćevapdžinica is a place that sells ćevapčići, a dish of small, grilled, kebab-like pieces of minced meat, popular throughout the former Yugoslavia, especially Bosnia and Serbia.

leave," said Taras. "We won't waste the whole day."

"And since when do you attend picnics?"

"I don't, but on Thursday, I think it was, I told Brajc he could go and hand in his notice..."

"You what?"

Taras explained to Alenka what had happened with Brajc.

"With what perverted sense of humour did you decide to send Brajc to investigate an attack on a gay club?"

"Lesbian," he corrected her. "At the time we still thought that the only victim was the disco ball in Monokel. And what's wrong with sending Brajc?"

"Apart from the fact that he is a chauvinist and racist?"

Taras shrugged his shoulders. Brajc was far less chauvinist, sexist and probably also less racist than the average Slovene, it was just that everybody got on his nerves. Gays no more than feminists or vegetarians, fascists, communists or advocates of political correctness, supporters of Maribor FC or Olimpija FC, or his former wife, or the guy she was with. If Taras had to work only with people he would dare take to the theatre with him, he would be working alone.

"Oh, well," Alenka sighed. "If that's the case, we have to go. But you owe me a film or a play, something long and torturous with dance inserts."

*

And although Brajc would announce his picnics with the words, "We'll just stick a steak or two on the grill..." there were hardly ever any steaks at Brajc's picnic because he simply didn't have the energy to prepare them. Ćevapčići, *pleskavica*, the occasional piece of chicken, a thigh or wings were his staple repertoire, accompanied with white bread. There was salad but the guests had to bring that, the same with desserts. This time the Ostercs brought along a potato salad.

"This way we can have a German picnic," Osterc tried to joke.

"Why German?" Brajc wanted to know.

"The Germans tend to bring along a potato salad whenever they are invited somewhere for dinner or a picnic."

"Oh? How do you know that?"

"When we went camping down on the Croatian coast last

year we had some very kind German neighbours and we invited them round for some chicken we had roasted. They brought along some potato salad and apparently they do that all the time," Maja Osterc explained.

Brajc listened to her attentively and nodded. He was almost ashamed that he had used to describe her as to how poison comes in small bottles, though it is also true that he always added that, "...and also in larger ones, as anyone who has ever met my former wife will well know."

Brajc's former wife was a tall woman, about Taras's height. When she and Brajc met, she played volleyball and was about two and a half stone lighter than now, though she was still quite a few levels away from the state of deterioration Brajc's body had been subjected to over the same time. They divorced three years after Brajc joined Taras's group when she went to live with her former trainer, and since then had not been attending the picnics organised by her former husband. Today she only dropped off their son Blaž, called Brajc to one side, explained something to him with much gesticulation, and drove off. Brajc watched her leave with a melancholy sadness that must have come as a surprise to anyone who had heard his comment when she parked in the yard.

"Here comes Cruella de Vil," he had said, loud enough for everyone to hear him.

Brajc was not a man who would keep anything to himself. In this light, as soon as he awoke from the dreamy stupor with which he continued to stare at the disappearing car, he went up to Osterc and his Maja.

"Do you know what she said to me? She said that the gym teacher had said that Blaž does not know how to run and that it might be a good idea to start working on that. What else? What does she mean – he doesn't know how to run?"

He took a look at his son who, as soon as he had arrived made his way to the table with desserts and began stuffing himself with the walnut croissants that Taras and Alenka had brought. Next to it was some shop-bought *potica*, a traditional walnut roll. Brajc liked *potica* but someone brought it almost every time and it seemed like a rather uninspired addition to the menu. Inspired by the Sarajevo ćevapčići story and the culinary memories of the union trip to Bosnia, he tried to remember whether there were any Bosnians living in his street whose wife might be able to make a *baklava* or some other sweet pastry. However the street he lived on was unfortunately so typical of suburban Ljubljana that even a gibanica from Prekmurje[16] would seem exotic. And anyway, Bosnians *also* got on his nerves.

"Blaž!" Brajc called his son.

"Mmm," muttered the sixteen-year-old who had so far been lucky that his calorie intake was directed to his height although signs were already indicative that he would, influenced by surroundings, develop an inherited roundness. And as far as influences from surroundings go, young Brajc didn't have it easy. If she wanted to become a lawyer, the former wife had needed to cut short her maternity leave and return to lectures. At least in the afternoons it was thus Brajc who was supposed to be looking after their child. Instead, however, of taking the boy out for a walk or to the playground, he would stick him on the sofa next to him in front of the TV and give him a biscuit, one of those filled with jam that he too loved. Thus the kid became used to eating lots of sweets even before his first tooth. A decade and a half later this kid moved just enough to look at his father, take a piece of *potica* and sit down on the bench at the table with all the desserts. During all this, none of his moves helped his father establish the correctness of the gym teacher's observations. Brajc thus beckoned to the younger of the Osterc boys who was kicking around a football with his older brother.

"Hey, hey, pass us the ball!"

The boy first looked at Brajc in disbelief and then his mother. When she nodded, he kicked the ball towards him. With reasonable skill Brajc stopped it with his foot, then picked it up and threw it towards his son. It hit the bench, bounced off and ended up around five metres away from Blaž who was just washing down the *potica* with orange juice.

---

16 Prekmurje is a rural area in eastern Slovenia, close to the border with Hungary. From Ljubljana it is the remotest corner of Slovenia. One of the iconic sweets from region with elaborate layers of pastry and four different fillings (poppy seed, walnut, apples & raisins, cottage cheese) is the Prekmurska gibanica, well known throughout Slovenia.

"Hey, Blaž, Blaž..."

"What?"

"Come on, pass us the ball!"

The teenager looked at the ball, looked at his father as if wanting to check whether he had maybe lost it, then just sat there indifferently, eyeing the dessert table. Judging by the expression on his face, he too would have preferred some baklava.

"Oh come on, for God's sake!"

"What?"

"Pass us the ball!"

Blaž looked at his father again and when he saw that he was serious, probably decided that the only way for him to leave him alone was if this one time he did what was asked of him; he stood up and dragged himself towards the ball.

"Come on, son, run, run, run!"

Blaž didn't pay any further attention to his father in an idiotic pinafore and just slowly continued making his way towards the ball.

"Just a few feet, a step or to, go for it, run!"

He didn't. He plodded along, reached the ball, picked it up, holding it as if it were something his hands had never touched before, carried it off to the Osterc boys, and dropped it onto the ground in front of them. Taras was hoping he was doing this deliberately to annoy his father and not because he really did not know how to throw the ball.

"Well," said Brajc when his son sat back down at the table. "Surely anyone can see he could do it if he wanted to."

Beside the Osterc family who came often if not regularly, because this way the parents could take a moment's break from the two wild primary school kids who played football, badminton, threw stones at each other or whatever, people at the picnic were also Brajc's nearest neighbours and some of their children who would come, stay or leave as they wished, since they lived just across the road. They also customarily left when something had to be done and sometimes came back, sometimes not. This way the number of people participating at Brajc's events fluctuated constantly. Not just from one event to the next, also hour by hour.

Taras and Alenka arrived at three when everyone was already there but not too long after the start of the picnic for them to be considered late. Brajc was just barbequing the second batch of ćevapčići and was sincerely happy to see them.

"Just on time," he shouted, waving the tongs in the air. "The second round will be ready in a minute. I'll keep some aside for you."

Alenka gave a sour smile. She never made an effort to be polite with Brajc whom she once described to Taras as a fat, lazy pig who makes no effort for anything and deserves all that has happened to him and all that probably will.

"Sometimes a little luck is what is needed," Taras had replied to this.

She had huffed angrily and forgot to ask him what kind of luck he had in mind and why Brajc, who was born with four healthy limbs and was not short of anything under the sun until he drank and ate his way to misfortune, would deserve it. Perhaps in this assessment of hers she was still influenced by Brajc's former wife who had called Alenka after their divorce, went out for coffee with her, and gave her her own detailed version of events.

"I'd rather not tell you all the things I found out about our dear Brajc!" she was outraged when she returned home though Taras was not really interested.

"Let he who is without sin..." he tried to say, only to exacerbate Alenka's response.

Taras had come to the picnic in his flip-flops and his usual light-coloured shorts but went and changed in the car when he decided to play football with Osterc's boys and a few other older almost-teenagers.

"Patrik, you can just sit and watch. On Friday you were so sick you stayed at home and today you want to play football?"

Patrik did not listen, of course.

Taras could not simply stand around and eat. He stood in the improvised goal and tried to defend it with the kids shooting at him from three metres away. He wore his baseball cap because the sun was right above them and the three fir trees and a silver birch in Brajc's garden did not provide much shade.

"Not a single fruit tree," Brajc's wife, when she still was Brajc's wife, used to complain. He promised her that he would go to a tree nursery and chose an apple or cherry tree, but then she left and he could not be bothered to look for trees.

"Isn't it much better to have all this space?" he turned the story his own way when participants at his picnic also asked him about it. "We can play football with the kids, breathe more easily..."

It is not as if he ever played football with the kids, not even his own, so Taras was surprised when Brajc appeared by the goal, well, the two sticks that marked the goal, waiting for an appropriate moment to talk to Taras so that nobody would overhear what he had to say. With the screaming kids who were trying to get the ball past Taras, more with scrambling towards the goal than shooing from afar, this was almost impossible.

"What's up?" Taras asked him when he noticed the fidgety Brajc close by and he kicked the ball far away towards the fir trees at the far end of the garden.

"Do you have a second?" Brajc asked as if this was something official and not his picnic.

Taras stepped out of the goal towards which a staggering horde of children were clumsily trying to kick the ball from the other side of Brajc's yard.

"Look," said Brajc, pointing to the table with food where a few guests were sitting.

"Yes?"

"Can you see Blaž? My son?"

"I do know who your son is."

Then Brajc repeated what his wife had explained about an hour earlier.

"Do you think that he really does not know how to run?"

"I don't know," said Taras. "He's sitting down."

"Yes," Brajc sighed. "He has been all the time. Could you help me somehow get him to move? If I go there, he will never listen to me. He never has done."

Taras looked at Blaž Brajc who listlessly sat on the bench playing with his phone. Then he noticed Osterc sitting in the shade of one of three huge sunshades that Brajc had got from somewhere.

"Why don't we play a parents-versus-kids game?"

"Yeees," the Osterc boys shouted, happy that they would be able to kick their dad.

"Parents against kids…" Taras shouted louder than was needed for Osterc to hear him, so he assumed Blaž Brajc must have heard him as well, even though he did not even twitch. Taras looked at Brajc who just shrugged his shoulders, so he went across to the teenager with the phone and tapped his shoulder.

"Uh?"

"We're playing football. Will you give your old man a goal?"

Blaž stared at him as if he was speaking to him in Albanian, so Taras repeated what he had said.

"Me?"

"Yes," he said. "You, and them, and me, your dad, everyone…"

"I don't know how to play football."

Taras patted him on the shoulder.

"You'll learn. Come on."

It did not sound like an invitation and perhaps this was why Brajc's son who was almost the same height as Taras, stood up and followed him, albeit confused and unwilling.

"We need another goal," said Taras and they found two wooden stakes in the shed which they used to mark out the goal at the far end of Brajc's lawn, slightly diagonally to the left because of the fir trees and the birch.

"Us," Taras pointed to Brajc and Osterc, "against you."

There were five children on the opposite team and the younger ones, including the Osterc boys, shrieked with excitement. Blaž just stood there, waiting for them to finish.

"Taras, is it not a little too hot for this?" Alenka asked.

"It is," said Taras. "But what needs to be done, needs to be done."

Brajc senior stood in the goal and they began. There were lots of screaming and pushing around and Taras, who had not played football for years, kept losing the ball when he tried to outplay one of the kids and then one of the others would leap straight at it, so the youngsters were soon in the lead. Blaž didn't move.

"Come on, Blaž, come…" tried Brajc who also didn't move

very much but he was in the goal.

Taras passed the ball to Osterc who lost it and his sons somehow pushed past Brajc. Taras was about to shout at Brajc to move his butt and at least try and save the goal but he somehow held back. Blaž was still standing there and had not moved. He looked as if he was about to burst into tears.

"It's not fair, there are more of you," said Taras and pointed at Blaž.

"He's with us."

He pulled him closer and said, "All you have to do is run up and down a little. When we go into an attack, you run that way, when we lose the ball you run back. If the ball comes your way, just kick it, anywhere, it doesn't matter, just kick it. Get it?"

Blaž nodded apprehensively.

"Great. Let's go."

Taras put the ball on the ground and began the attack, one eye on Blaž who still just stood there.

"Come on, come on, down there!"

Blaž moved and... No, this was indeed not a run. He moved his legs but almost without any kind of synchronisation. It wasn't left-right, left-right, but more like le-left, ri-right, a kind of skip during which the heels almost didn't leave the ground. It was terrible.

"Great, Blaž!" Taras shouted and kicked the ball as the older of the Osterc boys was rushing towards him, followed soon after by his brother. He wanted to pass the ball to Osterc but the boys were already upon him, so he kicked it to the other side towards Blaž who, in a world of his own, without watching what was going on with the ball, was galloping to the far end of their makeshift playing field.

The grass in Brajc's yard was considerably taller than it should be for a football match so Taras kicked the ball hard so it would reach even Blaž, but a metre away from his foot it bounced off a tuft of grass and shot up in the air towards Blaž. Taras worried that it would hit him as he moved, trip him over. Clumsy as he is, he might hurt himself in such a fall. Indeed, there was no sign Blaž had noticed the flying danger approaching, no signs that he intended to change the rhythm of his movement, get ready to stop it, kick it, or at least move out of the way. Plod-plod, plod-plod, he continued and, without seeing the ball that came flying at him from his right, hit it as he most certainly will never again hit a ball in his life. And the ball, as Blaž continued his le-left, ri-right towards the far end of the field, without even seeing or sensing what had happened, bounced off into the goal.

His first ever contact with a ball in his life and he scores! There are not many people in the world who can pride themselves on such a feat.

"Bravo!" Taras called out, ran up to Blaž and slapped his back after the boy didn't understand what he needed to do when Taras tried to high-five him. "See, it's easy."

Osterc came running and also congratulated him.

"See?" Taras shouted across his shoulder and with the corner of his eye caught Alenka running towards them. When he turned round towards Brajc, he saw him sitting down, holding the stake that served as a goal post. Then he let go of it and collapsed onto the ground.

CHAPTER 23.

"It aches. Here..."

Brajc pointed to his chest. He was covered with a sheet but his chest was exposed and attached to his pale skin covered with a few hairs were a couple of electrodes...

"I had some pain in the morning. It was as if there was something weighing me down. As if someone had put something inside my chest. Then, as I stood there, it felt like burning and I thought it was heartburn but then this heartburn moved up my arm and I thought it was strange. Well, then came a cramp. Darkness. As I collapsed to the floor I remembered that Alenka was also at the party and I prayed that she would notice what was going on. Was it her?"

"Yes."

"I thought I saw an angel flying towards me and this angel had her face."

Brajc was speaking slowly and paused between each word. Taras was sitting at his bedside and, just like Brajc, sweating. Despite the curtains being drawn to keep out the sun, it was unbearably hot in the hospital room. Taras and Brajc both kept reaching for the economy pack box of tissues and wiping their faces. As if the heat was not enough, Taras thought he could smell hospital lunch as well. He hated hospitals and could not imagine being in Brajc's place right now.

*

"We have conducted a troponin test and, as you can imagine, the level of proteins was high enough for a serious heart attack." Alenka nodded.

"Taras, it's not just you who's lucky," Dr Majda Juhant, the cardiologist at the Medical Centre in Ljubljana continued, "that you have Alenka. But also your colleagues. This... what's his name?"

"Brajc," Taras helped her.

"He has to thank her for saving not only his life but also a quality of life, providing he sticks to a few rules. It is now clear that she revived him quickly enough for no myocardial necrosis to occur. We conducted a PCI but an operation with a coronary stent, it seems, is not necessary."

"Which means?"

"This means he will get through this without any serious consequences until his next heart attack."

She looked at Taras.

"Almost half of them return, though they wouldn't have to. I think your colleague might well be one of those."

*

Alenka had reached Brajc just as he collapsed onto the ground next to the left goalpost and by the time Taras ran to the spot she was already pressing his chest with both her palms. Taras stood by their side, as confused as everyone else who gathered round Brajc's motionless bulk, trying to be useful by calling the ambulance and conveying to them what Alenka was shouting at him during resuscitation, that it was a heart attack, cardiac arrest. He stood between her and the other participants at the picnic, trying to act as a wall to give Alenka the space she needed.

After three sessions of stimulating his heart and exhaling air into his mouth, his stomach inflated, suddenly cramped, and Brajc coughed, shuddered, took a shallow breath of air, as if not quite sure which path to embark upon, the one returning him to everyone gathered around him on the lawn, or the one taking him somewhere else. He then caught his breath, coughed once again, and calmed, waking up and looking at everyone with confusion.

"Thank God," Alenka muttered and beckoned to Taras who kneeled down next to her and helped her hold Brajc's head.

"Someone bring an aspirin."

*

"Did he score the goal?"

Taras nodded.

"Upon first contact. Like Inzaghi."

Brajc smiled gratefully. Not that he knew who Inzaghi was, but if Taras says so…

"And they told the wife at school that he doesn't know how to run. Idiots."

He picked up the tissue from the side table, wiped his brow and looked at Taras.

"It's all shit, isn't it?"

"A heart attack," said Taras. "The doctors say that everything will be fine."

Brajc frowned.

"Nothing has been fine for a long time now."

Taras had to admit that this time Brajc was right. When he looked at the person in the bed in front of him, the combinations of the word 'everything' and 'fine' was not what came to mind. He looked both puffy up and haggard, his hair sticking to his forehead, he was sweaty, flushed and at the same time ashen-faced. It seemed that even just lying there in the hospital bed was a physical effort and that his body was fighting to get enough oxygen to his heart and other organs just as eagerly as those of cyclists on the last four kilometres of the Alpe d'Huez stage, only that with Brajc the molecules of oxygen needed to push through inches of fat, like water down a kitchen drain that has not been cleaned for decades. Brajc stared with repulsion at the heap under the sheets in front of him, his own stomach.

"When did this grow to this size?"

Taras could sincerely answer that it was there even when they first met, though it was true that in the last ten years it had gained in volume.

"I didn't use to have it. I used to be like you," he pointed with his finger at Taras or rather his flat stomach and pulled a face.

"Too many *pleskavicas*," said Taras and added, despite Brajc giving him a nasty look, "and all the rest."

"Yes, but why? I ate a lot before too. Why was it not like that then? It's not as if I looked after myself any better then?"

He shook his head.

"All the same, and then… this."

He sighed and stared at some indeterminate point on the wall opposite. It looked as if he was thinking. Taras stayed silent.

"I used to be like you," he repeated, "and now look at me."

However much he flattered himself, Brajc was never like Taras, probably not even at birth. He was always slightly podgy, though at one point in life he had fortunately grown in height and then his weight had been, for the first and probably only time in his life, within the limits of the recommended index.

"And it's not just this," he went on to say. "All is the same, but nothing is the same. When Ingrid and I met, I was drunk and she found this charming. Ten years later she divorced me. Apparently for the same thing. Who could understand it? Once she liked it, then she suddenly no longer did."

There was one other piece of luck Brajc had: that right at the time in his life when he was within the recommended body weight index, he wandered into some party organised by law students from which he took home the similarly drunk and young law student Ingrid, and, as he said, pumped her, and then, even before their child was born, in what Ingrid would later call her second consecutive bout of insanity, married her. They had their son and divorced before Blaž started primary school. By then Brajc was already very similar to today's Brajc, at least as far as his basic body contours and dimensions were concerned.

"The madness of youth," Brajc's former wife dismissed those ten years with a wave of the hand, unable to even remember or describe the first night she spent with the man who became her husband. "I don't know what I was thinking," she usually added with a slightly guilty conscience that vanished over the years. In those times Brajc could also be charming. In his own rough and primitive way, but still. And most of all, he was different from all the law students Ingrid had been going out with. At some party, when they were already an item, soon after they met, when she didn't yet know she was pregnant, one of these former dates walked up to her and patted her bottom, Brajc punched him, knocking off his glasses and then crushing them, and although her friends were appalled and she herself told him to stop and that he was overreacting, she knew very well, that at least at that moment, they were envious of her. When they had someone grab them by the arse, their boyfriends just laughed, dismissing it as a funny joke.

Brajc took a few deep breaths and then waited for a few moments as if he himself needed to process what he had said.

"And then, out of the blue... this."

He once again pointed at the bulk under the sheet.

"When did this appear? When did it all go wrong?"

He looked at Taras as if he was actually expecting an answer from him.

"What is it that everyone wants from me?"

"It piles up," said Taras.

"What?"

"Nothing, it piles up."

"Yes, but why does it not pile up with you? Why does it all go straight through the body and out of the arse in your case?"

"I am more active, do sports."

"Oh, come on! What about all those fat women who go jogging?"

Taras didn't see much point in trying to explain that they too will lose weight if they persist at jogging and Brajc took this as an affirmation.

"How did you manage to keep it down and I've failed so miserably? You are like I was when I was twenty. Why can you live like you always have and it doesn't show, and I can't?"

Taras laughed, though he didn't intend to. Like he had once laughed at one of the lessons at the Police Academy in early September, a lecture on police authorisation by Professor Zobec, for which he got a written warning, the third and last one before expulsion. The old man stood towering above him in front the board with 'A cadet should know the order with which a police officer gives instructions, and demands measures and actions that someone should undertake or stop undertaking,' on the board behind him. For some reason, unknown to him to this day, Taras found this hilarious and he could not stop laughing even when the old man had totally lost it and slapped him so hard that he fell on the floor. He had picked himself up and, still laughing, run out of the class with Professor Zobec shouting after him that he might as well go and pack his things because as far as he has any status at the school, Taras would not cross the threshold of the classroom again. Fortunately for Taras, Professor Zobec was temperamental but not wicked and when the case came up for discussion he demanded only a written warning before expulsion and Taras made sure he got through the remaining nine months till the end of the school year without any further outbursts.

Now, like then, he wanted to stop himself laughing but, just as with Professor Zobec, he just made things worse. He gulped on air and tried to hold it in his lung as if trying to swallow the laughter but after a couple of seconds the air and the laughter escaped into an incontrollable guffaw that made him unable to talk or even sit straight. He leaned against the bed, twisting with laughter. This was how Osterc and the nurse found him, found them – Taras, falling about with laughter, holding onto the side of the bed, gasping for air, and a surprised Brajc, staring at him in shock. When the nurse gave Brajc a querying look, he just knocked his finger against his head. Despite the laughter that was causing him to bend over, Taras noticed the gesture but it did not stop him. Nothing could stop him and even if there was something... This was the first time in a long time he laughed this much and he decided he would laugh it out to the end.

Monday

CHAPTER 24.

"How bad is it?"

Kristan was tanned and this tan went well with his silvery hair; he looked fresh, rested, and without worries.

"What did the doctors say?"

He should be congratulated. He did not begin with the rejected request for a search warrant and the reasons for it, his first card was Brajc. And although Taras knew that he was doing this for a purpose and that this purpose was not compassion, the anger he felt towards the chameleon on the opposite side of the table was inadvertently abating. How did he even find out about Brajc?

"Right then, I see," he said when Taras explained briefly what he had found out from the doctors and then sank into a few-seconds-long silence. Drvarič, who was sitting next to Kristan, more than ever looked like his bad copy. Kristan had on a light blue shirt, so light it was almost white, beige linen trousers, and, his legs crossed, he was also wearing linen shoes. The head of the General Police Directorate was not the immediate association triggered when he turned up. At this moment he would just as easily fit in in the café at the Hotel Palace in Portorož, or something similar in Cannes, and he would be welcomed gladly anywhere he would go in Barcelona. Next to him Drvarič looked even more tired and, though he was, despite the heat wearing a dark blue suit, somehow unkempt. He had been playing at being Kristan for a week and everything had gone wrong. How come, after all, he was – as Brajc would say (and at this thought Taras could not help himself but smile) – a cunt just like him?

"And what now?" he then asked. "Just three of you left, is it?"

Taras nodded.

"We're used to it, but we can't work anyway."

"Can't work?" Kristan seemed surprised.

Did he even know about the rejected search warrant?

"Oh, yes," Kristan eventually appeared to remember. "I heard that you had trouble searching the place on Župančič Street."

He looked at Drvarič as if it was his fault.

"Not searching the place," said Taras, "but with the search warrant. We didn't get one."

"Yes, well. We'll sort that out."

"Sort what out?"

"You'll get the warrant and you will be able to conduct the search at that idiot on Župančič Street."

"That Nazi?"

"That… idiot. I don't even know why the request was rejected. Some misunderstanding, it seems."

He was unbelievable. He went on holiday because of a threat to his position but came back with a new air of authority as if it was never doubted.

"And when will we get it?"

"Probably tomorrow, the day after at the latest."

He said it calmly, in passing, as if these kinds of complications were something normal, everyday.

"And what about the shooting at Metelkova?"

Kristan laughed.

"Did you read about it? The gay and lesbian community today protested about the direction of the investigations. They insist that we should first investigate any possible homophobic motives of the unknown shooter. You spoilt their party, Taras."

"Brajc and Osterc did."

"Whatever. What about this shooting?"

"Who is in charge of investigating the murder on Metelkova?"

"From today on, we are, the GPD. After this cockup we could not leave it with the guys from the station. Why are you asking? Would you like to take that on as well? Now that there are only three of you?"

Taras shook his head.

"You can keep it. Just asking."

He stood up and so did Drvarič. He was already holding the door handle when Kristan stopped him.

"Taras, do you have another minute?"

Taras nodded. What else could he do? Drvarič also waited but when he realised the invitation was not extended to him, muttered some kind of greeting and left Kristan's office. A miserable end to the previous week was followed by a miserable beginning of this one. He was at a meeting at the office of the Director of the GPD and never spoke a single word. He had not fallen this low in a long time.

*

"Taras...," Kristan began when Taras sat back down. "If I am not wrong, Cvilak is considering the possibility that the woman was not murdered but that she died of natural causes."

"Apparently he cannot decide," Taras lied.

"Well, that was what he said to me. And if this is the conclusion he reached, we are not technically looking at a murder, right?"

Of course, he was right.

"Basically, this is not the most important case in your career?"

"I didn't know I had a career."

Kristan decided to ignore this.

"I don't rank my cases according to importance. Besides, this is not my case."

"Of course you do," said Kristan. "Everyone does. That is why Drvarič entrusted this case to your colleague. In good faith that it cannot go wrong."

Taras shifted nervously in his chair. He was not sure where this conversation was leading and if he had to waste time, he could do it with someone else, not Kristan.

"He was not wrong. It's been a week since the murder, no more, and if all we can do with the guy who threatened to kill is chit chat politely, things don't move on."

"I told you that you will get the search warrant."

"It would help if someone told me why this is so complicated this time. To avoid future misunderstandings."

Kristan leaned across the table.

"This is not a time for heroes, Taras," he said meaningfully in a much lower voice than he had been speaking in. "It is a time for patience. There are four years until the next election, if indeed they get to full term, and four years pass quickly."

*

Tina came to work at eight and was not surprised to find the office empty. Brajc and Osterc would appear at around half past eight and Taras, freshly showered, filled with oxygen and the inner peace of someone victorious in a battle with their own self, fifteen minutes later.

She looked at the board on which – despite this being her case – Taras had scribbled a few names with question marks by them. Names of the residents of the block of flats overlooking the park, from the member of the Foreign Legion on the first floor and the young man with fascist tendencies on the third, to the woman with the dogs on the fourth. Barely legible and sometimes it seemed that even he was not sure what he had written or why he had written it.

Baloh, Jakin, Opeka. What could their motives be? A murderous craving in the former soldier of the special forces of the French Army, a hate murder for the second or getting rid of a rival in the third? She went over the apparent motives of those written on the board and in her mind added Taras.

"Because of my conscience which demanded that I end her suffering, your honour."

The first three no longer sounded so unbelievable. Besides, would a person who might kill someone out of some kind of principle, really try to lay the blame upon someone else.

She picked up the phone on her desk and called the Physical Investigations Department at the National Forensic Laboratory. People there did not like to be hurried, who did anyway, but she decided to ask them about the results of the tests on the gun Taras had taken from the former member of the Foreign Legion.

"Hopefully by tomorrow. We did however send you the results of the DNA tests."

"Where did you send them?"

They had emailed them to Taras. She asked them to send them to her also.

Looking at the board, she ticked off the first name on the list. Then she typed the name and surname of the Nazi sympathiser from the third floor into her browser and checked to see if there was anything new on his Facebook profile. His profile had been deactivated. Both his profiles had. On Saturday, when she had last checked and saved them, the skinhead was still very active, now, however – darkness. On Saturday he had added two screen shots of some computer games he was fanatical about, a shooting game, and a photo of a medal from Nazi Germany under which he wrote:

Knight's Cross for military valour – from Grandpa's collection.

She opened a new tab in the browser and put *Knight's Cross* and *military* in the search engine and found the site https://www.wehrmacht-awards.com with the description that this award was bestowed by Hitler personally, so the skinhead's grandfather with a Slovene surname was unlikely to have got it anywhere else but a flea market.

This was followed by images of weapons, both historical and their contemporary successors, for example the Panther tank from the Second World War and the modern Leopard 2A7, or the Walther P38 pistol and a modern Walther P5. The first picture was from some kind of archive, clearly taken from the internet, the second was photographed on a table and she tried to remember if it could be the table in his room. Light wood, imitation maple, and a part of a table lamp of white plastic in the top right corner of the shot. The next photo was a masked person posing with a pistol that could be the Walther P5. She zoomed in and indeed the metal frame under the barrel was oblique rather than right angled as in her Beretta. It could indeed be a Walther, such as the one used by James Bond before he switched to the more angular Heckler-Koch.

Final solution for many a problem, was written by the photograph.

And he had received three hundred and twenty likes for it.

She then came across a photo she would probably have

overlooked had she not seen it before, because it was not particularly interesting as such. The bench with the *Sieg heil* written across it. She checked the comments.

"Did you get her?" someone called *yoshi_perkua_gogi* asked.

"Deratting our town," *stalingrad_remember* wrote.

A "Well done!" was signed by *some painter_franc*.

At that moment Taras walked into the office.

"I've been to see Kristan," he said instead of a greeting.

"And? Did we get the warrant?"

He shook his head.

"No, not yet. Tomorrow or the day after."

He sat at his desk and only then did she notice the bag from a sports shop and a box inside it that could be nothing else but a pair of trainers.

"Been shopping have we?" she asked.

"Sorry?"

She pointed at the bag.

"Oh, yesterday morning. These aren't for me. They are for Brajc."

Tina laughed out loud. Taras remained serious.

"For Brajc?"

"He had a heart attack."

She stared at him as if checking whether this was just a bad joke. Taras was known for occasional gallows humour that was not even funny.

"At the picnic," he explained. When he described how Alenka had returned Brajc to the living Tina felt a sharp pain. Had Taras gone to the picnic with her instead of Alenka, Brajc would probably be dead.

"Osterc is with him and said everything will be fine. In as much as that is possible."

"You're naïve if you think he will ever use them," she said. "And why didn't you call me?"

"What difference would it make? It would just spoil your weekend."

He took the box out of the bag and opened it to show her the running shoes. Bright yellow. Only someone desperately without taste would choose this colour, or someone with an unusual sense of humour.

"I must think of myself as well, this way you can spot him from a mile away," he said, as if guessing what she was thinking about. "He won't go up Rožnik alone."

*

Silva brought the coffees and returned to her counter.

"We will get the ballistic results tomorrow. Probably," Tina said.

"I know, Golob called me. I was right that someone had recently used the gun. They found two traces of DNA."

"Whose?"

"I don't know. They are not in their database."

She stirred her coffee with the spoon though she, like Taras, didn't take sugar. Taras told her about the meeting with Kristan.

She smiled when she noticed the spoon in his hand. He did not use it to stir his coffee but just moved it from one side of the saucer to the other. Even more silly.

"Listen," he said. "Do we need to talk?"

She looked into his eyes and he nervously looked away.

"In fact there is no need. Everything is clear to me."

"Is it? Whatever we have, there is no need for the innocent to come off worse."

"The innocent..."

She smiled bitterly and reached across the table with her hand to stroke him on the cheek.

"It was just about sex, wasn't it?"

"I hope."

He paid and they left the café. She did not care whether Silva had noticed or not.

*

When they stepped out of the coffee shop Taras stopped briefly and she almost bumped into him. Instead of turning towards the station, he went the other way.

"Where are..." she tried.

He indicated that she should not say anything but follow him. They walked down Prešeren Street towards the south-west when an elderly lady stepped out of the front door of an older residential block. Taras jumped forward and held the door for her.

"Thank you," he said to the confused woman who threw him a suspicious look and continued on her way. He disappeared through the door and once again beckoned Tina to follow him.

It was dark and pleasantly cool inside. Taras found his wallet in his pocket and took out a visiting card, stuck it in the door so it could not lock, and then went to the right, behind the railings on the stairs leading to the top floors. He grabbed her hand and pulled her towards him, holding the finger of his other hand in front of his lips.

About ten seconds later the door opened and the card fell to the ground. The person who had opened it bent over to pick it up and Taras was already next to him. He pulled him into the hallway and pressed him against the wall. He was a younger man with a camera hanging around his neck and a bag across his shoulder.

"Hey, hey...!" he lifted his hands with the palms of his hands turned towards Taras. "This is my job, nothing personal. I have to eat. You know who hired me anyway."

"Give me the card," said Taras in an ice cold voice.

"No chance!"

The door against which Taras had pushed his follower was of massive wood and the walls were thick, but anyone walking on the opposite side of Prešeren Street would still have heard the two cries that happened almost simultaneously. The first came from the young man whom Taras hit across the face with his hand, the second was Taras who had forgotten about his tennis elbow. As if this enraged him further, he kicked the man from the side as he fell to the floor and he ended two metres down the corridor towards Tina. Then he approached him, stepped on the already smashed camera, stomping his foot on it a few times until there was nothing left of the Japanese technological wonder that was worth the weight of the materials it was made of. He picked out the memory card from the remnants and squatted next to the groaning and bleeding photographer.

"Now eat it!"

The beaten up man's eyes widened. Taras used the thumb and index finger of his left hand to pinch his nose and squeeze it.

"You have to eat, you said. So eat it!"

The photographer cried out and Taras pushed the piece of plastic into his mouth, twisting his nose further until he swallowed it. Then he let go of his nose and stood up.

He waited for the photographer to look up.

"If you don't leave me alone and if you ever try to continue to destroy my life, I will kill you! You and your patron. Tell him that. And there is no God or money that will prevent me from doing so. Get it?"

Tina had never before seen such fervent nodding or eyes this scared.

CHAPTER 25.

They walked back in silence until, right in front of the entrance to the building, Taras stopped and asked her, "What was I supposed to do?"

Tina gave him a tired smile.

"I am asking you seriously."

She did not know. She really did not know.

"You can't beat up the entire world. And I hope that you were not serious about killing them."

It sounded serious. The guy certainly believed him. He swallowed the memory card. God knows what the thing is actually made of.

"What was I supposed to do?"

Nothing. It's over now anyway. There will be nothing else for him to photograph.

*

Osterc was already at the office.

"How is Brajc?" Taras asked.

With unusual verbosity Osterc described Brajc's recovery. Less than a day after his first visit, Brajc's skin was no longer pale and saggy, as he said, but more healthily taught. Apparently he had started eating and told the nursing staff a joke about a man who didn't want to live to be a hundred.

"What joke is that?" Tina asked.

Osterc repeated it to her, replacing the word 'fuck' with 'have sex'.

"...who would want to live to be a hundred without food, drink and sex?"

Taras knew a better ending to the same joke. When the doctor lists to the patient all the things he ought to give up and the patient in return asks the doctor whether giving up all this means he would live to be a hundred, the doctor replies, "No, but it will certainly seem like a hundred."

"He sends his greetings," said Osterc. "And says he will be taking as much sick leave as he can get."

Taras sat at his desk and stared at the board. Pointing at Taras, Osterc gave Tina a querying look. He was still slightly red in the face.

"Kristan promised us the search warrant," he said before Tina had a chance to respond.

"And what now?" Osterc asked.

"We have this young Nazi who is showing off," Taras began without taking his eyes from the board. "Trying to convince the world he had something to do with the shooting. The more he does so, the more I doubt it. Then we have the old man from the first floor, or rather his gun that was recently fired, but of which the old man knows nothing or no longer remembers. We have a DNA sample, two in fact, from this gun and are waiting for the ballistic report and once we have those we will know whether we should try to find to whom these samples belong or not."

He spoke calmly, monotonously even, as if wanting to check the facts with himself as well as Tina and Osterc.

"Have I forgotten anything?"

"We have the woman on the fourth floor who secretly begs in her spare time," said Tina.

She told them about her run.

"Why would she shoot at the woman in the park?" Osterc asked.

"Rival on the same pitch? I know it sounds far-fetched. I'm just thinking out loud."

"Of course the person we are looking for might not be from this freshly painted building at all," said Taras. "They could have come to the park from anywhere."

"Today I checked the profile of this Ignac Jakin of ours again," said Tina.

She reached for her computer.

"His Facebook profile has disappeared but before that he published some interesting nonsense that I have saved."

After a few clicks, she turned the computer towards Taras and Osterc.

"Among his followers and those who liked his deratting in the park, as he called it, was also someone with a profile *Painter Franc*. I knew that I had seen this name somewhere and now that you mentioned this freshly-painted house..."

She clicked on a new folder and some image files in it, footage from the camera at the hotel on Župančič Street, checked her notes and ran the clip, stopping it when the van with *Franc Zupet, painting and decorating* written on drove by.

"Then we also have this."

She played the shot from the first camera from the moment the man in white came out of the passage and went towards the park, waited for the girl to appear, then skipped a few minutes and stopped with the arrival of the police car.

"I will talk to this painter guy. You remember, Taras, that Mr Baloh's flat was also freshly repainted when we called in on him?"

"I do. And one more thing. Someone sends Golob the photo of this second *Sieg heil*, the one from Metelkova. Let his guys find out whether it could be from the same author who also decoded the bench, if that is even possible."

"What should I do?" Osterc asked. "Help Tina?"

Taras looked at the board again and thought for a while.

"Do you need him?" he asked Tina.

She shook her head. He continued to stare at the board and then eventually turned towards Osterc.

"There are two things I'd like you to do. Your wife works in the library, doesn't she?"

The question was rhetorical. Of course he knew that she worked in the library.

"Can she check with her colleagues at the Oton Župančič Library whether Ignac Jakin happened to visit them on Monday between four and five? Or Nace Jakin? If he wanted access to their computers, he had to use his library card."

"Probably," said Osterc. "I will ask."

"She can also search for Marija Jakin," Taras added. "I doubt her son is a frequent visitor to the library."

"And the second thing?" Osterc asked.

Taras nodded, once again stayed silent for a few minutes, gazing into the emptiness.

"After that," he eventually said. "check Vadnal."

"Vadnal?" Osterc was surprised. "Did you not say that we were no longer working on that? Didn't the GPD take over that?"

"They don't have to know," he said, switched off his computer and tidied his desk.

"I too have a couple of things, Taras," said Tina.

"Yes?"

"Firstly, any information we gain in this way, even if it proves useful, will not be of much help. It won't be valid. We will not be able to use it anywhere."

"We can subsequently reacquire it in a way that will make everyone happy."

"Why not now?" she was surprised.

"Because of the tempo. By the time the court agrees, any kinds of traces will go cold. And the second thing?"

"I want to discuss the camera footage with you."

She surprised herself by saying it and it must have sounded odd as well because Osterc turned to her.

"Can it wait?" Taras asked, almost at the door.

No it cannot, she should have said.

"It can."

"Well, Wednesday then. I won't come in tomorrow."

She watched him leave and when he was already in the corridor, continued to stare at the closed door.

"What is it with this Vadnal?" Osterc spoke. "And which Vadnal was he even talking about? Senior or junior?"

*

Tina called the phone exchange and demanded the names of the police officers out on patrol on Monday night when they intervened at the bar in the passage under Nebotičnik. She was given two names, checked her notes, and called the first. A young voice answered at the end of the line. She tried to make hers sound more mature.

"Yes, me and my colleague went to check it out. Some guy had been drinking, he became aggressive and when they no longer wanted to serve him any drink, he threw a bottle at their window."

"And do you know who this guy is?"

"Yes, of course. He had been round there a few times in recent days and everyone knows he is working in that block of flats on Župančič Street, that corner building. He's a painter. We called the caretaker and he gave us his phone number. We gave it to our colleagues in Grosuplje, because the man is from Višnja Gora, and that area comes under their jurisdiction, and they sent two officers round to hand him a court notice. Do you need his details?"

"Yes, please." She gave him her email.

"Apparently he has quite a file," the policeman added as she was about to hang up.

"A file? Who?"

"This Zupet guy. When we called Grosuplje, they just sighed and said, 'No, not him again!'"

*

Taras persistently pressed the square button next to the surname Opeka. As he rang it for the third time, the intercom finally clicked and a "Yes, please?" came from the speaker.

"Taras Birsa, madam. Criminal investigator. I would like to talk to you if you could give me a little of your time."

"I was just about to take the dogs out," came crackling down the intercom.

"This won't take long."

*

"How can I help you, Inspector? I really am in a hurry."

After their initial barking the dogs calmed down and sat about a metre away from Taras, their gazes focused on the plate of biscuits in front of him. When Taras picked one up and brought it to his mouth, their pointy snouts followed his move. Taras stopped with the biscuit in front of his mouth and then moved it back towards the plate, then once again to his hand... The dogs, their snouts in coordination that any synchronised swimmer would envy, swayed along with him.

"And how's your health, ma'am?" Taras asked.

"Thanks, I'm managing," she said with the same cautiousness with which they had parted at their last meeting.

"I ask because the last time I saw you, you had problems with meningococcal meningitis or the consequences of, what was it?"

He noticed a moment's surprise in her eyes, confusion, shock, but she immediately composed herself.

"What is it that you are interested in, Inspector? Surely this is not what you came for."

Taras shook his head.

"No, not at all. I just mentioned it so you would take the time to talk to me. The dogs will wait, won't they?"

She nodded.

"Fire away. There's not much else that there would be any point in trying to hide."

"Have you lived long in this building?"

"I was born here."

She pointed to the door to her bedroom.

"There."

"Well, great," said Taras. "Then you will know all about everyone here?"

*

"This is what we have on Zupet."

The Commander of the Grosuplje Police Station looked pleased when he could place a thick folder with documents on the person she was interested in in front of his visitor from Ljubljana.

"Mostly they are offences in breach of public peace and order, but I assume you are not here because of those."

"This will do for a start," said Tina and nodded, meaning that she wanted to be left alone, which the policeman understood.

"If you need anything, give me a shout."

Judging by what the police reports said, Franc Zupet was someone prone to alcohol and violence. Five years ago he was stopped by police for a breath test and he locked himself inside the car when the policemen asked him to blow into the breathalyser. When they forced the door open, he fought them causing the first one who tried to grab him light bodily injuries for which he had to be taken to the Grosuplje Medical Centre. He was charged and sent to the district judge after getting drunk with local farmers, as it said, who drove to the bar next to the local shop with their tractors and ended their drinking by jumping, first on their tractors, then on a few cars. Bored by this they ended up pestering people at the shop. They had grabbed their shopping bags and thrown them in the air. By the time the police arrived they were already fighting amongst themselves. What an idyllic village, Tina thought.

Then there was a complaint by some Ivan Duh who suspected Zupet of damage to personal property, specifically his car. He had hired Zupet to paint his house and because he had not done the job to his satisfaction or on time, Duh did not want to pay him the agreed amount. A day after a furious argument an unknown perpetrator cut all four year-round Michelin tyres, model CrossClimate dimensions 225/55 R18 102, on his grey Peugeot 5008. Each of these tyres cost one hundred and fifty euros. Duh suspected Zupet who denied any wrongdoing when the police interviewed him.

A complaint followed from the local hunting club who had expelled Zupet from its membership on account of poaching and when he did not agree with their decision and verbally threatened 'nobody can exclude me from the forest and that they,' meaning the club's board that had taken this decision, 'should watch it if they ever meet him anywhere because there would be no witnesses.'

For these offences, except for the damaged tyres where it was impossible to prove that he was the offender, the local court in Grosuplje gave Zupet a six hundred euro fine that he had the chance to pay immediately in which case it would be reduced by half. When he refused, the fine had to be collected by court order.

He had once had his driving licence revoked for a year but he soon passed the control medical test and appealed to the court, which restored his driving licence due to the nature of his business.

This was not all. In the thick file Tina also found a breach of public peace and order complaint when he had organised a protest against the residents of a safe house in Višnja Gora. According to the report he and other protestors did not agree with the women there just lounging about. Though this is what it said, Tina imagined the words these people used were rather different, especially when she took a look at the attached photograph of the façade of the safe house on which someone had painted:

This is no spa lazy whores!

"It's missing a comma," Tina muttered.

The protests happened at the annual party organised by the local fire brigade, also attended, so said the report, by some of the residents of the safe house with whom a group of locals had got into an argument.

Attached to this was another photo, also of a façade of a house, though it was not the same one, with

Bitches go home!

written across it.

This could do with a comma as well.

She opened the last batch of documents in the folder. It was the report from the Ljubljana Police Department, the station where on Monday, the Monday of the murder, the waitress from the joint in the passage under the Nebotičnik accused Zupet of throwing a bottle at the glass wall of the bar when, soon after ten o'clock, at around 22:05 when she had no longer wanted to serve him because the bar was closing. This caused the glass wall to crack. This time he admitted to the act, saying that he had lost his temper when he could not get a drink after a full day's work.

"An interesting man, this Franc Zupet," Tina said to the Commander of the Grosuplje Police Station when she brought the folder back to his office.

"Were these reports all one would read they would state that the man is terrible, and in as far as they go I would agree."

"But there is a part that you wouldn't?"

The commander smiled.

"You'd be surprised, if you knew him. If you were to get to know him," he corrected himself. "He's a real hard worker, few people work so hard. Nobody else around here slogs as hard. He's done painting jobs for all of us. But when he has a drink, he becomes a different man."

"Nice words for a man who demanded that mothers with

children hiding from violent husbands move out from the safe house," said Tina.

"No, no, no... Don't get me wrong. I am not defending him at all. Whenever he did any of this shit, excuse my language, we certainly made him pay for it. Consistently and without pardon. But what it doesn't say in there was that a little after the fuss outside the safe house, Zupet was the first among the firemen who came to extinguish a fire that broke out inside."

"A fire? How did this happen?" Tina asked.

The commander smiled triumphantly.

"One of the charges fell asleep with a cigarette in her mouth. They saved her just in time."

"There were two photos in the file," Tina commented. "Of different houses, if I am not mistaken."

The commander shook his head.

"No, you're not. The building in the second photo is the local educational and training centre attended by secondary school kids with problems, often kids in trouble with the law."

"I don't understand what this has to do with bitches?" Tina asked.

The commander smiled with embarrassment.

"The place used to be reserved for problem girls."

"Right, great! And why is that photo in the file?"

"We assumed that Zupet had something to do with the graffiti, but we couldn't prove it."

"Did you send the photo to the NFL?"

"We didn't. We didn't want to burden them with something this..."

"Trivial?" Tina finished his sentence.

The commander looked at her tiredly. How could he explain that if they started wasting time looking for the author of every piece of graffiti in Slovenia, they might as well stop doing everything else?

"I'll do it," said Tina and grabbed the folder. "You can do without this for a while, can't you?"

Idiots, scumbags, liars, drunkards... she thought as she was returning to Ljubljana. She could include most of these people into at least one of these categories. And she will have to deal with them for the next forty years.

*

"Shall we begin with the first floor?"

Taras nodded.

"Right then... Franz Baloh," the old woman from the fourth floor set about giving details of all the residents in the building to Taras. "He moved here around thirty years ago. No, it must already be forty now! From Africa, apparently, where he was in some foreign legion."

"I know that," said Taras. "Did he move here alone?"

"No, with a daughter from his first marriage and a new wife, a black woman. It was the first time I saw a black woman in the flesh. She was much younger than him. You would not believe how quickly she learnt Slovene. There are foreigners who have lived here all their lives and still can't even greet you in Slovene. His wife was fluent after a year and in the end you could not tell the difference between her and a local."

"In the end?"

"She died ten years after they moved in. She got cancer and that was it. After that it was downhill for him. After the funeral, he became a different man."

"They didn't have any children?"

"No, that was it. She went to the doctor because they had problems conceiving, and came back with lung cancer. She had never even smoked."

"Baloh has a gun at home. Did you know that?"

The old lady shook her head.

"I don't know anything about any gun."

"Your nephew has one."

"Probably, he is a policeman."

"Baloh's flat has recently been repainted. Did he paint it himself?"

"No way," the old woman shook her head. "He can't even walk any more. The guy who painted his flat was the same guy who did the staircases and all the common areas in the building."

"Do you know him?"

"No. We've been trying to get someone to do it for a while.

Our caretaker is as lazy as they come. Did you know that we are the only residential block around here that is not even listed in the land registry?"

"Right," said Taras. "What about the second floor that is empty? Vasle, if I am not mistaken?"

"Yes, Majda Vasle. She was a banker, retired last year, died a month later in a traffic accident. Her son has now put the flat up for sale."

"The son? He does not live here?"

"No, he moved out about a year ago. He made some money very quickly, though I don't know what he does for a living. I do know he has a big car."

"And the husband, father?"

"I don't even remember him, he was here for such a short time."

"What was his name?"

The woman's forehead wrinkled for about a second and then she smiled uneasily.

"I don't know. It's been thirty years."

Taras wrote something in his notepad.

"Then we have the floor below us. Jakin."

"Yes, Dr Jakin. Well, he hanged himself."

"Hanged?"

"Yes. He had some kind of psychological illness and was constantly on pills. Then he got fed up of it all and committed suicide."

"When was this?"

"Just before the birth of his son. Isn't that terrible? It must have been… come to think of it, all this happened at around the same time."

"All this?"

"Yes, all this," the woman repeated. "The death of Baloh's black wife, Dr Jakin's suicide and the separation of the couple on the second floor."

"The Vasles?"

"That was the woman's name after the divorce. I can't remember what it was before."

"Perhaps Vadnal?"

The woman shook her head.

"I don't know. It's been so long..."

Taras wrote something else in his pad. He then put down the pen, looked briefly through what he had, and asked, "And how do you explain 'all this'?"

"This mess from thirty or however-many years ago?"

Taras nodded.

"As coincidence. Don't you believe in coincidences, Inspector?"

"I didn't use to," said Taras. "Now I am not so sure."

CHAPTER 26.

She did not know at exactly what time she had pressed the trigger. She was too drunk and stressed to make a note of it, so she now had to go through long minutes of footage of the pavement and the white car parked next to it, probably one of the smaller Opel models, and a black Mercedes behind it. In the background a grey stretch of road disappearing into the darkness. She could have fast forwarded the clip but didn't, as if she was afraid of what she would see. Then it came. The flash was stronger and much more distinct that the one on the footage from the night the homeless woman had died. She had expected this. In mid-June nights in Ljubljana are much darker at one in the morning than at ten o'clock in the evening.

She ran the footage again and then took a look at the clip from the night of the murder. Then both together, also putting the graphic representation of the sound on screen, one above the other. The undulation in the graph and the length of the flash were the same in both cases. Identical.

With one certainly being footage of the firing of a gun, there was no doubt about the other. One plus one...

Fifteen seconds later, the footage from the camera on the night of the murder, showed Taras's car driving off.

*

"So whose is this? Yours?" Taras asked.

They stepped out of the car with which they had driven across Vršič Pass, descended down the other side for a few kilometres into Trenta towards Bovec, then crossed the River Soča, past the settlements of Vrsnik and Na Skali, and ascended high above the valley until the driveable part of the road ended and

Malus parked his Fiat Punto in a yard with grass so green and soft that Taras almost felt it was a shame to do so.

"That would be great, but it isn't. Do you remember Weingerl?"

Weingerl was the president of one of the mountaineering societies in Ljubljana, clearly the one Malus belonged to. He must be around their age, but when Malus and Taras were competing in the mountains, he had chosen a career. He had begun with a rather original launch pad. Presidents of mountaineering societies that Taras knew of looked after various mountain huts that their respective societies were in charge of, making sure they did not fall into ruin, and were used as somewhere to organise their yearly meetings or any other parties whenever there was an excuse for one. For Weingerl, being president of a mountaineering society was a way of establishing business contacts and he was now General Director of the holding company owning most of Slovenia's power stations. Taras often saw him on TV.

"He never climbed anything more demanding than a grade three," he said.

"Four. He even climbed this one we are about to tackle. Though it's true that I pulled him along the worst parts."

He smiled.

"When he was president, we had it all. Besides, how many people do you know who would just give you the keys to their weekend house?"

Externally the house looked as it probably had done a hundred years ago when it was built as a shelter for shepherds bringing their sheep and goats every summer to the steep grassy patches among the beech and spruce, even larch at higher altitudes. Constructed out of wooden logs, its roof covered in pine shingles, and, what Taras liked most, without any satellite dish. It looked isolated but Taras knew that the various dirt tracks and paths indicated the presence of other similar houses, the owners mainly rich folk from Ljubljana. Some of them were descendants of earlier generations of Slovene climbers who had enjoyed coming to this area when nobody else was interested. These were later joined by university professors and later businessmen and politicians. With time the previously open paths were closed with barriers and signs saying *Private*.

When they reached the first such barrier further back down the road, Malus had a key to the padlock.

Malus now unlocked the house and invited him inside. Taras had to bend down not to hit his head on the doorframe. For a few moments before Malus switched on the light, Taras wondered whether there was any electricity at all in this place but when the lights came on he realised how very naïve he was, despite his thirty-year-long police career. Modesty and authenticity disappeared in an instant – Taras was now standing in a modern and tastefully furnished flat, that could easily feature in some interior design magazine. A light living room, despite its small windows, furnished with wood and other friendly materials, continued into a kitchen area with a counter and steps leading to a floor in the attic, presumably a bedroom, that could sleep a number of people.

"Cute place, isn't it?"

Aljoša came from behind the kitchen counter, opened the refrigerator and turned to Taras.

"Beer, lager, IPA, stout, or wine, white, red, orange, or a whisky, brandy...?"

"A Coke."

"Coke? Stop kidding me Taras."

"Or a mineral water, juice, plain water..."

He explained his problem to Malus.

"Well, that's an irony if there ever was one! The worst drinker among us becomes an abstainer."

"Well, I wasn't really the worst."

"Oh yes you were. You were drunk by the time we stepped out of the plane at Tribhuvan."

In as far as Taras could remember he was not the only one.

"Whatever... it's been a long time since my last drink."

"And you manage?"

Taras opened a can of Coke and toasted.

"Everyone should try it."

*

"I'm great," said Brajc, lying in bed, the sheet pulled up to his chin. He had pulled it up to cover himself as soon as Tina stepped into the room.

"I'm great now, but before I thought this was the end."

"Did it hurt a lot?"

Brajc shook his head.

"Not really... I mean, not that much. I felt a pain in the chest and it was as if it surged to my shoulder and jaw. It was not a pain that was unbearable. But the fear. It was as if I knew this was the end. Then there was darkness. Were it not for Alenka, we would not be talking here like this."

Her face must have reacted somehow and Brajc understood it to be surprise.

"Didn't Taras tell you that it was Alenka who revived me? Well, there's one who doesn't even know how to pride himself where pride is due."

"Oh, he did."

"The doctors say that the heart attack did not cause any permanent damage," Brajc continued and sighed. "If I stick to a diet and start working out."

He looked scared and for the first time since she had met him, Tina felt sorry for him. What happened to Brajc was his own fault but this did not mean he did not have the right to be afraid.

"But I have never worked out in my life."

"Taras..."

She probably wasn't supposed to tell so she hesitated for a while but then ended her sentence anyway, "Taras bought you some trainers."

"Really? But..."

Brajc thoughtfully stared at the sheet over his bulging belly.

"I don't even know how to use them. You just put them on your feet and start running, do you?"

She smiled. Had Brajc not looked so helpless, she would probably have laughed out loud.

"He said he would go running with you."

"Did he really?"

Brajc was touched and did not try to hide it. He crumpled the edge of the sheet and was silent for a while. Then he quietly said, "I don't want to hold you up, Tina. You have your own life.

No need to waste it sitting here with a fat old fool."

She stroked his head, his hair sticky with sweat.

"Don't be silly, Brajc. Are we or are we not colleagues?"

He nodded hesitantly.

"Besides, I want to ask you something."

He gave her a look of surprise.

"Go ahead. I'll be happy if I can help."

"Could Taras have killed the woman in the park?"

*

When Tina departed to visit Brajc, Osterc was left alone in the office. He was sorting out the paperwork to do with the murder at Metelkova. Mostly it was notes from interviews that Brajc and he had conducted and he tried to discern anything useful to give to Taras when they meet after he returns from wherever he was today. Anything that might link murder number one with murder number two.

However hard he tried, he could not find anything. No lead, no witness, no motive, however vague. Was Vadnal senior a drug distributer, as Brajc assumed, and thus a victim of competition?

"It's impossible that the old hippy on Metelkova didn't have a single joint on him," Brajc insisted. "They did away with him and took it all from him. What do you think he lived off?"

In as far as they were able to believe his friends, he had no major arguments with anyone and there was nothing missing from his backpack and room, or rather studio in which he had been living illegally. Who would get his space? They would announce a competition and allocate it to some other artist. Who would kill simply to get thirty square metres of work space?

"Anyone can apply and then a committee named by Metelkova City…"

All the people Brajc and he had talked to were regular members of the committee. And judging by the people who sleepily wandered around their hovels, as Brajc had called them, reluctantly answering the questions of two seemingly very different police officers – criminal investigators, then the candidates for the newly emptied space were probably not much different.

"There is nobody in this hairy bunch that would at least approximately fit the description of someone with the physical and mental characteristics for a perfectly carried out murder that we now have to look into on a bloody Sunday," Brajc had said after the interviews. "They wouldn't know the difference between a gun and a tomato if you didn't put a sign on them."

Besides, everyone they had spoken to had an alibi. Nobody was at home alone at ten in the evening. They checked what the dead man had been doing recently and decided he was not doing anything much. The last performance he had done was two years ago, entitled *The Homeland Is Blind*. Osterc checked the internet and found photos of a man walking around Ljubljana with his head bandaged, the bandage also covering his eyes, and an arrow supposedly piercing his skull. He was being guided around town by a young girl and in as much as he could see from the photo, she was someone they had already spoken to. This was also their only joint project. After this she had worked on her own stuff.

Basically nothing.

Osterc called his wife.

"There was nobody called Maria, Ignac or Nace Jaklin at the library on Monday afternoon," she told him without a greeting. "Will you stay at the office long?"

"No."

In fact, he had more or less finished for the day.

*

"Why would Taras kill anyone?" Brajc stared at her in shock. "You are joking, aren't you?"

Tina shook her head. She slowly, without stopping, told him what she knew. Of course she changed the part of the story that had taken place at her flat.

"We met on Čop Street when Taras was on his way home from shooting practice and when I mentioned the homeless woman in the park..."

"Oh," Brajc dismissively waved his hand after, contrary to her expectations, listening to her without interrupting. "There must be some other explanation. And besides, if I understand Cvilak correctly, nobody actually killed her. She died. He would be innocent of murder in court even if he had shot her."

"I am not the court. Any other explanation?"

"That someone else did it. That that flash you are talking about is not a gunshot at all and that the woman died a few minutes later when Taras was already in bed, smooching the angel who saved me."

It stung.

"I checked."

She told him about her night action and the footage from the camera.

"Fifteen seconds after the shot Taras drove off with his car parked in Župančič Street."

"Well, someone must have shot her ten seconds after Taras went past then."

She looked at him and he stroppily shook his head like a fifteen stone child.

"Taras didn't. And besides, you forget that our guns are in the database. If he had done Golob would find him before you had time to blink."

"It was Taras who gave Golob the empty cartridge case found at the kindergarten. And just as he was returning the gun to Baloh."

Brajc had to think to comprehend what she was implying.

"And now you think he ran up Rožnik, took a shot at the first beech tree with Baloh's gun and took that cartridge to Golob?"

"Theoretically, he could have."

Brajc sighed and seemed to collapse in on himself as he fell silent. A minute passed before he asked, "Tina, what is it that you want from me? To accuse a man whose wife saved my life and who bought me some trainers to extend it?"

"No, I want to find someone who could tell me that he is innocent. Who could tell me that he simply could not have done such a thing. That would be enough."

Brajc looked at her wearily.

"I am not the right man for that. I could not care less even if he did. You will have to find someone else."

*

Malus made up a bed in the attic. Taras looked at the low bunks and ceiling, went to the car, took out his sleeping bag and foam mat, and lay on the edge of the flat lawn. He had not slept outside in the open air for a long time. His sleeping bag was the same one he had used on the Dhaulagiri expedition, the couple of pounds of goose feathers in it were much more compacted than then but it was still too hot for this climate, so he undressed down to his underpants, wrapped everything else into the sleeping bag cover and used it as a pillow. He turned his trainers upside down so that the dew would not collect inside them overnight, almost proud of remembering this detail.

He would probably have fallen straight to sleep had it not been for the old smells that he had almost forgotten existed, which now transposed him twenty and more years into the past. The smell of plastic soaked with droplets of sweat, sun cream and a kind of homely stuffiness... This probably wasn't the same sleeping bag he had spent a night in on a thin ledge cut into the brittle but concrete-hard black ice on the West Face of Monte Rosa but after a while all of them smell the same.

Memories peeled themselves from the darkness into which he was staring, pictures of past ascents. Disordered at first, in the wrong sequence. Drejc washing his feet in... what lake was it? Drejc walking along the glacial moraine towards the West Face of Monte Rosa. Drejc at the end of a rope on a slope leading from the wall, in the darkness illuminated only by the flash from the camera and the torch on his helmet.

Perhaps this sleeping bag also post-dates the Eiger he climbed a year before Dhaulagiri, the climb that secured him a place on the expedition. He had tried six times before then on the North Face with various co-climbers and when winter began everyone was already teasing him about it.

"Hey, how's the Eiger?"

On his seventh visit he went there with Slavc. When the two of them, in their very Balkan old Yugo car had arrived in Grindelwald and he had peered up the stone and ice colossus rising for more than a thousand metres above Kleine Scheidegg pass, his stomach had cramped. We'll never get over this, he thought. Slavc, who noticed his ashen face, had to slap him on the back.

"What's this now? We'll crawl up this, what's come over you!?"

It took them two days to get across the wall and by the second night they were already bivouacking on ridge that leads up to the Eiger's 3997 metres altitude. They had thought that they would be able to dig a comfortable hole into the still steep mountainside but found that there was black ice under the thin layer of snow and, after two hours of hacking away at it with their ice axes, gave up and spent the thirteen long hours of the February night in a semi-awake state. Two kilometres below them, piste bashers were like giant beetles levelling the ground for Swiss skiers, above them, just behind their backs, Taras spotted a comet. When he mentioned it, Slavc told him he was hallucinating and he thought he really was until he heard on the radio when they were back in Slovenia, that there was indeed a comet close to Earth that would be visible to the naked eye in a few days' time.

Drejc abandoned climbing even before he did and was now a member of some kind of Slovene Hells Angels. He could not imagine him on a motorbike. When he was still climbing he had been around eight stone and everyone teased him when he could not find leggings popular at the time in of a size that would not hang loosely off his thin legs.

And Slavc is dead. Has been for twenty years now.

"If your fate is to hang, you won't drown," he used to say and that was how it was in the end. After all the Eigers and Dhaulagiris, he fell in some pointless ice falls in Tamar and broke his neck.

Taras turned in his sleeping bag so that instead of facing the blackness that was the forest during the day, he was now looking at the sky. Billions of stars were running away from him. How much further have they come since the comet, the name of which he had forgotten, hovered above them? It was as certain that they were moving away as it was that you would not hang if your fate was to drown.

There was something calming about this.

Tuesday

CHAPTER 27.

At half past nine Tina rose from her computer, told Osterc that she needed to check something and that she would probably be out for a while. Osterc nodded and pointed towards Taras's empty chair, as if to say, he's not here anyway.

She didn't go far. Once out in Prešeren Street, she walked down Šubic Street towards the Parliament, crossed Republic Square to Erjavec Street and stopped at a café nesting in the triangle between Erjavec and Igriška. She picked a table beneath a sunshade that offered her the best view and ordered a cup of coffee. From where she was sitting she could see the entrance to the paediatric clinic belonging to Taras's wife and if they stick to the opening hours advertised on their website, Alenka should probably arrive at the clinic at around ten.

She had to wait until ten past before she appeared on the pavement. She almost missed her, not really knowing what to expect, though subconsciously she was probably waiting for a white doctor's coat. Instead, walking towards her was a woman in a tight dark blue summer dress and, as she had done at the cinema, the first thing Tina thought was how neat and elegant she looked. She was wearing sunglasses and Tina was not sure where she was looking or whether she had noticed her, but as she was about to raise her hand to draw her attention, Alenka stopped.

"Tina, isn't it?"

Tina nodded and extended her hand to Taras's wife who

squeezed it and smiled.

"How come you are in this area?"

Tina had been thinking about how to answer this question if it arose, and until it did she hoped it wouldn't. How could she persuade a woman who she had only seen once before to sit down at the table with her and how should she ask her the question she was hoping to get an answer to? Should she say, 'Oh, I'm having coffee. Would you like one?'

"I'd like to talk to you."

Alenka gave her a puzzled look.

"With me? What about?"

"It will take five minutes."

Alenka smiled, pulled a chair closer and sat down.

"I'm listening."

Tina sighed and nervously held the cup of coffee in front of her. She was grateful to the waiter who noticed the new customer and hurried towards them.

"A white coffee with a little extra milk. Cold please. And a scoop of ice cream. Vanilla." She looked at Tina. "I skipped breakfast and it looks like I won't have a snack break either."

They waited in silence for the waiter to return. Two minutes of panic rushing through Tina's head. As if she was at an exam looking for the answer to material she had not revised.

"You said you wanted to talk to me," Alenka repeated.

"Yes."

Tina looked up from her coffee towards the coffee in front of Alenka.

"You probably know I was a witness last week at court when Taras was accused of..."

"I know."

"Then you also probably know that I gave evidence that none of what he was accused of actually happened in Bohinj?"

"I know that as well, yes."

Tina paused. She was nervous, so nervous that her hand shook when she lifted the cup of coffee to her lips and it clattered when she put it back on the porcelain saucer.

"I also know that you gave false evidence. I am certain that Taras beat up that idiot."

Tina looked up and for the first time since they began talking looked Alenka straight in the eye.

"You know? Did he tell you?"

"Of course I know. No, he didn't have to. Do you think I don't know the man I have been living with for the last twenty-five years?"

Tina shook her head. Of course not.

"But this is not what you wanted to talk to me about?"

She shook her head again. With even greater nervousness and uncertainty. Then she composed herself and looked at her again.

"I will discuss this with Taras as well, don't think that I am scheming behind his back. But the matter is so..."

She sighed.

"I'm listening."

"It is all so strange, that..." she smiled. "I would like someone to tell me that it's impossible, that I am missing something important."

"I'm listening," said Alenka once again with a slight smile on her tightly pressed lips.

Tina explained as she had done to Brajc about the events in the park and it helped that she had already talked about them once before. As she explained the dry facts about the camera footage and the only possible reconstruction of events that she could think of, she calmed down. She did not mean any harm to anyone.

Alenka listened and stayed silent even after Tina finished. When she eventually spoke she sounded relieved.

"This is not a theme for five minutes, is it?"

"No, but I had to."

Alenka used her spoon to take a large lump of ice cream and carefully drop it into her cup so that the coffee didn't splash over the edge.

"And you want to know, if I understand correctly, whether my husband killed that woman?"

"Nobody killed her. According to the report from forensic medicine, she died a natural death. It was after she died that someone shot her."

"But whoever shot her didn't know that at the time?"

"Very possibly not. And this is not about me wanting to get Taras into trouble or trying to harm him in any other way. If necessary, I will keep silent about the footage. I would just like to know."

Alenka used the spoon to mix the lump of ice cream, an iceberg on its way to southern seas, melting away in the coffee.

"Do you expect me not to talk about this with Taras?"

"No, I don't expect that. But he won't be back today and from what I overheard on the phone, he had apparently gone to the mountains. I will talk to him myself tomorrow, as soon as I see him."

"Right," Alenka smiled and dropped the rest of the ice cream into her coffee.

"Did you think he was right when he beat up that... what was his name again?"

"I did."

"How come? Were you not supposed to prevent it? I mean, according to your rule book, or whatever it is called?"

Tina shrugged her shoulders.

"I was."

"And why didn't you, if you should have?"

Tina wondered why this woman was always so in control? Alenka sat before her with a slight smile on her lips and from the moment she had sat down there was a sense that she was leading the game, all the movement, expressions, everything was controlled. Perhaps she should have joined the police.

"I thought that he deserved it. To some extent."

Alenka almost laughed out loud.

"To some extent? Why just to some extent? What did Taras even do to him? If I'm not wrong, he pushed his face in the snow?"

"Three times, and the third time he held it in the snow for so long I was afraid he would suffocate. He pissed himself when Taras finally let go."

"Why didn't you push him in the snow if you believed he deserved it? You could do it more moderately?"

What were these questions leading to?

"Don't eat yourself up over it, I would do the same. You see, Taras wouldn't. There are people who, how can I put it, simply don't have this luxury, this shifting of responsibility onto others. Of course Taras spoke to me about this case."

She smiled.

"In his own way. In a couple of sentences. Did you at any point regret it or was it hard for you to testify in Taras's favour, give false witness?"

Tina thought for a moment longer that she intended before shaking her head.

"That means at least a little. Why, though?"

"The man could have died."

"But he didn't," said Alenka coldly, dryly. "With his inherited empire this person will decide about the fate of many in his career. Perhaps it is better for these people that at least once to feel he a little threatened, scared for his life."

She mixed the remnants of the unmelted ice cream into the coffee and took a sip.

"You probably know that I am the owner of a paediatric clinic, one of the best known in Ljubljana?"

Tina nodded.

"Which means that Taras and I are now rolling in money, compared to the average Slovene. But for almost twenty years we didn't. I won't bore you with the details of how we moved the bills from one pile to another, hoping for a miracle. And this had its consequences. Not only for Taras, but me also. If I had to testify in Taras's favour, I would do it with a smile. Do not expect the kind of mercy Taras showed him from these people."

She looked at Tina and smiled as she probably would have done in court when she would say what Tina had said, "No, none of this happened."

"Indeed, there is another detail here, Taras's character line. He would, how can I put this... He would never attack anyone unprovoked and that is why he naively expects everyone to leave him alone. People confuse this with weakness and some of them, the more impudent among them, have a go at him, which is not in the least a good idea. I don't know whether you know, but Taras grew up in a foster family and he probably had more than enough of people kicking him just because they thought they could."

Tina thought of the photographer and his "Nothing personal..." and the flash in Taras's eyes triggered by "You know who hired me."

"And now as to what is bothering you. Could Taras, as I have just described him, a person who has to do what others wouldn't, have shot that woman?"

She looked at Tina questioningly, and when she got no answer, continued.

"Of course you know that Taras used to climb? Well, used to..." she smiled. "It seems this 'used to' is no longer accurate."

"I know."

"Do you know why he stopped?"

"The children, apparently."

Alenka smiled.

"Well, the children and money problems..." Tina tried again.

Alenka laughed and Tina fell silent.

"He stopped because he was afraid."

She checked her watch.

"If you're in a hurry..." Tina began.

"No, I checked the time because I would like to know if you're in a hurry. If not, can I tell you a shortish story?"

Tina nodded.

"Right then..."

She leaned back in the wicker chair, crossed her legs and gently rested her hands in her lap. *Pique, pique, pas de bourrée*, Tina thought to herself – she had dropped ballet in the third year of primary school. She would have bet on Alenka continuing it at least until secondary school.

"I met Taras at a party. I arrived at it with someone else but when I saw him, when we saw each other, the other guy didn't stand a chance. Taras turned up in some kind of jeans with a crease, as jeans were worn at the time, and I think his T-shirt was tucked behind his belt. If our Anja or Mojca were to turn up with a guy like that, I'd... I don't know what I would do. What could I do? So why did I leave with him then? Don't you find him a charming man?"

"He's my boss," Tina stuttered. "I have not thought of him that way."

Alenka gave her a look full of doubt.

"Well, whatever. There was a kind of energy I felt, though I don't normally go for things like that. At the time he was taking the exam for his criminal investigation course and talked about the bizarreness of your work that you have surely already encountered. To me, a girl from a good family, it inflamed the imagination. Then there was the climbing, from which he often returned like someone returning from war, bleeding, exhausted, but with a flame that burned him, not just warmed him, that is how strong it was, though I didn't want to have anything to do with that. And then there were parties, drinking and..."

She looked Tina in the eye and persisted.

"...sex that many a girl would envy, of that I am sure. Basically all the women I know."

She did not move her gaze and Tina had to force herself not to lower her eyes.

"We took care, but it didn't help and I became pregnant. We never thought of getting rid of the child. Everything seemed at the same time possible and impossible and we believed it would last forever, no matter what."

Why is she telling me this, Tina thought.

"Of course, it didn't. The first of Taras's friends died and we went to the funeral, then the second... It really felt like war. Then Taras's best friend died and I gave birth to Anja. One fine day, it was a Thursday, the forecast for the weekend was sunny without showers, Taras suggested a trip to Lake Podpeč[17]. He stopped climbing and ever since, until yesterday, he did not even look at the blue plastic barrel in which he stores his equipment. At first I was happy about this. Then I realised that he had paid a very high price for it. How can I be glad that my husband does not go to the mountains when he is missing a leg? Metaphorically speaking. Between us we have a never-spoken sort of consensus that he gave up climbing because of his family. He didn't though. He was scared."

"Why are you telling me this?" Tina asked quietly.

---

17 Podpeško jezero, a small lake on the edge of the Ljubljana Marshes, less than 10 miles out of town, a popular destination for short walks and strolls as it is also on one of the city bus routes.

"You asked me whether Taras would be prepared to put his own life on the line for an act of mercy towards a total stranger, if I understood you correctly?"

"Yes."

"And I am telling you that Taras is a person made of flesh and blood. Do you think he would risk the comfortable life he has thanks to my clinic because of a doubtfully demonstrated philanthropy towards someone who is not from his narrow circle of family and friends?"

She laughed.

"Do you know what Agatha Christie wrote, if I am not mistaken she placed the words in the mouth of her Hercule Poirot? After fifty, comfort is all that counts. Taras is nearing fifty. And there is one more thing. Taras can be very cruel towards the suffering of others. Do you know what he did when my father died? Regardless of what the man was like."

She waited a second or two.

"Nothing. He went cycling and even forgot to express his condolences to me."

She stirred the coffee even though the ice cream had long melted.

"I think he said something like – you knew he was going to die. In short, if you ask me, Taras is not the one you are looking for. There must be some other, quite rational explanation for all that mix up with the camera footage."

"What kind?"

"I don't know. I'm not a criminal investigator. Why don't you ask Taras?"

"I first wanted to make sure..."

"Did you not want to ask him because you are afraid that he might have actually done it or because you are afraid that he might resent you asking?"

"He's my boss. I suppose I was afraid of looking foolish."

Now Tina checked her watch.

"Thank you. I won't keep you any longer and I would also like to apologise for the other day when we met... It had been a hard day at work and I had had a few drinks."

She extended her hand across the table to greet her but was stopped by Alenka's icy voice.

"There is also something *I* would like to ask *you*."

"Please."

"Are you sleeping with Taras?"

In contrast to the voice with which she asked the question, the expression on her face seemed to be unaffected, almost curious. Tina moved her hand still hovering above the table, sat back down and tried to put all her energy into composing herself. She did not entirely succeed.

"What?"

"Are you sleeping with Taras? Are you lovers?"

"I don't understand why you would think we were."

It felt as if she was trying to buy time to find out from her what she already knew, like some small child, becoming entangled in an obvious lie.

"Look," said Alenka and it reminded Tina of the way Taras would say, look..., whenever he found himself in an uncomfortable position, with the difference that Alenka did not appear at all fazed. "I am a doctor and know a thing or two about the human nervous system. There are people who work like this..." she moved her hand in a straight line. "...and others who need amplitudes in order to achieve a balance. If you marry a man from the first category, you get a person who will trim the hedge and be happy with that, with Taras you get someone who..."

She drew a wavy line in the air.

"He used to sustain his nervous system with climbing..."

Her finger paused at the peak of the curve drawn in the air.

"...so he could then put up with the life that most people live, for a few days..."

Her finger stopped at a low point.

"...and again. Up and down. And then, all of a sudden, nothing."

The line she was drawing levelled out mid-air.

"Take a good look at Taras tomorrow morning when he turns up at work. His face."

"And why do you think I would sleep with him?"

Alenka smiled.

"He has mentioned you too often for my liking. And besides, ever since you have appeared in his life, I have the feeling that some of his former energy has returned."

She drew out a new curve and stopped at its upper amplitude.

"You didn't answer my question."

Tina looked straight into her eyes. Was that fear she could see inside? She could say yes and the fragile fortress before her would shatter into pieces.

"No," she said. "I am not sleeping with Taras and anything that is filling him with energy or whatever, has nothing to do with me."

CHAPTER 28.

At midday, after their climb, when they returned to the weekend house, he called Alenka and suggested they went swimming in Bohinj.

"Aljoša can drop me off in Radovljica, and you can pick me up when you finish."

"But that won't be before five."

"OK."

He had a rinse under the jet of cold water coming out of a pipe laid from the spring, under the forest floor, ending at a wooden trough.

"A new man rises," he said as he wiped himself dry and put on clean shorts and a T shirt. They went down into Trenta and found a place that sold pizza. They were both in a good mood.

"We could do this again, some time," said Aljoša.

"Twenty years pass quickly," Taras replied.

"Nothing wrong if it's sooner this time."

They arrived in Radovljica at three.

"If you want, I can keep you company. We can go for another beer."

There is still some of that mischief there after all.

"No need."

He could in fact have taken him to Ljubljana. He would be home at four and he could drive back out with Alenka, but he felt like being alone for a while. He strolled through the old part of town, found a bookshop and went inside. First he thought about buying a newspaper and finding some shade with a coffee but in the end thought that two hours was too long for a newspaper and decided on a book. The bookshop had a second-hand section where he found the first part of a biography on the Beatles. There was a dedication on page three: To Nataša for your great exam results, Grandpa and Grandma. He longed for the times when grandparents bought their granddaughters biographies of rock bands. In a dilemma between the Beatles and the Rolling Stones, he was firmly on the side of the Beatles.

Alenka was half an hour late and by the time she called him to come out of the old town centre that was closed to traffic, George Harrison had just been deported from Hamburg for being underage. His song *Something* was the one Taras liked most of all the Beatles ballads.

She arrived in her dark blue, almost black electric BMW. Taras could still not get used to it and dismissed it as a fad, but he was giving in. He preferred to drive his own car. His Citroën was like a truck compared to this. He could accelerate to one hundred after a ten kilometre run, this car did it silently in less than seven seconds. The bendy road from Bled to Bohinjska Bistrica was relatively empty at this hour and Taras took a rather sporty approach to its first curved section.

"For someone who should be enforcing law and order in this country, you are driving too fast," said Alenka. "Much too fast."

"I'm off today."

The water was almost too warm for an alpine lake. Like Ljubljana, the last time it had rained in Bohinj was at some point at the beginning of the month even though it is considered to be the wettest place in Slovenia and a saying goes that it is the place where rain whelps its young. Without any new downpours to disturb it, the surface water no longer mixed with the other layers and was now around twenty-five degrees. For Taras, who had had his fair share of freezing in his climbing days, this was just right.

"Doesn't it feel weird swimming here now when only in January you were fishing bodies out of the lake?" Alenka asked when the water reached her hips. Then she dived in and swam for fifty metres, before turning back towards the shore.

"That was a different lake."

Taras was not a good swimmer. Competitive swimmers would call him a bather and more than swimming, he enjoyed diving. Not deep diving where he had problems equalising the pressure or water getting into his nose. As soon as he attempted to go any deeper than a couple of metres, he could no longer stand it, so instead he stopped trying and tried to swim underwater for as long as he could hold his breath instead. He would choose a metre or so of depth and slide along the bottom, just above the flat pebbles, for as long as he could along the edge.

"How's the hand?" Alenka asked when he eventually joined her on the grass bank of the main beach. It was not crowded – it was only June, a weekday, and so late in the day that people were already leaving. The shadows were becoming longer and the heat was no longer as relentless.

He lifted his right hand in surprise and touched his elbow with his left. He had forgotten all about it. In the first rope lengths he had hammered in a couple of pitons and had to use both hands. He knew that because his right hand was still hurting then. What about after that? Did they need no more pitons or had the pain in his elbow eased?

"I am glad you went climbing," she said. "It's been a long time since I have seen you like this."

"Like what?"

"You know like what."

He leaned on his elbows and, probably for the first time since twenty years ago he had put his climbing equipment away in the blue plastic barrel, looked up at the peaks above the lake without feeling any kind of inner tension. Peaks in general.

Here's Johnny!

"How was it?"

"Fine. Surprisingly fine. A little weird to start with but then things went well. We exited the wall by eleven."

"Next time I would ask you," Malus had said as they lay on the patch of grass under the summit, "that we don't get up in the middle of the night for a route this lame."

Twenty years, even more, but it all seemed like yesterday.

"Aren't you hungry?"

Alenka had not eaten anything yet.

"Not even a snack lunch?"

"Not even a snack."

They put their towels in the bag and drove to the nearest restaurant. Taras was not hungry but ordered something and had a glass of water.

"Do you know what, I almost feel I should be drinking a beer right now," he said.

"With pasta?" Alenka put on an expression of horror.

"With anything."

He was climbing again and he could not imagine climbing and fruit juice.

They finished their food, ordered coffee and sat in silence for a while on the terrace overlooking the lake.

Taras theatrically opened his arms and sang:

Somewhere in her smile she knows, that I don't need no other lover...

"What?"

The people on the next table turned to look. He repeated the lyrics without the singing.

"*Somewhere.* A song by George Harrison." He pointed to the book he had bought.

"I see," she said. "What's it like?"

"Interesting."

It covered the period up to 1963, up to their first hits. Where could he get part two?

"Have the girls been in touch at all?"

"I spoke to Anja on Friday," she said. "She has two more exams and then she is free."

Then she would go on holiday down to the coast. Mojca would go on a student exchange to Holland for the summer. In early August they would return to Ljubljana for a couple of weeks during which, on Taras's insistence, they would find some student work. If Alenka had it her way, they wouldn't, though they admitted Taras was right after they had found their first summer job when they were fifteen.

"Do you know what I talked about with my own daughter today?" Alenka had said to him after Anja's first week at the bread counter at the Spar supermarket. "She said she likes Tuesdays most because pensioners get a discount and they are in no hurry, so she can take her time slicing the bread. And she told me that some people go to the supermarket more than once a day!"

Taras had always had summer jobs when he was young. In a ceiling beam warehouse at a brick factory under Pohorje where there was a small pond full of pike behind the factory gate. Sometimes someone from outside would bring the workers a couple of beers and they would let them through the gate and allow them to throw a line. Taras was sixteen when he had first gone there and had great difficulties loading the long, six-metre brick and steel brackets for ceiling fillers onto the pallet that a fork-lift would then load onto a truck. At the time Taras was around ten stone. The guy at the other end of the six metre bracket with steel reinforcement was six foot three and sixteen stone. He was always in a hurry and constantly shouted at him, "Hurry up, hurry up!"

As a young policeman he had once stopped there. The brick factory was gone, all that was left of it was a chimney. The pond had been filled in.

On the second day of her first ever student work Anja came home crying that her back hurt and that she was not allowed to sit down at all for the entire eight-hour shift. It was forbidden and she had to pretend to be working even if there was nobody at the counter.

"You'll get used to it," he had said, and she did.

"I met your colleague this morning," Alenka said.

"Tina?"

"She was having a drink in that café close to the clinic, so I joined her."

"And?"

"We talked a little, about your work."

"Remind me to fire her. She should not talk to unauthorised people about work."

Alenka smiled.

"And, what did she say about it?"

She looked at him as if she was considering something, then she just shook her head.

"Not much. Nothing that I don't know from you."

He nodded approvingly.

"Then we also talked about you."

"Perhaps I should fire you too then."

She did not smile.

"So how is work? How is the case you're working on going?"

He waved his hand and this time felt his elbow. As if the magic was gone. He pulled a face but was glad they changed the subject.

"It's not."

He made an effort to explain, though he found it tormenting and disclosing details was not allowed. He told her about the woman for whom Cvilak cannot decide the cause of death, about the problems with ballistics that do not allow him to entirely dismiss the old man in the wheelchair from his list of potential suspects, about the search warrant for the flat of one of the main suspects, in fact the only one, and the residents of the peculiar block overlooking the park that has changed its name four times in the last fifty years...

"And Brajc is out."

"But, if I understand this correctly, they promised to give you the search warrant for this guy you suspect had something to do with it?"

Taras smiled.

"If they first rejected it and then agreed to it, it either means they are clearing away something, or that the guy we want to visit has nothing to do with our case."

It was dark by the time they set off home. The road was empty and he wanted to once again push the electric wonder to its limits but the screen flashed a warning that he had already used up two thirds of the charge.

Wednesday

CHAPTER 29.

Tina reached the office at half past seven. Assuming that Taras would not go out cycling the morning after his climbing tour, she wanted to find him before Osterc turned up.

At a quarter to eight someone knocked on the door. She gulped, though she knew that Taras would not knock.

"Come in," she called out.

The door opened. Standing in the frame was an unknown man, about her age, tall and sporty, dressed in jeans and a white T-shirt. Despite the heat that was already engulfing the town, he appeared fresh – as poor old Brajc would say, washing-machine-advert-fresh. He smiled as one might smile to a friend.

"Yes?"

"Hi," he said. "I brought you the results."

He was holding a folder in his hands. Tina didn't immediately understand what results could possibly be in this folder, but he was already holding it out for her when he introduced himself.

"Stane Lokar, we were in email contact."

Trying in panic to think who this Stane Lokar, who spoke his name with such confidence and authority, could possibly be, she glanced at the folder that instantly reminded her - Forensic Handwriting Analysis.

"Nice to meet you," she said, smiling at him for the first time. "And this, I assume are your opinions of the three samples of handwriting we sent you?"

"Indeed. In fact they are not samples of handwritings but

graffiti of which two are sprayed and one is painted with a paint-brush," he smiled. "And I must say, I was glad of the stuff you sent us. I'm fed up of proving the authenticity of signatures on the wills of people who die suddenly."

He had a cute smile, which she instantly liked. It was genuine. There weren't many among her acquaintances who would not playact at least a little during a first meeting.

"Everything is written in the reports, but, if you want, I could explain a few things further."

She opened the folder, which contained a few pages of A4 and browsed through them. There were some titles of subsections in bold that she read: definition of task, definition of contested and comparative material, a list of internal accreditation documents that talk of methodology, a brief description of the methods used, presentation of a nine-point ladder of findings, description of material, each item separately, contentious and comparative, according to general characteristics – size, proportions, angle, evenness or not of application, then separate details of individual characteristics – general individual ones and detailed individual ones, such as shape of characters, linking, decorative elements...

She thought about how Taras, if at all possible, always allowed himself to be informed on the interpretation of medical and forensic evidence from the source – from the person who actually carried out the research. Now she sensed why. She lowered the folder.

"As I say, nothing any literate person would not understand, but if you want we could go over it here or even over a coffee," Stane suggested.

She looked at the pages again.

"With these things it's always a matter of interpretation, or rather – explanation. Besides, all my colleagues at the NFL are close to sixty. I'm fed up of listening to them moaning about how horrifically low their pensions will be," he added.

She checked the time, looked at the folder once again as if to check how much material there was in it.

"I'd be happy to do that," she said.

Having waited this long, she could wait for a few more minutes. She scribbled a message to Taras on a sheet of paper and left it on his desk.

They went to the café at Maximarket and sat at a table along its north side facing towards Parliament and was in the shade. Most of the other tables were taken by pensioners enjoying their morning coffee and Tina envied at least their tranquillity. She caught some of the conversation between them:

"...with these electric bikes I'm back in the game. You can't imagine how many I overtake on the way to Toško Čelo..."

She had to smile at the image of Taras that came to mind, sweat running from his forehead and chin onto the bike frame and the chain, and past comes an old man like this on his electric bike.

They ordered and Stane opened the folder.

"So, let's look at the graphology," she said, though she knew that the guy opposite her would not fall for that. He gave her a curious smile as if to check whether she really didn't know the difference between graphology and forensic examination of handwriting.

"If you'll allow me. Graphology is fake science," he said. "It looks at certain characteristics based on handwriting and has, from a scientific point of view, been totally discredited and is useless and not used in forensics."

"I know," she said. "I was kidding. I wanted to check out what I was told in training. If you want to work up a forensic who looks at handwriting, call him a graphologist. Like calling a meteorologist a weather man."

He looked at her with admiration and muttered, "I really have been with all these old men for too long. I think my sense of humour is in serious danger."

She smiled. Thinking about it, her own humour was also not doing very well lately, perhaps also because she's been hanging around an old man for too long.

"There is some research where some cunning guy from my profession sent the same text to a number of graphologists. He got a very different result every time. We don't use graphology, no one does in Europe and America. We all talk of forensic examination of handwriting, exclusively for the purpose of determining authorship. Who is the writer is all we are interested in."

"Well, then, what does the forensic examination of this handwriting of ours say?"

"It says that we have a few problems because of the limitations of our noble science. If we wish to give an opinion, we need comparative material. This differs from case to case, but let us make it clear that the lowest margin for the reliability of signatures is six samples and so much the better if there are more. It is true that you can sometimes determine authorship even from a smaller number of samples but in those cases we don't issue an opinion. With handwriting it is good to have at least three pages of writing by the same hand. You cannot compare lower case script with block capitals. Graffiti are a story unto themselves."

The waitress brought their coffees. They waited for her to leave. Stane emptied both sachets of sugar into his cup. Tina, as always, left hers alone.

"If you want, I can first give you the results of our findings and then we return to the explanations, but I'd prefer to go from left to right..."

"One thing at a time," she said. "No rush."

He nodded approvingly.

"So, what *is* handwriting? In principle handwriting is the act of motor memory. Like we learn how to ride a bike, for example, we also learn how to write. Through learning you get used to writing signs, for example, if we take a capital *N*..."

He turned the folder with the report upside down and wrote a simple capital N on the back of it.

"So, as you learn how to draw these basic shapes, you also begin distancing yourself from them, and what is created is individuality. This is greater with more complicated characters. The capital *I* is so simple it gives me a headache. There are only two possibilities – you can write it from the top downwards or from the bottom upwards, and very few people use the second option."

He sighed and rolled his eyes towards the sky.

"To be honest, I only know one person who does, and it's my fucked-up uncle. He's unbelievable, he does everything wrong, even holds the pen in a way you can't imagine. And he has some speech impairment. By the way, it has been proven that illegible or different handwriting and speech impairments are linked. Language is created in a certain part of the brain and writing is just a way of expressing it. Speech, writing, even thinking… all occur within language. What is interesting is that some theorists also see gesticulation, which is essentially also a kind of speech, as a kind of proto-writing."

He lifted his coffee cup as if toasting to someone who was absent.

"Perhaps that is why my eccentric uncle became a painter. He recently moved to some village down near the coast and now the poor villagers have to put up with his outbursts. He always paints naked and prefers to do landscapes. He's often so immersed in his painting that he forgets he's naked and walks into some village pub."

Tina laughed.

"Yes," he said. "Funny if you're not his sister, meaning my mother, who then has to rush around various police stations between Sežana and Postojna."

"At least he's not boring."

"No, that he is not. But if we return to the graffiti – handwriting on paper is very dependent on fine motor skills. Every person possesses some motor memory with which they form symbols, quite specifically and relatively distinguishable. Hands, especially fingers, are motorically the most developed part of the human body. The area of the brain controlling our thumb is as large as that for our entire leg. With writing such as this *Sieg heil*, which I would wish had been a little longer, the entire hand is at work. The detailed motor skills you can find when examining handwriting under the microscope are entirely absent here. What is preserved is the shape. If you write an *R* on paper like this…"

He wrote a large copperplate R next to the N and I, forming the letter with a single flow of the pen.

"…you will also execute it in the same way when writing on a wall. The shape generally remains the same or at least very similar. Some of my colleagues are very reserved about graffiti, others – among which I also place myself – less so. I have worked on some before. There is a lower rate of reliability but, if nothing else, it can provide some useful operational material."

He stroked the file.

"This, of course, will not stand up in court. It is all just operational material."

"I suppose I didn't expect it to. This case does not have a single solid thing to hold onto. Why would this be any different?"

He shrugged his shoulders.

"It's not our fault that this is so. I work with foreign colleagues a lot and when I see the materials they sometimes work with and what the courts demand from us, there is no comparison. I was at a seminar once and I had to laugh when I saw on the basis of what material they write their reports in England. Our courts would reject them before even reading through them. We Slovenes are a pedantic lot. We really stick to demanding standards. We try to assist the police and, if we have proof, we can write a report that will stand up in court, but most of the time all we can provide is guidance."

He opened the folder, looked through it and found the photos of both the *Sieg heil!* graffiti and the one from Višnja Gora about whores in spas.

"A paintbrush is better than spray. With a paintbrush the contact with the surface is still there and this contact involves at least the wrist. With spraying, the wrist is rigid. It's far easier to extract clues from a piece of graffiti written with a paintbrush than one that has been sprayed. When you spray, you don't get the connecting lines because you release the nozzle once you've completed the basic line of the letter."

He closed the folder and looked at Tina.

"So, to start with, what I can say with a relatively high degree of reliability is that here we are looking at three different authors."

"Three different authors? Hundred percent?"

He shook his head.

"I wouldn't talk in percentages. We generally avoid numbers. If you want to operate with numbers, you need to have the support of statistics and objectively measurable things, which this stuff isn't. Especially because handwriting as such is by its very nature variable and you need to take this into account. Numbers are not used. Even if we work on a system of probability ratios, we don't use numbers but merely put forward two hypotheses. One that the evidence points towards a common source and another that states that the evidence is such that it is more likely that it was written by someone else. And here I stand by my findings that these graffiti were not written by the same hand."

Tina scratched her head. If Taras suspected that Metelkova had something to do with their park, he wouldn't like this.

"Now to the more difficult question," he continued. "Is the author of any of these graffiti the same as the author of the text you sent me. It was a report on..."

"A statement from the report on a breach of public peace and order a few years ago in Višnja Gora."

"Yes, precisely. I stress, this is operational information that will not be of any help to you in court. Simply my opinion. So, the writing from this statement matches the graffiti..."

"Graffiti C? The one that says this is no spa, lazy cows?"

"I think it refers to lazy whores," he corrected her. "Yes, graffiti C."

"I know what you will say, but still: Can we, based on this," she pointed at the folder, "assume anything about the kind of people we are dealing with?"

"Then we are back at graphology. In retrospect, yes, but it's easy to be clever in retrospect. A simple case. When Bill Clinton stuck his dick in the wrong place, suddenly everyone knew he was a sex maniac and graphologists instantly recognised that this was evident in his handwriting. Of course nobody had picked up on anything of the sort prior to this. It has been proved that the same graphologist may give an entirely different opinion on the same manuscript when a controlled environment is absent. In one that is controlled, where all the media are blasting the same thing, this very graphologist will consistently give the same opinion, even if it is entirely misplaced. No, nobody who is serious about this can tell you anything."

Tina lifted up the folder and looked at the shots of the graffiti as if wanting to check for herself whether it still might be worth trying.

"The *Sieg heil* in the park was sprayed onto the bench, the one in Metelkova painted onto the wall with a paintbrush. Is it not possible that this is why it might seem they were written by two different people?"

Stane smiled.

"Yes, of course it is. There is a small chance that this could be so. This would be my honest answer in court. Here, however, between the two of us, I am confident that no, it wasn't the same person. Does that complicate the situation?"

She leaned back and sighed.

"I assume that my boss assumes it was the same person. I assume because I have no way of knowing what actually is going on in his head. He has no proof but when he reads this, he might change his mind."

"Birsa?"

"Yes. Taras Birsa. Do you know him?"

He shook his head.

"Not personally. Only from rumours. About half the people at Forensics hate him, probably also because Golob loves him so much. Now some ballistics software isn't working and we all avoid Golob who apparently owes this Birsa of yours some answers and is in a panic. What is he like really? Tough, is he?"

She thought for a while.

"Yes, in a pleasant sort of way."

Then she remembered the photographer and the previous guy kneeling in the snow.

"Until you step on his toes. Then he gets tough in an unpleasant way."

"And you? How are you doing at CID?"

"Fine. This was supposed to be my first independent case, it's summer and a colleague had a heart attack..."

"Brajc, yes, I heard."

"...there seems to be no rational explanation for the murder, therefore no motive and therefore no suspects. Everything we have managed to pile together so far is at best operational information..."

She hinted at the folder.

"...and with the change in government and our superiors

still unsure where the wind is blowing, we have more work with them than with what we're actually supposed to be here for. Beside this, I often feel that because the victim was a homeless woman and we don't even know who she is, nobody really cares. Sometimes I think not even my boss."

Her phone rang.

"Well, and now he's calling me."

She answered it.

"How far are you?" he asked without as much as a greeting.

"We've more or less finished. Are you interested in the results?"

"Later. Meet you at Župančič Street."

"What for?" she asked in a hurry, clear that he intended to hang up.

"Because," he said and it sounded almost cheerful, "they've found another former human being with a bullet hole in his head. Who do you think it might be?"

"I don't know. How could I know?"

"This time the French State Budget will breathe a sigh of relief. One pensioner less."

CHAPTER 30.

Golob, the forensic technician Marn, someone from forensic medicine whom Tina knew by sight but could not at that point recall his name, and Doles from the criminal prosecution service were all already in the room when she got there. Just as well the room was big enough for all of them. All their attention, though they were not all at that moment on top of him, was directed at the old man who was lying with his face in a pool of blood on the table in front of his chair. It was as if she was looking at a three-dimensional recreation of the Last Supper, with her colleagues the apostles in this scene and the dead member of the Foreign Legion Christ. Taras wasn't there.

She approached them just as Marn was removing the handgun from the dead man's hand. The Glock 19 that Taras had put in the plastic bag on their first visit. It was also put into one now. When Marn moved out of the way to put it with the rest of the collected evidence, Tina was able to see the top of the man's head with a now dried up hard trickle of blood coming from it. Instinctively she looked up at the ceiling and indeed noticed a small hole as well as bits of plaster on the dead man and all around him.

"Suicide?" she quietly asked Golob who was patiently waiting for Marn to finish his stuff.

"Judging by the wound, the position of the body and where we found the gun, I would say it probably is."

He formed a gun with his thumb and index finger and pointed it under his jaw.

"We also found a letter of farewell," Doles, the investigative magistrate, intervened and pointed to the door of a room Tina had not been in previously. "More like a farewell message. Taras has it. He's not alone. His..." he pointed to the dead man, "daughter is with him."

Tina knocked on the door and waited for Taras to answer, then she entered a dining room where Taras was sitting with the woman about his age but who, exhausted, looked much older. She was supporting her head with her hand and the exhaustion on her face seemed more like relief than sadness. Taras sat opposite her, holding a clear plastic bag with a sheet of paper, the kind of writing paper that used to be popular before it was replaced with universal white A4. He placed it on the table and turned to the woman. She leaned over it and glanced at the writing.

"How do you explain this?" Taras asked.

The woman shook her head slightly.

"I don't know."

Tina stepped closer and looked at the table.

"May I?"

He passed her the page. It could hardly be called a letter.

I had my reasons.

This was all that was written on the paper.

"I don't know," the woman repeated.

"Reasons for what?" Taras insisted and got another I don't know.

"Do you think that he wanted to tell you that he had his reasons for suicide?" Taras was relentless, "Or reasons for murdering the woman in the park?"

The daughter of the dead soldier of the Foreign Legion smiled bitterly.

"You don't give up, do you? How many times do I need to tell you that my father couldn't walk? He could not have killed her even if he would have admitted to the crime a hundred times. My father was a frightfully proud person. He'd rather you thought he was a murderer than someone who slept with incontinence pads."

"I didn't say that he actually shot her," said Taras. "What I'd like to know is if he wanted to say that he had done."

She looked at him and shook her head.

"I don't understand."

"Your father was a professional soldier, trained to kill. This was all he knew, all he was," said Taras. "Then along comes some-one and shoots a woman under his window, a woman who no-body in the block of flats wants and who everyone might prefer dead rather than hanging around outside their home. If anyone around here shot her, it could have been him. I don't think it's far from this to actually imagining in his head that he had done it."

The woman smiled.

"I don't know."

"Did he ever mention the woman in the park?"

"Yes, often, and you'll probably be happy if I tell you that every time he said that he himself would beg for a mercy shot in the head if he ever sank that low. But he did not kill her. Prove to me that he could walk and I will believe you, not before that."

"After our first visit we found traces of the DNA of two peo-ple on the gun. One, I assume is his, what about the second? Will it be yours?"

She shook her head.

"I doubt it. I never picked the thing up."

"Not even when you were cleaning?"

"I never opened his drawers."

Taras looked at Tina who shook her head. No, she had no extra questions. Then he turned to the dead man's daughter.

"Do you have any receipts from doctors, prescriptions for the medication he was on?"

"I have this," said the woman, pointing to her face. "All these years… I was young when I started looking after him."

When they returned to the room the deceased man was be-ing put onto a trolley. Osterc was in the room as well. He stood to one side while they loaded the body and took it away and waited for Taras and Tina to come and stand next to him.

"Never boring in this house, is it?"

Taras laughed, which was, considering that the door to the dining room where the daughter had stayed was open, anything but appropriate.

"Where is this going, Taras?" Golob asked.

"I don't know," Taras said and turned towards him. "Until I get the ballistic report for the one in the park, this is taking us to the era of Hercule Poirot. Perhaps I should organise a séance with everyone we think might be involved and try to confuse them with guessing."

Golob blushed which was all the more obvious because he was wearing white Tyvek protection clothing. He took off his gloves and muttered, "The programmer at the NFL has been given instructions to call me as soon as he finds out what is wrong and especially when he knows how long it will take to fix. He must give me an answer today and if he still doesn't, we will take the evidence elsewhere. You will have the report on the desk by tomorrow at the latest."

Taras looked towards the table with the dried up pool of blood.

"Well, now we don't seem to be in so much of a hurry, do we?"

Golob sighed.

"And as far as those two DNA samples go…"

"Today," Golob jumped in. "I promise that this will be the first thing I do when I get to the NFL. I've taken a sample and won't need to wait for Cvilak."

"So, let us say that one of them is his," Taras continued. "And if it is, are you saying the other one cannot be his daughter's?"

Golob shook his head.

"No, the DNA samples we found on the handle and trigger of the gun are DNA of two people who are not related. That much I can be sure of, without knowing who they belong to."

*

"Bodies are mounting," said Taras when he, Tina and Osterc got out into the fresh air. He said it as someone else might say: this dog of ours, we got it a flea collar but it keeps on scratching.

"Drvarič wants to see us," said Tina. "I'm sorry but despite the fact that formally I am responsible for the case, he wants to see you as well."

Taras took his mobile out of his pocket and checked the time.

"Won't manage it. I've arranged to meet Cvilak at the IFM in half an hour's time. I suggest you excuse my absence, tick him off and then we get together at the office at around two and summarise what we know before anyone else is killed."

Only now did Tina notice that they had all along been standing next to his bike that was leaning against the wall. He unlocked the massive lock, hung it across the handlebars, nodded and rode off. She looked at Osterc.

"Shall we go and see Drvarič?"

"All right."

Everything was always all right with Osterc. Not for the first time she wondered whether this was something you learned over the years or whether, like so many other things, it's a matter of talent.

*

Cvilak was still busy when Taras called in, so he waited in the conference room on the opposite side of the corridor. He sat in one of the chairs and, partly to pass time, partly because he felt he needed to, rubbed his thighs. Muscle pain from his climb, or to be more accurate, from his descent and walking back down hill, had set in and Taras knew that worse was yet to come. The second or third day he would be going down the stairs like a robot.

"Here I am," Cvilak appeared at the door and indicated with his hand that he should follow him.

Cvilak sat at his large desk, Taras on one of the empty chairs. He tried to remember what it was that he wanted to see him about. From a drawer in front of him Cvilak produced a folder and found a sheet of paper inside.

"So, here is the final verdict in the case of the unknown woman in the park. You are aware of the dilemma: did she die a natural death, specifically due to lung cancer, or was it a violent death following a shot to or rather through the head. By the way, what would you prefer?"

"If she had to die, I would prefer the first instance, without the shot in the head."

"Unfortunately what we might prefer doesn't come into it. We have what we have. I will tell you how my profession sees it and you will see what might be useful to yours. In order for you to understand my dilemma, you should know that we see death in our branch as a singular and final, irreversible termination of life and all life processes in the entire organism of the individual. That is the definition. With this we refer to the death of the individual which is only followed a while later by the death of all tissues and organs. When that happens we talk of a tissue or organic death, which occurs in different organs at various times after the death of the individual. As such, for example brain cells deteriorate very rapidly, the cells that make up the renal tubules are also very sensitive, more resistant are muscles and veins, even more so bones and skin. There is also what we call simultaneous individual and organic death, for example in large explosions, in exposure to very high temperatures, if someone falls into a smelting oven or a volcano, for example, and in serious injuries when the body gets crushed. I am simply stating it as a theoretical possibility because we cannot of course speak of any of these in our case. Are you following what I'm saying?"

"Yes."

"In our case we thus have irreversible damage of a critical number of neurons in the cerebral hemispheres because of the injury as well as extensive bleeding because of a ruptured artery. The organism responded to both. It bled from both wounds."

"Which tells us what?" Taras asked because Cvilak paused.

"It tells us that both occurred almost simultaneously. When one and the other happened to her, she was dying but had not yet died. Then I looked more carefully at each wound separately as if the other hadn't existed. The effects of the bleeding from the pulmonary artery were as expected for the stage of her illness. If I had been brought the body without the head, I would, without a second thought, attribute the death to lung cancer."

"What if I had only brought you the head?"

Cvilak nodded.

"Yes, well, if I only had the head, I would of course say she died from the bullet, but even so I would notice what I did, which is that the responses of the body to such a forceful breach – to spare you the technical details – was unexpectedly weak."

"It means," said Taras, "that the woman's cancer breached the veins and she was bleeding, and then someone shot her in the head. In any case before this so called tissue or..."

"Organic death," Cvilak helped him. "I would say even before that. Death from bleeding of such major blood vessels can occur within minutes, especially with someone as ill as our victim. A young, healthy person can lose two to three litres of blood, for a weakened, feeble old woman like ours, a litre is enough. Five to ten minutes after the ruptured artery. That is what I wrote here."

He pointed to the page in front of him.

"But was she dead by then?"

"She was dying. Had the irreversible termination of life in all the life processes of the entire organism occurred? No. Could it have been avoided or delayed by a single second if the shot to the head had not occurred? No."

"Is the person who shot her a murderer or not?"

Cvilak laughed and shook his head.

"Now that, you see, is beyond my personal competence."

Taras turned the page so he could browse over it, as if looking for an answer for the question asked. Then he turned it again and pushed it towards Cvilak.

"Come to think of it, mine also."

He stood up, nodded at Cvilak and made his way towards the door.

"Taras…"

"Yes?"

"There is one more thing I would like to talk to you about."

He pointed to the chair and Taras obediently returned and sat down.

"You can stop me and say it's not my problem, but I need to ask."

"Go ahead…"

"What the hell are you doing to Alenka?"

He wasn't shouting, he was whispering through clenched teeth. Taras would have preferred it if he was shouting.

"I saw her in town and I almost didn't recognise her. She was sitting in that place on Cankar Street and I don't know whether she looked more absent or more drunk. Who do you think brought her home?"

"Thanks."

"Don't you 'thanks' me!"

He was so agitated his face turned red, he angrily stood up, went to the sink and poured himself some water into a tumbler. He drank it and returned to the table.

"So?"

"We've sorted it out," said Taras.

Cvilak sat down and aggressively leaned towards Taras.

"You do know that you won't get another woman like that?"

"I know."

"You do know that she's a hundred times better a person than you, don't you?"

"I know."

"You do know that you're too old to be mooching about in rented bedsits and that your pay is too low for anything else?"

"I know that too."

"And you do know it's not fair to this kid either? What will she have from a person like you? What future does this thing between you two have?"

"None," said Taras. "That's why it is over. I told you, we've sorted it."

Cvilak stopped as if he was taking in what Taras had said.

"Over?"

"Yes. Over."

Taras stood up and had reached the door when he stopped for a second time.

"I almost forgot," he said. "I wanted to ask you a favour."

"Yes?"

"You received another of my clients in refrigeration today. An elderly gentleman, suicide with firearm. I would like you to also examine his legs."

"Legs?"

"Yes, legs. Spine, hips, knees, muscles... Everything that keeps a man standing. I would like to know whether he could walk."

Cvilak nodded.

"I'll see what can be done. If he had any serious injury that X-Ray will pick up on, then I'll be able to give you an answer, otherwise I doubt it."

Taras held the handle and opened the door.

"Taras..."

Cvilak was standing behind his desk, wagging his finger at him.

"I know," said Taras. "It's over."

*

He was unlocking his bike when his phone rang. With one hand he was removing the chain, the other looking through his backpack and when he finally found it, it fell out of his hand and shattered on the ground. He swore as he pulled the chain out of the spokes where it had become entangled and two passing medical students just leaving a lecture gave each other a look of surprise. Had it said Golob on the screen?

He picked up the various pieces of his un-smart phone, put in the battery, mounted the casing over it and pressed the button on the top right in the hope that it had survived. It had. He entered his code and tried to return the call. Engaged. He put the chain away in his backpack and tried again. Engaged.

He sat on the bike and drove off. At the first red traffic lights he tried again. This time Golob answered.

"Hi, Taras! I called you, it rang and then stopped."

"I dropped the phone."

"Oh, I thought you couldn't talk, so I called Tina."

"And you called her because...?"

"I called her, or rather I tried to call you, to tell you how incredibly happy I am because Evofinder is finally up and working. And also how, I wouldn't have thought it, but it was worth the wait. I can barely wait for something like this to get to court, just let various people like Petan try to doubt my ballistic reports again."

"You called me to tell me whether the bullet cartridge case in the park matches the gun of the dead man Baloh, didn't you?"

"Indeed," Golob sounded happy.

"And you will tell me that it does, won't you?"

Silence for three to four seconds.

"How did you know?"

He didn't, but someone had shot at least one bullet from Baloh's gun, and the park is closest for a man who is unable to walk.

CHAPTER 31.

When he returned to the office he found Tina and Osterc there. Tina looked embarrassed.

"What did Drvarič have to say?" he asked.

"He said he would rather wait for you."

Taras rolled his eyes and muttered something Tina did not understand but was probably just swearing.

"When will this man let me breathe? I have long learnt not to expect him to actually help with anything but it would be progress if for once he wasn't talking non-stop shit and trying to be clever..."

Like previously he ended the sentence with something unintelligible. Again she could only assume that he was swearing.

"I'm finding it ever harder to just grin and bear him. I bet you whatever you want that the next half hour will be a complete waste of time."

"He is concerned that you might not follow any instructions he would give to me."

"What, and if he gives them to me I am more likely to?"

*

Drvarič was in a good mood. On the desk in front of him he had a copy of Cvilak's report and, once they all sat down on the chairs in his office, he turned it towards them and pointed to a paragraph in the typed text.

"She died a natural death, didn't she?"

"She did," Taras agreed just to get it over with as soon as possible.

"Therefore this is not a murder? OK, so we tick this off. Now there is no need to concern ourselves with that idiot, is there?"

"Which idiot?" asked Taras.

"The one bragging on Facebook that he will... I don't know what. Everyone on Facebook seems to be bragging about something these days."

"The Nazi?"

"Well, he's not really a Nazi because of one stupidity, Taras!" He didn't mention which stupidity he had in mind.

"No need, is there?"

"We still don't know who shot the woman."

"Well, but now it's not important any more." Drvarič stopped and thought for a while. "Although the GPD did ask me why we haven't visited this 'Nazi' as you call him. Perhaps it would be a good idea to pay him a visit. You have the search warrant, don't you?"

"No," said Taras. "How could I have it?"

"Oh, yes," Drvarič sighed and produced a white envelope from his drawer. "You weren't here yesterday, so I put it away."

"I was though," said Tina.

"Yes, that's true," said Drvarič, holding the envelope for a few moments before pushing it towards them into a sort of no-man's-zone between Taras and Tina.

"Well, here you are. When will you go and visit him?"

The question, like the envelope, was directed somewhere into the space between them. Taras looked at Tina and raised his hand slightly at the elbow with two fingers extended.

"May I suggest at some point towards the end of the week. Tomorrow we still have a lot of work with this Baloh guy."

Drvarič nodded and a shadow descended across his face, Taras would say a shadow of genuine worry. Worry was in fact Drvarič's only authentic emotion.

"It would not be right to keep them waiting now that they..."

He frowned. "Does this thing with Baloh spoil anything for us?"

Taras stayed silent. So did Tina.

"Well, does it?"

"Everything points to suicide," Tina took pity on him. "He wrote a brief note which we could understand as a hint that he had shot the woman in the park."

For a second Drvarič's brow darkened but then it dawned on him.

"Oh, well, see, that's even better."

"Of course we cannot know for sure until we get the ballistic report," said Taras.

"We know," said Tina and fell silent when she saw Taras's face.

"What do we know?" Drvarič was quick to ask.

She bit her tongue but it was too late. And anyway, it's Taras's fault. How is she supposed to guess what she can and what she can't say?

"We received the ballistic report for the dead man's gun. It is this gun that shot the bullet which…" She wanted to say… murdered the woman in the park, but she paused…

"Went through her head," Taras helped her.

"Really?" Drvarič was pleased. "Well, you see, how things sort themselves out."

Tina wanted to comment, but Taras got in first.

"Yes, indeed sometimes they do."

"I will let Kristan know that we've sorted out this mess and that there is no need to delve into it further."

"Right," said Taras.

Tina glanced sideways at him and he pretended not to notice.

"Well, it's summer," Drvarič sighed. "Sometimes I get the impression that we are the only people working. When are you going on holiday? Have you put in your requests?"

"Second and third week in July," said Taras.

"Down to the Adriatic?"

"Corsica."

"Wow! A beer there costs seven euros."

Taras smiled.

"Well, not that that would mean anything to you," Drvarič added and talked about Corsica for about a minute. His wife and he had hired a car and got stuck in a traffic jam between…

"What's that road between Francardo and some mountain pass?"

He tried to recall the name of the road where he had come

across a truck which did not want to move even a little to one side and their encounter caused a queue of impatient drivers to build up behind them. He couldn't remember and gave up.

"You should take Alenka to Bonifacio. It's a town right on the southern tip, built on the top of some limestone cliffs. Crazy."

"I will," said Taras but Drvarič had already turned to Tina.

"What about you?"

"I don't know. I haven't made any plans yet."

"Osterc?"

"The kids are going to summer school down to Premantura on the coast, we will stay at home. There are things to do round..."

Drvarič was no longer listening to him.

"And how is Brajc doing?"

"He's being sent home today," said Taras. "He got off lightly."

"If I may," Osterc jumped in. "I'd like to get off a little early today because I need to get to the hospital. He asked me to take him home."

Drvarič nodded and then paused as if he had momentarily forgotten why he had called them to his office.

"Well, if that's it?" Taras stood up and turned towards the door. Tina picked up the envelope with the search warrant.

"Yes, of course," said Drvarič.

He watched them leave the office, wondering what on earth he had forgotten to tell them. It all seemed to go too well for it to bode well.

*

"Now, here is what we'll do," said Taras when they had all returned to their desks. "Anyone needing a coffee get one now, then we'll put our phones on the desk, all of us, me included, switch them off, and have a chat. Is the coffee machine working yet?"

Only he and Tina went to get coffee.

He insisted that they really switched off their phones.

"I'll go first, you two let me say what I have to say. If you think of anything, if I miss the point on something, note it down and you can tell me at the end, OK?"

"In fact," said Tina and waited for both of them to turn to her.

"I would like to start, if I may. As far as I know this is still my case and whatever we do here will reflect on me and not on you two."

Taras looked at Osterc whose face was as expressionless as usual.

"All right, Taras?" Tina asked.

He nodded and shrugged his shoulders, as if to say, of course.

She stepped to the whiteboard, picked up the sponge from the shelf below and wiped away everything that had so far been written on it.

"Ooof," she could hear Taras groan but paid no attention to him.

"I too have felt from the very beginning that I cannot breathe. Perhaps I should have gotten all this out earlier."

She took the marker and wrote *Mici* on the board.

"This is the only name we have. In any case, it's better than *unknown woman*."

Under this name she wrote *Baloh* and under him *positive ballistic test*, *DNA* with *X2* in brackets, and the word *admission* with a question mark next to it.

"So, we have the woman in the park who was shot. What the court decides about her will depend on what Cvilak gives them. We don't know the actual cause of death and until we're given other instructions, we are also not really interested. We have a weapon used in this and a suspect who is the owner of this weapon. The problem is that he was apparently not capable of committing this crime, whatever it is, whether murder or desecration of the body, because he was an invalid, or incapable of walking."

Under the word *admission* she wrote *unable to walk*, also with a question mark.

"I have spoken to Cvilak and asked him to pay attention at the autopsy to whether he could walk or not," said Taras.

"Well, that's the next point I wanted to say. I want all..." she almost said all four of us, but her gaze focused briefly on Brajc's empty desk. "All three of us to know what each other is doing rather than me having to guess in front of Drvarič what I can and cannot say."

"*Mea culpa*," said Taras.

"We," said Osterc and also corrected himself. "The two of us have been together for ten years. We almost do it telepathically."

"And I don't like to explain things that I am not convinced of myself," said Taras. "That's all it is."

"Golob and his team found DNA traces of two people on the gun," Tina continued. "Tomorrow we shall know whether one of these belongs to Baloh or not. The daughter who looks after him also had access to the gun but if the one sample belongs to Baloh, the other DNA cannot be his daughter's. These relationships can be determined from DNA samples. So, if Golob confirms that one of the samples belongs to Baloh and Cvilak also tells us that Baloh was capable of leaving the first floor and returning without anyone's help, then we shall slowly close the file and begin to prepare the case for court."

She looked at Taras as if she was expecting him to object.

He didn't and she continued.

"What though, if Cvilak says that his daughter was not mistaken? Who else could have had access to the gun?"

She turned to the whiteboard as she spoke and wrote a new name onto it.

"It could have been the painter and decorator Franc Zupet from Višnja Gora. He was doing some painting in the block of flats and when we first visited Baloh his flat was also being painted. Not by Baloh himself, of course. Or?"

"No, certainly not," said Taras.

"Then we also have someone who calls himself Painter Franc online becoming all enthusiastic with the posts of Ignac Jakin, who is our next name."

She wrote Jakin's name next to Baloh and under it bulleted *photographs and posts*, *Facebook* and *Instagram*. She also wrote *Slovenske Novice* and added a question mark.

"Why did you tell Drvarič that we would only call in on him towards the end of the week? Why not tomorrow?" she asked Taras. "We have a search warrant, let's check his GSR particles, compare his DNA with that on Baloh's gun and that's it."

"I was intending to do it tomorrow. I just wanted Drvarič to spread the rumour that we are not that interested in him."

"Is that why you told Drvarič that the case is more or less

concluded?"

"Isn't it better that he and all his whisperers think that it is? If nothing else, it'll get them off our backs. Beside those..." he pointed at the whiteboard on which Tina had written DNA, GSR next to Jakin's name "...I would add testing, a polygraph test. It won't do any harm."

"We'd need to book that a day or so in advance," said Tina.

"Yes, well," Taras muttered. "I did it on Monday."

"And when was I supposed to find out about it?"

He sighed and tapped his fingers on the table.

"Let us make clear where we stand. Nobody will be happier if you conduct this the way you think it should go. But get on with it. Someone has to..." he looked for the word and found it, "...dictate the pace."

"Is there anything else I don't know?"

He nodded.

"Indeed there is a minor thing. Tomorrow morning I am meeting up with a colleague from Sova[18]. Before we step into any more shit, I'd still like to know why we didn't get that warrant. I suggest, only suggest, that you two go and find Zupet and then we can go and visit Jakin."

Tina wrote *polygraph* next to Jakin and stepped back to look at the board.

"Have we forgotten anything? Do we need to add Mrs Opeka from the fourth floor? What's her name again?"

"Marija," said Taras. "Like Jakin's mother. I don't think we do. I visited her the day before yesterday," he gave Tina an embarrassed glance, "to get a kind of chronicle of their building's community. By the way, who will you take with you for the house search tomorrow?"

"What do you mean?"

"Me or Osterc? We don't all three need to hang around there."

"You, of course. You visited Jakin with me the previous time."

"I am asking you because in that case, Osterc, I'd ask you to look through my notes and add precise dates for everyone. When they were born, died and things like that?"

---

18 *Sova* is the acronym by which the Slovenian Intelligence and Security Agency (*Slovenska obveščevalno-varnostna agencija*) is most commonly referred to.

"Of course," said Osterc. "What about Vadnal? Am I still looking into him?"

He turned to Taras and when he didn't respond, looked at Tina.

"I have nothing on that," she said. "It's not even our case."

"Did you find anything?" Taras asked.

"I looked through the material Brajc and I gathered and his personal data in the register. He was registered as living in a multi-residence house in Moste. I called there but nobody knew him. If he ever lived there, it must have been years, perhaps decades ago and he never bothered to change his permanent address."

"Did you try his former wife?"

"Not yet, should I do that?"

"Why do you even think, or rather" Tina corrected herself, "assume that the cases are connected? Just because of the *Sieg heil* writing? I found out this morning they were not written by the same author."

Taras smiled uneasily.

"Even *assume* is too strong a word. But, just think about when the first graffiti was done."

"The day we discovered the woman's body, before half past four in the afternoon," said Osterc.

"Yes, it must have been there then because someone sent a message about it to *Delo* from the Oton Župančič Library at half past four. What about the other one?"

"At night. The report by Pestner and his guys does not mention it and they were there immediately after the shooting."

"Precisely. And because, if I understand you correctly, Tina, the authors are not the same person, there are theoretically three possibilities: that it is a coincidence, that we are looking for an individual or a group that has begun attacking a certain kind of people, or that there is someone in the background who wants to divert the attention at Metelkova to someone else, in this case the neo-Nazis. How could they have thought of this?"

"The newspaper," said Tina. "You forget that *Slovenske Novice* had it on their front page."

Taras smiled.

"I didn't forget. You are forgetting that the issue with the article about the murder of the homeless woman in the park and the photo of the *Sieg heil* bench was published a day after the graffiti appeared. The second writing happened in the night, the evening of the day we discovered the body, when nobody would have seen the article. The author of the second sign must have seen the first *Sieg heil* somewhere else – live."

"Why didn't he then send a photo to the papers?" Osterc asked. "If he just wrote it, there's not much point."

"I don't know," said Taras hesitantly. "Perhaps it was enough that we knew about it."

"How did he know we knew?" Osterc asked.

Taras looked at Tina who shook her head.

"Taras, this is your fixed idea. I don't have a clue."

Taras stared out of the window overlooking the façade of the Natural History Museum, scratched his week-old stubble, then waved dismissively, "Right, no point. Just a fixed idea of mine. Forget about Vadnal."

*

At four Osterc checked his watch and announced his departure.

"I'm going to collect Brajc to take him home."

"The nurses will be grateful," said Taras. "Say hello from me and tell him that I will call in to see him in a day or two."

"There is another possibility," said Tina as Osterc was already at the door. "Who says that whoever wrote the *Sieg heil* on Metelkova didn't send this one to *Delo* too?"

"What do you mean?" Taras asked.

"Perhaps he did send it but they didn't publish it. They don't publish everything they are sent."

Without saying anything, Taras reached for his phone, switched it on, and searched for the phone number he wanted. Then he dialled the number from his landline.

"Hello Valič," he greeted the journalist and continued without giving him a chance to even return the greeting. "Tell me, was the photo of the bench with *Sieg heil!* on it that you published the only one of its kind you received last week?"

When he had thanked him and put down the receiver he

looked at Tina and smiled.

"The following day they received another photo from the same address. He no longer has the mail and cannot remember the precise time, but it was before twelve. My respects, Ms Lanc."

He turned to Osterc.

"You will ask your wife to help us again."

"And what am I looking for this time? Probably not for this Ignac's membership card, or am I?"

"No," said Taras. "Ask her to check which name appeared twice. Both on Tuesday and Wednesday."

*

"How simple most things are when they are explained to us boneheads," said Taras when Osterc left. "Once again, respects, Tina."

"Oh, it just occurred to me."

"And how did it occur to you to visit Alenka? Apparently you spoke to her yesterday?"

She gave him a questioning look.

"It wasn't by chance, was it?"

She reached for her laptop and searched for a file on it.

"There is something I want to show you. Something I should have shown you before."

CHAPTER 32.

"This."

She showed him the footage from both security cameras and put in front of him the page with her notes on the times and description of events.

He looked at it without saying anything. First the information from the camera at the GPD on Štefan Street and then that from the camera on the hotel.

"And this is supposed to be the gunshot?" he asked.

"Yes."

"Are you certain? It could be anything."

She then showed him the shot from outside the hotel taken during her night action.

"This is from my Beretta."

"What did you do?"

She told him, what and when, and he looked at her with surprise, almost admiration. He seemed amused by the whole thing. He looked at both shots again and wrote out a few numbers on a sheet of paper.

"But I told you I didn't shoot her?"

It sounded like a question.

"Taras, I lied for you in court and I will do it again, if necessary. I was there when you pressed the man's head into the snow for so long he pissed himself. Yesterday you forced someone to swallow an SD card. How am I supposed to know..."

"What I am capable of?"

She stayed silent.

"And why would I do this?"

What is she supposed to say? Out of mercy towards...

"You talked about that cat that could not be helped... What did you do with it?"

"I know someone who maintains that people are not cats."

"And I know someone who says they are."

Once again he checked the notes on the times.

"You know that our guns are traceable? They are all in Golob's Evofinder."

"I know."

"Surely you don't think that I managed to trick him?"

"You wouldn't have had to."

He thought for a moment and then nodded.

"I was the one who brought Golob the cartridge case, wasn't I?"

"And you had Baloh's gun at the time. And perhaps you don't remember what you said when we first met, on that drive to Bohinj?"

"I do remember that you came to the first meeting in a mini and you then changed into jeans and brought some gaiters with you."

"You spoke about how terribly stupid criminals are and always leave traces behind, and how that if you ever lose your job and join the criminals, you will collect cigarette butts from bars and leave them around as decoy evidence?"

"Oh, that?"

"Yes, and if we leave this aside; how is it possible that you didn't see or at least hear anything in the park? Where on earth were you?"

"I was sitting in the car with headphones over my ears, listening to Mötorhead from the *Discman*."

"You what?"

"At full volume."

"Listening to Mötorhead?"

He repeated what he had said. He spoke in a jaunty, happy voice. It really seemed as if the whole thing was amusing him.

"And as far as this footage goes... Things are not always as they seem. If anyone were to accuse me of murdering the woman in the park, I would use this in court myself."

She gave him a puzzled look.

He stood up, glanced at her legs under the table as if to check what she was wearing on her feet, grabbed his backpack and walked to the door.

"I'll call you in fifteen minutes, we can meet in the park. Change into trainers on the way."

*

"Ready?"

"For what, Taras?"

He was waiting for her next to the bench where the woman had been found and was holding his phone. It was almost an hour since he had left the office, not fifteen minutes. He gave her the keys to his car which she took hesitantly.

"I didn't have a clue that this was what was bugging you. I thought that that it was to do with that talk of ours just... as a talk. But that I would kill someone like this? That would be too much even for me."

"Taras..."

"No, no, it's fine."

He wiped away the droplets of sweat that were appearing on his forehead, and lifted the page he was holding in his hand.

"According to the data you made a note of, I had two minutes and twenty, or in fact, let us be accurate, twenty-one seconds to get from Štefan Street to this bench, and then fifteen seconds to shoot the woman and drive away. Right?"

"I can't recall the precise numbers right now."

He showed her the sequence of events with the times she had written out.

"Right," she nodded. "That'll be right."

"Two minutes and twenty-one seconds is enough for the walk from the underpass to the bench. I measured it as I was waiting for you. Easily, I didn't even have to run. Now let's see about the second stage of my supposed murderous hike. My car is over there, parked in the very same spot it was parked last Monday. Do you know how hard it was to find the owner of the car that was parked there before and persuade him that he needed to move his vehicle in the interest of a criminal investigation?"

"Taras, I am not saying you did shoot her. I'm just saying that..."

"That you can't, given the evidence..." he waved the page in front of her face, "...see how anyone else could have done it."

She did not answer him.

"You see, that is why I am the chief criminal inspector and..." he feigned unease, "also the owner of that vehicle over there."

He raised his archaic phone and placed his thumb on the button in the middle.

"You have fifteen seconds to convince the jury of my guilt."

"Come on, Taras!"

"Start counting from my signal to the moment the car drives out of the parking space."

She looked at the distance from the bench to the car.

"You don't need to be Usain Bolt for this. You will lose."

"We'll see. Ready? Three, two, one, go!"

She thought the whole thing was silly, but she ran. If this is how he wants it, let him! In a few seconds she reached the low stone wall of the park along Župančič Street, jumped over it, ran across the road, round the car, and thrust the key into the door... She tried to turn it. It wouldn't turn. The lock was jammed.

"Slowly, turn it slowly," Taras was shouting from the other side of the road. "Did I forget to tell you that the lock on the driver's side doesn't work? You can lock it but not unlock it. It is possible if it is raining and it gets wet, otherwise it doesn't turn to the right at all. I should have taken it to the mechanic long ago to get him to oil it or something, but I didn't. And it didn't rain at all on Monday, if I am not mistaken?"

She returned to the park and they walked back to the bench together.

"Murder of Old Lady, take two. Three, two..."

Once more she rushed towards the wall, more determined this time, jumped over it and stopped on the pavement. Driving past her, wildly honking its horn, was some kind of large urban crossover.

"It's true that it would be easier at night," said Taras when he came after her. "Should we wait till the evening? It will be easier with the heat then, as well."

Tina returned to the bench without saying anything.

"So, take three. Three, two..."

She ran wildly towards the car, reached it without problems this time, unlocked it from the passenger side, ran round the car, sat at the wheel, pushed the key into the ignition, turned it... Vroom, vroom... the car jolted for a centimetre or so and then came to a halt. She once again turned the key and the same thing happened.

"Wait, wait!" Taras shouted from the opposite side of the road.

Moodily she waited for him.

"Look, this is a diesel, an old, tired diesel. Its glow plugs need a little time. You turn the key slightly to get them going, like this, then you have to wait for the light to go off. If you don't wait, the engine just dies. It takes a few seconds for it to warm up, but who cares, what's a few seconds, eh?"

"Not quite there," said Taras when she managed at her fourth attempt to actually move the car. "Would you like to try again?"

"How long?"

Droplets of sweat had also appeared on Tina's forehead.

"Perhaps we should come to conclusions on the basis of more data. A single measurement would easily be dismissed at court."

"How long?"

"If I can read this thing correctly," he pulled a face and blinked at the phone, "it says 29.84. You are only fourteen seconds and eighty-four milliseconds short of the record. Are you sure you wouldn't like to try it again? With a little hard work, you might get closer to it in two or three years."

She looked at him wearily, though she wanted to laugh.

"We'll go for coffee, you're buying. And you will wait for me because I need to pop home and change."

As she stood under the shower she felt she was washing away something much heavier and dirtier than sweat. He hadn't killed her, he hadn't shot her, she kept thinking and was suddenly ashamed for having even considered the thought.

She stepped out of the shower, dried herself with a towel and ran into the bedroom where she had left her phone that was now ringing. It was Taras.

"Your doorbell is still not working," he said.

She should have hung up. She should have told him to wait downstairs. She should have, but she didn't. She pressed the door release button.

*

"Alenka knows," she said.

They had been lying on the bed for a while, staring at the ceiling.

"I know."

"And?"

Taras stayed silent.

"She knows, and at the same time hopes that it isn't true, and if it is, that it will end," she said. "And when she will no longer be able to turn the other way, you will move away because she will kick you out."

With accentuated irony, she added, "And will we then start living together happily ever after? With kids and all that?"

He stayed silent.

"I could leave Aleksander. It wouldn't be nice, but I could. You cannot leave Alenka. And that's it."

He sighed, continued to look at the ceiling and began talking without turning towards her.

"Over the last few days I have tried to take a look at myself from a cloud. In my wise old age, I have learnt that this helps when a person gets lost. After all, I am a criminal investigator. I have spent my life learning how to see things from a distance in order to get the entire picture."

"And what did you see?"

He saw a man, frolicking around with a much younger woman. A beautiful young woman with whom he also likes to talk just as much as he likes removing her knickers. He then takes a shower, gets dressed, puts on his shoes and leaves with a mixed feeling of triumph and guilt, at a ratio of around ninety to ten. When he reaches the car it is fifty, fifty, by the time he gets home it is ten to ninety. Then he says to himself, never again, until the following morning when he once again sees this young woman and his solid promise begins melting away like April snow. It is like tempting an alcoholic every day with an open bottle of beer.

She would probably not like this comparison.

If he climbs up one cloud further, he sees a man to whom eventually sleeping with her and trying to meet her for coffees in dark corners of various cafés not frequented by friends, acquaintances and colleagues, constantly nervously looking over his shoulder, is no longer enough. How wonderful if he could take this young woman to the cinema occasionally, a weekend down on the coast, or anywhere where he could introduce her to friends and revel in their envy. If he could sleep over rather than just sleep with her. This much to start with. Children? Again? From this cloud it seems impossible, but usually these things change fast and perhaps he might then even have a son.

"You should have had a son," Alenka said often.

He mocked people who were not strong enough to give up their bad habits that destroy them. Brajc and his greed and laziness. And now, was he any better? He will not mention this comparison either.

If he climbs yet another cloud higher, he sees Alenka and her tears as she looks at photos of their thousands of moments together, arranged in a confusing but beautiful album, and he cannot imagine a life without her. Thinking that she might one day simply disappear from his life, all the previous images just fade away. Until the next day.

"Well, what did you see, Taras?"

He turned to her and smiled.

"I saw someone in a hurry."

Thursday

CHAPTER 33.

Taras sat in the corner of the café and kept checking the clock on the wall. Silva had already put a cup in the coffee maker but he told her to wait a little with his order. After five minutes of sitting at an empty table, he thought that he spotted the acquaintance he was waiting for through the large glass front on the south side of the café, but the guy just walked past, so he was no longer sure. He called his number but it was unavailable. Five minutes later he appeared and Taras could have sworn that it was him the first time round.

"Did you miss the place the first time?" he asked him after they had greeted each other.

His acquaintance smiled, "I've missed a lot of things, well, that's why..."

He glanced around the café, eyed over Taras's cycling backpack that was hanging across the back of his chair, and noticed the coatrack that now, in mid-summer, looked pretty useless in the corner at the end of the short serving counter.

"Is your phone in your backpack?"

"Yes," said Taras.

"Remove the battery."

Taras sighed, pulled the phone from his backpack and showed it to him.

"Oh, what kind of MacGyver-phone is this?"

"Wouldn't it be enough to just switch it off?" Taras asked.

"That's what the Saudis in Istanbul thought, if you remember that small matter, but it wasn't."

After Taras had removed the battery and SIM card, his acquaintance stuffed Taras's backpack into his own bag and hung it on the coatrack about three metres away from their table.

"We did some experiments when I was still working on stuff like that and nothing spoils a recording more than the gurgling of a coffee machine. Everything else can be removed with filters, this is impossible."

For years Taras and Alenka lived near a railway line and he could imagine what his acquaintance was saying. It had seemed that every time he wanted to listen to something interesting on TV a train passed by. And as if on cue, Silva switched on the machine to make Taras's coffee.

"White coffee with cold milk," his acquaintance ordered.

"Where are you now?" he asked him when Silva brought the coffees and disappeared behind her counter.

"Still at Sova, just that I have been moved to the archives where, if I can use a metaphor, I shuffle files around. They would probably prefer if I didn't even go to work but I will not afford them the joy of dismissing me unfairly. We will see who endures longer. I can stay sorting out files until I retire, if that is what I decide. Besides, in the twenty years I've been at the Agency I helped set up, I have created quite a collection. There are thousands of photographs with names and all the other associated data. Upon any possible sign of trouble I might come across in life, I have no qualms about them ending up on the internet. I would make time for it. What about you?"

"No change. Ljubljana PU, violent crime and sexual offences, mostly murders. I imagine you know why I asked to meet you?"

His acquaintance nodded.

"I heard. Because of this woman in that park. What's the name again?"

"Of the park or the woman?"

"The park. The woman, as far as I know, doesn't have a name yet."

"Everyone calls it whatever they want. It has been known as Lenin Park the longest."

"That's the one next to Figovec Inn?"

"Yes."

"You always knew how to step on a mine, Taras. Do you do it deliberately or does it just happen?"

"Talent," said Taras. "I even try to avoid it, but it seems there's no other way."

"What exactly are you interested in?"

"Why I initially did not get approval for my request for a search warrant for someone called Ignac Jakin, and why I got it later?"

"Because of a mix-up," his acquaintance smiled.

"Meaning?" Taras asked.

"A mix-up," he repeated. "When a new master appears there is panic at the top. T'was ever thus. For a while now nobody has known where to put this Nazi apprentice. Or perhaps they were just testing the ground, seeing where they might be able to place him. You know why a dog licks its own balls?"

"What do you mean, didn't they know where to put him? Is he not a member of one of these neo-Nazi groups?"

"Yes, he is, but... *ganz unten*. Only just recruited. It took a while for those who panicked to check who he is, how high up he is and whether what he did, or was supposed to have done, was a lone act or whether he was following instructions. It's summer and New Age Nazis also like to go on holidays. Very much, it seems."

"Right, let's slow down," said Taras. "What exactly are we talking about?"

"We are talking about what is happening all around us. You're not blind."

He sighed and gave Taras a quizzical look.

"Do you want to hear the whole long story before I tell you whether this person indeed killed the woman whose case you are handling, or would you prefer just a simple yes or no?"

"Did he?"

"I don't know."

Taras laughed. Silva brought them two glasses of water and they waited for her to return to her bar.

"Tell me," said Taras. "Clear my horizons."

"Thank you. Every so often I feel the need to trust someone. It is a kind of self-verification, to make sure I am not crazy. I've been following this story closely. I still am."

"Go ahead," said Taras. "Perhaps you'll discover that the blooms of evil have also already settled in my body."

His acquaintance laughed.

"I think you know that you are immune to that. People like you don't march along. I have yet to meet someone so allergic to crowds. I remember Alenka moaning how you have panic attacks every time you go close to a shopping centre. By the way, how is she?"

"She's fine."

"Give her my greetings."

Taras nodded and tried to remember what his acquaintances wife's name was, if he was indeed still married, but he didn't have to because his friend was already talking again.

"The story begins years ago," he began. "When today's masters first became the caretakers of our country. Years ago and with our agency. We were the first. It was with us that they tested the assault on the state. At the time they put one of their own at the head of Sova. This is not strange in itself, everyone does it. The problem wasn't that he was incompetent or because he was just being loyal, the problem was that this person was and still is a neo-Nazi. There are photos of him where he appeared in public with his head shaved in the company of these skinheads. Just type his name into Google, add Nazi, and you will find it. The only difference was that he was wearing a blue jacket and they wore black. But because these photos were about fifteen years old, we dismissed it as the madness of youth. We were all mad when we were young, we both know that..."

"I dunno. My memory is fading."

His acquaintance laughed.

"Mine has also always been rather selective. Well, the dumb ones then go on to join the Nazis, the less dumb ones regret it until the day they die."

He poured some sugar into his coffee and stirred it.

"Honestly, have you never wanted to hit your bike across the head of some migrant from further South in the Balkans when they were behaving in Ljubljana as if back home some village near Doboj?"

"You forget that I'm a policeman. We actually did things like that."

This time he laughed so much that he spilt a few droplets of coffee on the table.

"Yes, I forget. At the time I was still studying anthropology and was spreading around images of a multicultural paradise. Well, basically, we thought this person would come to his senses but then it began. Clearly every new head puts his own people in key positions and it is expected that there would be some kind of purge which is nothing to do with capable-incapable criteria but politically acceptable or not, but this guy... You see, Slovenia is a small place and if they bring a new colleague into your department who says over morning coffee that Hitler had the balls to do such and such, then you know that the man at the top is certainly very much a still active neo-Nazi. Without any trace of finesse. Hitler had the balls? What can you even say to that? And you will have to work with this person. I think we were unique in Europe at the time. But nobody paid much attention."

"Did you not even think about throwing him out of the office?" Taras asked. "For a start."

"I don't doubt that you would have done so and unfortunately that would also be the only appropriate response. I just told him he was an idiot. He laughed at me and then reported me to the boss. He also laughed and said I was taking things too seriously and that I should not see things as just black and white. That we need to consider everything in a balanced manner. That was just about the time the state broadcaster also began using the word."

Two men walked into the shop. Taras's acquaintance eyed them over and watched them as they looked around the place, choosing where to sit.

"Paranoia is not as hard as many people think. It befits the natural state of humans, we have just become lazier over our comfortable millennia," he said when the newcomers chose a table at the opposite end of the café.

"Very soon we realised why they had sent us this man. The task given to the new general director was in fact not to do his job. At the time Slovenia was buying quite a lot of weapons and any intelligence service of any decent state would be bound to monitor the purchases of military material. Even the Minister of Defence warned that he had arms dealers wandering round his building, yet our service did nothing at all. It didn't even check up on the people who were involved in the deals, even though it should have investigated everyone – from what and how much they drank, what car they drove around in, the weekend houses they were buying, the drugs they were pumping into their veins, who they were sleeping with... No, we were not interested in this. All we were interested in was finding any kind of stuff with which we could throw shit at the former president of this country. This was two times difficult for us because these idiots actually believed such stuff existed but that it was not possible to find it because we, the old force at Sova were hiding it all from them."

Two teenage girls walked into the café, probably from the nearby Economics Faculty, though students were not among the regulars at this place. They preferred the joints along Ig Street and Taras liked it that way. They sat at a table close to Taras and his interlocutor but wherever they would have chosen to sit in this small café, they could not really be far from them anyway. Even before ordering they brought out their phones and began sharing shots.

"Should I ask them to also put their phones into the bag?"

"You can joke as much as you want, Taras. Where were we?"

"Arms sales."

"No, we covered that. You know the outcome, anyone with half an ounce of brain does. Stick the messenger in jail, the only one to get locked up, everyone else is free, some of them here, most of them in the Cayman Islands. But we were talking about neo-Nazis. So, very soon we had a whole litter of people around us who esteemed Hitler's balls, and we could only thank the fact that they were truly completely incompetent at doing the work they had been chosen to do for any freedom or autonomy that we managed to hold on to. Then we still managed to complete the report on the activities of extremist groups in Slovenia that Sova is obliged to hand to the Parliamentary Commission for the Supervision of the Intelligence and Security Services. Before it reached them, it of course landed on the desk of our General Director. There was no response for a while – of course he was waiting for instructions – then he returned it to us saying that it was imbalanced, that there was no mention of left-wing extremism. Of course there wasn't, because there isn't any in Slovenia unless you include people like the organisers of the annual pride parade. They actually told us to take photos of all the anarchist *A*s we could find in Ljubljana and find their authors or at least possible authors..."

He laughed and circled with his hand in front of his face.

"Crazy. We resisted and because at the time they were still not that confident, they stopped, we didn't have to go collecting *A*s but it still ended up in the report. Together with demonstrations of a decade earlier against the Bush-Putin summit in Slovenia, entirely benign and outside the time frame that the report was supposed to cover. In its original form the report on right wing extremism was eleven pages long. Only four came to parliament. By comparison, for example, the Austrian report is sixty-five pages long. And what they did publish in the end was a secondary school essay. And do you know what's interesting about it? It's funny, but any average person can easily discern which parts are original, meaning the stuff we wrote, and which parts were added later, by them. Do you know how? Simply by looking at the sentences and grammar. These people never use compound sentences and commas."

"And what was on the missing seven pages?"

"In a roundabout way, what concerns you and your difficulties. In a small town – there's no need to name it because you can also google it – there was a youth section of a party, some of the members of which were neo-Nazis. They attended various events, some of a more sports and recreational nature, others different, and of course everyone in this town knew they were neo-Nazis. What was new was that we found out that these neo-Nazi members were being trained at military training facilities. The initiative came from the party and the idea was put forward by someone who lived close to the training facilities and had access to the structures of the Slovenian Army, so he could organise training sessions at times when the ranges were not being used. The Slovenian Army was basically their sponsor. At first it provided the space, later even the instructors."

"I read about this," said Taras. "Didn't they sort it out though?"

"They didn't do anything. The explanation was that they were doing it outside work hours. The idea was in fact not even that original. Similar processes were taking place at the same time in the Czech Republic, Slovakia and Hungary. In their cases, the motives of the politicians, the people in power, as to how to use these people are much clearer. It is not even about simple ideology any more. These young people probably feel good for being under the auspices of someone because they know that when their sponsors come into power, they themselves will be able to do whatever they want. They will be able to sow terror and division, threaten political rivals, basically do anything to maintain a permanent impression of being under siege and thus keep their party in power for as long as possible."

"Did they shoot the woman in the park?"

"One thing at a time. Allow me the joy of explaining. When things go so far that we start counting ourselves, I will call upon you as a witness. You know, when they start handing out veteran pensions."

Taras laughed.

"First we need to win."

"Justice always wins," said his acquaintance. "It is always the same and always ends the same way, only that it takes time and a lot of damage is done in the meantime. But, if I can continue, the connection between the hard core of the party and street hooligans is the party's number two. He is their ideological godfather, a figure who works as an inspiration. There is a photo of the visit of the youth section from this small place to Parliament, meeting both the neo-Nazi and the number two. Because of the authoritarian structure of the party, it is always clear who's at the top. If you want to know what direction the party is going in, any party, you need to look at who is number two. About a year ago, number two in the party was replaced because the old number two had become too popular and was, as we would say, removed by promotion when he was sent to Brussels where he is leading a very comfortable life. The choice of the new number two, and with this also the direction of the party, coincided with the trial where the leader was accused of corruption and also sent to jail. As you know, protesters gathered outside the court at his trial and it then became clear to him that this is a support base that he could mobilise. They were mostly old men. We followed the trial and the protests and... that's nothing. With these people you cannot break up a demonstration, you can't even get your own honest folk to counter demonstrate. Do you remember the anti-government protests a few years ago?"

"I do. I was on call at the station, waiting for the call. We all were."

"If you stop the footage of neo-Nazi demonstration disrupters at the right point, you will find the face of one of those who visited number two in Parliament. Or, if you remember the events before the revolt, when a group of unknowns came to Metelkova where the banners for the demonstrations were being made, and left their Molotovs and stones there? Fortunately, this was noticed by the people there and they contacted the media. It was reported on before the police even got to Metelkova. As you know yourself, there are people in Metelkova who maintain good, or let us say tight contacts with certain members of the police force. In the style – we're here, we acknowledge the occasional joint, but we're trying to maintain some kind of order and make sure there's no trouble. Don't send us your *jugend* to shit on our heads and everything will be fine."

"I know. When Metelkova was being created, I was one of those policemen."

His acquaintance nodded, "Well, indeed. And after their visit following the report because of the Molotovs at Metelkova, one of these policemen told me, 'We know what this is about.' Of course there are costs involved in training these people. All these activities cost money. Those spoiling the demonstrations got fifty euros per head, which is bizarrely little. At about the time the recruitment of these hooligans happened, the party began to come up with hate statements, it began spreading intolerance through social networks which had a specific effect. These statements could then be found on the websites of Slovene neo-Nazi organisations. Basically, they provided an ideological scene that has become the basis for organising people in the field."

"An interesting story," Taras admitted. "Why don't you go to the media with it?"

His acquaintance gave him a hurt look.

"Where do you live, mate? All this that I am saying – this is the fifth time I'm going over it – can be found by clicking twice on Google. This is all public. When journalists found out that neo-Nazis were active in the party's youth wing in this small town and began writing about it, the party suddenly informed the public that the youth section was being abolished. Officially because of a lack of active members. If you look at the reports by the executive committee of the party which are also not hard to find, they indicate the exact opposite. These people were very much active even after the official abolition. They were supposedly abolished yet you can still read that the executive committee thanks some of their neo-Nazi members for posters and such. Of course state TV did not report on it. Good converts discovered that cooperating with the right-wing is worth their while, even though the Right was not even in power. Sometimes this is not even so important."

"Interesting," said Taras. "And why am I now allowed to interrogate that Nazi and was previously not given the warrant?"

"This party war I am talking to you about doesn't work to order, or it does so very rarely. It works on instincts, tries to guess things, and sometimes gets it wrong. This is why the masters in the background are tolerant towards it, prepared to forget the occasional unnecessary, overextended stupidity. If nothing else, it comes in handy when defining their new limits. After the initial confusion and a reflexive response which was protectionist, they calmed down and realised that your client, if involved, did this on his own and that now when they are in power, this could spoil their plans. They visited him, I think the day before yesterday..."

"Who did?"

"I don't know. I assume it was a delegation of older Nazis who are anyway in a kind of intergenerational conflict with their younger members. Previously they got on their nerves because the young neo-Nazis tended to put comments on Facebook they shouldn't have, which was rather hypocritical because they were doing the same, just that their channels were not as dynamic. I don't know what they found out but by the fact that you got permission for your visit I can assume not much. I don't believe they would let you near the guy were this in any way to compromise them."

"I believe only that the world will come to an end once, I just don't know yet when this might be," said Taras.

"It could come sooner than you think."

"I also doubt that this guy is capable of realising his wet dreams," Taras continued. "But if it looks like a duck, flies like a duck and also quacks like a duck – what else is it if not a duck?"

"Our latest news is that that you do already have the right guy and that you've deposited the search warrant into a special device called the waste paper bin."

He imitated Taras's supposed throwing of the search warrant into the basket by throwing a sachet of sugar onto Taras's empty saucer. Taras always moved his cup from the saucer onto the table. A sturdier foundation.

He picked up the sugar, flicked it into the air and caught it in his hand.

"I don't know. That wouldn't be environmentally friendly."

CHAPTER 34.

"That's in Dravlje, isn't it?"

"Yes, our golden neighbourhood."

"Golden?"

In her memory Tina had a group of blocks of flats in various colours, most of them in hues of blue.

"It's golden for us," said the caretaker. "Absolutely nowhere else uses the amount of money they need for maintenance."

She put the phone back into her handbag and looked at Osterc.

"We're going to Brilej Street. Apparently he's there."

Tina drove, Osterc sat in silence with an expression that Tina, as a computer graduate, would describe as *basic setup*.

"How's Brajc?" she asked to break the silence.

"Fine," said Osterc.

Was this what Osterc was like or did he just stop talking because by mentioning Brajc this was neither possible nor desired? Fortunately at this time the traffic from the centre of town towards the suburbs was low and the journey took barely fifteen minutes. They found the right number and parked right next to the painter and decorator Franc Zupet's white van. She picked up the file from the Grosuplje Police Station and the file with the report from the National Forensic Laboratory to which she had added some of her own pages, and followed Osterc who was already on his way towards the entrance to a dark brown, ten-storey – she counted them – block of flats.

There were two lifts, one with odd and the other with even numbers – a system she had never seen before – and they first took the one with the even numbers right to the top, stopping at every second floor. Osterc would jump into the corridor and check whether the painter was working there while Tina held her finger on the door button. They only found him on their way down with the lift stopping at odd numbered floors. On the fifth floor a man in white overalls was painting the ceiling of a long corridor that had never seen a single ray of daylight. The entire block of flats was one of those architectural accomplishments the interior of which brought catacombs to mind. The man was wearing – Tina could not imagine why – a switched on head lamp.

"Good morning," said Tina and held up her ID. "We will need to speak to you for a few minutes."

He carefully stepped off the ladder and, roller in hand, stared at Tina's ID, hoping it would vanish. His white overalls and white hat had paint all over them and she noticed his blond hair sticking out at the sides. There were patches of fluff on his face and if Tina hadn't known that he was already thirty, she would have thought him younger.

"So, what good news do you bring?" he asked when he reached the floor.

"No good news," said Osterc and at that moment the light in the corridor went out.

"See?" said the painter, his headlamp blinding them. "I can't get it to stay on all the time. It's driving me crazy. I've never painted with a lightbulb on my head before."

Tina reached for the nearest switch and pressed the button but instead of the light coming on, it rang a doorbell. She sighed, looked for another switch, the right one this time.

"Yes?" they could hear someone ask from behind the door.

"Sorry, ma'am," Tina said hurriedly. "Pressed the wrong button."

"What?"

"Wrong button..."

"I'll call the police," the old woman behind the door started shouting. Tina shook her head and showed the painter the folder she was holding.

"Let's go outside. I would like to show you something."

He obediently followed her into the lift, staring at the folder just as he had stared at her ID. Tina deliberately looked straight ahead and didn't pay him any attention, just like Osterc, who probably wasn't doing it deliberately but out of habit. They stepped outside and Tina led them towards a bench between two clusters of blocks on a tiny patch of lawn under a scrawny maple tree that still managed to produce a little shade. She pointed to the bench and the painter sat down.

"Do you know this?" she asked, opening the folder and finding the page with the photograph of the graffiti in Višnja Gora: *This is no spa lazy whores!*

The painter grimaced but didn't answer.

"And this?" she continued, producing a new page from the folder, the report he must have written following one of a number of times he had been brought in to the Grosuplje Police Station.

He looked at it and once again pulled a face.

"Our experts have compared them and found out that they were written by the same person."

She showed him the part where Lokar had compared the graffiti with the writing. Of course it also said there that due to the small basic sample only a weak connection might be established and used only for operative purposes but she did not think the painter would notice or understand even if he did.

He didn't notice. He stared at the ground with embarrassment.

"But I also painted over it."

"You what?"

"I painted over that..." he pointed to *This is no spa lazy whores!*

Tina looked at Osterc. This was going much easier than she had expected.

"Why did you even write this shit?" Osterc asked.

The painted sighed and looked at him. Tina sensed that he was relieved that Osterc had taken over the questioning.

"We were at a fair organised by the local fire brigade on the football pitch close by and these women from that place were there. We danced and then we stopped. I don't know why. I can't remember, I was drunk."

"What about this?"

She put one of the two *Sieg heil* graffiti in front of him.

"This isn't mine," he said.

"I'm not saying it is. Our experts also say as much."

The corners of his mouth turned up scornfully.

"Are you often drunk?" she asked, not wanting Osterc to move on to something safer.

"Once a week," he said frankly. "Whenever I finish a big job. Surely I have a right to that?"

"Was the last time on Monday night, or have we missed something?"

He gave her a weary look. If he had dared to, he would ask: 'Why are you pestering me with all this?'

"Monday? I suppose so, if you say so."

Tina looked through the folder. She didn't really need what she was looking for, but let him have the feeling that the file contained his entire life.

"A while ago they threw you out of the hunting club?"

He remained silent.

"Because of poaching, if I am not mistaken. When they caught you, you threatened the members of the club that you would kill them all. Were you drunk then also?"

"Have I killed anyone?" Defiantly he raised his head.

"Have you?"

She glued her eyes to his face. Was that hesitancy she noticed, even if only for a brief moment?

"Who would I kill? I haven't killed anybody."

"How do you know? Drunk, you might have killed someone and don't even remember it."

It most certainly was hesitancy. He waited for her to go on but she didn't want to. What she wanted was to hear his response.

"I don't know what you're talking about?" he eventually said with caution.

"Can you tell us about your last bout of drinking after finishing the block on Župančič Street?"

This confused him, though Tina could not tell whether it was because he had something to hide or because he would need to tell them what happened.

"You can start with your arrival at the bar in the passageway between Štefan and Cankar Streets."

He flapped about with his arms as if trying to conjure up the words the police woman was demanding of him.

"Yeah, what is there to say? I came there, I dunno what time. I finished that place close by... Not as big as this one here... But it was hard work and hot as hell... so I went for a drink. Then I drank there, I don't know how long, and apparently also broke something which I also paid for, check if you want to, if you don't believe me... And that's that."

He took a deep breath as if he had just come swimming to the surface from great depths.

"Let me help you," said Tina and once again looked in the folder. "You came to the place at half past seven and left it at ten. If you want to have the precise time I can give it to you in minutes and seconds."

He gave her a surprised and also already worried look.

"You drove off from outside the block of flats on Župančič Street – drunk undoubtedly – at five minutes past ten. So?"

"That'll be 'bout right," he muttered.

"And now to what we are really interested in. We want to know what you did in those five minutes. Any normal person, however drunk, would need what, about two minutes at the most to get from the bar to Župančič Street?"

"What could I have done?"

"Any normal person coming from the bar in which you made a fuss and according to what the waitress told the police, smashed the large glass wall, shouting at the same time that..."

She found the right page in the file.

"...all lazy sods, commis, faggots, immigrants, tramps and teachers should be shot..."

She stopped and with a faked disbelief repeated, "Teachers? Where does that come from?"

"They get all summer off and I have to work."

"I see," she gave him an encouraging smile. "So do I. Well, anyway, any normal person would need much less than five minutes to get from there to your white van parked in Župančič Street."

He stared at her. He did not understand.

"You needed almost five minutes. I repeat, if you want the precise time I can look in the file."

His worried eyes jumped from her to Osterc who had folded his arms in his lap and was nodding.

"I don't see why..."

"Why we would be interested in this?"

"Yes."

"We're interested because during this time that you were staggering around that area someone murdered a harmless woman. Just as harmless as those lazy whores at the spa in Višnja Gora."

Zupet was silent, hunched up.

"Why would someone want to kill someone as unimportant as a Ljubljana tramp? Unless, of course they were drunk and hated tramps. So much that they went shouting out loud how they should all be shot. So much that they posted a like on Facebook to some disgusting message about the murder."

"Oh, that," he dismissively waved his hand. "That was just fooling around."

"You call applauding someone who brags about killing a person just fooling around?"

"Yes, it's just writing. I didn't kill her. I read about someone shooting this tramp but that could not have been me. What would I shoot her with? A paintbrush?"

"Did you also paint Mr Baloh's flat?"

"Yes, but I didn't kill him either. I heard about it though."

"Right. Baloh, however, had a gun in a drawer in his flat and if you had access to the flat you had access to the gun."

"I don't know anything about any gun."

Tina looked at Osterc who just nodded which probably meant she should just continue.

"Where were you for those five minutes?"

"If you can't remember here, you might remember at the station," Osterc intervened in the conversation.

"Hang on, hang on..." he almost cried out. "Getting there. Look, I went to the car, I know as much. Then I went inside the house, though I don't know... Yes, I do know! I'd forgotten the ladder that I can't fit in the van any other way other than across the front seat. I was about to drive off when it dawned on me that I had left it in the building."

"Oh, come on!" she said. "Dead drunk you remembered the ladder and made the effort to go and fetch it? Who opened the door for you?"

"Right. It's not anything special but still costs something. I won't be buying a new one every time..."

"Every time you get drunk? Who opened the door?"

"I don't know. I can't remember. I was drunk. Ask the people at the flats."

This was going nowhere. Even if he had somehow managed to get Baloh's gun, when and how did he return it to his drawer? Slowly she put all the pages back into the folder.

"We will check," she said. "Of course I suppose nobody saw you, did they?"

"Yes, they did."

Her hand straightening the pages stopped.

"You can ask that guy."

"Which guy?"

"I met a guy in the building. We almost bumped into each other in the corridor because I couldn't see to one side because of the ladder."

"A man? Around thirty? Shaved head? Was he coming or leaving?"

"I can't remember what he looked like but his head certainly wasn't shaved."

"Which flat did he go into?"

He shook his head.

"I don't know."

"What floor was your ladder on?"

Once again he shook his head.

"I didn't kill this woman, believe me if you want to, don't if you don't. I was pissed, that I admit. I smashed that window, but that's been settled."

"Just as well," she said. "And we can settle this matter too, if we want."

He raised his head and waited.

"Give us a sample of your saliva so we can check whether

you held Baloh's gun or not."

"And what if I refuse?"

"No worries," she said and Zupet began to rise from the bench. "No worries at all. We do have various connections with the tax and trade departments though. You do have everything in order, don't you?"

He sat back down and stared at her for a few moments.

"Where should I spit?"

CHAPTER 35.

"So, Tina," said Taras when he briefly explained to her and Osterc about his meeting with the acquaintance from Sova. "Shall we go and visit this unimportant Nazi or just forget about it? We can do that now."

He was looking at her as if whether she would pass the test or not depended on her answer. He really did not need to do that.

"You believe that Baloh didn't kill, or rather shoot the woman?"

Taras shook his head.

"And Cvilak can't help us?"

"No," said Osterc who went to the autopsy. "He said that he cannot be certain."

*

"Tell Taras," Cvilak had said after finishing the autopsy, "that this is like that seagull that the Americans placed in a wind tunnel. All they discovered was that a dead bird doesn't fly. Same with our body. All I can say for sure is that Mr Baloh, in the state he is now, cannot walk."

*

"And your colleague from Sova says that our Ignac Jakin almost certainly didn't shoot, regardless of all the posts and bragging on social networks?"

"That's what he thinks. Assumes. Concludes."

"Do you believe him?"

"I believe that..."

"Yes, yes. You assume, conclude, that he is right?"

Taras nodded.

"Shame," she said. "I was rather hoping it would be him. But I will not miss the joy of visiting him one more time, armed this time."

Taras smiled, took his gun with its holster out of his backpack and mounted it on his belt. He knows me better than I hoped, Tina thought. Then Taras, as if in a classroom at school, raised his hand.

"I have one request," he said.

"What?"

"Can I conduct this thing?"

"Do you think I can't do it myself?" she asked.

"With all due respect. Half a year at the CID. Opposite you will be a lawyer with fifty years of experience."

"How do you know which lawyer he will call?"

He smiled.

"I know. Believe me, I know."

*

"Taras Birsa from the Police, ma'am. With a search warrant."

He stood at the silent doorphone for a few seconds until a response. He sensed her surprise, almost shock, despite the device distorting the voice considerably.

"What was that?"

"Taras Birsa from the Ljubljana Police Directorate. I have a search warrant," he repeated.

"But…" came from the speaker though the sentence hung mid-air and he could hear the lock release. He pushed the door open, held it open for Tina, the forensic technician Marn and his two assistants, and followed them up to the third floor. The woman was standing at the door like some kind of last desperate defence against invaders. Taras gave her the search warrant which she initially only glanced at but he insisted that she took it and read it properly.

"They said you wouldn't come."

"Who did?" Taras asked.

She didn't reply.

"They were wrong. You have the right to a lawyer being present at the house search. Do you have one?"

The woman went to the wardrobe where there was a phone

on a shelf. She picked it up and clicked a number in her phone book. With a tired look, Taras sat down on a chair and beckoned to Tina to sit down as well.

"Marn," he called the forensic technician who was standing by the door with his assistants, "Go for a coffee. I'll call you when the lawyer arrives."

"Good morning Mr Miheljak," said the woman. "This is Mrs Jakin. They told me I should call you if..."

Taras knew Miheljak, everyone did. He was one of the older generation of Slovene lawyers, from the contingent that in Yugoslavia got Jehovah's Witnesses out of jail and defended those detained on the basis of Article 133[19]. He must be over eighty, was a funny and pleasant man but with a blind spot. Whenever a conversation veered into politics or themes abused by politicians, he turned into a passionate defender of Sloveneness as he understood it. There was no argument with which you could get to him. Taras had encountered him at hearings three or four times and, in as far as he could see, he was simply becoming worse over the years. More and more often he would intertwine the defence of his clients with a political dimension even when the acts for which they were in court were mostly and firstly criminal. It did inadvertently occur to Taras that this kind of blindness might be a kind of defect, something with chromosomes or ageing, for which a kind of cure would be found at some point in the future.

The woman leaned silently on the kitchen counter and watched them. She appeared fragile, but to Taras it looked as if she would attack him if he dared enter her son's room without permission.

"It's your son we are interested in, not you," he said with a smug smile, as if this was not clear from the search warrant. "He is at home, isn't he?"

She nodded.

"I thought so."

He put his phone on the table and took his book out of the backpack, found the right page and began reading.

---

19 Article 133. Hostile propaganda of the Criminal Code of the Socialist Federal Republic of Yugoslavia, colloquially known as Verbal delict (Verbalni delikt), often inferred when political opponents of the Communist system were prosecuted.

Two hours to the minute after the call, Miheljak appeared even though his office was barely a street away. During their wait Taras had almost finished his book. The Beatles had returned from Hamburg and were considering their next moves. He hadn't known that this was the first time they nearly broke up. To begin with, Tina observed Marija Jakin who was still leaning on the counter, looking emptily ahead, then she began browsing her phone and spent the next hour and a half reading the day's news.

The lawyer entered without greeting, surprisingly lively for his age, shook the woman's hand and shouted at Taras.

"Whatever you did, asked, found, demanded... before my arrival, whatever my client might have told you... is not valid."

"Good day," said Taras. "How are you?"

He found his phone in his backpack and called Marn. Miheljak paid no attention, stepped to the woman and asked her something quietly. She pointed to the door to the son's room and Miheljak, without knocking, opened it and disappeared inside. Taras waited for Marn and his assistants to come to the flat, then he followed Miheljak.

He found him sitting on a chair next to the bed, leaning towards the skinhead who had propped himself up on a pillow against the wall, sunglasses covering half his face. The posters and pictures above his bed were gone.

"Are you Ignac Jakin?" Taras asked.

"My client will answer only when I will allow him to."

"Are you Ignac Jakin?" Taras repeated the question without paying attention to Miheljak.

The man with the sunglasses sitting on the bed looked at his lawyer and, when he nodded, replied with a yes.

"Can you take off your sunglasses, please?"

Once again he looked towards the lawyer.

"What for?" Miheljak asked aggressively.

"Because I would like to make sure it really is him. With these glasses he could be Michael Jackson as far as I know."

With a glance that was somewhere between contempt and caution, Miheljak paused for a second or two, as if needing to think of the meaning of the explanation, and then nodded. The skinhead looked at Miheljak, then Taras and then Miheljak again, who nodded once more.

"He has that right," he said.

Hesitantly, as if expecting that a cavalry would appear to save him from the Indians if he delayed, the young man moved his hand towards his face, grabbed the white frames of his unusually dark glasses. Taras would expect glasses like that from one of his contemporaries at Metelkova. His hand stayed on the frame for a few moments and then, with no help forthcoming, he slowly took them off, holding them about twenty centimetres in front of his face, ready to wear them again as soon as permission to do so would be given.

There was a massive purple swelling where his right eye should have been, with little but a line in the middle behind which was probably an eye, if it still existed.

"Wow!" said Taras. "What's this?"

With the corner of his eye he glanced at Miheljak who was trying to hide his shock.

"Who did this to you?"

"I did it myself," said Jakin without waiting for Miheljak to nod. "A branch in the park."

"Have you been to the doctor?"

He shook his head.

"Would you like to report it?"

"Didn't you hear him explain that he hit it on a branch?" Miheljak intervened.

"I see," Taras feigned surprise and turned towards Marn. "You check for this branch."

"Why that?" Miheljak protested.

The caution in his voice was now much more evident.

"Because, considering the nature of his injury, I would like to establish that what your client is saying is the truth and that he is not with his claim covering up a criminal act according to Article 123 of the criminal code of Slovenia which talks of grievous bodily harm, if I am not mistaken."

Miheljak sighed irritatedly and sneaked a glance at his watch.

"Is anyone in a hurry?" Taras asked.

"No, no, not at all..."

"Well, then we will take our time. You need to be thorough

with these things. If inspecting the site takes two hours, then two hours it is."

Miheljak stared at Taras for even longer this time and although his expression was frozen, his eyes showed that there was a fierce battle going on within. He ended with a tactical surrender. He nodded to Jakin.

*

It took them around twenty minutes to walk all round the park and establish that no branch was suitable for such an injury because no branches were low enough to hit the eye of a man of a height of around five foot nine. All had been sawn off so that children wouldn't climb onto the trees and be exposed to further danger. After twenty minutes of walking, the participants were all sweating and Miheljak was close to collapse. The forecast was that temperatures in Ljubljana would reach forty in the shade that day and it was evidently correct. In most of the park the trees were so sparse that they didn't really offer much shade anyway.

"Try to remember," said Taras to the skinhead. "If necessary, we can do another round. I'm sure we can find the spot."

He turned towards the trees where they had started their investigative walk when Miheljak grabbed his hand.

"Listen, Inspector..."

He pulled him to around three metres away, almost pleading with him.

"Would it not be possible to arrange this..."

He fell silent but Taras did not make it easier for him.

"To arrange this?"

"In a civilised manner?" said the old man.

"Absolutely. We can walk round the park two or three more times, then we will file a report for self-inflicted injuries, take him off to A&E where he will give his own statement, and so on. Is that what you had in mind?"

He turned round and Miheljak once again grabbed his arm.

"Listen, Inspector..."

Miheljak's thin hair that had previously been combed to cover most of the baldness on the top of his head had now matted into a few tousled knots that inelegantly hung towards his collar down one side of his head. Taras too was all sweaty but he was a good thirty years younger and was at least wearing a short-sleeved T-shirt. Miheljak had been enduring all this torture in a not-even-so-thin dark blue suit that now hung off him almost as matted as his hair.

"Look, tell me what you want and I will try to accommodate you."

Taras looked at him and then turned his gaze somewhere towards the treetop of a nearby horse chestnut, as if trying to decide, then he turned back to Miheljak with an upbeat face that did not hide ridicule.

"A normal house search where you will sit quietly in the corner and leave us alone, samples, fingerprints, DNA, GSR-particles and a polygraph."

The old man twitched.

"You know that the polygraph won't help you at court if you are thinking of taking this innocent boy to court."

"I know, but still."

Miheljak looked around the park and then at Taras.

"Between us. He is prepared to admit that he is the author of the graffiti on the bench but he has nothing to do with what you are really interested in."

"Even so."

The lawyer nodded tiredly, took his phone from his jacket and moved a few feet away. As he was on the phone, Tina approached Taras.

"Should I call an ambulance or will you take pity on him?"

"I didn't start this."

Miheljak put away his phone, turned towards Taras, and nodded.

"You win, Inspector. Can we now go into some shade?"

*

Ladislav Mozetič, or Lado, as his colleagues called him, was a pedantic man. This, after all, was something one might expect from the Slovenian Police's chief polygrapher. He was thus now, an hour before the arranged arrival of his new client, as he called those he was testing, checking a few last details. Taras Birsa had called him on Monday and told him to get ready. He did not need to explain what he was dealing with. After the article that appeared in *Slovenske Novice*, everyone in the building on Litostroj Street housing the Ministry of the Interior knew what their colleagues at the Ljubljana Police Directorate were investigating.

"Will you send me the documentation?" he had asked and received the reply that it was already all waiting for him in his inbox. He read through it and on the same day went to the park and found the bench. It was not hard. It still had the *Sieg heil!* written on it. He sat on it and sat there for a while, even closing his eyes, as if trying to transpose to the time when the victim was lying on the bench and her executioner approached her.

Above his work desk he had stuck a motto: *Staying silent appears like an affirmation but is most certainly not a denial.* He wished his clients to see it, just so they did not get any clever ideas at the last moment about silence being golden and such like.

He had a colourful career behind him. He had started out as an ordinary policeman, was promoted to criminal investigator, became the chief at the police station in Šentvid, and then, ten years before retirement, an opportunity arose for something new. At an age when most of his colleagues had begun to count down to retirement, he went to Zagreb, to the world-famous expert polygrapher Zvonimir Ros, and after a few months of training became an expert in asking questions at twenty-second intervals, trying to find the truth.

It was because of this sign that he took those he was about to question into the room with the polygraph through his office and not through the door that led to it directly from the corridor.

He would stand up, open the door and enter his kingdom. On many faces that entered this room for the first time, he noticed surprise, even disappointment. They probably expected something like the interior of the Apollo. Instead there was a single computer on the table, just like any other computer to look at, behind it a chair for the polygrapher, and by the wall close to the door two more chairs, wooden and uncomfortable. One for the person being tested and the other for their lawyer. This is where they sat during the conversation he would conduct before the testing during which he tried to sense something of the tested person's life stance, attitude to the actual event, an insight into their origins and the life's circumstances in which they had grown up, moulding their character. Only after this conversation was he able to compile the test for each client, unless the person to be tested had already proved unsuitable. Not everyone was a suitable candidate to sit on the sofa on the other side of the table and the computer, in front of a large screen on the wall. The graphs on the computer screen were totally unpredictable for drunks, druggies, and also pregnant women and teenagers in the most difficult years.

He checked that the program was working and then set up all the other connections on the table. Breathing sensors – one for the thorax, another for those who breathe using their diaphragm, among whom, interestingly, there were more women than men.

Next to them he placed the blood pressure gauge, sweat electrodes, as they call them, though they are, not strictly speaking that. The spiked rings placed on the index and ring finger, connected to electrodes and the computer, monitor the changes in the microconductivity of the skin were his favourite part of the polygraph system. Not only his – this method has been proven as the most reliable in sensing the changes that occur when a person is lying. Next to them he also placed the electrode with a clip-on probe that measures the oxygen saturation at the fingertips. When a person is stressed the body responds by stopping pumping oxygen into the peripheral parts, trying to keep it in the internal organs and muscles. To fight, to flee. He checked the movement sensors built into the chair – the seat and the hand rests, and the plate in front of it where the interviewee places the soles of their feet.

Everything was working properly, everything was ready.

People often asked him how reliable the polygraph is and did so with the incorrect assumption that what he aims at is the interviewees humanness, morals.

"Apparently psychopaths can trick it?" they guessed and assumed that a psychopath would not feel anything when asked the question 'Did you kill your mother?' and that the machine would thus also not detect anything.

Quite possible, but if he asks him instead:
'Did you kill your mother
– with one bullet,
– with two bullets,
– with three bullets…

It would not be the love towards the murdered mother but the fear of the consequences of their answer that will send the lines on the graphs up into their heights, especially if the one on the polygraph chair could be facing thirty years in prison. If you stick to the rules, the polygraph is much more reliable than any eyewitness accounts, even though neither the defence nor the prosecution are allowed to use information obtained this way at court.

*

When Tina was returning from the toilet, the sign TESTING IN PROGRESS was already switched on. Worried that her steps might interfere with the sensors on the device behind the door, she tiptoed into Mozetič's office where Taras and Miheljak were waiting for the testing to finish. Taras was holding his book, browsing through it for the interesting sections that he might want to read again. Miheljak was shuffling some pages and then put them away in an old-fashioned leather briefcase. He turned to Tina.

"I gather you are heading this investigation. How come you released this pit bull on me?"

He glanced towards Taras and smiled. All that was missing was a wink.

Taras didn't respond. He must have heard him but didn't look away from his book.

Friday

CHAPTER 36.

Brajc woke up at seven. How unfair this world is, he thought. Whenever he had to get up this early, he wanted to sleep, now that he could, he can't. He looked at the list of essential medication he had been given when discharged from hospital, took two yellow-blue capsules with some long name he had no intention of remembering.

He sat at the table and began reading the brochure they had also given to him, one explaining the basics of a healthy lifestyle to cardiac patients. He did not need it. All the things it listed that he should be doing were precisely those Brajc hated, all the things they listed that he shouldn't be were those he enjoyed. This was a rather unpromising start.

A healthy diet that will protect your heart contains less fat, he read, especially saturated fat from animals, less sugar and less salt, and more protective substances, fibre, vitamins, minerals and water. Fibres, vitamins, minerals and water? None of this sounded as if it would taste any good or taste at all. He continued reading, hoping that he would come across some surprising piece of information, for example that ćevapčići contained lots of fibre and water, alas, he was disappointed. Fruit and vegetables, full-grain bread, cereals, lean meat and fish. No bacon, no eggs. Nothing with which he had nourished himself every morning ever since he could remember.

He went to the kitchen and opened the refrigerator. It was full of frankfurters, various kinds of sausages and salami, vacuum packed prosciutto, cheese, a full-fat Emmentaler, processed spreadable cheese, butter and eggs. Everything in the fridge was included on the list of things he was supposed to avoid, everything stared at him hatefully, everything wanted to kill him.

He closed the fridge door and sat at the table, opened the brochure again and wrote a list of items he was supposed to eat and would have to buy and the things that could be prepared from them. Once he finished he browsed over his list and shook his head. It might be possible to live off this, but it certainly wasn't food. He thought of the people who persist with this kind of diet day after day for their entire lives and considered the incredible amount of willpower they must have not to break their regime. He hadn't even begun and it was crystal clear that this task was too difficult for him. They were asking him to jump over Everest, but he could not even get off the ground.

He opened the refrigerator again and took out three eggs and some butter. For a moment he thought about frying them in oil that he must have somewhere in the cupboard above the sink, then he dismissed the idea – if you're going to rise you might as well shine – and threw the usual quantity of butter into the frying pan. He sat at the plate rolling his once-so-beloved eggs round his mouth, angrily crumpled up the brochure and threw it on the floor. All they had managed to do was to turn him off his only joy in life. He stubbornly chewed on and swallowed his mouthful, put the plate in the sink, picked up the brochure from the floor and put it in the waste. Then he sat back down on the chair, put his elbows on the table and buried his face in his palms. The labyrinth in which he had found himself was too large. He would never find his way out of it.

He sobbed, silently at first, so that someone not knowing what this was about would think it was a cramp that eased and then returned. These cramps were soon joined by snivelling and eventually tears. They rolled down the inside of his palm, down his wrists and dropped onto the smooth surface of the varnished wooden table.

It was totally impossible that anything could in any way get better or change. Never again would things be as they were.

There was no point in any of this. There long hadn't been.

Through his tears and fingers he noticed the phone on the table. For a while he stared at it through the gaps in his fingers, then he removed his hands and wiped away the tears.

"If someone doesn't call me in the next minute, I'll go and shoot myself," he thought to himself.

The thought was terrifying and alluring at the same time.

"If someone doesn't call me in the next minute, I'll shoot myself," he whispered to himself.

He sneaked a glance around the room, as if to check whether anyone might have heard him.

"If someone doesn't call me in the next minute, I'll just get it all done and over with!" he shouted.

He extended his neck to check the time on the phone. Seven forty-two. The chance of anyone calling him at seven forty-two was miniscule even when he wasn't on sick leave, now it was basically zero. He stared at the numbers, waiting for the two to change to a three. What would happen when it did? Will he stand up, stroll into the bedroom, open the drawer in his wardrobe, the one lowest to the floor, pull out his police weapon... Will he?

He closed his eyes and kept them closed for a few seconds. Then he opened them again. Seven forty-three. Nobody had called and nobody would. His hands shook. Nobody will ever call, not just now. Not at seven forty-four, not at seven forty-five, never. He is alone, he has no one, and they have taken away all his joy.

Then the phone rang. It was so unbelievable, so magical, that for a few long rings he just stared at the phone, afraid of picking up the receiver.

An unknown number.

"Yes?"

"Hey, Franc, where the hell are you?" a strange voice asked.

"Who?"

"Where are you, mate? Everyone is waiting."

"I'm not Franc," said Brajc.

"Oh, shit, sorry," he heard and then the caller hung up.

Confused, he placed the phone back onto the table. Does

this count?

*

"What are the chances of the DNA test proving it's a lie?" Tina asked.

Taras and she were sitting in the Pisker coffee bar, waiting for Osterc. He should have been there by now but he called to say he was held up and would be a little late.

"Should I come to Pisker or to the office?"

"Come to the bar. I can switch off the phone but if he appears at the door to the office I can't pretend he isn't there."

He didn't say who he was thinking about but he didn't have to. Both Osterc and Tina knew.

Apart from the usual pests, like the one Taras did not want to mention, and their unwelcome interventions, their day was going fine. They had completed the house search and when whatever results from it would be ready, they will respond accordingly, but to do so they would have to wait at least until the following day. All they had now were the results of the lie detector – they were available instantly.

"What would the DNA prove as a lie?" Taras asked. "The polygraph or Jakin?"

"In this case is this not the same?"

*

"So," Mozetič said once he had finished the testing and the lawyer had taken Ignac Jakin away. "I devised the test according to what you wanted to know, Taras, with a few limitations that I had to take into account considering what I knew about the case."

He unfolded a graph drawn across a number of pages.

"I set him most questions according to the method of recognisable or, as we call them, Japanese tests, which our Eastern colleagues insist are the only appropriate ones and say all other methods are scientifically unfounded. I would not agree with this entirely because we often also carry out misleading tests or credibility tests and we have also used them to a certain degree here."

He unfolded the first sheet with a graph towards Taras and Tina.

"This question which was 'Was the gun you used to shoot the woman in the park...'" And he listed six different handguns.

"As you see, the testee reacted to the Walther 5 and not to the Glock 19 which has been proven as the murder weapon. We also know why. From the material you sent me it is evident that he had been arranging to buy a Walther, which means that he simply recognised this weapon. The same thing happened when I showed him six different guns on the screen and asked him the same question. A longer pause from the end of the question to the beginning of his answer, shallower and faster breathing, an increased heart rate, not to mention the graph on the microconductivity of the skin."

He pointed at a very high peak in the curve.

"So he didn't react to the right gun?" Tina asked.

"No, it doesn't mean anything to him."

He placed another large sheet with graphs on the table.

"More interesting are the responses to the question 'Did you kill the woman in the park?' I assume the testee could not have known anything about our dilemma on whether the woman died from the gunshot or because of her illness."

"No," said Taras. "He couldn't have."

"Again I asked him six questions in which I hid the woman in the park between five other persons. The woman in the shop, the postman, the journalist, the worker on the street and his own mother. He responded only to his mother. How is she?"

"Alive," said Taras.

"There was no deviation when he was asked about the woman in the park."

"Excuse me," said Tina. "How could he have admitted to the murder of his mother? A murder that hadn't even happened?"

Mozetič smiled.

"He didn't admit to the murder of his mother. He only reacted to the question. Perhaps he wants to kill her."

He opened up another sheet in front of them.

"Once again, as you requested, Taras, I set him another question. This time whether he has *planned* to murder the postman, the shop assistant, his mother... and the woman in the park. Here we have a definite reaction at person number four."

He pointed to the graphs and indeed at number four they all became wavy.

"And number four is?" asked Tina.

"Our homeless woman in the park. There was some reaction at number two, who is his mother, but very weak."

"And what about the graffiti at Metelkova? He admitted anyway that he wrote the stuff on the bench."

"And our test confirms this. Did you write the *Sieg heil* on the wall of the block of flats where you live, the bench in the park, on the building at Metelkova, etc.? He reacted only to the bench in the park."

"What are the chances of his fooling us?" Tina asked.

"That is what the movement sensors are for. If he had put a pin in his shoe, which is what they most often try, we would sense that."

"Did you ask him whether he knows who the murderer is?"

"As you requested, Taras. Well, here I made an exception and began questioning him according to the credibility method, meaning a series of unrelated, control and throwaway questions, and the answer was – no. It seems he has no idea who the gunman is."

Tina nodded and looked at Taras who continued to examine the curves on one of the sheets. She was not sure which one.

"Does this fit in with your expectations?" Mozetič asked.

"More or less," said Tina.

"Which part more and which part less?"

"I didn't expect it to show that he was the one who shot her but I more hoped than assumed that he would know who did. So our neo-Nazi theory is out."

"And yours, Taras?"

"It does, unfortunately."

He finished looking at the sheet and put it with the others.

"What we are left with is the DNA tests and the gunshot residue. If they are both negative, poor old Baloh will prevail as the guilty one. It won't be the first time that an innocent man will get the shit end of the stick."

He looked at Tina and smiled.

"Though it can't be shittier than the shit that has already happened to him anyway."

*

Taras greeted Osterc who sat down with them. He placed a sheet of paper on the table and beckoned to Silva who nodded. Green tea, what else. They waited for Silva to bring a glass of hot water, Osterc unwrapped the teabag from its plastic wrapping and dipped it in the glass.

"Osterc, did you ever drink coffee?" Taras asked.

"No."

"Have you even tried it?"

"No."

"How come?"

"I can't drink something that dark."

Taras shook his head as if trying to assess his answer, though among all the arguments for and against any certain food, drink, or whatever, this was one that was not that hard to understand.

"How did it go in the library? Have you found anything?"

Osterc nodded.

*

This time he did not just drop off his wife and drive on to work but outside the library where she worked squeezed his car past a wooden marker stake onto the grass. He was not the only one. There was little left of the supposed lawn anyway.

He followed his wife who took him to the reading room and told him to wait there.

"The boss doesn't know anything about this and it is better it stays that way."

She returned a few minutes later with a folded roll of paper in her hand.

"Is there this much of this stuff?" he asked.

"The first time you knew the precise time, these pages show the visits of the entire morning."

He browsed through the list of numbers and next to them the names of people who had visited the Oton Župančič Library last Wednesday morning.

"Can I check this here?"

It was quiet in the reading room at this hour and it had air-conditioning.

"You can," said Maja Osterc, "just make sure no colleague

sees what you have on the table. If anyone appears pretend to be reading the newspaper."

He waited for her to leave, then he brought from his bag a pencil and the list of visitors to the library after four o'clock last Tuesday. He aligned it with the list of those who visited it the following morning and underlined the first name on the first list. He ran down the names on the second list. With a computer this puzzle would be solved in seconds, here it will take... well, a long time.

*

"What did you find?" Taras asked.

Osterc was about to tell him but Taras's phone rang.

"What's up, Brajc?"

Taras listened and nodded twice. His face showed surprise. He circled with his index finger on his temple and pointed to the phone.

"Saturday morning," he said.

Then he gestured with his finger again.

"At six o'clock in the morning, Brajc. Set your alarm clock."

He put down his phone and looked at his colleagues.

"You won't believe what I have just lived to hear. Brajc called me to ask whether I really had bought him trainers and asked when he could test them. I can't believe it!"

"Perhaps something is wrong?" Osterc asked.

"Rain forecast for Saturday," said Tina. "Apparently it will make up for lost time."

"A good deed a week, sends the doctor..."

Taras tried to find something appropriate that rhymed with week, but all he could think of was 'bleak' which made no sense in the sentence. Perhaps 'up the creek'? Slightly embarrassed he turned to Osterc.

"So, you found something?"

Osterc gave a slight nod.

"It probably isn't anything shocking. There were quite a few names. Not that many on Tuesday's list but definitely on the list from the following morning. There were seventy-five on Tuesday between four and five, both at the book and computer sections, but their system does not separate between the two. I had to compare these seventy-five with a hundred and twenty who came to the library on Wednesday morning. To make things easier I started by looking at the men only."

"Why the men only?" Tina asked.

"Statistics," said Taras instead of Osterc. "Normally it is men who do the shooting."

"And the women who visit libraries," said Tina.

"There was no match with the men. So I worked on the women and Tina is right, there were far more than the men. Here one name stood out."

He put the two lists on the table and straightened them. On both all the names were ticked and on each a single name was marked with a yellow highlighter.

"Here, this is it."

Taras looked at the name.

"She's probably just some pensioner who visits the library every day," Osterc pondered.

Taras shook his head.

"This lady certainly could not have visited the library."

"How do you know?" Tina asked. "Do you know her?"

Taras shook his head again.

"No. All I know is that this lady is dead."

CHAPTER 37.

Majda Vasle.

She had a guilty conscience as she wrote the woman's name on the whiteboard. She was not her discovery.

"Your handwriting is much better than mine," said Taras. "Now I at least know what is written on the board."

Not only that. Taras was right. Once again. There was a link between the two crimes that he picked up on while she was preoccupied with seconds that did not lead them anywhere.

"Who is she?" she had asked, confused. "I mean, besides being the owner of the flat on the second floor of our block of flats?"

Taras looked at Osterc who was sitting at the computer, waiting for the device to wake up.

"I assume," said Taras, "with great probability, that Osterc here will be able to confirm that she is the mother of Jakob Vadnal who is the son of Robert Vadnal, who, as we know, died a sad death in his unofficial residence on Metelkova."

"It's starting up," Osterc was fidgeting. "I've already asked for a new computer but apparently it's not our turn yet. Next year."

"If you poured coffee over it, you'd get a new one straight away," said Taras. "Or green tea. How come you hadn't checked Vadnal's wife?"

Osterc blushed. If Drvarič were to shout at him that he was an idiot, he could take it calmly and think about the protective aluminium cap for the blades of his lawnmower. If Kristan were to slap him across the face, he could handle it, he was after all the Director, but this remark by Taras hurt.

"I was working on this," he yelped and passed Taras a piece of paper across the table. "Sorting out the data for the people in the block of flats and I forgot about Metelkova."

Taras skipped over the list of names with dates. Dates of birth and deaths of some of the people in the block of flats. He took a marker to make a note on the board but Tina stopped him.

"All this time I thought that you could at least read what you write on the board. I think I'd better do this."

He sat on his chair and waited for Osterc's central register of population to open. Tina had to tiptoe to reach the top of the board. Then she suddenly stopped.

"There must be a mistake here," she said and turned round.

Taras peered at her absently. He was waiting for Osterc.

"Here, just a minute," said Osterc.

"What kind of mistake?" Taras asked.

"With the death date of Dr Jakin and the birth date of his son."

"A mistake?" Osterc asked.

"Look at these dates. The date of the father's death and the date of the son's birth."

Osterc stretched his neck, looked at the numbers and wrote them down on a piece of paper.

"I am certain I copied them out correctly. But I can check."

Taras was looking at the board and judging by the manner he was moving his fingers, in that unique way he had, she concluded he was calculating. He did not count on his fingers the way any ordinary Slovene or Westerner would but the way he had learnt in Nepal – with the thumb of the same hand along the joints of the other fingers and once he had also told her how to count to ten in Nepalese: *ek, dui, tin, char, paanch, chha, sat, aath, nau, das.*

"Ten months?" he was surprised.

"Yes, and as far as I know," Tina nodded, "pregnancy in the human species lasts nine months."

"Is it possible that it might have been ten?" Taras asked. "Some take their time arriving."

Anja, for example was born a week late.

Osterc was typing away in the register, shaking his head.

"Both dates are correct."

"Which we can interpret in two ways," Taras summarised, "either the young lout is a medical phenomenon or the deceased Dr Jakin is not his father."

He once again conducted his unusual counting ceremony and nodded.

"What does that mean?" Tina asked.

"I don't know what it means," said Taras, still thinking. "But I would certainly like to know who his father is if it isn't poor Dr Jakin."

"Robert Vadnal was married to Majda Vasle who lived in a flat in Župančič Street in Ljubljana," Osterc said. "They divorced in January 1988. He was never officially registered as living there."

"Although he did. For a short time," said Taras. "At least our witch from the fourth floor says so. She also told me that all this mess, this nest of interesting people happened within a very short period."

He checked the dates. Baloh's wife died in early September 1986, Dr Jakin died the following April and his son was born ten months later, in January 1988. That was also when the Vadnals divorced. At about the same time Jakob Vadnal was born. All in less than a year and a half. Thirty years later it did indeed look as if it all happened at once.

"Do you know when Vadnal left home, if we assume that the know-it-all grandma is not mistaken and he really did live at Župančič Street for a while?"

"His son said as soon as he was born. Apparently he has never seen him."

"Yet he still has his surname?" Tina was surprised. "Can either of you explain this to me?"

"Perhaps he wanted a father," said Taras. "Some people can't do without one."

Tina turned towards him, Osterc also. He smiled, possibly

with embarrassment.

"Just as I can't do without a coffee right now."

He returned with a cup of coffee, placing it on his desk.

"I forgot to ask you if you wanted one too."

"It's fine," said Tina. "What do we do now? Will we visit Vadnal junior and ask him about... But that's not our case?"

Taras leaned on his desk with his elbows, rubbed his eyes with his fists and massaged his forehead with his fingers.

"More than whose case this is," he said thoughtfully, "what I'm interested in is why Vadnal junior would kill Vadnal senior?"

"Kill?"

"Kill. Shoot. Murder... Who else, if not him?"

"If he wrote the mails and sent them with the *Sieg heil* photos to *Novice*," Tina was thinking out aloud, "then he probably tried to divert attention from the murder at Metelkova. And if he was trying to do this..."

Taras nodded.

"But why would he kill him? Revenge because he left him?" Tina continued.

"And he would wait thirty years for this?" Taras asked. "Didn't he have any other problems?"

"Maybe it had been bothering him for a long time and then he had a momentary inspiration with this woman in the park," Osterc suggested. "The painter we visited yesterday said that he met someone in the building that night. Brajc believes there are drugs in the background. Perhaps father and son were more connected that we think."

"Brajc always thinks there are drugs in the background," Taras rejected him. "He worked in Narcotics for ten years and won't get rid of this fixation until he retires!"

Then he smiled and shook his head.

"Canvass. How silly of me. No window overlooking the crime scene should remain unquestioned. Blah, blah, blah. Why the hell didn't I stick to this?"

He turned to Osterc.

"Osterc, my friend, we will once again need to get to Vadnal junior. Get your necessaire and let's go to buy some bitcoins."

He probably felt that she was annoyed because he looked at

her as he filled his backpack.

"You're right, Tina. This is not your case. Instead, why don't you think about the new possibilities for your case that open up in light of our new discoveries?"

They disappeared down the corridor and Tina thought that he would probably die if he ever let on what was going on in his head. Besides, it wasn't his case either. She looked at the whiteboard. What light, what new discoveries?

*

"Call his secretary, so we tell him we're coming," said Taras as they sat in his Citroën.

"He doesn't have a secretary," Osterc shook his head. "At least there wasn't one when Brajc and I visited him last time."

He searched for the phone number of Jakob Vadnal's company, Las Cripto... something.

"Tell you what, no need," Taras waved his hand. "I don't know why, but I have a feeling he won't be happy to see us."

*

"He will probably be busy," said the woman at reception at the Crystal Palace.

"Why's that?" Osterc asked.

When they were here on Friday with Brajc, she didn't even know Vadnal, she barely knew about Las Criptomonedas.

"Fifteen minutes ago three gentlemen arrived and were also looking for him. Since they have not yet returned, they are probably still with Mr Vadnal."

They knocked on the door with the LC sign on it and when nobody replied, they knocked again. A man appeared at the door who according to Osterc's description could not have been Jakob Vadnal. Despite this Taras asked.

"Jakob Vadnal?" and showed him his police ID.

The guy, tall and neat who, despite his suit, could not hide and probably didn't want to hide his muscles, raised his eyebrows.

"He's busy," he said.

Taras waited.

"No problems. We will wait for him. In reception."

He pointed past the body-built man, though he could not

have known whether there was a reception or anything like it in the office or not.

The guy, probably unwittingly, moved a step to the side and Taras pushed past him. He found himself in the space separated from the larger office by a glass partition. Beyond it there were three people sitting at the oval table. A man with a black, neatly trimmed beard at the top of the table, and either side of him a clone of the man who had opened the door to Taras and Osterc. Taras waved his police ID at them through the glass partition.

The man who had opened the door for them stepped past them, entered the office and closed the door behind him. He leaned towards the other three at the table. The men next to Vadnal glanced towards Taras and Osterc and nodded briefly. They stood up and one of them leaned across to Vadnal and whispered something in his ear. They then all walked straight past Taras and Osterc without saying anything. The last of the three at least nodded.

"Good day," Taras greeted him when he opened the door without Vadnal inviting him in. He walked across to the large oval table and showed him his ID again before, once again uninvited, sitting on one of the chairs where Vadnal's acquaintances had sat previously.

"I hope we are not interrupting anything," said Taras, "but business is business."

"You've already been here," said Vadnal.

He was pale, there was a patch of perspiration on the front of his shirt and his hands shook.

"Not me. Only my colleague," said Taras and pointed at Osterc. "A few new things have appeared and we had to visit you again. Is there something wrong with you?"

Vadnal suddenly stood up. For a moment Taras thought that he would run away.

"I need to go to the bathroom," he said, almost ran through the glass door and disappeared behind a wooden door with a WC sign on it. He returned a minute later, refreshed and composed. Were it not for the sweaty patch on the front of his shirt, one would think that a different person emerged from the bathroom.

"How can I help you?"

Taras briefly explained about the woman in the park.

"Have you heard about her?" he asked.

Vadnal shook his head.

"How come? It was all over the papers."

"I don't read the papers often. Financial ones, yes, but these things are usually not mentioned there."

"Lucky you," said Taras. "We can't avoid them. Just as we are obliged to visit anyone who could tell us anything about the case."

"And could I tell you anything about it?"

"Well, after all, you do live in the block of flats above the park. The painter who worked in the building met you that very evening when the murder occurred."

For a moment Vadnal stared defiantly at them, then he looked down at the table.

"What day was that?"

"Last Monday."

"Perhaps I just came to check on the flat. I don't live there. Haven't lived there for a long time."

"Well, whose flat is it, then?"

"Mother's. I mean, it's mine now, Mother died earlier in the year."

"And, if I understood correctly, you didn't know your father."

Vadnal shook his head.

"How come you chose his surname?" Taras probed.

"I didn't choose it. I was given it at birth and was stuck with it."

"Your parents divorced. You don't happen to know..."

"Excuse me, Inspector," Vadnal interrupted him, "but what are you trying to find out with this questioning?"

Taras smiled and looked at Osterc who was once again in a state of motionless attention. He prodded him with his elbow and laughed again, then turned back to Vadnal.

"See, that's what I call professional deformation. I get carried away and begin pestering people as if this was an interrogation. I apologise."

Vadnal nodded ever so slightly.

"Back to the flat. Apparently you are selling it. Or you were selling it, or something?"

The expression on Vadnal's face remained unchanged but Taras thought he could sense a nervousness. Who knows what the sensors of Mozetič's device would show in this case?

"Why are you interested? Are you thinking of buying it?"

"Oh, no, no way," Taras laughed. "Far too expensive for me. We're talking about a lot of money, aren't we?"

"A fair amount," said Vadnal.

"So, are you selling it, or not?"

"I am," said Vadnal, though he didn't really sound convincing.

"Well, yes, sorry for badgering you with all these questions," said Taras and smiled. "I almost forgot why we came here. So, you were there on Monday, you were seen three minutes past ten. A minute or so earlier, a brutal crime was committed in the park. Did you hear or see anything?"

"Nothing."

"Did you know the woman?"

"No."

"No?"

Vadnal looked at him. He tried to appear indifferent.

"What do you mean? Surely I know who I know and who I don't?"

"You did say that you didn't even know about the murder. That all you read is the financial papers."

Vadnal shrugged his shoulders.

"Perhaps I heard about it and then forgot. Basically, I don't know who the woman is."

Taras looked around the office and his gaze stopped at the nude on the wall. He gave an approving nod.

"Kelman, isn't it?"

"Do you know his work?" Vadnal asked.

"Not really. I just know he's top. Expensive."

Vadnal nodded.

"The most expensive."

"And how is the cryptocurrency business lately?"

He turned from the painting to Vadnal, looking straight into his eyes. This time Vadnal didn't look away.

"Depends, Inspector. It's fine if you know what you're doing."

"I never understood these bitcoins," Taras continued as if he was chatting with a friend over a coffee, "how..."

"How their value is determined?" Vadnal interrupted him with a slight intonation of ridicule.

"No, not that, in fact. It's clear they are worthless. What I don't get is this thing about mining. These blockchains, is it?"

"Why do you want to know that?" Vadnal relaxedly crossed his legs that had until then been firmly on the floor. He was on his own turf now. "Why would you be interested in the technical applications behind cryptocurrency? Are you perhaps interested in how banknotes are printed, where coins are minted, how much money is in circulation, how often banknotes are replaced, when bank machines are filled...? Why then would stuff like that interest you with cryptomoney?"

"I can touch ordinary money."

"All you touch is the paper, or that little metal that is worth even less than the number on it. Like many others, you are condemning bitcoins because they are considered as an exclusively speculative investment. In Europe, the United States, partly in Russia, and in Japan, this is a speculative investment, so what? We have a stable monetary system, substances we live off, wages, and we can afford things such as bitcoins as a little extra. A kind of asset class. As an extra income. This is what we are best at. Well, at least some of us. If we lived in Zimbabwe, Venezuela, anywhere in Latin America, or even in places like Turkey, as it seems after the last crisis, we would be very happy if we had access to crypto currency. Why? Because crypto holds its value. If your money is worth less by the day, you buy crypto and this way preserve at least some of its value."

Taras looked at him with admiration.

"See, Osterc," he turned to his silent colleague. "What could we could do with this knowledge? We certainly wouldn't have to chase around scoundrels for a mere grand and a half a month."

With a smile on his face he turned back to Vadnal.

"Though it is true that the value of bitcoins recently fell from twenty thousand to a mere six. Someone who was overdoing it could find themselves in quite some shit, wouldn't they?"

Vadnal sniffled. His runny nose seemed to be giving him some trouble but in a gesture he seemed to be used to, he squeezed it and breathed in at the same time and managed to contain it.

"A cold?" Taras asked sympathetically.

Vadnal nodded and sniffled again.

"I mean, if they were too greedy," Taras continued. "Apparently we Slovenes have a tendency to get carried away in this area?"

"It's nothing to do with greed," said Vadnal and once again there was a sense of ridicule in his voice. "There are investments with stable returns that are less speculative, such as bonds, property, and so on, then you have shares and the much riskier security bonds, for example, junk bonds or something similar, then expert financial instruments and right at the end commodities which are very volatile, for example oil, and after oil also crypto currencies. This is called the usual diversification of a portfolio. With these latter ones, the rule is that you invest as much as you can afford to lose. If you stick to this, what can happen to you?"

Taras was nodding keenly.

"Were the three men before us investors?"

*

They walked past reception and returned the magnetic cards when Taras turned and smiled at the girl behind the counter.

"Excuse me, I assume that your system notes all the arrivals and departures from the building?"

"It does."

"Might you be so kind and trust me with a piece of information?"

"I am not allowed to," the girl shook her head. "You would need a court order for anything like that."

"I know, I know, of course I know," Taras was quick to say. "But I don't need any list from you or anything. Nothing on paper. Just a small favour. Mr Vadnal whom we have just visited, says that he was here last Monday and Tuesday afternoon and late at night. You would be doing me and him a huge favour if, merely as a formality, you could confirm this. I know, of course, that he wasn't lying."

The girl hesitated briefly, then clicked something on her keyboard, waited for a while, clicked something again, looked up and nodded.

"From two to midnight, both on Monday and Tuesday."

"Thank you, you're a treasure," said Taras.

*

They drove back to their office in silence. Taras navigated the main road leading from the trade park towards the town centre, deep in thought. Osterc in the meantime was fiddling with the clock on the dashboard of Taras's car. He could not believe it was still on winter time.

"The clocks will soon change back," Taras shrugged his shoulders but Osterc still set about pressing buttons that Taras had never even touched before.

"Thanks," he said when Osterc had finished.

"He no longer has his watch," said Osterc.

"Thanks," said Taras again, not paying much attention to what Osterc was saying.

"He no longer has his watch," Osterc repeated.

"What?"

"Vadnal. When Brajc and I visited him the last time, he was wearing a watch for which you'd almost need a gun licence. Now he wasn't wearing it."

CHAPTER 38.

"I don't know what watch it was. I don't know anything about watches," said Osterc. "I've been known to take the odd clock apart in the past, an alarm clock – they're larger and you can put them back together again. But alarm clocks have disappeared now, anyway."

Taras nodded and at the crossroads, despite being in the middle lane, switched on his left indicator. He looked at the driver in the car next to him but the man looked persistently elsewhere. An elderly man of around seventy with an elderly woman next to him, probably his wife. He stared straight ahead, his wife also. Taras waved at him. Nothing. Taras pushed in in front of him with the front of his car and the old man went wild. It was as if Taras had pressed an invisible button. He did not take his hand off his horn and when Taras didn't move back he drove half a metre towards him and nearly touched Taras's Citroën with his Passat or something, grimacing and threatening him with his fist. Taras found his ID in his backpack, opened the window and held it up in front of the wife's faces behind the glass. She was not waving her hands about but her face was no less angry.

The woman strained her eyes, turned to the driver and said something. Just as he had a few seconds ago suddenly become animated, he now switched off. He lifted his hand off the horn and stared straight ahead across the bonnet of his car.

Taras drove in front of him and, once he was in lane, waved to the man to thank him. He didn't respond.

"Aren't we nervy?" Taras muttered.

"Aren't we going to the office?" Osterc asked.

"No, we're going to visit someone who knows a few things about watches."

*

He parked under the castle. With Osterc they crossed the square in front of the Puppet Theatre, walked past the south edge of the market to the Cathedral of St. Nicholas and stopped at a tiny watchmaker's shop on the opposite side of the road, almost as small as the shop next to it which specialised in selling Krainer sausages.

Taras pushed the door open and stepped into the small shop which appeared even smaller because it was so full. A path led through the glass cases with clocks and watches, a kind of mini labyrinth which would not allow two people coming in opposite directions to pass each other. Through it Taras reached the counter where a young man sat at a computer. He greeted him.

"Is your old man here?"

The man pointed to the door behind him.

"Where else?"

Taras introduced Osterc and gestured towards the door.

"Yes, of course. He'll be happy to see you."

Taras knocked gently, then opened the door and entered with Osterc close behind him. In a small room a small, round man sat at a workbench, staring at something in front of him. It was not clear what because his body hid his work surface. When the door creaked he half turned towards them, lowered his head and peered at the visitors across his thick glasses.

"Oh, Inspector!" he seemed genuinely pleased to see him. "What brings you here? We haven't had any troubles for a while now."

Taras smiled, walked across to the old man and gave him his hand. He introduced Osterc.

"Now it's we who have the troubles. Or..." he corrected himself "...more of a riddle. I think you might be able to help us solve it."

"I'm all ears," said the man and indicated they should sit down. There were three chairs in the room, each one different. Taras had the red upholstered one, Osterc a wooden one painted blue, the old man stayed on his three-legged stool without a backrest.

"We are looking for a watch. We would like to know what kind of watch someone who we are interested in was wearing. And, following that, what might have happened to it."

He pointed to Osterc.

"It was big," Osterc described the watch he had seen. "And looked fancy."

"I see," said the rounded gentleman. "That is not much help to us. Fancy in what way?"

Osterc sighed.

"It sparkled. If I saw a picture of it I would probably recognise it, but like this, without anything, I cannot seem to bring it up in my mind."

The old man nodded and took a small laptop from the shelf behind his work desk. He clearly didn't use it often as it had accumulated quite some dust. He opened it and switched it on.

"It will take a little while for it to get going," he pointed at the computer. "In the meantime tell me a little more about the person who was supposed to have worn it."

"A young social climber," said Taras. "Came into some money quickly. There is a painting by Slovenia's most popular and most expensive contemporary painter hanging in his office."

"But he is not specifically a watch lover?"

Taras looked at Osterc who shook his head.

"Probably not."

The old man lifted his stool and moved it closer to his visitors, then sat down and held the computer on his lap.

"It means we're not looking for watches such as, for example, the likes of Patek Philippe, notable especially for their elegance? Watches not intended for the nuveau riche but those born with a silver spoon and who don't care what other people think about it? We are looking for watches for people who own a BMW X5 or an Audi Q7?"

"A Porsche Cayenne," said Osterc and upon noticing Taras's quizzing gaze added, "I checked it in the register. New, not second-hand."

"There are quite a number of watches that would fit a man like that," the watchmaker continued. "This one, for example, would be a first, most obvious choice."

He showed them the screen.

"Rolex. First possibility. Most Rolexes are made of steel and even though they are status symbols and in high demand, they are not extremely expensive. We are looking at watches up to ten thousand euros. I would not, however, describe them as sparkling. Of course there are also gold Rolexes but these are quickly into the range of twenty to forty thousand euros, for the simple reason that they're gold. Technically they are the same. They are much shinier though."

Osterc took a look and shook his head.

"That watch was different."

"No worries," the old man nodded. "There are plenty of other candidates. A second possibility in such circles is a watch of the Breitling brand. It has a large, noticeable version called the Chronomat for people who like to show off."

A watch with a winged logo and the word Breitling in among three tiny dials with hands built into the basic blue dial appeared on screen.

"Breitling used to advertise with pilots, that's why their logo has wings. Recently they've gone in a different direction. With a new owner and new director, they turned more to life style. Their motto now is air, land, sea. Meaning they still cover aviation, but also car racing, even cycling, and diving. Does the man you're interested in engage in any of these activities?"

"We don't know," said Taras.

"If it is made of steel, such a watch costs up to eight, nine thousand euros, with a gold strap its price quickly increases to thirty, even thirty-five thousand euros. A gold watch with a plain strap, around twenty thousand."

"It wasn't blue," said Osterc.

"There are various colours but all are in these hues. Black, grey, there really aren't any really bright ones in their range."

He entered a new name into the browser.

"The next kind popular in these circles are Panerai. They're not gold, but they are rather big. The Luminor model has a recognisable arch across the crown. This arch used to be something used by divers to give extra protection to and tighten the crown.

It is a recognisable feature which is why the watch was so popular with poseurs. People with money who want to show off and are not after a watch that might suit them but one that can let everyone else know how expensive it is. There is no gold version of Luminor. They cost between four and in some cases even over ten thousand euros. From experience I know that these people buy the cheaper ones. Why give twenty grand if one for four looks the same?"

"No," said Osterc. "I think that it wasn't round."

"You don't say," the old man almost jumped. "At last, some information. So, it wasn't round. Was it square?"

"No, it wasn't square either."

"Of course not, I'm only joking."

He was already opening a new page on the computer and showed them.

"This one perhaps?"

Osterc looked at the screen carefully.

"This is more expensive than a Rolex and also very successful in these circles. Audemars Piguet with their Royal Oak model. Even just the steel version costs more than twenty thousand euros. The model Royal Oak Offshore is a particularly large watch with their characteristic eight-sided lunette. This is this ring round the glass. Unfortunately, it is also worn by people who don't know why the watch is this way, they don't know the history or its technical properties, all that matters to them is that it's large and expensive."

"This was it," Osterc nodded. "Eight-sided."

"Who is their representative for Slovenia?" Taras asked.

The old man shook his head.

"You can't buy this watch here. There was a representative for Slovenia but a watch dealer from Trieste seems to have been very influential also globally and he managed to argue that the rep in Slovenia was too close to his turf. Anyone who wanted such a watch will surely put in the effort and drive the eighty kilometres to Trieste to buy their watch there."

Taras looked at it. As a child he had been given a blue watch for his confirmation, Vostok, a Russian brand. It worked for a month and then they went to the shop to have it replaced. The second one also worked for barely a month and, because the watchmaker was out of Vostoks, he got a green Poljot. This one also didn't work for long. Taras, who was about seven or eight at the time, wore it anyway, so he wouldn't be the only one in class without a watch. At least he could set the date in the tiny display window to the correct one every day.

"Royal Oak has one of the most beautiful stories in the history of watchmaking," the old man continued in a melancholy voice. "Gerald Genta, the famous Swiss watch designer, created it for the Basel Fair in 1972. He had been given an order to design a slightly more modern watch and he more or less drew this one overnight. It was initially thought it would come out in a single series intended for Italy. He was enthusiastic about the eight-sided shape and in one way or another began incorporating it in all his new designs. He died a year before his famous product turned forty. What is interesting is that, when it was first introduced, this watch was more expensive than a gold Rolex, even though it was made of steel. But people like your man are usually not interested in this. Because it was so successful they later produced a version called Offshore with another designer. This is much larger than the original – at the time most watches were around thirty-seven, thirty-eight millimetres in diameter, even less. The watches sold as men's watches at the time today look to us as if they were designed to be worn by women. Fortunately watches are now getting smaller again, for a while it looked as if we were going towards gas gauges. Royal Oak is forty-two millimetres in diameter and there is an even bigger version, which is also very high and has an integrated strap. You cannot remove the strap. I find this is too much. Wherever you reach towards with your hand your watch hits first."

"And if a person like this found themselves in financial trouble," Taras asked. "Where would it be easiest for them to sell it?"

The old man scratched his head. On the bare skin above his glasses. He only had a sample of hair left. Tiny tufts above the ears.

"The first option would be to his colleagues. But this is less likely. With good watches, age isn't important. A good watch is a good watch. But these new money people are crazy about new models, when something new comes out, they buy it and include their old watch in the deal. Despite the fact that many an old model that is no longer being produced, keeps its price more easily. A snobbish, consumer reflex sets in, they change their old watch for a new one, pay the difference, happy to get rid of it, although in the long term this is an even worse financial loss for them."

Taras shook his head. If it went to his colleagues, they would never find out.

"Any other possibilities?"

"There is a world platform for selling watches, it's called Chrono 24. You can find any make and model of watch you want there, and they list a price, whether it is used or new, whether it has its certificates or not. We can have a look."

He opened the web page advertising luxury watches for sale, clicked on a tab with the Audemars Piguet brand.

"Here, eight thousand, eight hundred and seventy results for Audemars Piguet, three thousand two hundred and three for the Royal Oak Offshore model. But selling things through this portal takes time. Is your man in a hurry?"

Taras thought of the three neat and brawny clones.

"He's in a hurry."

"He could have taken it to some watchmaker here in town to sell for a commission, but again, that is not really a rapid route. Not for someone who needs money quickly."

"Let us say that he is in a great hurry."

"Then he would take it to a pawn shop. You can sell things quickly there but at a great loss. I have a friend who has an arrangement with pawn shops in Ljubljana and its surroundings and they call him whenever a watch appears and the contractual period expires. Someone in financial trouble pawns a watch they bought for ten thousand euros, gets six for it and then the pawnbroker sells it to someone like my colleague for seven thousand euros. He takes his time and sells it on for nine."

"Do you think you might be able to call this colleague of yours? If such a watch were to appear at any local pawn shops, he would probably know?"

"Of course," said the old man, went to his workbench and

found a black book in a drawer.

"I should have long digitalised this," he said to Taras and Osterc as if in an apology. "My son keeps telling me to do it, but I can't be bothered to type it all out."

He dialled the number with his mobile and got the owner. When he explained what he wanted and three 'mhmmm's later he put down the phone and turned to the criminal investigators.

"Your watch is in Litija," he said.

Taras smiled and turned to Osterc.

"Our lad is in trouble. In deep financial trouble."

*

He escorted them out to the street.

"And how's business otherwise, in these times?" Taras enquired. He did not want to say, in these times when any electronic device from scales upwards gives us the precise time.

"You'd be surprised," said the old man. "Watchmaking has never been as popular as it is today. Never before have so many expensive watches been sold, unfortunately also because any drug or anabolics dealer can choose what they want online. Previously only those from rich families where a particular attitude was maintained knew about them, or watch enthusiasts. If you wanted information, you had to go abroad and do your research... Now we have the internet. Now every buffoon can be clever."

They shook hands.

"I hope I was of help. Just like you were of help to me then."

"It's my job," said Taras.

"Many people wouldn't, even if it was their job."

*

It was hot in the car. It had been parked in the sun and when Taras opened the door a wave of heat blasted them as if from a furnace. He opened all the windows, even the ones in the back and as he waited for the temperature to fall below the level at which proteins coagulate, he called Tina.

"What's up?" she asked.

"We will be at the office in ten minutes. I'd like to ask you a favour."

"Tell me."

"Can you check who the owner of the flat on the second floor of Župančič Street is? The one that used to belong to Majda Vasle."

"I've already done so," she said. She could not stop herself saying, "Even though this was not supposed to be my case."

"And?"

"According to the only information I could find, the owner is apparently still Majda Vasle."

CHAPTER 39.

"The mother?"

He looked at the whiteboard where it was written that Majda Vasle had died on 12 January. In parenthesis Tina had added that she had been in a traffic accident.

"Where did you check?"

"In the property register..."

"No, no," Taras shook his head impatiently. "The property register is a summary of a number of sources, it is not always reliable. Why didn't you check the land register?"

"Because," she said slowly, emphasising every word, "this building is not entered in the land register."

"What do you mean it is not in the register?"

Before he even finished his sentence he remembered. What was it the busybody on the fourth floor had said? That they had a lazy caretaker and that the block of flats had still not been entered into the land register.

"I see," he said and nodded at Tina, repeating this 'I see' another three times.

He typed property registry into his browser to see what would come up.

The property register lists the details of the people who are possibly the owners of a property. It gives details for flats and other parts of buildings that are not listed as separate entries at the land registry.

Possible owners. This was not of much help to them.

"But," Osterc spoke. "If he was not really on bad terms with his mother, he must have inherited the flat. He is the only child, the woman was divorced and he should thus also be the only heir. And half a year later, surely the probate proceedings are done and over?"

"Not necessarily," Taras shook his head. "Probate proceedings occur at best eight months after death."

At least when Taras's father-in-law had died it had taken that long.

"Perhaps this is why young Vadnal has become so jittery. Perhaps he's not the only heir. What if Vadnal senior had something there?"

"As an heir?" Tina was surprised.

Taras shook his head.

"No, as a co-owner. This," he pointed to the screen where he still had the site of the State Geodetic Administration with the property register open, "tells us only who paid the tax or, what is it called, the building land development fee. Robert Vadnal could well be a co-owner. When they moved into this flat, they were still married. If only we could check the purchasing contract..."

"Taras, you're forgetting two things," Tina interrupted him. "Firstly, that we are not looking into the murder of Robert Vadnal..."

"It is possible that he also shot the woman in the park. He was here at ten in the evening on Monday."

"And you forget," she continued. "That he has an alibi for Metelkova. He was in his office all that time."

"I am not forgetting it at all."

Vadnal had an alibi not only for Tuesday but also Monday. At 2am he was buying and selling electronic mist.

"But we know that, despite this, he was at the building on Župančič Street at 10pm on Monday. We have a witness who I wouldn't use as reliable evidence in court, but Vadnal did not deny being here anyway. And if he could have been at the flat on Monday even though the system at the Crystal Palace says otherwise, then he could just as well have been at Metelkova on Tuesday. What if the woman on the bench was just a rehearsal for his father?"

"With Baloh's gun?" Tina asked.

Taras stepped to the whiteboard and wrote FLAT in block capitals on it.

"If only we could... Perhaps one of us can pretend to be a potential buyer..."

He looked at Tina.

"You're the only one he doesn't know."

"Are you suggesting," she said in a resigned voice, "that I call him and arrange a meeting because I urgently need a flat?"

Taras shook his head.

"No, no. Nobody would believe you that you are buying a flat for four hundred thousand euros. Tell him you are representing an elderly couple who are returning to Slovenia after years of living abroad and urgently, very urgently, need a flat in the centre of Ljubljana."

*

FLAT for sale. 100 m² in town house, close to centre and Tivoli... Price: 425,000 euros.

I can get this down to at least four hundred, she thought for a moment, as if actually intending to buy it.

She was not sure how estate agents dress so she wore what she had worn for her job interview only that she did not wear tights under the skirt that Taras had branded a mini. She imagined they might carry around folders in which they keep plans and layouts of properties with the square footage of the rooms, but this was probably in cases where they are trying to sell a flat and not, like her, trying to buy one. She took a notepad and a fountain pen. If you're buying a four hundred thousand euro flat, you don't go to the meeting with a biro.

She was out in the street at ten to nine. She was nervous.

Five minutes before the arranged time, she was standing on the pavement outside the door. The door opened and first two dogs appeared and then the old lady. She did not have time to hide, all she could do was greet her and hope that she would not start talking to her.

A minute to nine a white Porsche Cayenne came driving down the street at a much faster speed than appropriate. The driver did not even try to look for a parking space, just turned onto the pavement and stopped. A man fitting the description she had been given stepped out of it. She refrained from waving at him and waited for him to get closer. Only when he began walking towards her did she make a step towards him.

"Jakob Vadnal?"

"The very same," he said and offered her his hand.

"Tina Lanc."

She did not see the need to give a false name. At least she wouldn't make a mistake.

He unlocked the front door and for a moment she shuddered. What if she met someone else in the corridor whom she had already spoken to?

"Have you been in this long?" he asked, as if sensing her nervousness.

"Two years," she said. "I studied computing and psychology but what can I do when there's nothing suitable in my field of work."

If you are forced to lie, try to incorporate at least some truth into the lie, she had been taught.

They reached the door to the flat, a solid wooden door which creaked when he opened it. Tina breathed a sigh of relief once they went inside. The first, most dangerous part of this mission was over.

"Perhaps the hinges need oiling," he said. "But you know what it's like when you don't live in a place any more. You barely find time to fix things where you live."

*

He showed her around the flat. As for the layout and size, it was identical to the one below it and the two above but other furniture and the way it was placed made it look different. It was furnished carelessly, a little of this, a little of that. A leather sofa in the living room, in front of it an old-fashioned dark wood table, against the wall a smooth wardrobe, perhaps even formica. As if each piece had been added separately. When one piece became too worn it was replaced with one that happened to be in fashion at the time. The kitchen and the dining corner were covered in wallpaper, the other walls painted, some green, some even brown. Despite the lights being switched on and the light coming from outside, the flat was very dark and gloomy.

"As far as the price goes," Tina began, "my clients would be interested to know whether there is any leeway?"

"Leeway?" he feigned ignorance.

"Any chance of lowering it."

"That depends," he said. "It depends on how serious buyers they are. How soon could they transfer the money?"

"You can get thee hundred and fifty in two days, if we reach a deal."

He shook his head and left her waiting for a few seconds.

"We could probably meet somewhere half way. Two days, you say?"

"On the condition that all the paperwork is in order."

He nodded.

"It is, though there is a minor technical detail. You see, the flat is registered in my mother's name and she died in January this year. And the way the courts work here, the probate proceedings are not due until September. I am the only heir though."

"Well, then we shall speak again then. Of course I will need to search elsewhere in the meantime. You must understand that."

"No, no, don't hurry!" he almost cried out.

His cool vanished so suddenly that she could not hide her surprise. Any real estate agent would probably also be unable to.

"All this can be sorted out. If your clients really want this flat, we can go to a lawyer and make a contract that will take into account all the circumstances. Why wait a month?"

He began explaining the complicated legal manoeuvres with which they could come to a satisfactory agreement and to both his and their benefit circumvent the Slovene courts. She tried to listen to what he was saying and waited to interrupt with the sentence she had ready in her mind.

"In any case, I would need to take a look at the original purchase agreement."

"Why?"

"What do you mean, why?"

She smiled. You did not have to be a real estate agent to know that without this any discussion about buying a property ends. Was he really so naïve not to know this? So desperate?

"I don't have it here."

His top lip quivered nervously.

"Then call me when you do."

She turned towards the door. He jumped after her and grabbed her by the shoulder.

"Where are you going? I didn't say I cannot bring it. I have it in the car. Wait here and I will go and get it."

He almost ran to the door. Before disappearing in the hallway he half tuned to her and pointed at the sofa.

"Make yourself comfortable. I'll be straight back."

She waited for his steps to die away on the staircase, then found a paper tissue in her handbag and began opening the drawers on the cupboard closest to her.

*

He only ran for the first few steps, then he stopped and slowly continued down towards the ground floor. He unlocked the door to his car, sat inside and took the cardboard folder from the glove compartment. He stared at if for a few seconds, then closed it and got out of the car.

At the front door he came across an elderly neighbour who was returning from walking her dogs. He needed to wait or the woman to walk into the corridor, not simply push her out of the way.

"Oh, Jakob, what are you doing here? I haven't seen you in a while."

"I came to check on the flat," he said and felt his voice tremble. "Air it a little."

"And now she is with you?" she continued nosily.

What did she mean?

"Ms Lanc, is she with you now?"

"Do you know her?"

"Yes, of course, she's a policewoman, a criminal investigator. She came to see me about that woman murdered in the park."

"Yes, of course," he muttered. "Excuse me..."

He turned round and made his way to the car. He ran for the last few metres. He sat at the wheel and was about to press the ignition button when he stopped and got out again.

There was something in the flat that he could not leave behind.

*

Tina heard the steps in the stairwell and immediately afterward the door creaked. She closed the drawer, the last one in the first cupboard, and took the two steps to the nearest sofa and sat down. Just in time. Vadnal returned with the folder in his hands, came closer and handed it to her.

She took it and opened it. As she browsed the first page Vadnal stepped behind her and she could hear him open the drawer. She turned round to see what he was doing and for a brief second saw Vadnal holding something in his hand that was fast approaching her head.

*

She woke up with a headache. Her head hurt so much she didn't dare open her eyes, afraid her skull might fall to pieces. From behind her closed eyelids she heard movement, someone next to her was moving about, and then she heard a kind of blunt chopping noise. She raised her head that had previously been drooping over her chest.

Slowly she opened her eyes. One eye first, only just enough to allow a little light. Then the other. Only with half the success. It was glued together, covered in something sticky. When she eventually opened her eyelids something viscous trickled down her cheek to the wide piece of silver tape that was stuck over her mouth.

He was sitting at the table with a gun in front of him, a wallet next to it. He was busy with a pile of lumpy white powder that he was chopping into fine dust with a plastic bank card, arranging it in lines. There were some pills next to the pile of dust. Five pills arranged in a pattern like the five dots on a die. Four in a square and one in the middle. Next to the pills were a glass of water and a lit candle, the only source of light in the room. He had switched off the light.

He looked at her for a moment.

With the powder he created five lines, a few centimetres long, then returned the card to his wallet and took out a hundred-euro banknote. He rolled it up and leaned across the first line, sucking it up his nose, then gathering what powder was left from the first dose and rubbing it into his gums above his top teeth.

She was seated on a chair, her hands wrapped behind the backrest and tied at the wrists, probably with the same silver tape as her mouth and her feet around her ankles. She tensed her body and then gave up. There was no chance she could break free alone.

She could follow her jailer only when he leaned across the table, otherwise he was, like her, just a silhouette in the semi-darkness. She tried to figure out how much time had passed since she had fallen unconscious, but there was nothing to help her. It could have been a mere fifteen minutes, it could have been many hours. It was night outside.

He began with the pill at the centre. He looked at it, leaned across a new line of powder, sniffed it and used his index finger to rub his nostril. Then he picked up the pill and swallowed it.

He was gathering up the courage. Three more lines and three more pills, that was all she had. She did not want to but she couldn't help herself. She cried.

*

Taras was sitting in the car in darkness and silence. He placed his Beretta on the driver's seat and waited. He could see the light on the second floor and also the entrance to the block of flats and tried not to look away for a single second. He felt guilty for having involved Tina in all this, so he had decided to at least do all the rest the right way.

He had arrived at Župančič Street at half past five when people began leaving their work and there were more empty parking spaces around. He found one that was right and parked Osterc's Fiat Stilo there. He did not want Tina to recognise his car and feel that he was standing at her back. Even so she was rather too confident when they parted and he had tried to explain who she was up against.

"He has killed and will again if he has to. Let him show you the flat, the original contract, thank him, tell him you will call him, we hand the case over to Kristan and goodbye."

He was not sure she fully understood.

He returned home by bus, had a shower and watched a match. During half-time he checked his gun, trigger, breech... Checked and loaded. Everything was in order.

At eight he sat on the bus and was half an hour later having coffee under the large trees in the garden of the Slovene Writers' Association. At quarter to nine he stood on the corner at the Finance Ministry and watched out for Tina and Vadnal. She arrived at five minutes to nine, greeted the woman from the fourth floor who was taking her dogs out for a walk and fortunately didn't stop to chat. Vadnal appeared exactly at nine. They shook hands and disappeared into the building.

He waited for three minutes and went to the car. Vadnal had left his Cayenne on the pavement. He thought about calling the tow truck but he restrained himself. When he sat in the car, the lights were already on in the flat. Three of its windows looked out to the north and it must get dark inside long before the light is too low outside.

At half past nine Vadnal appeared at the door. He almost breathed a sigh of relief, expecting Tina to appear after him but Vadnal went across to his car alone. He took something from inside it and went back towards the block of flats where he met the woman with the dogs at the door. He must clearly have forgotten something because he immediately afterwards ran back to the car, sat in it, and a minute or so later made his way back to the building..

At nine fifty-three the lights in the flat went off. He waited for them to appear at the door. A minute, two, three. He looked up towards the window of the flat and noticed a faint light coming from them. He grabbed his gun from the seat and leaped out of the car.

*

Vadnal was swallowing the pills in half-minute intervals and her only chance was that his head exploded before he came for her. The way he was going, there was a chance it would. His movements had become jagged, almost manic, his gaze wandered from the table with the drugs and the gun, to her, and it seemed he could not hold back any longer. Before sniffing the last line, he grabbed the gun, lifted it, looked at it again and put it back down.

This can't be happening, was all that she could think. Just that. It can't be happening, can't be happening, can't... No plan, no point. She had not had a chance to experience anything, had never wanted to harm anybody, people don't just die like this. Not at her age.

Then she heard the door. Damned old door. She hoped that the creaking noise would not reach through the crystals of cocaine that had settled on Vadnal's sensory receptors, but in vain. He twitched and turned in the direction from which came the clear and telling creak of the unoiled door.

He stepped behind her and held the gun up to the back of her head. Deliberately or just because he didn't realise it, so hard she would have cried out if she could. Instead, all that came from her mouth and through the duct tape was a barely audible groan. The footsteps stopped briefly, then continued and slowly the second door opened. Behind it stood Taras holding his gun, lowered against his thigh.

For a moment he seemed confused, almost as if, in the light of the candle that flickered when he opened the door, he did not understand what was going on. He twitched and she thought, almost hoped, that he would throw himself into the dark... Vadnal burst into laughter.

Taras stayed where he was. He calmed himself, looked up at Vadnal who was stooped over Tina.

"I will count to three," said Taras.

Vadnal pushed the barrel of the gun harder against her head but she could barely feel it now.

"One."

Vadnal laughed.

Taras's hand with the gun rose up to his chest, joined by his left hand.

"Two."

He was guffawing.

She closed her eyes and lowered her head. Not to make herself smaller and expose Vadnal... She wanted to believe that this was not why she did it, but didn't. She knew what was coming and that nothing and nobody in the world could prevent it from happening.

The pressure on the back of her head eased, the gun moved away from her.

She could not remember if she turned towards Taras or threw herself at the table. Taras did not wait until three. She knew that he wouldn't.

It was silly, but what she thought about was his elbow.

Saturday

CHAPTER 40.

Dawn was breaking above Ljubljana. Anyone stepping out onto the terrace at the Nebotičnik skyscraper at four o'clock in the morning at the end of June would be able to see a slightly lighter darkness in the distance and sense the first colours of the awakening day. In town, down in the streets, it was still night. And if they were to look from the same terrace towards the north, they would see a light on the seventh floor of the building next to it and the silhouettes of three people in the window.

One of them was Taras. He was sitting next to Drvarič and both were in front of Kristan who was sitting at his desk. He could kill for a coffee even though he had had three at the Medical Centre where he had taken Tina. Three, but small, tasteless and weak from the hospital coffee machine. The tension was easing and he was beginning to feel tired. There was nobody at the General Police Directorate to make one at this hour.

"So," Kristan began after he had stayed silent for almost a minute, leaning with his elbows on his desk, scratching his forehead and two or three times sneaking a glance at Taras.

"Tell me, please," he then began, "that you have a good reason and an even better excuse for this tonight. That it was only and exclusively in self-defence."

Taras told him what had happened in a few sentences. From the moment he stepped into the flat to the shot.

"Why didn't you come to us?"

"I just wanted to check whether our theory made any sense. If Vadnal senior had not been at least partial owner of the flat, we would have been left without our only motive."

"And was he?"

Taras nodded.

"The sole owner. I don't know why and how come the flat was registered in his name, but it was. When they signed the contract, the wife had only the right to use it. There was no way the flat could be sold while he was still alive."

Kristan turned towards the window. It was beginning to get light outside now. He thought for a while.

"At eleven I will have around thirty journalists not counting the technical staff that come with them, all in the conference room. And although I would personally wish to handle this differently, I am left with no choice but to declare you a hero."

He looked at Taras.

"It will be best for all of us this way. I don't know though who will want to work with you in the future. Drvarič…"

From the inside pocket of his jacket Drvarič pulled an envelope and wanted to hand it to Kristan. He in turn just pointed towards Taras.

Taras opened the envelope, took out the sheet of paper, read it, then put it back in the envelope and handed it back to Drvarič.

"At the same time, while we all smile and hug, I will announce before everyone your temporary suspension and an internal enquiry. As a formality in any such case… Whether it will stay a formality, remains to be seen."

Taras appeared indifferent. Probably deliberately.

He was tired.

"Is there anything you want to say before we start on the details?"

Taras could not hold back. He yawned.

"Excuse me," he said when he managed to close his mouth again. "There are two things. Firstly, this letter was written on Thursday. It can't have anything to do with what happened yesterday."

He yawned again.

"And secondly?" Kristan asked impatiently.

"It's been a long night. I could have left earlier but I chose to write the report. If possible, I'd like to withdraw until eleven. I would not like to fall asleep during all the smiling and hugging."

*

"What are you doing here, Taras?" Golob asked him. "I thought you were with Kristan?"

"No more. I'd like to see the results of the DNA tests. You mentioned that you would have them at eight."

"I shouldn't now be showing you these."

Golob raised his hands as if trying to fend off Taras with his open palms.

"You can before eleven," said Taras. "At eleven there will be a press conference at the GPD where Kristan will explain to journalists what happened in their neighbourhood last night and also tell them that I am suspended."

"Until eleven?"

"Check if you don't believe me."

Golob looked at him, eyes half closed, then waved his hand.

"In fact, what do I care. Nobody informed me. Until I get this by mail, it doesn't exist for me."

He produced a folder from his drawer and pushed it towards Taras on the opposite side of the desk. Taras opened it and browsed through it.

"Surprised?" asked Golob.

With a motionless face Taras stared at the piece of paper and by the mere fact that he could not take his eyes off the relatively few words written on the page, any averagely intelligent person could assume that something had surprised him.

"I shouldn't be at my age, but yes, I admit, I am a little."

"Do you need an explanation?"

Taras shrugged his shoulders. He was about to get one anyway.

"So, as you requested, we analysed the DNA from the Glock 19 pistol belonging to Franz Baloh, which turned out to be the weapon used in the murder of the woman in the park."

Taras raised his hand as if in a classroom at school.

"It has now already been decided that she died due to her illness. Yesterday it was leaked to the press and at eleven it will be confirmed at the GPD. As I see, the first DNA belongs to the owner of the gun, Franz Baloh."

"That is right. The second DNA is unknown and is also not in our databases."

Taras nodded. This part he understood without Golob's explanation.

"Then," Golob continued, "you also requested the DNA analysis of the deceased Robert Vadnal and the DNA analysis of Ignac Jakin and any possible correlation. Clearly you expected a match?"

Taras nodded.

"Might I ask why?"

"Thirty years ago there was a big mess in the block of flats. Some were born, others died, others divorced and moved out. I thought that all this was somehow connected. I thought that Robert Vadnal was Ignac Jakin's father."

Golob shook his head.

"No, he isn't. Does this spoil it all for you?"

Taras sighed and stood up. He could not be bothered to listen to Golob's lecturing. Not today.

"It spoils the symmetry. But who says there should have been symmetry here anyway. Thank you."

He stood up and started walking towards the door but as he grabbed the handle, Golob added, "There is something else, though."

He turned round.

"Sit down Taras, I think you will be surprised a second time."

*

"Taras Birsa, ma'am, from the Police."

She waited for him at the door, half hiding behind it. A frail single mother with an adult son who spends all his days in front of a computer. Poor woman.

"Yes? My son isn't home."

Only half her face appeared behind the door. Enough for him to notice the black bags under her eyes.

"I am not here because of your son. I came for a visit."

This confused her. For a moment she hesitated, then stepped a small step backwards and timidly asked.

"A visit?"

"A coffee and a little talk."

She didn't like it but eventually opened the door and indicated to him to follow her.

"I can only make you a Turkish coffee."

"Right."

She went to the stove, filled the coffee pot with water and put it on the hob.

"Milk?"

"No, thank you. No milk, no sugar."

She waited for the water to boil, removed the pot and stirred in the coffee. She placed it on a small wooden tray, put a cup and saucer on it and placed it on the table in front of Taras.

"Was it hard for you, alone with a child?"

She looked at him with surprise. Since he continued talking, he probably wasn't even expecting an answer.

"I have two daughters. My wife... Well, I call her wife, even though we're not married. She didn't work for a while and we had to get through on just my pay package. Sometimes I didn't know how we would pay the bills. And at the paper factory you probably earnt even less that we did at the police."

She did not sit down with him. She stayed at the kitchen counter.

"I am not the most systematic of types. I follow my nose, as we say. If possible, I would live without numbers. But I do have a girl on my team who studied computers. I am also unfortunately someone who tends to keep things to themselves. When, however, I entrusted her with what I had found out in this block of flats, she immediately spotted a small discrepancy. Would you like to know what?"

She did not respond but again Taras did not expect an answer.

"But about that a little later."

He lifted his cup, took a sip of coffee and put it down on the table next to the saucer she brought it with.

"Good coffee." He nodded approvingly. "Let's first finish the part about life as a single mother."

He looked around the room.

"Does that thing even still work?" He pointed at the ancient TV standing on the chest of drawers. "Though your son has a nice LCD on the wall in his room, and his computer isn't bad. Very good, in fact, if I am to believe my colleague with a degree in computers. He was never deprived of anything, was he?"

"I tried hard that he wouldn't be," she said dryly.

"Well, considering the way things turned out, it might have been better that you wouldn't have tried so very much."

She looked at the floor.

"You know that the lie detector and the DNA sample proved your son innocent of involvement in the death of the woman under your window?"

"I know."

"What you don't know, though," Taras continued, "is that the polygraph showed that he in fact intended to murder her. It's extraordinary how two people got the same unusual idea almost at the same time."

He leaned back, folded his arms and stared at the woman. She was still gazing at the floor.

"By the way, the polygraph also showed that he wants you dead as well."

She raised her head. In her eyes, on her face, there was pain, blunt like an old scar. This was nothing new to her.

"Dead," he repeated. "Isn't that terrible? After all that you've done for him. Do you know what it was that…"

He smiled.

"Do you know what initially blurred the picture for me? My colleague and I came to see you, everyone in this block of flats, for what we call information gathering interviews. I didn't think of it as coming to visit suspects. Not at all. Somehow it didn't fit in. An old town block of flats with local names that have been here for generations… and outside a cold-blooded execution of a helpless woman. What kind of beast must a person be to do this and why? Then, bingo, even on our first visit to your downstairs neighbour, the deceased Mr… What was his name again?"

Here too she was silent.

"Baloh, isn't it? Well, we discover a gun with him which is almost still smouldering. He agreed we could take the gun in for analysis, but I remember sensing an uncertainty as soon as he did. He wasn't sure he was doing the right thing. As if he knew that he should not have given it to us, though he did not know exactly why. Do you know the feeling when you reach for a glass with your hand and the moment you touch it you know that it doesn't bode well, that you will break it? But you can't do anything about it? The hand goes its own way."

He leaned on the table again, this time with one hand only, and he scratched his head with the other.

"No? It happens to me sometimes. Well, then, two floors up, here was your son who fitted the profile. Thirty something, mentally still a teenager who wants to prove himself in front of others like him, and a neo-Nazi supporter as well... Something you are undoubtedly very proud of?"

He stopped.

"Are you?"

"He's my son."

Taras nodded.

"And motherly love is unconditional, of course. My colleague searched his computer. Did you know what she discovered? I can read it out to you."

He took a cardboard folder out of his backpack and placed it on the table. He took a page out of the first batch of papers it contained.

"This is his web correspondence. I won't tire you with dates, which we diligently noted, or with all of it, because there is quite a lot of it. I would, though, like to read you two or three sentences. This is what he says in one of his posts.

"A tramp has been lying under my window for three days. A smelly old woman. If they don't take her away soon, I'll sort it out for them. Straight onto the compost heap.

"Of course we say lots of things and don't actually do them. Well, your son didn't stop.

"Well, the rubbish men haven't come and clearly won't," Taras read on. *"We need to finally get the Let's Clean Up Slovenia campaign going. Can anyone help me get hold of the right equipment?*

"Then there were a few jokes on the same theme, as well as suggestions of which an interesting one was that he should acquire some hydrochloric acid and douse the old woman with it. Some of them mentioned Auschwitz and similar places, in between there was an answer by someone whom we also intend to visit. This is what he says:

"Call me and bring five hundred euros.

"For five hundred euros one can buy a 0.32 calibre gun on the black market, most commonly the Crvena Zastava brand from Kragujevac. We used to call them *Little Bee*. It's not brilliant but you can kill a man with it if necessary. Your son, supposedly would get his hands on a Walter P5 for that money. Congratulations!"

He turned the sheet towards her across the table, pointing to the paragraph concerned, as if she would be able to read it from where she was standing.

"Your son got this message last Monday morning, and the woman was shot that same evening."

"Baloh shot her," she spoke. "He shot her and admitted to it. Why don't you just leave us alone?"

"You're talking like my boss. 'Leave it, Taras, why bother, the murderer admitted to it and then killed himself. This happens all the time.'"

He tried to imitate Drvarič, though he wasn't particularly successful. Brajc was a much better impersonator than he. Even Osterc was.

"Someone shot her with Baloh's gun. Was it Baloh? It would be difficult, since he couldn't walk. What do you think? You knew him, could he have done it?"

She didn't answer.

"And another detail. Would a professional soldier after using it have forgotten to clean his weapon? Impossible, however demented. Does a dog forget to salivate if you stick a steak in front of it?"

With feigned embarrassment he added, "This about dogs was not the nicest thing to say, but you understand."

He shook his head.

"No, but he didn't have to walk. Someone else could have used his gun. We found traces of another DNA on his gun, you see. The DNA of someone who could have used it according to his instructions, or at least with his knowledge... Or the DNA of someone who could have taken his gun and then returned it without his knowledge."

He stopped and looked at his cup.

"No more coffee. Will have to hurry."

Carefully he placed the cup back on the saucer.

"Who would take the gun from the drawer and later, after using it, return it? The daughter? She had access to the flat, she could have been cleaning, picked up the gun and left a trace on it. She could have gone to the park with it... But she didn't. The DNA was not hers.

"Your son? He had a motive, had clearly expressed the wish and had even taken steps towards its realisation, but – did he also have access to the weapon? Could he have gone into Baloh's flat? Could he have sneaked in with a trick? How could he have known where the gun was or that Baloh even had it? And, of course, why would he then be looking for a gun on the internet? I considered all this even before we conducted the DNA test."

She stood calmly at the counter, her face impassive. What if she wasn't even listening?

"As you know, there was another incident yesterday in the flat below you. A man died who had shot his father on Metelkova. Due to some minor detail, I long thought that the perpetrator was the same. That the person who shot the woman in the park and the one who killed the man on Metelkova was one and the same."

He smiled.

"There was some mathematician, I have forgotten his name, who was into quantum physics, or whatever it's called, and he maintained that the correct equation must be beautiful. I also think along those lines. I like patterns."

"My son didn't kill anyone," she said.

He did not pay attention to her words.

"Your husband committed suicide. May I ask why?"

She grimaced.

"Depression. He suffered from it for a number of years and had tried to take his life a number of times before."

"Was it anything to do with the fact that you had a lover?"

"Who says I had a lover?"

She stared at him defiantly.

"Do you know what my pedantic young colleague noticed, the girl who likes numbers?"

"It seems you are about to tell me."

He smiled at her encouragingly. Finally, she has come out of her shell.

"She noticed that there was ten months between the death of your husband and the birth of your child, your son."

Her eyes rolled towards the window overlooking Župančič Street. It must have been well insulated because they could hardly hear the traffic below. She stared out of the window for a few seconds without really looking anywhere, and when she turned to Taras again, an entirely different face was looking at him. A face ready to bite.

"Is this what you came to tell me? I met a person who understood me because he had been through something similar. It happened when my husband was already dead."

"I know it's not nice delving into these matters, but what can I do, a job is a job. Who is the boy's father?"

She did not answer.

"It could have been the murdered Robert Vadnal, who we, around some corners, found out used to live here but divorced your neighbour Majda Vasle and moved out. For a brief period she too used the surname Vadnal. They divorced after the birth of your son. Someone might think that the two could be linked. After comparing DNA, however – his we could get easily, your son's, because of your friends in high places, unfortunately with more difficulty – we realised that this was not so. Robert Vadnal was not your son's father and here my expectations of the two cases were finally shattered. Shame, the pattern would have been beautiful."

With the spoon that she had unnecessarily brought with his coffee, he mixed what was left in his cup.

"So many questions, and no answers. Then one hopes that some might be found if we discovered who the unknown DNA from Baloh's gun belonged to. I'll show you."

He pulled another sheet of paper from his folder and placed

it on the table.

"This is what the DNA profile of the unknown sample from the handle of the gun looks like. And here..."

He placed two similar pages next to it.

"...are the DNA profiles of your son and Franz Baloh. Lines, lines, lines... They don't mean anything to me, so you will have to trust me, what I am telling you is the result of the work of experts."

She merely threw a quick glance at the pages on the table.

"When I first visited you, I had a feeling I had seen your son somewhere before. It was a kind of fleeting feeling that... Well, it's almost funny. It was not a feeling that I had actually met him anywhere, and this confused me. I could not place him into any context, but he looked familiar. When I returned to the police station after my first visit, I looked at photos of all young offenders and tried in my mind to make them older. He wasn't among them. It was a strange feeling, so hazy that I should have just dismissed it, but it didn't go away."

Once again he delved into the folder and brought out a photograph. He placed it on the table in front of her. The photo of the soldier of the French Foreign Legion with two friends.

"You must have noticed the likeness yourself, haven't you?"

The man in the photo was smiling, his hair short, a narrow face and thin lips.

"If your son didn't have his head shaved, I might have realised earlier."

"If I had known that this was bothering you so much, I would have told you myself at the time."

"No, you wouldn't have. Your son doesn't know, does he?"

She stayed silent but this time she did not look down. She stared straight into his eyes and Taras had to make an effort not to look away first.

He placed the index finger of his right hand on the first page.

"I allowed myself to be informed. I hope I will know how to repeat this correctly. You see, our cells contain forty-six chromosomes, of which half come from the father, the other half from the mother. I have forgotten why, but there is some mix up, complication, in the way men inherit their chromosomes, but it is possible to look at certain key characteristics such as blood group and things like that, to determine blood links between a father and son."

He smiled with embarrassment.

"If our experts were to hear me now... Anyway, apparently on the basis of these tiny lines here, it is possible with great reliability to establish that the deceased Mr Baloh is the father of your son."

"I know he is," she said scornfully.

"What you might not know is that the mother's line can also be traced, in fact... oh, I don't know, very far, far back. With a hundred percent accuracy. Something to do with mitochondria. Don't ask me how, please."

He pointed with his finger to the DNA of her son and to the unknown DNA on the gun.

"And this here is what we might call a perfect match. It means..."

His finger touched the DNA results for Franz Baloh.

"The father."

Moved to the DNA of Ignac Jakin...

"The son."

And to the third DNA.

"No, not the Holy Ghost."

Sunday

CHAPTER 41.

"I was surprised you called?" said Taras. "So you finally decided to do something?"

They were sitting on a bench at a table at the inn on Rožnik. Both on the same side, under the roof, with the rain pouring down across the other side. Brajc longingly glanced at the notice at the door saying: Fresh *flancati*[20] daily.

They were the only ones outside the inn, which was still closed. Both were soaked since it had rained on them for the entire run, all forty-five minutes of it. Three quarters of an hour to run up Rožnik! Taras's patience was being put to a serious test.

"For some time now, even before all this," Brajc sighed, "I had been saying I needed to change something."

Taras nodded.

"Do you think," said Brajc, finally taking his eyes off the notice, "that I will be able to live normally and all that afterwards?"

"What do you mean normally?"

Brajc sighed, making some kind of circles in the air with his hands.

"Normally with food, and things like that?"

"If you'll exercise, you will be able to eat anything you want."

"Really?"

"Really."

Brajc sank into deep thought. His brow furrowed as he considered this.

---

20 A traditional Slovene carnival food, deep fried pastry covered in sugar.

"If I understand correctly, I am already exercising, am I not?"

"When you'll be able to run up Rožnik, from then on."

"I see..."

"Yes."

Disappointed, he abandoned the thought of *flancati*. It was too early anyway to buy them. Why don't they put away the notice when the inn is closed? The curtain of rain in front of them persisted. If it continued like this for another hour, there would be floods after a month of drought.

"And how will I know I am running?" Brajc asked.

"What do you mean?"

"How will I know that I'm running? That I'm not walking?"

Taras gave him a suspicious look. He did not appear to be joking.

"When you will have at least one foot in the air all the time. That's the definition of running."

Brajc furrowed his brow and stared at the surface of the table in front of him. Ten seconds later he looked up, his brow smooth.

"You really got me there for a while. That's impossible!"

*

"How are things?" he asked Tina.

Her head and right cheek were bandaged. One of her eyes also had a patch over it.

"Concussion and two titanium plates," she said. "Twelve stiches right next to the eye. Apparently I was lucky."

"And otherwise?"

"Stop taking the piss, Taras. Laugh is the last thing I can do right now."

She was lying in the dark in a single room at the University Medical Centre trauma department. If there had been anyone else in the room, they would not have allowed Taras to visit her on a Sunday at half past eight in the morning. He sat on a chair by her bed. A puddle formed on the floor from the rain trickling off his anorak.

"I knew you would shoot."

She spoke slowly, pausing in between each word. He had put the flowers he bought at a petrol station on the table by the bed.

"He hit me across the head but it is my jaw that hurts. I will have to eat through a straw until I die."

"You'll be like new in a week or two."

He had spoken to the doctor.

"We will first need to wait for the swelling to go down and see the results of the injury. Then we can decide how to proceed. She may need extra surgery, she may not, it is hard to say anything specific at this stage."

He reached out with his hand and stroked the skin on her cheek with the back of his fingers. The only part of her head not covered in bandages.

"Do you know what I did when I came to, tied up on that chair? I ran my tongue over my teeth. I was worried he had smashed them. Isn't it interesting? What I was interested in moments before death was what I would look like."

"You'll look like before. Beautiful."

"How did you know he wouldn't shoot me before going for you?"

"You were the only thing between him and me. Why would he do that?"

"Because he was so stoned he didn't even know what he was doing? Did your hand not shake at all at the thought that I was in between you and him?"

Stupid question, would she rather have seen it had?

"Honestly..." he paused for a moment as if trying to remember. "I don't know what I was thinking at the time."

With difficulty she smiled.

"Have they suspended you?"

"First they congratulated me."

"And assigned you a psychologist?"

"Yes."

Once again she smiled slightly.

"Shame I can't be present."

"I refused one," he said.

She gazed at him with her one open, large, dark eye.

"Does it not bother you that you shot a person?"

He frowned and shook his head briefly, shaking it as someone who has suddenly smelt something repulsive.

She nodded.

"It wouldn't bother me either," she said harshly.

She pushed herself up on her elbows and Taras helped her readjust the pillow.

"You don't yet know how the other story unfolded?" he asked her.

"Unfolded?"

"The DNA from Baloh's gun, that second sample, belongs to the mother of our neo-Nazi, Marija Jakin."

"The mother?"

He nodded.

"She intercepted her son's correspondence on Facebook and decided that she would, in her own way, prevent him from any stupidity. That was the expression she used – stupidity."

"And how did she get to Baloh's gun? Surely he isn't...?"

He nodded and finished the sentence.

"...the father of her son."

She nodded ever so slightly with her head.

"Was she a Nazi too?"

"No. She's nothing. She worked as a sales assistant in the nearby paperworks all her life and never refused anything to her son, anything that was within her power. She never said no. This she saw as a virtue. When I asked her whether she had ever thought that this 'stupidity' could have been prevented in other any other way, she said..."

He smiled.

"She used an interesting phrase. She said, *I had my reasons.*"

"Was that not Baloh's parting message?"

"It was. What did he mean by it? I don't know."

"A crazy house," she said.

"Has been for some time. When Osterc sorted the data and you noticed the ten-month pregnancy, I thought of Robert Vadnal. I thought he was the father of this Ignac and that this was the reason his wife threw him out of the flat thirty years ago. And if his real son hadn't tried to divert us by writing that second *Sieg heil* and sending emails to newspapers to try and get us off his tracks, he would have managed it. He more or less gave himself to us."

"All's well that ends well."

They were silent for a while. Taras stared at the edge of the bed.

"Little Red Riding Hood, why do I have such a big eye?" she tried to break the silence.

"Drvarič showed me your letter."

He waited for her to speak but she didn't.

"He says you have arranged for your transfer to computer forensics. Yesterday afternoon Glavan from that department also called me because he didn't want it to look as if we are stealing each other's staff."

"I was going to tell you," she said more slowly and quietly than before. "I wanted to wait for this to be over."

She stroked his hand.

"I had decided even before the shooting. And not because of this thing between us."

She shook her head.

"Or at least not just because of this. When I came to the department half a year ago, I wondered whether I could become a criminal investigator. A successful criminal investigator. Now I know that I could. I think I could actually become a good criminal investigator. I could, but I don't want to. I don't want to live with the conviction that I am surrounded by madmen, lowlife and future victims. If I stop now, perhaps I won't."

She looked at him.

"Will we miss each other, Taras?"

"Computer forensics is not at the other end of the country. We'll see each other occasionally, I'm sure."

She smiled.

"Perhaps indeed."

*

He didn't have an umbrella. He had used one twice in his life and forgotten it on both occasions. It would not have helped him much anyway. The rain was so heavy and persistent that the road in front of him had turned into a river. There was no point in trying to run to his car, five hundred metres away. He huddled under the roof of the bus stop and decided to wait for the worst to pass. He nodded at the other people standing under the plastic roof, two women and a man, all holding rather sad-looking, soaked, banners. *It's about our children*, one of them read.

He watched the drains, the gutters that could no longer take the water. It was now spurting like geysers from them. The new river was slowly breaking its banks, splashing over the granite kerbs onto the pavement. From under the roof of the bus shelter he looked up at the sky, the dense, continuous greyness. There was no sign that the rain might abate soon.

It seemed that it really was trying to make up for lost time.

In order for the story, fictional from first to last word, to remain within the margins of plausibility, I have to thank many people, most of all: Dr Jože Balažic, Head of the Institute of Forensic Science in Ljubljana, Dr Dorijan Keržan, Director of the National Forensic Laboratory, Dr Blaž Stres, Associate Professor at the Biotechnical Faculty of the University of Ljubljana and the University of Innsbruck, Bojan Kuljenc, President of the NGO Kings of the Streets, Bojan Levič, a clock and watch expert, editor of numerous horological publications, the journalist Erik Valenčič, the lawyer Marjana Manfreda, the information technologist Klemen Bajc, the financial advisor Gregor Karlovšek and a few others who wished not to be named. This would not have been possible without their invaluable help.

Tadej Golob, the author